EMMALINE DARLING
The Curse of FaeKing

BOOK 1

EMMALINE DARLING

The Curse of FaeKing

K.E.NAPIONTEK

For Mom and Dad,

You encouraged the little girl to dream.
That dream took flight and touched worlds unseen.

CHAPTER 1

THURSDAY AFTERNOON

The details of my mother's death highlighted the *Peninsula Daily News*, describing her whimsically as '**floating in a mass of reeds along Lake Crescent's shoreline,**' summing her lasting image up as a '**Modern Arthurian Tragedy**' while reinforcing the lakes legend for '**rarely giving up its dead.**'

That is, until now.

'Steve Barren, a seasoned botanist, and educator at NatureBridge Olympic National Park stumbled across the distressing scene Monday morning, around 6:00 AM. "[She] looked ethereal, straight out of a storybook. I almost mistook her for the Lady of the Lake," Barren told Officer Crowe during an interview, comparing the recent passing of Dawn Darling to Port Angeles's most infamous ghost tale of Hilly (Darling)

Mortimer. Surely Barren had connected the family tragedies together. The Darlings are well known to share a reputation with Crescent Lake, the perpetual hot spot for their hardships since the disappearance of the town's founder, William Dyrling, in 1810.'

'Dawn was released to her family Wednesday evening, November 4th, after officials pronounced her passing was due to a previously diagnosed illness. Police assured residents that the deceased had passed quietly and was taken to the Clallam County Medical Examiner where the victim was identified as local Dawn Daphne Darling. The family will have a private service on Thursday. Details found in obituaries.'

My grandparent's paying the reporter off did nothing to smother town gossip. Instead, the act rekindled the old expression *Darling Curse,* something my grandparents were overcompensating for, using my mom's funeral to gloss over yet another Darling stain. I could almost hear her laughing at the grossly excessive display. *Or maybe that was just me.*

We huddled, shivering, under umbrellas gathered about the mahogany casket while listening to the hollow rings of a sermon echo somberly above the storm chatter. Visiting relatives stood with strangled tolerance, having slithered out from under their various hiding places to mark the ending of another cryptic occurrence in our family history. Friends of my grandparents held a social obligation to attend, filling in the gaps where a few of my preoccupied aunts would have been. Teenage cousins leaned against tombstones, glued to their phones. The group was meager sizing for how deep our roots tied into the town.

I watched them shuffle about while the preacher continued to cough up mothballs.

Didn't anyone else find it odd that effort had been taken into laying out sheets of plastic grass?

They could display the box dipped in gold, and still, the ugliness would have oozed shamelessly from the cracks, reminding us of why we gathered at Ocean View Cemetery today.

Shoes squelched through the muddied earth, splattering the presentation with light satisfaction.

I was getting distracted...

"Em," There was a voice muttering through the sticky layers of my thoughts. I shivered harder, curling fingers about the hem of my coat. "Em," they whispered again.

The torrent stilled enough to register my best friend staring down at me; a peculiar expression graced his striking features. His rusty red locks were now windswept from the afternoon showers. One thing you could always trust was the weather being unreliable in the Pacific Northwest.

"Hmmm?"

"You're spacing out again," James nudged me slightly, causing my unsteady ankles to buckle.

"Jamie," I shot back with a little bite. "Where's Abby?" My gaze combed through the small crowd of mourners, searching for a pink raincoat.

"The vintage handbag confiscated princess Abby," He gestured to my grandmother who had the tiny blonde securely gripped about the wrist.

My disdain for Darleen was clear, but I was trying to keep my manners. Fighting in front of guests would have been the wrong move. The woman was old, but that didn't stop her from having a silver tongue. She could break a man twice her size with mere words. Proof of this stood beside her with a desolate expression on his face, sipping from his 'coffee' mug.

I tried hard not to imagine the inner dialogue running through her mind. Her eyes ticked back and forth while she noted each imperfection in the sermon. Thin-lipped and irate, another Darling tragedy was not on Darleen's agenda. The rain was falling heavily, bruising petals, wilting ribbons, and staining the exposed pictures. The uninvited guests were offsetting proportion count for the meal after the ceremony, her brand name heels, ruined, and her youngest grandchild was squirming. This just wasn't Darleen's day.

I smirked, finding amusement from the ordeal until she caught me watching.

Tearing away, I overlooked the branch barren pines, observing the grey hews of sky melding into the even murkier depths of the Strait of Juan de Fuca before us.

Motioning distractedly to the wasted tree line, I whispered to my companion. "You know what they say. The bluff is crumbling more and more. It won't be long until locals found coffins smashed against the beach side. Hope Grampa bought extra insurance," I snorted. Not that it helped that the cliff had the nickname 'The End of the World,' irony had a stronghold here.

"Oh yeah, THAT'S an enjoyable image," James jeered, fighting mockery with sarcasm. "I'm sure Dawn has room. Let's add you alongside her. Won't that be a fun ride?"

"Alright, I get it…"

4

He rolled his eyes, confirming any doubts of normality I had. The rest of the grievers stared at me with appalled expressions. Gram was livid.

Had I been that loud?

Sobering my attitude, I tried to behave like a lovely little mourner and shifted attention back toward the droning preacher; after all, the grandparents had done most of today's preparations, and it wouldn't do to seem ungrateful.

Family tiptoed around me in large circles, afraid my lax exterior was leading into a mental breakdown. They weren't so far off. My reality had become the cousin to my lopsided sanity, and they were linking arms, one skip away from diving off of *The End of the World.*

Instead, care was averted to my baby sister. Young as she was, Abigail was a fiercely independent 3-year-old with her own set of ideas about the world. The infinity of death was something her vivid imagination found unbelievable. Finding it hard to comprehend that someone could simply cease to exist, and with Gran feeding her beliefs about heaven, the girl was becoming even more cynical in her grief. No child wants to hear their mother was residing somewhere other than with them, and she had burning questions I was not emotionally equipped to explain yet.

"Could the deceased's family please step forward, share words before we end in prayer?" They turned to me in succession, staring out from under dripping umbrellas with mixed sympathy. Oh right.

I tripped toward the blossoming coffin, burning anxiety radiated up from my chest, encompassing my ears, throbbing loudly. My brain sputtered off, and I stared, panicked, at the green roughage below.

"Emma," an arm wrapped protectively about my shoulders, lending me enough support to pull a small bottle blue Anemone flower from my tousled up-do. I twirled the blossom between my thumb and forefinger, searching for words.

"Emmaline," Gram hissed impatiently.

My jaw clenched. "Mom… will be missed," I managed, shifting my gaze to watch Gram gesture for the preacher to continue. Abigail wriggled from her confines, dashing through the circle of people to grab at my side. She hummed quietly to herself. No one else spoke. I focused on my hand running along her forever-tangled locks and placed the small cobalt bud atop mom's permanent resting place. The flower seemed to refuse to blend against the lavish bouquet of cream. They closed for prayer shortly after, a practice foreign to Abigail who strolled about me with an arm tightly coiled about my legs.

The storm raged like heavy drops of tears. Even before the sermon ended, people were scurrying toward their cars, queuing James to scoop up Abigail and wrap her within his coat. My heels stayed planted firmly before the casket, watching as it was being ushered quickly into the ground.

"How'll she breathe?" I heard Abby ask.

"Sssh," James mumbled. "We'll talk in the car."

The more I focused on that idea, the more claustrophobic I got. *I was sending Mom off into the ground, unwillingly.* I felt sick.

"I want to watch," I called over my shoulder, knowing James would hear and lead my sister off to the car where she could sit warming up by the heater.

No surprise, my grandparents left without saying a word. Even as I bent to pick up some soggy dirt to toss into the pit, they left me alone to watch the final descent of Dawn Darling's body. The splatter on those perfectly arranged flowers was gratifying, even the grit against my palm was calming. None had directed me to throw the earth, yet the religious act oddly consoled, despite how contradictory it was to my raising.

"I'm driving!" James called across the cemetery.

Turning my head, I peered to my best friend distractedly. He leaned against my worn Volkswagen beetle, rain-spattered and rolled down the leather of his jacket, while black slacks hugged his ankles where water had soaked through the material. He had settled Abby into her car seat where she was playing with her botched doll, Agatha. The red head's expression was brooding. Thick eyebrows furled above dark eyes, observing me intently.

I shifted to the hole again, torn between going after James and lingering to see the entire burial. Sighing to myself, fighting against the weather, I had the morose urge to pull out my phone and take pictures.

"Emma!"

"Just a sec—!" Listening to the clicking of several dozen frames taken of the scene, I pressed close while sheltering the screen from the drizzle. I had a feeling I was missing something.

"Emma, come on!"

7

Distracted, shivering and excitable, I flipped my thumb along the blurry images, turning to the car obediently at James's call. Walking precariously alongside graves, I abruptly halted.

"Emma! You're getting soaked!"

Hairs rose across my body, too engrossed in what I was seeing. The ghostly silhouette of a distorted figure emerged behind the casket, slowly approaching the camera's focal point with each picture. The only distinct feature of the individual was their top hat, then nothing.

"What?" I breathed, twisting around to look after me.

As if dissolved with the showers, no one was there. Someone visiting a grave shouldn't have been this alarming.

"Emma!" James was suddenly beside me, sounding urgent.

Lurching breathlessly, I dashed to the beetle, spooked.

He ran after me, "Emma!? What's the matter?" Scrambling into the Volkswagen, I locked the door behind me, kicking off my shoes. James peered at me from beyond the glass. I wouldn't look at him, too mentally scrambled and pumping with adrenaline. He finally veered around the car and got inside.

"Thanks for being here," I quickly commented before he started in. Tense, I settled against my seat, staring fixated at the rearview mirror. Abby was tucking the end of the toilet paper sheet she had wrapped Agatha in; mummification in a pinch for a little girls form of grievance. When she looked up, we exchanged blank looks.

James quietly started the engine. Putting the car in reverse, he flipped an illegal U-turn. "You're insane and soaked. What were you looking at?"

"I thought I discovered something," I lied, slipping my phone between the seat and my thigh. "You scared me," I continued slowly, catching my friend's expression, watching his brows furl in concentration. "Thanks for coming. It would have been worse without you."

"I'm glad I can make a shitty situation stink less?" He kept his view to the road. "Em, what happened?"

"Just what I told you."

He seemed to relent after a minute. "Next time, bring an umbrella. And don't wear heels, you looked ridiculous."

"Thanks," I said blandly. "I'll take note."

Friendship with James Beasley was eccentric at best. We met our freshman year of high school. He was the cliché new guy, instilling a rather passionate sentiment of either love or hate within his onlookers. Charming, mysterious, and senselessly cool; people obsessively pawed after him, wanting into his selected company. That wasn't me. I had no interest in the dark cloud of gossip that hovered around him, too guarded by my own family baggage to bother; yet somehow, despite all my careful avoidance, I always bumped into him.

It was that summer, after freshman year, that I stumbled across him alone at the park. Sporting a grossly swelled eye and cracked lip, James wasn't the usual alluring picture girls fawned over.

Knowing he had signs of a jaded past, personal preservation kept me from intruding within his space, but it was Mom who pulled him into the house, fixed him up with a poultice and mug of chamomile tea, before prying him for information. That's when she unraveled the sparring match with his dad, someone who didn't take kindly to James's clever mouth. After that, we intentionally ran into each other, and that seemingly murky cloud, shriveled to a mere watermark.

"What did you think you saw?"

"Huh?" Large raindrops slapped against the cracked windshield of my beat-up Volkswagen, while the wipers uselessly tried to preserve a clear view of the road. I had been leaning my head against the window as we zoomed along carelessly down the street at 60-miles-an-hour; cops were predictable and lax in rural areas.

"The thing you thought you saw."

"OH, Right," I flipped the radio on. "I thought saw someone."

"And?"

"Well, they disappeared," I shrugged. "So, obviously I was mistaken."

"So… they vanished in a cemetery?" He offered me a grin, wiggling his eyebrows, "*Ghost*?"

"Oh, shut up," I shoved his shoulder, causing us to swerve, "Jamie!?"

"You made me do it!" he retorted hotly.

"Why are we yellin'!?" Abigail chimed.

We both calmed down. Turning to peek at my sister, I poked her foot. "Why are *you* yelling?"

"Cuz…" she huffed with no further explanations, loosely holding onto her doll, which had the unfortunate run-in with some scissors a few days ago. Judging by Agatha's physical state, I was sure the toddler was having a hard time processing the week's events. I wasn't sure how to approach her about it.

"So… did you see your cousin Crystal there? She's getting pretty hot."

When the little blonde seemed to lose interest in our conversation, I shot him a look. "Crystal is also sixteen, perv."

"Well, she dresses like a twenty-something."

"That's why they call it jailbait my friend. You're gross." He gave me a sideways stare, and I shrugged, "Just saying."

We were both in our twenties. With the way he was going, sooner or later something would occur, one with an underage persuasion. "You'd like her older sister more," I diverted the conversation. "She's away at college, but I'll introduce you this summer."

He offered a goofy grin at the proposal, validating I had deterred him successfully from examining the cemetery incident further. Smiling to myself, I became quiet. Listening to the soft rock channel I tried my best not to think. I yearned to curl up on the sofa and zone out in front of the fire.

"Emmy," chirped a voice behind me, chubby fingers tugged lightly on my hair.

"Abby?" I responded, surprised she had made it this far without chattering away in the back seat, a conversation that was often insightful for a child her age.

"D-dat man was dressed funny." She didn't bother to stop playing when I turned to gaze at her. "Why didn't you-you go see him?"

"Well," my gut twisted oddly, searching for the right words for a response. "I don't know Abby. He left before I could say anything."

"But he-he was waiting." She insisted, looking up at me with disapproval.

"Yes," I replied, brain power fizzling. "He didn't wait after the sermon."

"Yah-uh!"

"So, you both saw the ghost?"

"Ghost? No ghost!" Abigail tossed her head dramatically. "No ghost, Jamie. A person!"

"I think you corrupted her." James raised a brow, looking at me.

"I did not," I groaned.

"Maybe you're thinking about the weird guy wearing the crazy-ass scarf?" I smacked his arm unceremoniously, and he made a noise. "Sorry, just crazy scarf."

"O-oh, Jamie said the word!"

"Yes, yes, he did."

Abigail held out her hands in expectation. I snickered. "He'll give you the money when we get to Gram and Grampas. Okay, Crab Cake?"

James feigned an expression of utter tragedy, which made the babe squeal with delight.

"Promise, Jamie."

"I promise." He responded solemnly.

"Turn here." I gestured to the left.

It was amazing how long a habitual route could seem when all you wanted to do was run away. Potholes filled with muddy rainwater were a game of hit and miss while we

12

drove down the darkening trail. The area was a lovely but a common sighting in the Pacific Northwest. Pine and maple overhung the graveled path, surrounding the large, robust house at the end.

My mother's childhood home glowed from head to base like a gloomy jack-o'-lantern in the fall weather—cars and trucks looped around the parking lot, snuggly sitting beside each other with limited room to budge. Leaves littered the scene in a light blanket of warm colors, some already settling on the recently parked vehicles.

Absentmindedly, I sat chewing on my nails. "I think I have the right not to go inside," I muttered, slipping down in my seat.

"But— I'm hungry! Aren't you hungry Abby?"

"Ya!" she exclaimed, already kicking her legs to get out of her booster seat. I could feel the tips of her shoes pressing into the back of my chair as she stretched.

"Besides, you are supposed to make an appearance." The spindly young man slipped from the car, looping around to grab my sister before I could protest.

"James! Come on— wait!" I watched them dance in toward the house. They ignored me entirely. Begrudgingly I got out and slammed the car door, flinching at the creak of protest. The old thing already had enough problems without me adding to them. I patted her rusting white hood apologetically before heading inside.

The afternoon's unusual incident at the cemetery had left me chill and drained, and for once, I welcomed the stuffy, overheated atmosphere of my grandparents. Regret quickly changed my mind when a crowd of strangers and undesirable family members in attendance swarmed me.

Was the group getting larger?

Nodding, smiling politely, I exchanged short condolences with passing individuals. Worming my way through the dark-clothed bodies, I made for the stairwell leading upstairs; taking a few steps, I turned to glance over the sea of heads. I located James in the dining room nibbling away on pieces of meat and cheese from the food table. Abigail had only been with him for a short while. After he shoved a dollar into her princess purse, Gram scooped her up and took her into the kitchen.

Quickly taking out my phone, I texted James.

ME: PIG! Get Abby away from Gram!

He perked up when he received it, cheeks plump with unchewed food. He didn't watch for me until a moment later with a hint of a grin. He shoved a piece of ham into his already full face, demonstrating his lack of urgency.

Honestly, you'd think he'd act more somber at a wake. I flipped him the bird, knowing very well that I needed to pull myself together quietly before I erupted in front of the wrong audience. He knew I didn't choose to be here. I told him stories about Gram and her history of diluting my mother's character to suit her interests. Gram enjoyed few things in life, but degrading others was a skill she took pride in. Now that my mom was gone, I was the next in line of fire.

"Emmaline?"

I let out a silent exhale of stress, shifting my gaze slowly to present a controlled smile.

"Oh! It *is* you. For a minute, I thought I saw a ghost."

14

"AH… Mrs. Evans. How nice it is of you to be attending."
There's that word again.

We observed each other mutually until she responded with a simpering expression and a calculating gaze. I shifted my weight, adjusting for a nasty impact. "Oh really, it's the least I can do for your grandmother. She is in such a state, the poor thing."

Swallowing the acidic words lodged in my throat, I gave a cordial nod.

"That's nice Mrs. Evans. Gram is lucky to have such a supportive friend." Slipping slowly down the staircase, I was attempting to pass her, trying to give the impression I'd seen someone familiar, seeking to escape her insufferable attention. *Where the hell was James!?*

"Emmaline, dear…" She was staring intently at me, not giving an inch to let me through. "Everyone was so surprised to find Dawn was as sick as she was. Barely even saw her out and about. Then when she did—oh goodness, what a scene. Then to pass in such a horrific way and at the VERY Lake, your father went missing? Darlings have had such misfortunes." She shook her head, reaching out to pat my hand which rested on the railing. "Dory hasn't uttered a single detail about what ailed Dawn or the bizarre incident…" she trailed off, looking pointedly at me. *What? Was she expecting me to fill in the blanks?*

Her sight glazed over for a split moment, reveling in her overindulgence to petty gossip. I had to give Gram points for keeping mom's privacy. Then again, it was probably to save face. My mom had already caused the family name enough slander for Gram to not sit as comfortably in her position with the town's social hierarchy.

"Mom wanted normalcy as much as possible." Past tense wasn't getting any easier to establish. "There isn't anything wrong with being private."

"When someone is that mentally disturbed, it's bound to raise questions, Emmaline. The fits were a concern after all."

My face felt hot. Whether it was from being put on the spot or due to the sheer nerve of this woman, I stared at her for a long seething point.

Files from the coroner stated that my mother had been sick for a long while before she passed. A tumor the size of an egg was pressing on her brain stem, causing hallucinations about bizarre and otherworldly things. She downplayed her migraines and her occasional spasms. Even on the days she forgot to pick up Abigail from daycare, there was always a reasonable excuse. It wasn't until *The Episode* that we found out what was going on.

I had managed to coax her to the grocery store with us when she had her first public breakdown. I had gone to the deli with Abigail to order us beverages when I heard her screaming shrilly at the top of her lungs. Rushing back, I found her sprawled in a pool of spilled honey. The barrel lay off to the side, oozing the last bits of its bowels across the cemented floor. She was shaking her fist at the dairy cooler, yelling nonsense about blind eyes, terrified. After that, she shut herself inside the house.

Numbness shrouded me, pulling a gauzy curtain across my senses. We fought our way through her final weeks of life in mechanical motion, preparing for the inevitable. She was going to die. We just didn't know when.

"There is no doubt that Lake Crescent's water runs deep through your veins. Perhaps she took some advice from your ancestors."

I clenched my fists to my sides, opening my mouth to retort.

"Oh, Mrs. Evans, I haven't seen you since high school. Are you still lubing old ratchet cocks and carefully stroking hammer springs?" The woman went sour, regarding James as he sidled up to the stairwell to lean against the rail. While James's banter was playful, his dark eyes were sharper than usual.

Mrs. Evans was best known for her long, overextended, guest lectures at the local schools. With her overly zealous appetite for vintage heirlooms, she earned herself a rather vulgar reputation amongst the students she frequently berated. "A fine-tuned clock piece is not a lude act, Mr. Beasley." His name was acidic on her tongue. "Lubrication is a perfectly normal term for the preservation of historical artifacts. You'd know this if you listened to the whole lecture." Her nostrils flared, glancing between us.

"Well, you are the expert of cock pieces. When you've stroked one, you've done them all."

I bit my inner lip to control my jaw from dropping.

"Clock piece, Mr. Beasley!" she corrected him. "Your mother should have fed you a heavy-handed treatment of lye soap." She turned her nose up, trying to preserve her composure. "I shouldn't keep you, Emmaline. I'm sure you

17

have more guests wishing to greet you." She twisted around and walked away hotly.

"I think she just implied my mom should have poisoned me." James seemed unimpressed, peeking up to give me a look over. "She didn't bite you too hard, did she?"

"No."

"No shits were given?"

"None," I smiled a little.

"Good," He gestured over his shoulder to the group of guests. "The waters are swarming with stuck-up prunes."

I policed the crowd mulling in and out of rooms in the house. They carried small china plates filled with finger foods, whispering behind the rims of crystal glasses and funeral pamphlets, staring in our direction.

"I don't know half of them. Why are we even here?"

"Your Gram would hold it against you otherwise," He drawled, raising a brow. "Besides, I'm not prepared to deal with your complaining... or hers."

I reached to flick his nose, only to catch sight of a white top hat amongst the grey scale of funeral-goers. I was going insane.

"Do you see that?" I pointed vigorously, feeling the crawling sensation of eyes observing us.

"See what?" James was back to his concerned voice from earlier.

"The white top hat!" I snapped pushing passed him with sudden enthusiasm, frustrated by my irrational fear.

"Alice, don't run down the rabbit hole," He mumbled meekly after me.

Ignoring him, I combed through the rooms, growing desperate to prove to myself that I wasn't crazy. Through and through, I looped about the expansive house, but there was nothing to find.

Nothing.

I was left mystified, thinking of spirits again.

Shrugging off my still-damp coat, I stood exasperated before a large windowpane facing the river. My eyes ran along the dripping beads of rainfall, the scene appearing to melt before me.

"You lost the rabbit." My friend concluded, sidling up beside me and popping a piece of garlic bread into his mouth.

"I don't know what I'm supposed to do." The impulsive energy I owned had all but leeched out of me; I was beginning to feel melancholy with the weather.

"You don't have to do anything, Em. I thought you knew that?"

Scratching absent-mindedly along my arm, I shrugged. "I'm tired," I wanted to believe there was something else in life other than the pain left in my mother's place. Perhaps the top hat was just a symbolic hallucination; my mind was telling me I was reaching for answers I couldn't yet grasp. There was no escaping this embittering suffocation clawing up my stomach.

"That's normal."

"I'm angry."

"That's normal too."

"I don't feel normal," I gave him a look. "I want to punch something. I want to break a bottle and carve out my heart.

19

Leave it for the birds. Watch them peck away at my freaking misery."

"Emma..."

"Don't," I held up my hand, clenching my jaw. "Not yet. I can't." The floodgate I had opened quickly slammed shut and locked. It wouldn't do to have anything toppling out quite yet.

I pointed at the window, nostrils flaring. Focusing on the riverbed, the man in the top hat was standing, waiting for me, mocking me.

"There, he's down at the river."

Were my delusions taunting me? Had the Top Hat been a illusion fabricated to keep my busy mind occupied from reality? Was I sick like countless Darlings before me?

Meeting the vision head on, I left James thoughtlessly behind and ran out the back sliding door, on along the deck, and down onto the sloping trail that led toward the riverbed below.

The thundershower sent a prickling sensation down my exposed skin. Murky, swirling waters of the creek rumbled angrily at me, sparking disturbing images of my mother struggling for air in Lake Crescent's cold depths.

I stood, staring into the raging whitewater, no pale man in sight.

'Would you forgive me if I lost you to the faeries?' Her voice murmured in the recesses of my thoughts. I could still recall her scribbling in her journal that day, propped up against a plush throng of pillows overlooking the thicket behind our house. She had been drawing ink figures with wings and black eyes.

Laughing nervously, I wasn't sure what to say to that question. Mom looked very serious, so I was worried she was having one of her episodes again.

'Faeries mom, why would you lose me to the Faeries?'

Had she recalled the time I was lost in the woods as a child? Search parties traipsed through the undergrowth for hours trying to find me. It wasn't until later, after she had left to look herself that I had been found by the local officials. Dad once said she had gone a bit crazy then too. Now I imagined she was mixing traumatic memories with fragments of old story books.

'To escape them of course, please don't hate me, Emmy. I didn't understand! I had no idea it would end like this...' Her hands were cold when I squeezed them, trying to reassure her. *'I tricked Him once, you know? Him and ALL of them, but I don't think I have enough time to keep Him away. I've made such a horrible mistake.'*

Her pen dropped and rolled down the cushions, ink smudges permanently marking a particularly lovely purple cover. I went to grab it for her, but she tightened her hold, pulling me close to stare wide-eyed.

It was because of my grim curiosity I humored her. Now it would forever haunt me.

'How did you trick Him?'

'I hid what was most precious to Him, in the last place He would ever think... or want to look.'

I had to settle down and reevaluate what I was encouraging. I wondered if I should have tried to change the subject.

'Take care of yourself, Emmy. Never let them fool you.'

I snapped into reality. My nails dug into my forearm, gaze staring intensely at the gushing water. The color had turned a muddy hew from the overflow.

"'Take care of myself...'" The downpour muted my voice. "That's funny," I responded cynically, sagging down into a squat, falling into a sense of defeat.

For a long stilling minute, I stayed in my contemplating position until my feet grew prickly, signaling me to rise. As I stood, I wrapped my arms tightly about myself.

"Good morrow to you. I believe... you were looking for me?" A brogue accent washed across the rain chatter.

Tensing, I turned to take in the aristocratic gentleman before me. Tall, slender, impeccably dressed, his skin was the pigment of snow, with the facial hair to match. When he took off his top hat, I realized he was ashen from head to toe. The only intensity that seemed to mark his person was his amber eyes, flecked with gold.

"Emmaline Darling." That wasn't a question, but he was expecting an answer.

I nodded.

"Good." A pale hand rose to greet me at eye level, wiggling a vanilla envelope between the index and middle finger. "This is for you, Miss Darling." He paused in waiting. "I believe you should take it."

My mind was struggling to return to my body, trying to comprehend what was happening.

"W-who are you?" I stumbled out, willing my hand to rise so he could settle the letter onto my palm.

"That is not relevant to this moment in time." I was took caught up in the drops of rain freezing against his body to notice what he was saying. They clung like gemmed facets of intricate designs, swirling about his shoulders and powdering his collar. What wasn't sticking to the masterpiece adorning his body, bounced off to land on the ground about his feet, dissolving almost instantly. "You have been served, Miss Darling."

"Wait, what?"

A puff of cold air escaped his smiling lips, his teeth reflecting sharply despite the gloomy lighting. Tipping his hat in my general direction, he turned and walked down the trail.

CHAPTER 2

THURSDAY EVENING

Everything stilled. Even the downpour quieted itself long enough for my body to catch up to my brain. Clutching the envelope loosely, I took in a steadying breath before bolting after the stranger.

He couldn't have gotten far.

My bare feet pressed against the moss-laden flooring, feeling water pool about my toes as I slipped along the path.

Even with the woods molting in decay, green was ever prominent. Towering pine trees and crawling undergrowth adorned the wet mulch, copper-toned leaves peppering the pathway in disarray.

The stranger should have been easy to spot. The trail was narrow, nestled between a hilly thicket and the swelling river. Unless he went off the beaten path, I could catch up to him before he started his way toward the house.

"Hello?" I halted in the pathway's middle, just a few yards away from an old stone bridge where fallen trees were clogging the underbelly. I listened acutely to the rustling fern patches, trying to hear the direction it was coming from. "Who are you?" I called out hesitantly.

Snickers erupted, encompassing the forest in a wave of foreboding.

"Hello?" My tone was wary this time.

"*Little Darling dressed in black, will she make a tasty snack?*" A soft voice gurgled near the rushing water.

Inspecting the newly toppled embankment, where the river pooled in a section, I saw a set of large round reflective pupils. "*Shall I grab her by the hair? What a simple way to snare…*"

I gripped the note close, listening to the laughter rising in the ferns. "Who are you?"

"*Drag her home make her groan, fill her up with heated stone.*"

"You're disgusting," I breathed.

"*Eat her digits, limbs then eyes… watch her as she slowly dies.*"

Staring in horror, I screamed as something grabbed my shoulder.

"Emma!?" I was immediately kicking on instinct, registering James only after he seized me by both shoulders. "Are you hurt? Did someone hurt you?"

"There's something in the water!" Focused, he turned to the bridge, glaring intently. I clutched at him desperately when he tried to approach it. "Don't! It's threatening to eat me." I could feel my eyelids widening, stinging at the effort.

"Emma," He peeled my fingers from his arm. "Go back to the party," He instructed, picking up a sturdy looking branch to snap it in half over his leg.

The cracking echoed, sending a shudder through me. "I mean it," James warned.

Gradually, I shifted up the trail, watching my friend make his way calmly over the slick logs. He held the tree limb out like a harpoon.

What was going on?

"Emma," he gazed after me, face shaded by his damp curls. He swore when I wasn't budging. "EMMA, GO!" He suddenly brought the splintered end down, slicing through the surface of the stream.

There was thrashing and squealing. I caught sight of gangly disjointed limbs before an ink-like substance stained the water, as it spilled over the rim of the logs and washed downstream.

Creaking of branches resounded above us, showering dead leaves as animals scurried off from the struggle. There was no more laughing.

Disturbed about the occurrence, I eventually shook myself free from the scene and took off to my grandparent's home. There was a man. There was an envelope. I had physical proof that this was happening. *I wasn't crazy.* But I had just left my best friend behind.

James remained absent for 23-minutes and counting. When he found me, I had tucked myself into a wicker chair on the porch, a champagne bottle settled between my thighs.

I ran my sight along the surface of the gifted envelope, tracing the indented scrolling that spelled my name, 'Emmaline NovaLee Darling.' The back, sealed with a waxy substance, had an emblem pressed into the center. I couldn't quite make it out, but the entirety of its existence felt wrong.

The weight of the man's appearance weighed heavy on my mind. He unsettled me to where I was white knuckling the chair, taking heaping gulps of air to calm myself.

Was I overly paranoid? If I thought about my day long enough, I was sure I could convince myself this had been nothing more than an extremely odd occurrence.

Compulsive thinking drove my nerves into shock. My finger skewered the sealed fold of the letter as I inwardly battled with what to do with it. The man's tone still rang in my ears, '*You have been served, Miss Darling*,' as if he had some legally binding documents to relay. If so, what could he want?

"Red Riding Hood, Red Riding Hood, where is your coat? If you're outside, you'll surely be soaked." A soft, raspy voice sang against my ear—hands wrapped around my shoulders, pulling me against the chair. My body gave a slight jolt in surprise, immediately slamming my veins with adrenaline until James peeked overhead, a puckish grin gracing his features.

"What is that?" He gestured to the message.

"I hate you," I jerked from his grasp, shoving it quickly aside. His eyes were darker than ever, causing shivers. I turned from his grinning face. "You don't sneak up on people like that. You have no idea…"

27

"What happened, Emma?" He came around, plopping down on the chair's footrest, stooping over to stare at me intently. "Who gave you that?"

"Someone at the party…"

"What is it, a card?"

"More than likely, what else could it be?" I sounded more uncertain than he was.

"Are you asking me?" He threw me a strange face. "Let me see."

I twisted, staring at him. "You want to talk about a sympathy letter, now? You just harpooned someone!"

"Em—"

"What was it?"

Shoving his hands into his coat pockets, the redhead gave me a side look. "You wouldn't believe me if I told you."

"At this point, I think I'd consider just about anything."

He frowned, rocking on the balls of his feet, acting uncertain. I hung on his words.

"Deranged raccoon," He said quietly.

"What?"

"Rabies…" he drew out with bated breath. "The thing was crackers."

"James!?"

"I told you," he repeated.

"We need to leave." I rose, gripping the bottle to look around irritably. "Now, before I really start freaking out."

My friend's expression changed, mood sobering. "Sure, I'll get my coat. Meet you at the front door."

Stuffing the envelope into my damp pocket, I didn't respond. As I made my way inside, I tried to avoid the stares and the whispering.

"Crab Cake," I found the blonde tot raiding Gram's bag for loose change and mints. "We need to go, okay? The house will be cold."

My sister wiggled in her seat, scrunching up her nose to give a grumpy face. "No Emmy," She grumbled. "No. We should stay."

"Abigail." My mental endurance was dangling by a loosely fabricated thread. "We are going home."

We stared each other down until finally; I tossed her over my shoulder. Pink bloomers flashed a section of the guests while I carried her off to find James. Her protest was in the form of refusing her coat by cleverly keeping her arms rooted to her sides until I manually dressed her. Getting a whine when I zipped her jacket clear up to her chin, she defiantly yelled when I pulled her hood over her head. Making her upset was not on my list of fun things to do; we were both just missing mom.

Sighing, I kissed her forehead.

"I'll bring her out to the car. You go say bye," James ordered lightly.

I hadn't the heart to protest. After wrapping my sister up in his coat, swaddling the babe, off he took her giggling into the night. At least someone could make her happy.

"Gram…?" I made my way into the kitchen, winding around small groups of passively chatting individuals. I spotted her sitting with a few of her friends at the table, mugs of decaf coffee and fat-free edibles laid before them in a

29

pleasing display. They all gave me the same look over, beady expressions piercing in the soft fluorescent glow.

"Emmaline, I see you've taken my granddaughter. Were you not staying tonight? Do you honestly think it's best for your sister right now? This is an important moment to feel comforted and safe for a small child that has lost someone."

"Yes," chimed one woman. Mrs. Kimberley, a particularly characterless highlighted blonde with the telltale signs of an overly pampered housewife. "She should stay in a home that can give her all the comfort only a mother is able to provide."

Most of the women at the table were a decade younger than my grandmother, but that didn't stop them from fawning over the Darling patriarch. Insanity marked the name in history, but power and money seemed to sway loyalty.

They all clucked and nodded their heads in agreement.

The term 'whipped' came to mind…

"Plus, it would give you a chance to soothe yourself after such a long week." Mrs. Porter added.

"Get your affairs in order," Miss Maycomb hummed.

"Not that she did much to help in the preparations," Gram pursed her lips against the rim of her cup. "But yes, of course, if that gives you any sense of release. By all means…" Her clipped tone was a trigger of a mental shutdown. I shrunk in her controlled company of onlookers. One comment after the other stuck into me, with rusted arrows weighing me down.

"I'd like her to come home with me tonight, Gram."

"Never mind what you would like, Emmaline, it should be what's in her best interest. And is it?" She inquired again

30

with insistence, "Really? After all, you'd be living alone in that unfinished house all by yourself. Everything is as your mother left it. Don't you see that's a bit too much?"

"James Beasley has been staying with us. He's a good guy and has helped out a lot."

The chickens were squawking and pecking again.

"Scott would have shot the boy on the spot if he caught him in Anne's room," Mrs. Kimberley shook her head at the notion.

"Young women are so forward this day and age," Mrs. Porter hid behind her mug of coffee, giving sideways glances toward Gram.

"If my daughter ever let a boy stay the night—" Josephine Smith started.

"The idea is unsuitable for a young woman and a little girl." Gram finished, clipped.

I shifted, shoving my hands roughly into my pockets.

"You're making me sound like a slut. We're friends. Nothing is happening." I didn't think this conversation deserved an audience.

What the heck was she trying to imply?

"Then why haven't I met him?" Gram stared across her mug, slim fingers sparkling with her gold bands.

"You have…?" I watched her, confusion apparent on my face. "Hey, Grampa," I saw him in the corner of my eye, shuffling into the room to head for the makeshift bar on the kitchen island.

"Emma," he spoke good-naturedly. "I was wondering when you'd be back up from the river."

"Yeah," I shivered at the recollection. "Actually, I'm just about to leave."

"So soon?" he swirled a cup of brandy in his hand. "We have plenty of rooms. Have a glass, spend the night," Even as he offered a wrinkled smile with the raise of his drink, his eyes seemed dull.

"I suggested that, Albert. She doesn't seem to want to stay here tonight," Gram interjected.

He ignored her and stretched his arm over the island, holding out the beverage with an insistence I never knew he was capable of.

Hesitantly, I took the drink loosely in my hand. "Abby wants to go home." I lied, stiffly twisting my upper body to examine the flock. The table of women gave me the urge to explain myself to gain sympathy. "She's taken to sleeping in mom's room." That wasn't a lie.

"I would cut that quickly," Mrs. Evan's said sharply from the doorway. "Children are to sleep in their beds, the light out and no thumbs in their mouths." The hen's bobbled in agreement.

Wanting to take that perfectly groomed head of hers and shake it like a Magic 8 Ball, I instead choked slightly on a portion of ice while downing the offered drink. My stomach curled in on itself, and I regretted my decision instantly. *Bad idea.*

I discarded the glass on the island, swiveling toward the door. "I gotta leave, thanks Grampa," I could hear Gram's chair as she moved to stand.

"I'll walk you to your death trap. I wasn't able to say goodnight to Abigail." I tried to overlook her, hugging my wet coat closer while a light hum of the alcohol washed over me.

Jerking into gear, I pushed roughly passed Mrs. Evans, making my way hastily toward the exit. Gram chased after me, catching up only after struggling on a raincoat.

"Emmaline!" she called out, hooking her hand about my arm before I could slide into the passenger seat of my car.

"What?"

"We have a room set up for her. She would be comfortable here." Ignoring her hard expression, I tried getting in.

"Her place is home, with me." I didn't bother hiding the curtness this time.

"Girl," her head followed me into the Volkswagen, causing me to sit uncomfortably pressed against the seat. "Look me in the eyes when you are speaking."

"Gram, it's not going to happen! Okay?"

James leaned across me to grab the handle of the door. The motion caused the older woman to straighten in alarm as if she were only just realizing he had been there. Who did she think was driving?

"We're leaving now. Hey, thanks for the lovely service, Mrs. D!" He spoke as if we were conversing about the weather.

I rejoiced silently when she grew indifferent to his words. Finally relenting, Gram retreated from me, ignoring him entirely.

"I'll be calling you, Emmaline," She added. "If you don't pick up then I will be forced to come over. I won't let you turn into a shut-in like your mother!" James closed the door with a creak of the rusty hinges. She smacked my window, irritatingly, with emphasis.

Twisting, I glanced behind me to see if Abigail was still settled securely in her car seat. Mrs. Evan's stood on the doorstep, blatantly watching the drama unfold from afar. *Creeper.*

Rubbing my churning stomach, I shifted to the front, frowning. The ride home was quiet, my mind replaying the events of the funeral until they twisted nightmarishly together. Getting Abigail ready for bed was an eager distraction, and a hot bath was well overdue after the mucky service. Somehow she had splashed mud in crevices and cracks that shouldn't have been exposed to puddle water but, then again; she was an avid jumper.

I brushed her hair and tucked her into Disney pajamas. Lining her bed with mom's pillows, we took the time to build a canopy of sheets, reheated leftovers for snacking during a soft and reassuring conversation.

I was there. I wasn't going anywhere. Yes, I'd be in the living room if she got scared. Gram was definitely NOT sticking me in a box. If she needed water, she could get it from the bathroom. No, I promised I wouldn't leave her alone at home. They could string me up by my toes, lock me in a cage, or drop me on a lonely island. The island, Abby added, was inhabited by polka-dotted flamingos, with talking pet dogs that guarded a cave full of treasure, and still, I assured, I'd find my way to her.

The girl finally fell asleep after such a fantastical story time, giving me the freedom to slip downstairs. I was thinking James had left when I found him slumped forward, on the couch, staring absently at the TV screen. A bowl of a four-day-old shepherd's pie loosely cradled on his knees. He had made the fire; acknowledging it had grown cold. Something he never seemed bothered by, always overheating.

"You should go home." He was looking worn out. It must have been hard work taking care of us. "Sleep in your bed tonight. The couch isn't comfortable."

"Are you kicking me out?" He mumbled through a mouthful of food, giving me the same disinterest he had been showing the TV.

"You've been here for weeks. I figured you'd want to, you know, go home. Breathe? Have space?"

"What kind of ass would leave you two here alone?" He ran a hand through his thick hair, waves bouncing back into perfect placement.

"I guess…" I followed his example and reclined gradually into the couch, mulling over what he had said.

"You still haven't opened it?" There was a moment of rustling. Before I could register the question, James had torn into the mysterious envelope and carefully tugged out the contents.

My first instinct was to slap the letter safely out of his reach, save him from something vile that could spill out upon its opening. *That was irrational though… right?* I retracted myself, just the same.

Unfurling the hand-pressed parchment he leaned forward in rapt concentration, reading each word carefully. By his lack of speech, it was hard to register what he was feeling. My nails were in my mouth by the time he finally glanced from the paper, turning his intensity over to the envelope to examine the emblem on the seal. In the lamplight, I could vaguely make out dark amber wax imprinted with the shape of a shrub.

"Is this a joke?" He cracked an odd smile. His irises seemed to swallow the whites of his eyes, darkening his expression.

I gave an involuntary shiver. "W-what... what are you talking about?"

James tossed the note at me, making me scramble for the paper to read it myself. "Who gave that to you?" he snapped, springing up to storm toward the stairwell. "Fucking idiots, I need to check on Abby."

My heart fluttered with the rise of anxiety, hands shaking as I clutched the crumpled edges of the letter. I skimmed the tarnished red print, transfixed on the curves and flicks that flowed pleasingly.

Emmaline the Cleverly Hidden,

Are you mourning her—your mother?

Perhaps that is too forward of an inquiry. We doubt time has passed long enough for your tears to dry, but our tolerance grows thin, and her recent passing has freed the way to a most anticipated reunion.

Truly, you are an occasion worth the wait. How long has it been?

Of course, we wouldn't expect you to remember, your mother had assured that. Regardless of old wounds, we hope to encourage your curiosity along this journey. Join us in a game and seek the truth lying rooted in the wake of your mother's death. Return to us what she has stolen, and we will relinquish the one we have taken. Your presence is most anticipated.

Until then,

Hands clammy, I barely noticed the smear of blood soaking into the edge of the note, distracted by the words, now disjointed in my thought process.

"EMMA!" James' panicked voice repeatedly bellowed from upstairs.

My heart seized in my chest, causing my jaw to strain with the muscle tension spreading down my body. I could barely breathe, frozen in my state of confusion.

"EMMA!?"

I lurched off the couch. My fingernails scraped the grain of the floor as I tripped up the stairs in haste, following the dread stricken cry of the redhead.

Was she gone, or worse… dead?

37

Shuddering, I followed his voice, finding him pulling apart Abigail's vacant room. I stood foolishly, viewing him search through her toy-filled chest, gutting out drawers, searching inside the closet and under her bed. James grappled the pillows, striped sheets from her mattress, and mangled the bed in his frenzy. I watched an item topple from the blankets.

Dipping down, I scooped up the strange-looking object: a nob of molded honeyed wax, seeds stuck where eyes may have belonged, with bits of hair protruding out in various places.

James had since stilled himself, staring with a rigid understanding. "Give that here," He demanded.

"What is this? What does this have to do with Abby?"

He ignored my questions, taking the item to storm off down the stairs.

"Where's Abby?" I took after him, tracking him to the living area where he stood in front of the fireplace. "Why are you going through her things? What is that thing?"

"What the hell does it look like?" He gestured vehemently with it clutched in his palm before swinging open the door to the fire and chucking it begrudgingly inside. The doll quickly melted, hissing and spitting within the heat.

"JAMES!?" I seized his arm, shaking it in my frustration and fear.

"Abigail is gone," He growled at the stove.

"She wouldn't be hiding inside her sheets or drawers." I rationalized. "She could be playing hide and seek. She could be outside," moving toward the foot of the steps, I shouted her name and waited, listening for any scurrying, shifting, or giggling with the creaking of floorboards, but there was nothing.

"Do you genuinely believe that?" He questioned, watching with bewilderment. "You got a letter stating kidnap!" He took hold of my shoulders, dark irises severe. "Do you remember who gave you the note, Em?" He shook me to attention, "EMM!?"

Children don't just disappear out their beds from a two-story house.

"No, I... No, I don't," I lied again. My gut churned.

What was that thing he threw in the fire? Why was I lying to him?

James watched me closely as if trying to decipher whether if I was withholding information. "Did someone threaten you?"

I shook my head, gaping at him. *Not directly anyway.*

He finally dropped his hands after the intense moment of pause, pulling out his phone.

"What are you doing?"

"Calling the police?"

I grappled for it, panicked.

"The f—Em!?"

"Please," I picked obsessively at the skin around my nails. "What if they're watching us? What if they'll hurt her if we call? I know it's crazy but don't call just yet.

"If we don't do it now, it'll look like we have something to hide." He deflated after seeing my face. "Go…" He gestured dismissively.

I tried to ignore his pressing stares while we searched through the rooms. We were helpless, grasping at straws.

39

What did any of this mean?

James snatched the letter up, rereading it for any signs. "Flowery context filled with nonsensical bull." He growled. "What is this?" He indicated to the bloodstain. "Did you cut yourself?"

"I uh... I think?" I was absentmindedly fiddling with my hands.

"On what?" he demanded

"There's something sharp, like glass in the wax." I gestured to the envelope, shrugging, hardly seeing the importance of a scratch. "They want to see me."

"Em, that's what makes it more dangerous. This flamboyant jerk thinks you stole from Him. Do you consider that as someone in their right mind? When they resort to kidnapping to meet you?" I tried snatching it from him, but he held it high overhead. "We can look it all over when the authorities get here."

"James, what if we call and we never see her again?" I gave his side a shove. "This FK said they're just keeping her to make sure I meet them! And we've got nothing to offer the police other than my blood on a letter."

"A letter with a piece of glass shoved in the wax! Anyone with half a brain could put two and two together."

"Yeah, and you trashed her room. Is that a part of the protocol? And what the hell did you throw away, huh? Face it. The whole thing looks shitty." I spun around, crossing over into the entrance hall for a sweatshirt and flashlight.

"What are you so afraid of?" James deliberately followed. "The police are there for a reason."

I felt claustrophobic, *trapped.*

"I'm going to go look outside…"

"Think about it," he pleaded. "We don't even know how they got in much less get her out without being seen."

I shivered. Those were similar thoughts I had about the Pale Man. *How quickly he had come and gone without drawing attention to himself? Why didn't he jump me at the party when I was alone in the woods?*

Despite how agitated I felt, James' overbearing brother act hadn't been taken for granted. The night held a bitter taste, and the narrow path of my flashlight was little comfort in the shadows.

Shuffling along the damp grass, I tried to focus on the pinpricks of heat that settled through my toes. My mind was reeling, tumbling over itself in a hyperactive jumble of obsessive babbling. Law enforcement was not equipped to handle unearthly men that froze rain by mere contact, right? They don't deal with creepy rhyming monsters hiding under bridges or disembodied laughter in the trees.

If James indeed had known what happened, he'd think I was lying, or worse, mentally unstable. *I wasn't my mom.* Closing my eyelids, I shivered a yawn, drawing my arms closer to myself.

Searching had gone across the neighborhood. We echoed Abigail's name throughout the alleyways and circled the local playground, hoping to glimpse blonde hair. There was nothing—no sign of her running off or there being a struggle.

It was as if she merely *vanished*.

My last option was the thicket behind our house. I hadn't considered it as a possibility because Abigail had been strictly taught it was a dangerous area. The growth was dense, hiding the sharp incline to a ravine. Lofty grass hung over the edges making a deceitful impression of where the ground ended. If a toddler were to go traipsing through the woods at night, she would easily tumble down and hurt herself.

Climbing carelessly over the worn fence dividing our backyard from city property, we pushed through the thick underbrush and on into the trees.

"Stay." James broke the silence when we found our way to the edge. "You've done enough today."

His words were so absolute I physically felt myself shutting down. I stood foolishly barefooted, watching silently as he slipped off into the dark pit below. The flashlight beam swung in and out of view as he shouted out my sister's name, sending dogs howling into the crisp air.

I knew the area well. The ravine stood as a former dumping ground for non-decomposable items during the 40s to early 70s. As a preteen, I used to walk along the rusted scrap metal that lay scattered wedged between its rock covered bedding. Scavenging, I would dig for hidden oddities exposing broken plates, medicine bottles, porcelain baby doll limbs, and utensils; it grew into an eclectic hobby for a quirky kid with no friends.

My favorite spot was the old Dodge cab-over that jutted out beneath a sizeable billowing willow. Long tendril branches curved up and over the rim of the gully, curtaining the perch during the spring and summer.

James had been down there for over 15 minutes. If he had not encountered anything by now, I knew she wasn't down there. Abigail was mischievous, enjoying hide-and-seek like most little kids but she'd never shy from James's voice.

By the time my friend had found his way back up the steep incline, Abigail's disappearance had settled as a twisted mass inside me.

I was such an idiot.

Frustrated, we quietly trailed into the yard and around the house. I sat on the steps of the porch, flexing my toes, attempting to regroup a plan of action. I would have never noticed the massive silhouette standing along the street if it weren't for the creak of a rusty mailbox hinge.

Glancing up, I did a double-take and leaned to stare up at the oversized object shifting uncomfortably in front of me.

"H-hello?" There was a strained whine as if the being wasn't sure how to respond. "Who's there?"

Maybe if I didn't encourage a conversation, it would go away?

The porch boards flexed under James from somewhere behind me.

"*Pardon, didn't mean to ssstartle,*" returned a low whispering hiss. We both took in a sharp breath when the stranger moved to stand beneath the lamplight.

Hairs rose along my neck at the sight.

Hazy light hit the rear of the beast's broad shoulders, illuminating its tawny fur. They seemed to peer down across a long knotted nose, hooded eyes staring thoughtfully toward me.

"*You can sssee through my glamour?*"

"I…" my voice dissolved.

What were you supposed to say to a supposedly nonexistent creature of supernatural capabilities?

James swiftly switched on the porch light, directing his lantern into the being's face. Seething, it recoiled from us.

43

"Stay the hell back!" He ordered, brandishing the beam as a sword.

"*Isn't it a bit rude to be pointing bright lightsss into innocent bystandersss eyes? You really ssshould control your imp, Emmaline.*"

"Sorry!" I squeaked helplessly.

Waving us off, they made their way toward Mr. Weatherly's front lawn, grumbling about humans being a hazard to society; a long thinning tail trailed behind its body, autumn leaves clung to the tuft of fur at the tip. The scenario became even more bizarre when the beastly thing walked up the steps and into the house, mail tucked under the crook of its arm.

"That THING lives at your neighbors?" James stared in disbelief. "If it lives there, then where is Weatherly?"

"Actually," I slowly found my words. "I think that is Mr. Weatherly."

"You're shitting me."

"No. No, I'm not."

"How could you possibly know that?" He countered. I didn't have a straight answer for that, perplexing my friend further.

"How could that large *Thing* be next door and we hadn't even noticed? I'm pretty sure I would have noticed a long time ago if your neighbor was a Sasquatch!"

"Troll…" I concluded.

"I don't even want to know how you came up with that. Has this happened to you before Emma? Tell me the truth."

"James."

"Emma. Have you seen this before?" The excitement was swelling in his neck, flushing his ears and giving him a nervous shoe tap. "I'm going batshit crazy…" he paced. "How do we even know *He* doesn't have something to do with Abby's abduction? Huh?"

"I'm not sure…" I curled my fingers about the railing, slowly rising from my spot.

"How can you be so calm? You wanted to play Nancy Drew, well, there's your incentive!" he pointed to Weatherly's house.

No one had awoken from the others yelling. Even the yowling dogs had stilled.

"Let's… get inside. We're exposed out here."

I knew we would not find Abigail that night, but our sudden discovery left me to ponder a large window of fantastical possibility.

"Dreaming," The redhead concluded, plopping onto the couch. "This is just a dream. We're dreaming, Em."

But it wasn't a dream, nor was it a figment of my imagination. My curiosity itched to sneak over and peek into the window of Mr. Weatherly's homestead but felt insecure standing alone in a world I realized now I knew nothing about.

CHAPTER 3

FRIDAY MORNING

I woke startled to find myself in the living room, my phone vibrating across the coffee table while David Bowie's 'Dance Magic Dance' filled the space with unnecessary chatter. I grappled for it, pawing clumsily at the screen with my fingers. "Hello?" My voice was rough with cotton tongue."

"Darling!"

"Sunshine?" My eyes popped open to a painful jumpstart when the sun hit my face. *What a wakeup call.* I felt like I had just pounded shots the night before. "What's wrong? Did something happen?" Shuffling around in haste, I tried to comprehend the other's excitement.

"No, no, nothing's wrong," She crooned softly in her charming Asian lilt, "But you certainly *are* late."

"Oh. Oh no, Sunshine I'm sorry," I struggled up the steps for some fresh clothes, intent to pull on the nearest thing possible and rush to work.

"Darling, Darling, do not worry!" She was one of the few who used my surname affectionately. Perhaps it was because she and her husband came to Port Angeles after the pre-established superstitions. "Eugene took your shift! You've had a hard week. We are fine for you to take time off. Be with your sister." I felt the knot twist in my gut, recapping last night's devastation. "We are training Jordan and have Heather to help with weekends. No worries. Have the break you need."

"Thank you Sunshine, tell Eugene thank you for me," I walked toward the kitchen, nearly tripping over James who had been sleeping on the floor near the loveseat.

Shaking my head, I propped my upper torso against the island counter, settling to a comfortable slouch. "I—uhm—should at least get my paycheck. I would have gotten it on Wednesday, but I kept Abigail out of daycare for the wake."

"Come by when you can." There was some muffled talk on Sunshine's side of the line. "Eugene's keeping it in the back for you."

Starting the coffee with one hand, I smiled against the phone. "Thank you, so much."

"Yes, anytime Darling, rest."

I hung up after my goodbyes, sighing in relief. A fraction of stress cracked and tumbled off my shoulders at the thought of not worrying about work until Monday. Not that Easy Street was a stressful environment; although, pushing out hot drinks to a morning rush was a bit of a mind trip, having time off took complications out of the equation so that I could focus entirely on Abby, finances be damned.

Sitting with a mug of freshly brewed Sumatra coffee, I pondered the words James had said to me the night before.

'How do you know HE doesn't have something to do with Abby's kidnap?'

My brows furled, gazing into the recesses of my cup.

Why hadn't I called the police as he had asked? Even in this new world, where monsters were becoming a reality, that didn't mean I shouldn't abide by the law. I had no reason to doubt their capabilities, right?

My anxiety level told me otherwise.

What was I afraid of?

My grip tightened on my coffee. *I was a mess.*

Needing a distraction, I ambled out of the kitchen, around James, and up the stairs. Intent to be productive and dress, I placed measured steps down the hall but found myself caught, gazing into Abby's room.

I took in her empty bed, willing her body to emerge from the stack of pillows—grumpy expression included. As if I had forgotten we were just playing a game. Numbing silence settled against the knowledge of two rooms bare.

Refusing to cry, I tore away, marching into my ever-cluttered room to peel off the grimy funeral dress I had slept in. A shower would have been nice but too much effort. With little recollection, I mechanically picked out clothes from the piles on the floor, shrugging on a fairly wrinkled attire.

My mind wandered aimlessly along the various colored streaks that filtered through the pane of stained glass above the bed. Distracted, I prepared to leave out without a second thought, only to catch a glimpse of myself from the vanity mirror.

"Brush your hair, Emma," I shook my head, grimacing at my reflection. Dropping to the edge of the mattress, I tore forcibly against the bedraggled locks, beating my frizz into submission.

I ran my gaze along the nightstand, noticing the book settled to the corner—*Mom's diary*. Perhaps the mystery shrouding its existence was what kept me weary. The lock was shut, and the key had been missing since her death. While I was tempted to pry the thing open, damaging the journal didn't seem worth it. Maybe mom lost the key on purpose, unless, she was buried with it.

That wasn't creepy at all.

"Em?" James called up the stairs nervously. "Em, are you there?"

"Yeah, I'm here," I left my thoughts with the book and made my way into the living room.

Even with a night of restless sleep, with wrinkled clothes and pillow hair, James was extremely good looking. He was a tall, willowy creature with a toned core that often sent the women purring after him at the gym. His jawline was sharp with high cheekbones to match. Thick arched eyebrows framed his chocolate irises that were so heavy they appeared black. If it weren't for the usual impish grin on his face, his looks could cut you deep to the bone. James Beasley was a whole breed of his own.

"Hmmm... coffee?" he gave a hopeful gaze to my mug.

"Yep," I gestured casually toward the kitchen. "Just don't use the whole honey bear this time."

He cackled like his old self, flitting off toward the drip coffee to create his syrupy concoction.

Snatching up the kidnap letter, left to the coffee bar the night before, I followed him back into the kitchen to settle beside the table overlooking the backyard. I observed James as he bounced about the mustard-colored room. The 70s style wasn't exactly my favorite décor, with faded daisy borders lining the maize tiled walls below the painted cabinets; it had been untouched since my parents moved in. Bizarre carpet and wood floors covered the entire development. Fixed, stained glass accented windows, while speckled ceilings with gold glitter graced a few of the more obscure rooms. The master bedroom had a mirror on the beam above. Mom had plenty of opportunities to upgrade the house, but it stood as a statement against everything Gram was. Not to mention a memorial of the way dad had left it.

"You're over-thinking again," James folded up onto the chair before me, knees tucked up to his chest. "What are you doing today?" His demeanor had sobered, giving me the impression that his words carried more meaning than he was letting on.

"If you're asking about work, Sunshine called. I have it off."

"Good because we're calling the police."

I held my cup up with both hands, looking across the rim to the window. Responsibility gnawed at me as a realization hit me. "I'll need to tell my grandparents." Rubbing my face, I felt uneasy. "Let's just… get this over with."

"Like pulling off a Band-Aid," he added.

I shot him a look.

After James contact the PA law enforcement, I had the pleasure of calling my kin. I wasn't sure what I was expecting, but there was a lot of quiet on the other side of the phone.

"Are you still there...?" I leaned against the door, ripping the skin around my nails while mildly observing a police car parked in front of the house. "I said—"

"I heard what you said," Gram gave a clipped tone. "We'll be dressed and on our way shortly."

"Right... okay." My shoulders sagged. "Hey Gram, do you know anything about a key found on mom—Gram?" I looked at the screen, realizing she had already hung up.

James gave me a peculiar look as he passed. Despite only one police vehicle showing up, the house became the neighborhoods highlight of the afternoon, not to mention a personal nightmare. My grandparents weren't here, and three officers were now reviewing the evidence and crime scene. Making myself useful I offered them a bottomless pot of coffee.

"I'm sorry for yur loss Emma."

Glancing up, I studied the cop momentarily. Shoester was the officer in training, a healthy-looking young man only a few years senior. While we shared a few art classes back in school, I doubted that was where he had remembered my name. Anyone could pick out a Darling as if we had it stamped on our foreheads.

"Which one," I countered. Sympathy wasn't a strong suit of mine.

51

"I, well... yur mom." Blinking timidly, he eased against the counter to watch me flip the coffee to brew. "It looks like it only keeps going downhill for ya, doesn't it?"

"Shouldn't you be working?" I shot him a look, involuntarily shivering; they held the door open, letting the chill roll through, despite how hot I ran the stove.

"I didn't mean to offend, Emma. It's just, with yur dad, mom, and sister, you know, and those things people say about the Darlings..." He straitened awkwardly with an empty mug in hand. Snatching it angrily, I hastily refilled his coffee. The maker hissed with indignation as the black liquid sizzled onto the hotplate.

"I think you should just go do your work, Shoester." Shoving the drink back into his hands, I made him jump. "And leave the curiosity card at the door." He was still a superstitious local, despite his job title.

"Erm, right..." he lifted his cup and nodded in thanks, quickly shuffling off to join the other two officers.

I looked to the clock; Gram was unusually late.

The police made a full search of the house. They checked every room, working through a systematic procedure to ensure the situation was handled as professionally as possible. I watched the officers bag the letter, regretting not copying down its contents. Fingerprints were obtained on the window and doorknob from Abby's bedroom. Pictures were shot, things were moved and disassembled. I pulled out the most recent photos and videos I could find of her.

Where were my grandparents? The officers wanted pictures of my father, and they needed to know they were looking in the wrong place. Ethan L'Wren was filed as a missing person, but everyone knew he was dead. He *had* to be. When he vanished, they found his truck near Lake Crescent Lodge; encouraging the old native tales of angry spirits that drag victims into the deep glacial waters. *Never to be seen again.*

As a kid, overhearing the various slanderous undertones given to my father, paired with the lights of law enforcement, imprinted my first bitter taste of being a Darling.

The men buzzed softly to themselves about the legitimacy of a real hostage situation. The letter stated compensation for returning Abigail. There was no telling when another messenger would show.

My anxiety ran high, to where I had every intention of grabbing my keys and heading toward the exit. Even if the house was chill, the strangers tracking in and out began to close in on me, smothering me.

"Miss Darling?" Officer Crowe questioned, looking up from his paperwork to give me a raised brow.

Couldn't I take a breather?

"Yes?" I swiveled where I stood, beginning a slow meandering to the middle-aged man.

Clean cut graying hair and deep grey eyes, Crowe had laugh lines hiding behind his groomed stubble. I wondered if that was a sign, that he was more than just the badge on his uniform.

"I'd like to go over your witness statement again. I'm looking at it, and something seems… vague."

My cheeks flared with the idea of confusing facts. I didn't want to get caught up in telling too much.

"Oh?"

"Yes. Nothing we can't clear up. Is there a room we can go to sit and talk?"

"Yeah sure… Upstairs." I pulled myself up the steps, guiding him into the master bedroom I gestured to the small wicker table situated before a large window overlooking the mountains. "Is this okay?"

"More than, thanks." Sitting he began to spread out the papers before himself.

Closing the door a bit, I tried not to fidget. I was having a difficult time talking to the police officer directly. "Miss Darling, could you state your general information and the relation to the missing child in question?"

"My name is Emmaline NovaLee Darling. I'm twenty. My birthday is November 23rd, 1991. Abigail LaMay Darling is my younger sister."

"Address, city, and county you currently reside?"

"1413 West 18th Street. Port Angeles, Washington. Clallam County."

"Born of Dawn Darling and Ethan L'Wren?"

"Yes."

"And your sister?"

"Mom… never said," I admitted.

"All right," He wrote a few things down on a small pad of paper before leaning back in the bamboo chair. "Now, if you can, please recall as much detail of what happened yesterday, was there anything suspicious going on? Did you see anyone strange at your mother's funeral?"

"I thought I had already placed that all in my statement. We were at the funeral, nothing happened."

"Ah," Crowe stared at what I now knew to be my witness account. "So, what is this you say about seeing something odd just before leaving then? You write, 'it was probably my imagination.'" He peered up at me with an expression I couldn't quite put my finger on. "Mind talking about that Miss Darling?"

"What... is there to tell? I thought I saw something..." I shrugged my hands into the pockets of my hoodie, digits fiddling with my cell.

What kind of mayhem would I unleash if I was to show him the photo I took of The Pale Man?

"Emma," Crowe replied gently. "Is there something on your mind?"

Staring at the table my hand slid from my pocket, cell phone clutched within my grasp.

"There was a man..." I clamped my jaw shut when a knock came to the door. Officer Crowe seemed calmly agitated by the interruption, but he consented the others entry.

"John?" Officer Harper, who was Crowe's partner, peered in. "Sorry, but we have something I'd like you to look at."

He rose and smiled apologetically. "We will have to continue later, Emmaline."

Nodding quickly, I followed behind the two men, curiosity getting the better of me as they slid into Abigail's room. The door was gently shut behind them, but they weren't concerned enough to check when the old door didn't stick, leaving me leeway to push slightly against it with my shoe to listen.

"The window was sealed shut," explained Harper.

55

I couldn't see what they were doing. The door wasn't opened wide enough to view the scene, but the two men were huddled near the far wall, facing Mr. Weatherly's house.

"Looks like ice…" Crowe stated.

"It's cold, but it isn't enough to freeze a window shut," Harper replied. "Take a look at this…" there was a moment of pause before a murmur of questions broke out amongst them.

"If this is a drug, it isn't anything I've ever seen before," Crowe spoke.

"It's reflective." His partner stated. "Possibly just glitter of some sort. This is a little girl's room."

"Bag it," concluded Crowe. "You'll have to have Shoester get a ladder to continue dusting the exterior of the glass. Get some samples of ice too. Just in case. Looks like code 207 could be forced."

Eyes widening in alarm, I quickly turned when someone walked up the steps. If I wanted to get out for a breather, this would be my chance.

I headed down the stairs quickly, trying to pass Shoester but he caught me by the elbow.

"There you are…" He quickly released my arm. "Uhm, your grandparents are here Emma…"

There went my escape plan.

"Oh?" I turned my head, to watch my grandmother grasp the post of the rail with a handkerchief.

She peered up with a look of utter concentration. Her eyebrows were stitched together, freehand cradling a purse against her chest. When we crossed gazes, she shook her head.

"Emmaline, come downstairs. Go on Brandon, tell John and Paul."

Shoester gave me a look of open pity, doing as he was told.

Confused, I descended the steps. My hesitation quickly bled into dread when I turned the corner to greet my family. Words caught in my throat, losing meaning in a jumbled mess of hysteria.

I gripped the wooden railing watching Grampa stand comfortably, hand in hand, with a creature posing as Abigail. Waxy and stretched, it was as if their skin was having a hard time fitting to its bones; like a sweater, shrunk in the wash and forced to mold over a body now twice its size. Her eyes bulged a little too much making them owlish, pupils dilated and unblinking.

There was the image of my sister being skinned alive so that this thing could step into it like a wetsuit. I was going to throw up, and there she stood *smirking.*

"Grampa…"

"Everything's okay Emmaline." He mumbled.

"Grampa, you need to get away from that thing."

He frowned, watching me.

There it was.

That same expression Shoester had.

"Emmaline," Gram gripped my wrist, "I think you need to sit down and breathe."

My mouth was dry, eyes fixated on the monster. I hadn't heard the officers descend the stairs until Officer Harper passed me.

"Abigail Darling?" He looked to the girl and then to Grampa.

"I'm sorry Paul. There has been a grave mix-up, and unfortunately, your time was wasted," Gram replied.

"No," I said firmly, staring at Gram, despite how tight her grip was getting. "That's **NOT** my sister. We spent all night looking for her. Where's James?" I looked around.

"Yesterday was a taxing ordeal," Gram continued, focusing on the men before us. "Emmaline was withdrawn, disappearing down to the river during dinner with the funeral guests. When she found her way back into the house, she wanted to leave, and insisted on taking Abigail with her. I pressed for her to stay the night. Emmaline is a grown woman, she's made it plain she will do as she pleases, but little girls need security."

"That's not true, Gram! That's not true! She left your house with James and me. Then she got kidnapped, right out of her own bed!" My heart was racing, eyes darting between the group, "Where's James?!"

"Emmaline…" Grampa spoke sternly. "Who on earth is this James you keep speaking of?"

"James Beasley, in the report you made?" Officer Crowe looked over the paperwork he had brought with him, the witness account.

"He's been in the house the whole time!" I stared at them.

"Emma, the house has only been occupied by the four of us," Shoester muttered.

"James gave you a report. He was the one that called you in the first place." The room was quiet, save for raspy breathing coming from the creature clutched tightly about Grampa's hand. Then it dawned on me. "I'm not making this up. He's real. You… you don't remember?"

"I think you should sit down, Emmaline." Gram yanked on my elbow, pushing me onto the chair in the entrance hall.

This was only the beginning of a mental shutdown. Murmurs bounced around me, discreetly trying to debate what to do. Everything came to a pause at the sight of the disfigured creature. The police tucked away the evidence that stated the intent of kidnap, filing reports and packing up their tools.

Whoever FK was, they had a severe lack of manners.

"Emmaline… You're tired, stressed… confused." Grampa tried consoling me. He leaned in, giving my shoulder a gentle pat. "Let's just smooth this all out. Chalk it up as a simple mix-up. Then you can come back to the house with us and spend a few days."

"No…" My voice was hollow. I could hear it. A part of me wanted to grab the evil little beast and force it to break the hold it had over everyone. "It's been stressful." I parroted. "I buried my mom. Just need to clear my head."

"That's very understandable," Harper interjected, offering a sympathetic look. "No one is accusing you of anything, Emmaline. I think it would be best if you took up your grandparents' offer… or we can bring you to the hospital, let you stay the night for some assurance."

Crowe seemed to slip from the bowels of the kitchen then. He walked in careful strides as if he were approaching a frightened animal ready to bolt. "Miss Darling. I was hoping to take a few more minutes with you to finish our discussion. I'm sorry we were interrupted earlier." The intensity in his grey eyes was sharp but straightforward, nothing to hide there.

Harper, ever watchful, gave his partner a slight shake of the head in disagreement.

Should I lean on Officer Crowe? Was there something in my story that rang through to him? If I could get him alone, talk rationally to him, maybe, just maybe, he'd begin understanding what was going on.

"Yeah," I rose deliberately, looking into the living room at the creature playing with Agatha. My lip curled in disgust when they took up the doll's arm and popped it from the socket. "It's fine. We'll talk now..."

Guiding him up the stairs, I quickly pondered the risks involved, anything to keep me from looking utterly foolish... but really, I had very little else to lose, and my reputation wasn't that stellar, to begin with. "Has someone been in my room?" I noticed a light faintly glowing under the crack of the door. A shadow cast itself across the line, making it clear someone was inside.

Without waiting for an answer, I quickly walked further down the hall, nudging open the door with the sole of my shoe—hoping for James.

"Well..." Crowe started.

Shoester looked up from beside the bed, my mother's journal sat unopened in his hands.

"What are you doing?" I scolded. My emotions lashed out as I snatched the journal from his hold, "Out."

"Emma, I—"

"**OUT**! You had *no* business!"

"Now, Miss Darling," Crowe held up his hands in guard. "Harper asked him to look in here."

"Why? And why pick this up?" I waved the book erratically toward him.

Shoester stuttered out a nonsensical ribbon of jitter. The seasoned officer surveyed the scene with an air of unconcern.

"You think I'm lying," I stated.

"I don't think anything," Crowe sighed softly. "But you must admit this seems strange." I tried interjecting, but he held up his hand. "Look at the facts, Miss Darling, half of your report is false by the sheer presence of Abigail, which creates suspicion on the rest of your account."

"You have evidence."

"We do." He nodded. "And we will look into it. But plainly, you are under a significant amount of stress. My best advice is to come with us to the hospital and have an evaluation. Your grandparents stated that the family has had a history of mental disorders."

"I'm not crazy."

"Then let's rule anything out that might pose a threat to the investigation. This letter you have, it makes your house unsafe. I can't force you to go to your grandparents, but it is in your sister's best interest to stay with them."

CHAPTER 4

FRIDAY EVENING

Isolation was an unsettling distraction from the muddled plateau I had placed my feelings; trying to remind myself that my grandparents were somehow brainwashed, and that James had a valid reason for disappearing. I had to believe I could make it through the night without losing my mind.

Time drudged slowly on while lying limply to the hospital bed. The afternoon comprised a physical and mental examination, followed by a slew of various deficiency tests to rule out anything unexpected. At the end of a very long arduous wait, I had been told I was functioning normally, and, despite Gram's insistence of psychosis, the diagnosis was classified as 'Complicated Bereavement Disorder.'

I was clinically depressed by the loss of my mother. The hospital, by law, could not keep me through the night unwillingly, although their advice strongly suggested I stayed for peace of mind. With nothing better to do, I slowly settled into the reality of my situation. I was alone and needed to find a solution.

I pressed my palms firmly against my eyelids until pinpricks of light formed amid the darkness, thinking hard. *Whispering woods, The Pale Man, Mr. Weatherly, F.K., and The doppelgänger, what did they all have in common?* No one saw them for what they were.

I took up my phone, scrolling anxiously through previous days of conversation with James to reassure myself that he was real. He was. I could vividly recall his face. Tell you how long he'd been growing out his hair, the story behind the scar on his eyebrow. The brand of the stupid jacket he had been obsessing over until he broke down and bought it. James wasn't a figment!

Who could brainwash several people into believing a person didn't exist; to make them blind toward such a monstrous creature, who now posed as my sister, and to bend the truth and write a different story?

Rolling sideways, I dropped onto one socked foot, then to the other. Straitening, I drug my sight around the room, found a pen and pad of paper, before flopping onto the chair near the window.

At least I had a great view…

Me: Where are you? I texted James.

I needed to think.

Weatherly was a clear target for consideration. Our houses were close, and Abigail's windows were facing the old man's home. With a bit of work, anyone could have taken a ladder to the side and snuck up through the window. Even if there was no clear motive for kidnap, I had to admit that a disturbed mind rarely had reasoning behind their actions.

Tapping the pen against the window in thought, I stared out into the harbor, watching the oil rigs pull in for maintenance.

I had an itching feeling in the back of my mind.

There had to be a *pattern. Connection. Web.*

Drawing out the moments that stuck out, I circled The Pale Man and doppelgänger, pointing them toward F.K., who appeared to be the anonymous ringmaster of the entire fiasco. Weatherly stood on his own in the page's corner, hovering with the Whispering Woods. I wondered where I could go from there. I was no detective, yet here I was, musing over the possibilities of who took Abby.

Pulling up the search engine from my phone, I typed *Troll*. Immediately the distorted pictures of internet pop culture smeared the first few inches of the screen. I scrolled down, reading the definition of Troll:

'Noun: Troll
Plural noun: *Trolls*
Trolls are a mythical cave-dwelling beings depicted in folklore, as either a giant or a dwarf, typically having a repulsive appearance.
Synonyms: *goblin, hobgoblin, Gnome, Halfling, demon, monster, bugaboo, ogre*
'The storybook trolls who live under a bridge.'

There were thousands of results.

Distractedly, I ran my eyes across the first few explanations of an *Internet Troll*. I ticked away at the pages on the screen, concentration lacking as I passed domains dedicated to movies, games, and news feed somehow linked to *Troll*. Folklore was too far and few in between, attracting fanciful topics holding no substance. None of it appealed to my curiosity. Nothing jumped out in connection to my plight.

Changing tactics, I backtracked.

Entering, **Pacific Northwest Trolls**, it was then that my interest peeked.

Images of the troll's statue under the *Fremont Bridge* in Seattle, Washington popped up, followed by sites dedicated to *Troll Holes* and *trolling*, a form of fishing tactic. Five sites down and a website by the domain name of 'P.N.W. Ghouls and Goblins: A simple guide to the fantastical secrets within the Pacific Northwest,' stole my attention.

Tapping the link, I felt a sense of eagerness, watching the simplistic website upload onto the screen before me.

Sage green and cream-colored background framed an amateur's collection of obscured pictures dedicated to the lush dripping landscape of the Peninsula Northwest. Most all had red circles showing some unfocused point in the shot they claimed were supernatural sightings. I didn't take the time to read their captions but instead focused on the writing of the author.

In a highlighted entry, it read:

'If you believe in the existence of Faeries or have been, in fact, pixy-led yourself, trust this when I say... you are not alone. I will take you on the shocking retellings of the well-hidden secrets within the PNW while advising tips and tricks in keeping your life Faery-less.

P. Whimsy'

I licked my lips.

Faeries...

Pressing on a subtitle to the left of the posts, it led me into a long list of various creatures this P. Whimsy took the time to classify, describe, and warn his audience of.

There were easily hundreds of posts dating clear back to March 2001, a dedicated blogger with 15 years of constant monthly content.

With no other leads, I scaled the long list and settled to reading P. Whimsy's 'Troll Findings,' happy to find there was more than one reference.

The first classified Troll was known as a *Buggar*. It went, 'Buggars, possibly migrated to England as German Trolls but is more predominantly classified as a shapeshifting Goblin.' There were no noticeable traits other than the shapeshifting, which I noted, before moving on to the next column.

'Duergarrs, were Dwarf Faeries, who showed Troll-like behavior by preying on Travelers.' My mind trailed to images of my neighbor cooking up Abigail as a late-night snack.

"Fee-fi-fo-fum," I quickly squashed my mental disturbances.

The next was 'Illes *(pronounced Eels)*,' they were particular species that, 'were hairy and dark in color. The dangerous characteristic of this species was their shapeshifting abilities, in which they used something physically alluring to snare their prey.' Coming in contact was *highly ill-advised*.

In my thirty minutes of expertise, the next few species weren't even worth noting. Nothing seemed to describe Mr. Weatherly's grizzled appearance, and I wondered if I was also pointed in the right direction.

Leaning forward I rubbed my eyes, feeling them cross in the strain—the last mentionable post I was debating whether I would take the time to digest. I had onset restlessness about my so-called detective work.

Tapping my pen distractedly to an irregular rhythm, I curled back against the seat, giving a satisfying pop to my upper spine while I stared up into my phone for the final installment that P. Whimsy offered.

It proved to be the most fulfilling content so far:

'Trolls also referred to as: Trolds, Trows, Berg People, Hill Men, Rise, Jutul, and Tusse, have been a part of folklore as long as humans have had oral storytelling. They have described Trolls as tall bipedal creatures with shaggy, rough hair covered in moss-like growth.'

'They are primarily carnivorous beings only eating human flesh if their natural food supplies have declined dramatically. With this said, goat and mutton are their favorite meats or other faeries that are plump and robust in flavor.'

'Trolls are reported to hate humans, animals, and other Faeries which make them mostly reclusive by nature, claiming areas such as caves, ponds, bridges or long abandoned buildings as their own. Trolls are also said to find humans ugly and would never steal them for mates whom they regard as worthless. Fortunately, you would never catch a Troll going willingly into a human home, believing them to smell terrible.'

'If you come upon one, do not run from them for they can sense fear. Like any bully, you will only make your situation worse by attempting to flee. Outsmarting them is your best defense and leverage, for there was never a Troll who did not enjoy a game of riddles. Fortunately, Trolls have never been particularly smart, just tricky. If you find yourself with Troll problems, make a deal to match a riddle for the right of safe passage. If they lose, they will begrudgingly honor your contract and leave you be.'

'These days, Trolls rarely manifest outside of the Fae Realm, due to the over-accumulation of humans; however, don't let that fool you, they are closer than they seem. I do not advise contact.'

Something utterly extraordinary was happening—something supernatural. Lamp lights suddenly flickered on, just as the sun dropped to the West of the Olympic Mountains. No longer able to sit, I rose from my seat and pressed my forehead against the window.

Picking at my fingers again, I stared plainly to my reflection. I could feel my heart pulsing loudly up my neck, tightening my jaw. There was a heavy cocktail of desperation and adrenaline coursing through my system. My hands shook in need to prove I wasn't what they thought I was.

Despite the risks, if Weatherly was indeed a *Troll*, then he was the first stepping stone to regaining my life.

Pacing the room, I peeked out the door then checked my phone. Where was James? I slumped back into the chair, stretching out in restlessness.

"Stay... or go?" I mused out loud, observing the white plastered ceiling until my eyes crossed.

There was a light tap on the window…

Then a second.

A third...

Peeking over the arm of my seat, I watched with disinterest as tiny pebbles bounced off the glass. Some idiot without a phone was trying to get ahold of a patient in the building.

My phone vibrated unexpectedly. I jumped slightly, peeking to the message alert.

JAMES: Look down, dummy

Rising, I gazed downward, regarding James's overdramatic performance of attention with disinterest. The headlights of a car passed by, spooking him into the bushes. He waited a long moment before he was back to texting me, waving his screen light in my direction.

Abruptly, I wasn't interested in seeing him. I plopped back down and promptly neglected to reply.

JAMES: Em. I've come to rescue u! He finally sent.

Yeah right… I gave his name a sour look.

JAMES: I can't go in

JAMES: Visiting hours are over, he added seconds later.

JAMES: Em

JAMES: Em...

JAMES: Emmmmmmmmmmmmmmm!

JAMES: I can't explain over text

JAMES: Can U pls reply?

69

ME: That's funny, considering you never answer my texts

JAMES: I deserve that

ME: Where the hell have you been!?

JAMES: let's talk in person. Can u pls come out?

ME: I'm not going anywhere until you tell me where you've been!

There was a long pause. Enough to give me doubt he'd respond.

JAMES: Dads

I focused on the screen, and a sizeable sigh escaped my lips. I relented.

EM: I'll meet you outside... might take a while

JAMES: I'll b waiting

The process was sluggish. 10:23 PM checkout wasn't the normality for hospital. By the time I had gathered my things and signed release papers, it was almost 11:00.

I slipped nervously out the sliding doors, hugging my coat like it was a stuffed animal. *What if I had just imagined it all?* I stared at my phone screen for reassurance.

"Emma," James called lightly, waving halfheartedly from his leaning position against the red Toyota truck he drove, still handsome with his guilt-stricken expression.

Climbing into his vehicle, we made a long silent trek back to the house. When we arrived, the windows were dark and empty, blending the dwelling against the backdrop of the thicket beyond.

"Em—" He started, turning the vehicle off to settle us into an uncomfortable quiet.

"You weren't there, I needed you," My voice was stronger than I had expected—cold even.

"I'm here now."

Staring hard at the dashboard, I hugged my clothes closer.

"That's not good enough." I turned to glare at him, faltering when I saw the discoloration forming along his cheekbone.

"James…"

He turned toward me. The lamplight reflected in his eyes, revealing the glassy telltale signs of distress. "I fucked up."

"Shit, what did he do?" I flipped on the overhead light, trying to get a better look at his face.

"I told him he was a piece of shit for the things he's done, that he could go screw himself." He was excited and terrified at the idea he'd just stood up to his father.

"James, you don't jab a bear."

"I was angry and being an idiot, I left," he gestured with his head to the back hutch where the seat was crowded in stuffed duffel bags. "I'm now homeless," he stated bewildered.

"You aren't homeless," I observed him from the corner of my eye, taken back.

"Well, guess I could sleep in my truck." He said feebly.

"Oh, shut up and get in the house." I pinched the bridge of my nose then shoved my coat in his arms. "I need to do something—and I don't want questions."

"Okay..." he stiffened, staring at me intently before he fumbled for the keys.

71

"Just, get the fire started, will you?" Sliding from my spot, I waited impatiently for him to gather his things and walk toward the house.

"Be careful Emmaline," he called out tentatively.

Staying placid, I didn't respond, knowing he wanted to follow me.

Not tonight.

Waiting for him to close the door behind him, I took off down the narrow pathway between my house and Mr. Weatherly's. Unlocking the gate, I hooked a right into a small orchard. Congested with weeds, they drooped miserably with unpicked apples. An old Ford Coop sat sunken and depressed, long forgotten amongst the little weather-worn figurines peeking through the unkempt backyard.

Marching carefully up the warn porch steps, bypassing an earless stone bunny, I settled to the door and knocked quickly before I lost my nerve.

Leaning back on my heels, I waited.

There was no answer.

I did it again.

One by one the lights snapped off inside. The more persistent my knocking became, the swifter the house retreated into darkness.

"Mr. Weatherly!!!" I pounded until my cold fingers tingled.

Why did I give James my coat!?

I glanced over to my house to see if James had taken to snooping. So far, I didn't notice a mop of red hair poking out amongst the curtains. "Mr. Weatherly, you need to talk to me!"

Nothing.

"I know what you are," I prompted. Remembering Trolls couldn't resist a good game. "Let's make a deal. I want to play a game of riddles with you!" I really thought that would have worked.

The neighborhood quieted to my bantering, and the house kept still.

Maybe the gossip hadn't spread yet about today's events...

"I'll report you to the cops, Weatherly. They'll come and question you."

My heart curled into a knotted throb as subtle creaking floors sounded just behind the door. "I'm serious," I warned.

The light flickered on above me.

Stepping back in anticipation, I waited for the sound of a lock shifting back. I was disappointed again.

"I just want my sister back, can't you understand that? I know you must have something you can tell me, anything."

Perhaps my plea struck a chord. Unlatching clicks added to the metal grind of chains sliding and dropping away. After an agonizingly long pause, the door creaked open a fraction from its frame.

"*Ssstop yelling and pounding at my door, it'sss giving me a headache,*" The voice came again like a soft whistling wind, filled with dark foreboding.

I stepped back, startled.

"You really are Mr. Weatherly?" I asked meekly. "You aren't his pet or something, right?"

"*I never mistook you for a fool, Emmaline... do not make me regret such reservationsss.*"

"Can I come in?" I tried not to flinch in his honestly.

73

"*If you mussst…*" There was movement.

Giving myself a few seconds to collect myself I finally pushed the door open, just enough to slide inside. A cocoon of pitch black swallowed me whole. I felt suffocated as an odor clung to the walls, reeking strangely of wet dog and rotted wood.

"Can you turn on a light?"

"*Emmaline,*" there was a warning in that soft voice.

I quickly closed the door, regretting the action. *What had I gotten myself into?*

"Are you really Mr. Weatherly? Or… or did something happen to him?"

"Oh, how insightful you are," they chuckled. "*Hmmm… that was two questionsss. Which would you prefer me to answer?*"

"Both," I answered honestly.

"*Either, or,*" I heard a heavy shifting from my form. "*Wasss this why you came here, to interrogate me, or, perhapsss, was it something a little more meaningful you were after?*"

"My sister, I think you know something about her disappearance."

"*Oh, you do, do you?*"

"Yeah," I adjusted awkwardly. "This… guy with strange eyes and the ability to—" I hadn't said it out loud yet. "Freeze rain," Yeah, that sounded insane. "Found me at my mom's funeral then gave me a letter."

"*Did you open the letter?*"

"Yes. It's from someone who calls themselves, FK."

"*Oh, I sssee… Well, that IS a stroke of bad luck, now isn't it?*"

"Is it?"

74

"You drew blood, of course, am I presuming there wasss some afflicting implement on the letter? Hidden?" They didn't answer my question.

"Yeah…"

"Then you have doomed your sister." My heart sank to the recesses of my stomach; his words were so calm and resolute. *"Nasty Faeriesss and their slippery fingersss."*

"W-what?"

"Hmmm, I sssurmised you already knew." Even in the dimness, I had an unsettling idea the other could see me. At least my eyes had adjusted enough where I knew there was a vague outline standing before me. That or I broke into an old dead man's house to hallucinate.

"You're a Troll." That was a statement, not a question.

I hadn't touched a fantasy book since I was a preteen, vaguely recalling creatures of lore. I was no expert; yet, here I was, pointing fingers at a massive creature I had never seen until recently.

There was another bout of stillness before the being changed positions.

"Finally, clever girl…" they seemed a bit disgruntled. *"But not entirely accurate in your sleuthing; however, I'll give you points for intuition."*

I wasn't sure if They were trying to play me. *Oh, They had a sense of humor.*

"Then, what are you if you aren't a Troll?"

"I am a being, caught between two worldsss." His voice murmured across with regretful reminiscence. *"A pawn in a large game of twisted truthsss and deceptionsss, I am no one important other than a guide."*

75

I leaned forward, afraid to miss something they would say. "Who are you to guide?" I asked in a much softer voice.

"That is a good question, isn't it?"

"Why let me into your house if you refuse to tell me anything? What's so bad about giving a straight answer?" *Was this how it would be from now on, elusive behavior, speaking in riddles, rhymes?*

I was growing frustrated.

"You threatened me to allow you into my dwelling. What wasss I supposed to do to ssshut you up? Would you have preferred I slaughtered you on my stepsss? Perhaps, I'll drag you deep inside my home, rip you apart limb from limb? Boil your flesh for my soup, and grind your bonesss for my bread?" There was a sinister snicker. *"What a mess that would make..."* Paling, I backed fully to the door. *"Oh, don't be sssuch a baby, Emmaline. I prefer chicken if you must know. Besidesss, I wouldn't kill you, less I wanted to cease to exist myself."*

"Explain, please?" My voice croaked. "Is there some code against killing humans or something? Or are you supposed to guide me in the right direction?" I wasn't sure I would want to go in any direction they led me toward.

"A code, to not kill humans? Yesss, yesss I suppose you could call it that; although, it's become more of an unspoken order—new leadership these daysss. Oh, of course, if a few humansss go missing from time to time, it's not that big of a deal in the entirety of things..."

Running a hand through my hair, I gripped hard at the roots to ride through the brief urge to stomp on the beast's foot. I came to get answers; I reminded myself. "Are you," I began slowly, trying to remember the letter. "My guide?" That was direct.

"You, would be who?"

"Emma, Emma Darling! Are you my, Emma Darling's, guide?" I could practically taste the smugness in the air. This must be pent-up conceitedness he'd been harboring in the years hauled up in this old rickety house of his.

"*Yesss, I am.*"

I let out the breath I had been holding. If this was the work of FK, they were failing at managing their henchmen. "Why would I, Emma Darling, need a… magical being to guide me?"

"*To be led in the right direction, sssilly girl.*"

He tempted me to grab the earless rabbit outside and beat him over the head with it. *I think I was getting slightly aggressive lately…*

"Why do I, Emma Darling, need to be led in the right direction?"

"*Because you would fail otherwise, it's obviousss you have no clue how to handle yourself around othersss, such as me.*"

"Trust me. I won't have much of a problem if they are all grumpy old men that hide in the shadows like a coward." A rumbling growl reverberated throughout the room, sobering my mood just enough to keep from roaring back. "Don't give me that… you can't hurt me, right?" I folded my arms, glaring. "You've made me into an idiot this entire conversation. I think it's only fair I'm allowed to dish it back to you. Tell me what you have to say. Guide me where I am to go. But don't play me for an airhead, Weatherly."

"*Basssle.*"

"What?" My brow furled, taken through another setback of emotion as I stumbled into confusion.

"*My name is not Weatherly, it'sss Basle. Weatherly was the previousss owner of thisss establishment, who, unfortunately, met his demise many years prior.*"

"Base-el? Basil?" I instantly thought of the herb.

"*No, no, no.*" There was a disgruntled noise. "*Bah-sss-EL. Think of a lamb who bahsss. Think of the letter which is 'L.' Basssle.*"

"Basle," I corrected myself, earning a rickety sigh. I felt the awkward pause after his introduction. "Basle," I thought carefully. "Where has FK told you to guide me?"

"*Ah, we are getting to the more important questionsss, finally. Never assume the origin of intention, however.*"

That was unsettling. What was he trying to say? Didn't FK send him?

"If FK did not send you, Basle, who did?"

"*That, unfortunately, is one question I am not in the liberty of answering.*"

"Basle," I groaned.

"*I can only guide you in the right direction, Emmaline.*"

"Then where is the right direction!?" I refuse to apologize. He was insufferable. Gripping the doorknob I had every intention of walking away. I wasn't getting anywhere at this speed.

"*When the sky shines full of moon, beneath the town the market's boon. Knocking twice, and utter the word, will get you through to the Bazaar of Myrrd.*"

"Why is this important?"

"*Although I cannot tell you what you ssseek, go to The Market of Myrrd tomorrow night and look for a being by the name of Almarik. Ssspeak to only him, ask your questions wisely. Chances are he knowsss a great deal about your situation.*"

I peered closer, frowning when I couldn't extract anything from his face within the gloom of the room. I didn't understand why he couldn't tell me himself. *Was it not safe? Was someone watching? Perhaps, the one who stole my sister?*

"Why can't you help me...?"

"*I am sssimply the watcher in the night... the beacon of light when you don't know where to run, nothing more and nothing less.*"

"Then what is the word to get into *Myrrd*?" the name sounded so abnormal rolling off my tongue. "Where is *Myrrd*? Where can I find it?"

"*I will leave you with one more riddle and then I will bid you farewell. High upon the throne, the monsters perch on stable stone. Sharp teeth gleam with envy, its eaten bones of many. While it sleeps, it guards the keep. Down the steps is what you seek.*"

Would I remember all of this?

Basle must have seen the look on my face, feeling the floorboards shift beneath us while he changed weight from foot to foot restlessly. "*Do not think too awfully hard on it Emma. The Fae existence is a mind bottling experience to grip. You will learn. As for Myrrd, it resides below the Port of Angels.*" Even with the slight bite of impatience, I could now hear the sense of duty conveyed.

He wanted me to know I could trust him, rely on that he was giving me honest help and direction. Even if he was a shy creature—which hid away in the dark—I felt I could trust his word.

Since there was no longer a conversation rolling, I figured he was waiting for me to leave. I peered closer.

"*Emma,*" he gave a light warning.

"Basle," I countered. "I need to look you in the eyes."

"*What could that possibly accomplish?*"

"Have you ever heard of the phrase, the eyes are the windows to the soul? I want to trust you, so I need to see who I'm dealing with. You can't believe I'd just blindly follow your instructions, do you?" *No pun intended.*

"*You sssaw what I looked like the other night...*" There was stiffness in his voice.

"Not clearly."

"*What doesss it matter to you, so as long as I tell you what you need?*"

Giving a tentative smile, I slipped a hand behind to slide across the wall, searching for a light switch. "What's the issue? I'm sure you're the best looking Troll-thing out there!" I found a few power toggles, and, one by one, flipped them up.

The crackling of fluorescent bulbs filled the room, finishing with a resounding hum as the lights adjusted around us.

I quickly tried blinking away the spots of darkness. Turning to the creature, I nearly jumped out of my skin. He looked infuriated. Enraged. Basle's black lips curled back in a silent snarl, revealing harsh, jagged teeth from within. I would have bolted smartly from the spot only I was rooted from shock and fright.

The whites of his eyes, so haunting against the pale green of his irises, were wild with contempt for me. His face, elongated with a matted mane of cascading fur, had a long twisted nose and drooping dog-like ears. Basle stood much like an ape. His massive figure, forced to bend down from the low leveled ceilings, held him well over my height. Incredibly intimidating, it wasn't long before I felt the hairs on the back of my neck stand on end.

I stepped back from his monstrously hairy form to press against the door. He shifted from me in return, angling his face away.

"I'm sorry Basle. I didn't mean to shock you."

"Jussst... Get. Out."

"But Basle..." There was something to his eyes I couldn't quite put my finger on.

"*GET OUT!*" He roared.

I hopped to. Like wolves were snapping at the soles of my feet, I flew across the yard and in through the back door of my homestead. I had to lock the entrance and close the windows that surrounded me before I could even remotely calm down.

CHAPTER 5

SATURDAY MORNING

There was little sleep to be had. Morbid details of goats roasting alive across a bonfire consumed my dreams; their child-like screams echoed in my ears as masked beings danced around their sweltering bodies, laughing gleefully through the crackling flames, gangly figures jerking to a tuneless dance...

'**Emmaline...**' a voice whispered in my ear, jerking me from my nightmares.

I found myself alone fully clothed in a curled spot on my bed. Shaking, I laid staring up at the ceiling hoping to return to sleep, but exhaustion wasn't enough to pull me back.

Nerves shot, I settled for a cup of reheated coffee in the kitchen. Glancing over my hospital scribbles, I tried recovering bits and pieces from the night before.

Myrrd was a foreign word that ended with an awkward roll of the tongue. It left me tumbling around and around in the entirety of my situation, ending up in a muddled mesh of more questions than I had started with.

What sort of place was Myrrd? Why did I have to find this individual, Almarik?

I still needed to remember the clues Basle had left me. I was still feeling guilty for blowing it with him.

"Idiot," I muttered to myself, swirling the pen tip distractedly to the corner of the page. "Full moon... monsters with sharp teeth..."

What was I, a hero? I scoffed.

Think, think!

I abused my forehead, tapping it rather bluntly with the end of my pen, attempting to shock some brain cells into action. "Knocking twice, saying the right word would get me into *Myrrd*..." If *Myrrd* dwelled below Port of Angels, which was just one of many names bequeathed to the town, then he must have meant the market took place in the older parts of downtown. *The Underground... but which entrance was the right one?*

Channeling high school history, I could recall a brief discussion on Port Angeles's early years. Back in the later 1800s, the downtown area had begun the process of building on top of itself to escape the eroding ocean tides. Flushing an entire hillside downward, in what we now call, *The Sleuthing of the Hogback Hill*, what wasn't lifted was entombed. That is, until recent years when they were reopened for guided tours.

If monsters were real, then that's where they'd be. The problem was that there had been a handful of places saved and I had only one day to figure out the right one.

Not bothering to change, I grabbed my notes, half-charged phone, and headed out the door to visit *The Chamber of Commerce*, the home of the local 'Historical Tours.'

Knowing the *Chamber's* hours were a hit and miss during off seasons, I wasn't sure if I could even find the right information on a Saturday morning.

Down Railroad Avenue, my weary little Volkswagen could be seen puttering along the road as I slowed to peer intently at the small red-bricked building established almost flush to the road edge.

Even as the darkening skies lifted with a tinge of morning light, it had been showering, painting the ground with a thin sheet of gloss.

It was hard to see inside the building, but one thing was obvious, they weren't opened.

Slipping from my still-running vehicle, I jogged around the side to peek into the windows. I could just make out the floor to ceiling rows of various colored pamphlets, decorating the walls like mismatched tiles.

They didn't open until 10:00 AM.

The disappointment was pressing on my shoulders, but at least they were open on Saturdays, Sunday's and Mondays they were closed.

Luck, whatever that was, seemed to be on my side at that point. I only had to wait it out until then. My next venture was coffee. The current debate was whether I wanted to grace my lips with the heavenly black elixir that was Sunshine's gift to mortal man or avoid confrontation with my boss altogether.

Parking along Oak and First Street, in front of *Country Acre*, I sat in my car to watch as the rain drizzled down lazily in the early morning hours. Port Angeles ran on its own proper time of 8:00 AM to 5:00 PM during winter. Nothing was open aside for *Easy Street*, and I was attempting to avoid work as much as possible.

Flipping on a Canadian soft rock station and leaning back, I decided to wait it out for the remaining hour it took for the market to open its doors for a cup of Joe.

I hadn't realized I fell asleep until the sudden sensation of panic rose along my spine. Eyes darting quickly, I twisted to take a peek at my surroundings, only to realize I had a molten pair of irises staring through my side window. Sharp teeth visibly grinned through the glass.

The Pale Man had once again made himself known.

Glaring, I locked the doors quickly with a flip of the switch, an action only proving to amuse him further. I rolled my window down just enough to speak to him.

"For fuck's sake! Who and what are you?" *You tell him!* I congratulated myself on the hint of venom in my voice.

"Ah, Miss Darling, I see you have wisened over the past few days. May I ask how you have been fairing as of late?"

"How the hell do you think I'm fairing?" My fingers twitched in the desire to grip his collar and give his head a few smacks against the car. If the bug chipped further from the abuse, it would be well worth the damage. "Where the hell is my sister you monster?"

Tilting his head the top hat shaded his pasty skin from the shower while beads formed detailed designs about the rim.

85

"Sidhe," He corrected me lightly. "Nonetheless, Fae will do just fine. I would caution you on your words, Miss Darling. While I revealed myself to you, I have not to others. Which means," he drawled on. "You are yelling at empty space."

Damn monsters, boogiemen, and faery freaks.

I checked the clock, realizing it was around 8:30 AM. I had only slept over an hour. No one was up this early. Even if a cashier was looking through the window, they could have easily mistaken me for yelling at a seagull—we were infested.

"Humans with their silly paranoias," He chuckled beside me, as my attention returned to his almost translucent form. *Perhaps he had mistaken my distractions for fear?* "Calm down. You shall be fine."

"Oh really," I laughed sarcastically back at him. "Says the snatcher of small children."

"I did not steal the little Pisky."

"Why should I even believe you?"

"You don't. Need to that is. However, it is hard for a Fae to lie." I gave him a suspicious look over. "Twisting the truth and telling a lie are two different things, Emmaline. You can always find truth in the Faery tongue, but are often too misled by the enigma of its contents."

"Then what would you call taking Abigail from me?"

"Borrowing," he replied without a skip of a beat. "She'll return to you."

It was hard not to roll my eyes in exasperation, another supernatural trying to tiptoe around the subject at hand.

"Then why have her, what do you want?"

"I truly want for nothing; I really couldn't care less about your fate. It is my Master who requires knowing the state of your humanity."

Master? That isn't weird at all.

"Then… I suppose they would be the mysterious FK?"

There was no reaction to the other's face, merely a polite nod. The conversation all but fizzled into an awkward staring contest.

He watched me expectantly. "Well?"

"Well? Well, what?" He confused me.

"Your health, your emotional stability as of this point in the game?" he drawled again, looking bored.

"Fine," I ground out. *What an ass.* "As fine as I could be with my sister stolen from me." I peered closer. "Is Basle in the same league as you and yours?" Despite everything that transpired last night I had to make sure about who I was dealing with.

He observed me, eyes growing intense before he leaned back on his heels and looked skyward thoughtfully.

"Basle, the large matted hermit?" he stated. "He has approached you?"

"He's my neighbor." I glared. "You didn't think I wouldn't see a large lumbering creature roaming around my neighborhood? I'm not an idiot, and I don't sit well being forced into a scavenger hunt, scraping for goddamn clues to get to the end of the puzzle. You can tell your *Master* that."

"Speaking of which, I am here to relay another," He finally glanced back with a sardonic tooth-baring grin.

Hand raising slowly, his palm pressed against the window of the car door. The cold spread from his skin, slowly crystallizing and frosting the surface. I shrank away in alarm, watching his fingers curl over the crack of the window.

"On her death, fate was cast through dealings of the past," He murmured, breathing a heavy cloud of air. "Secrets inked with blood and tears, marking pages filled with fears. Bound up tight, then tucked away, hidden safely from the Fae."

"W-what?" My stomach felt upset again. I watched the other wearily, gripping the seat my body was halfway sprawled across.

"Miss Darling, have you ever wondered why this was all happening to you in the first place? Did you presume it was just bad luck?"

"I haven't gotten that far."

There was a careful expression on his face.

"Miss Darling, there is no coincidence within your circumstance, just a carefully calculated chain of events leading up to a climax that concludes the fortune of your being."

"What the hell have I ever done to cause Him, Her, THEM, whoever, to steal Abigail?" Hooking a hand to the steering wheel I hoisted myself back over, feeling my body tensing. "You've brainwashed my family and made me look insane."

"That isn't anything new to a Darling, now is it?"

I growled at him. "You have no right!"

"And yet, HE did." The Pale Man replied. "I wonder, how is our little Changeling fairing with dear Grammy and Pappy?" He simpered. "I expect it isn't *that* charming." Not waiting for an answer, his nostrils flared as he inhaled, body going rigid.

Somehow I knew what was about to happen before it hit. Ducking down, I curled up as a blast of cold air blew into the car, making it groan in protest while it rocked slightly to the strain. The mist above solidified, showering the roof with an overwhelming rhythm of sharp taps, before rolling off the sides and melting onto the ground.

"Tick Tock, Miss Darling," He called.

I was too overwhelmed and frozen to watch where he went. Scrambling for the handle, I spent the next few minutes trying to pry the door open. When that didn't work, I then turned on the engine enough to get the window down so I could crawl out the driver's side.

Predictably, he was gone.

Grabbing out my things, I shut the car off and quickly scooted inside the natural market, sighing in relief as the heaters wafted over my form.

I needed to stay calm. He was just there to deter me. Get me off track. I had to stay focused. Shifting to my notes, I walked a full loop around the produce, chanting a mantra in my mind to, *stay calm.*

Passing the laden barrels of citrus fruits, shelves of bagged greens, open-faced coolers of artesian cheeses and marinated goods, I found myself before the deli.

"Morning, what can I get for you today?"

I peeked up, gazing back to the young brunette with large solemn eyes and a pale complexion, paranoia was settling in as I wondered if she was a monster too.

She smiled faintly at me. *Was I looking twitchy?*

"Drip with room, please," I slipped out my wallet and clumsily fished around for coins, glancing around distractedly.

The store had over 40 years of service to the community, making its own historical footprint within the peninsula. One of the veteran employees were bound to know the information I was after, or, at least that was what I was telling myself in my moment of desperation.

Old rustic farm equipment and vintage cooking implements lined high ridged shelves that elevated the stained cedar rafters above. Small town roots of hospitality and tradition ran deep in the store's foundation, making it a hub for tourists to venture through as an attraction when coming across on the ferry from Victoria, Canada.

The main fascinations to the interior were the two fully functioning tractors stationed atop fortified structures, huddled silently to watch over the building. Like metal gargoyles perched atop the corners of old cathedrals, only wood and stone held them back from toppling to the floor below.

Paying, I settled to a table beside an old-fashioned mantelpiece comprised of large river rocks.

Conundrums were stacking up like unpaid bills, unsightly but necessary. Rewriting the second riddle to my dilemma proved harder without a sufficient night of sleep.

I gulped down the burning mouthful of coffee while bringing up the search engine. I had a split-second fear of thinking P. Whimsy's website was an illusion, until 'Faery Protection,' popped up as a recently updated post.

With pen and pad poised, I relaxed a fraction.

'When crossing the Unseen, we need to safeguard ourselves from the worst of their whiles, lest we are lost to them forever...

I have gone through the measures of assuring these are accurate full proof anti-Faery protection, as they have been passed down through oral legends from sources anonymous.

THE 3 RULES OF FAERY PROTECTION:
1. Never EVER drink or dine on the foods of the Faery Folk.

2. Carry Iron. Iron is poison to Fae and should be used as a precaution.

3. Discover a Faeries true name, and you have the power to cast them away. (*i.e., The Tale of Rumpelstiltskin*)

ANTI-FAERY PROTECTION CONTINUED:
4. "Place a nail in your right pocket when going outdoors."

NOTE: They primarily make Nails of steel, which is a refined metal derived from iron ore.

5. "Place Rowan berries in your pocket to keep from being swayed by Fae influences."

NOTE: Other names include Mountain Ash or Witchwood. They are fast growing bush-like trees, branded by their vivid red berries.

6. "4-leaf shamrock will break a Faerie's spell over the mortal who may carry it."

7. "Keep a Besom, a witch's broom, near the hearth of your home to keep unwanted spirits from entering through the chimney."

8. "Wear green while visiting a forest to keep from being toyed with cantankerous Fae."

NOTE: Red is ill-advised to wear for it draws Fae near you rather than away.
9. **"Use salt to cover entrances to guard your home of spirits."**
NOTE: Keeping it in your pocket to make a ring about you if encountered by them.
Best Wishes,
P. Whimsy'

The list wasn't long. Most of its contents seemed obscure, but I've never had to deal with pest control quite like this.

What Whimsy was suggesting, seemed far too out of my reach at this point. The only things that seemed workable were the nails and salt I could easily find in the kitchen. In my youth, spotting a 4-leafed clover took hours, hours I didn't have. Rowan Berries were an anomaly that I wasn't even sure grew around these parts. I wasn't confident I could afford the time to go in the outback and find out.

I had to remind myself that the two riddles from two different sources took president over protection. Whimsy's words were all but useless if I couldn't get into *Myrrd*, and while running face into danger didn't sound appealing, Basle's tips may lead to solving the second riddle that The Pale Man offered. Unless, of course, they were all tricks from the same source, but that was a rabbit hole I was unwilling to jump into less my brain permanently fried from the web.

Dragging myself up off the seat slowly, I took a measured look around, unabashedly sizing up employees who looked old enough to know local downtown history.

Within the labyrinth, I followed the hand-painted signs toward the east end, settling before an extensive library of gallon jars, filled to the brim with various alphabetized herbs. Its size swallowed the gentleman operating the station.

"May I help you?" He peered over his spectacles, flamboyant attire somehow befitting the green apron he wore. I quickly shoved my notes into my pocket.

"Well…" *how was I to start?*

"You must be new." He cleared his throat while pulling on a pair of disposable gloves, skimming across the herbs while chatting. "Country Acre is a family-owned establishment, dating back over 40 years. Starting out as a small store it since has grown into what you see before you by the loyalty of the community," He gestured around. "Natural to organic foods, we hold an array of artesian goods that cannot be found anywhere else." Gimmicky came to mind, but it was plain I picked the right individual.

Plucking up a small container, filled a fourth of the way with dried rust colored berries, he took his time slowly uncapping the vessel.

"It's a beautiful store," I played along, mesmerized by his handwork of dropping each dried berry into a plastic bag, individually by tong.

"Did you come from across the way?"

"Where?" I blinked up at him.

"Canada, Victoria?" He offered with a quizzical expression.

"Oh yeah, just been walking around, it's a quaint area," I agreed. "I heard there was an underground?"

"Indeed!" The man perked up. "There's a section connected to this very building. The employees have coined it, 'The Dungeon.' It's quite the sight."

"Really. Is it opened for the Historical Tours?"

"Nah, the owners don't like people going in there, it's stuffy, and well, dangerous if you don't know where you are going."

My fingers picked lightly at the wood of the counter while I mulled around his words.

"But here I am, rambling away. Is there something else I can help you with?" He leaned closer, pupils shifting while he dropped the bag of berries abruptly in front of me.

"What's this?" I leaned away cautiously.

"It's what you wanted, wasn't it?" He gestured with his head, "Mountain Ash."

"No, I..." my voice trailed off, excitement rising to the thrumming of my quickened heartbeat. *Mountain ash... Wasn't that Rowan berries? Had I asked him for those?*

"Is there something else I can help you with?" He implored.

If it weren't for the past few days, I would think he was a bit crazy.

"Password..." I mumbled. "The password," Reaching up, I drug the bag slowly off the counter to eye him unblinkingly for fear he would disappear.

"Thistle..." He chuckled in amusement. "Is an excellent herb, don't you think?"

"Um, yes."

"When all else fails, Emmaline, look up..." I followed his movements, my eyes resting to the John Deere tractor quietly

94

overseeing us. A hoe leaned to its side; sharp teeth protruded menacingly.

"How did you know my name—" Glancing back, the man had already disappeared into the stacks, beyond the counter.

What was really going on in this town, I wondered, a tinge of dread dusting my mind. Dragging my head back upward, I stared hard at the machinery towering over me.

I just wasn't so sure about anything anymore...

CHAPTER 6

SATURDAY AFTERNOON

I left the store feeling lower than ever. Barely noticing the rain, I crossed the road and made my way along the sidewalk, paying little mind.

"Emma?"

I registered a doorbell tinkling with the creak of floorboards. Snapping into myself I realized I had walked right into *Easy Street*, a few buildings down.

"Heather?" I was expecting to see Eugene and Sunshine sitting patiently behind the counter, waiting for customers to slip in.

"Now that we've established everyone's names," the brunette gave me a feigned look of amusement.

"Sorry, I didn't realize you switched to morning shifts."

"Yes, since college started. What can I do for you?" She openly eyed my cup of coffee with judgment.

"O-oh… yeah," *well at least Sunshine didn't witness my act of betrayal.* "I'm here to get my check."

"Sure thing, Eugene left it on his desk, in case you dropped by."

"Thanks." Shoving a hand awkwardly into my pocket, I walked deeper into the House before she had time to strike up an obligated conversation.

Pulling back the curtain, I crept into the kitchen to follow the narrow aisle leading into the back office. Grabbing my check, I hovered impatiently, trying to anticipate Heathers next move.

The young woman appeared to be staring blankly out the door, picking slowly at the blueberries of a scone. She flicked them off to a napkin with a slow and steady rhythm of movement. *Odd.* That was the word of the week.

I snorted.

Despite my mental peanut gallery, I still had to physically pull myself from my rooted position to try sneaking out the back. As if the building heard me, a jarring sound of clanging metal shocked me into a momentary awareness.

Grimacing, I listened intently, trying to decipher where it had originated. The wall was thick; thick enough to stop sound from carrying over from the neighboring business, and it was too faint to be coming from the kitchen. Heather didn't seem phased, so I doubted it came from outside.

Was it the basement? The lengthy room, in all of its bare bones, was a neatly placed hazard zone for those who hadn't mastered its trails.

Converted into a workroom for Eugene's various wood related hobbies, towering stacks lined the walls of boxes filled with tools and scrap pieces for later creations. In the few times they permitted me to descend the steps, I could understand why it was designated as a 'no entry' region for employees.

Another clatter of metal sounded. Heather barely batted a lash.

Sighing, I crossed into a dimly lit lounge to take a peek into the 'employee's only' door. What appeared like a waste closet was a cleverly disguised stairwell leading to the room in question. Rolling the garbage can out of the way, I tugged up on the false flooring, descending the worn stairs with trepidation.

Thick heavy air consumed my lungs, coating it with the chemical odor of fake pine to mask a mold problem. Upon restoring the building, Eugene had discovered that the previous business owners were using the downstairs for a grow room. Needless to say, there was no proper draining system to dispose of the waste. While he gutted the place and pulled out the debris, it still had lingering darkness.

I pulled on the cord, watching the light flicker on, swinging with the momentum. If I were to get slaughtered, then this would be the part.

The eeriness was enough to make me run, but my curiosity outweighed irrational ideas of boogiemen hiding in corners. There was nothing scary about a hoarder's paradise, *right*?

Holding my breath, I crept deeper. Looping about the labyrinth of miscellaneous items, I approached the back of the room where the retired elevator cab had settled. There, I found the group of offending metal.

Placing my cup to the ground, I returned them to their rightful spot against the wall. When my work proved successful, I bent to take up my coffee, only to snag my keychain against an offending object.

Flinging from my pocket, they tolled shrilly against the pipes.

Oh, hell no.

Something scurried across the floor in fright. I grappled for my keys distractedly, poles toppling everywhere in an irregular chorus of ear piercing rings.

"Shit!" There was more scuttling and soft scratching, as the thing tried getting out of sight. Wrestling for my phone, I switched on the flashlight APP, running the beam across the ground. I wound the lanyard roughly about my knuckles, waiting to release it on the scampering vermin. At that moment, my phone exposed a shivering figure pressing up against the side of the elevator. Large saucer eyes stared back at me.

That was NOT a rat!

I stepped back, stumbling over the rods, gasping. The creature gave a raspy startled noise; lips curling back to expose small sharp incisors.

"H-hot…" they pleaded softly.

Confused, I shuffled back.

"W-what?"

"H-h-hot…" they hid their face, a long thin tail curled about its form, hugging the end close for security. The further I kept the light on the being, the more restless it became.

"Are you talking about my phone?" I redirected the cell light to the wall, watching them calm enough to take another shy-eyed look toward me.

"Hot..." their rounded face nodded, small folded ears twitching in recognition.

"Erm... Okay, hot," I agreed. "Do you live down here?"

"Hot."

"Yeah, hot, I know." I gestured around. "Were you the one that made all the noise down here?"

"Hot..."

"Yes, hot. I get it. The flashlight was hard to handle," I frowned when it hid its head, showing long nimble human-like fingers when it covered its ears.

This was surreal.

Hunching over itself, Hot seemed only a few inches above ankle height. Bottom heavy, squat legs and long arms curled to their body in the attempt to appear smaller. *How long had they been down here?*

Looking around, I noticed red straws and a few coffee filters, stained with use, scattered across the ground.

"Hot, were you upstairs?"

They perked up. Their all-consuming eyes regarded me with a new form of curiosity.

"Hot," they agreed, slowly uncurling from their tense position to gather their fallen spoils.

"Do you go up there a lot?" I recognized a pattern.

The compost was always being sorted through; discarded straws from sloppy customers would go missing off the floor. Tables, I thought, needed washing were picked spotless before I had the chance to touch them. The small spaces under machines in the kitchen were always immaculately clean. All this time I thought Sunshine was overdoing it.

"Hot."

"Hot, can you say anything other than 'hot'?"

Looking put out, the small creature held out their free hand to show raw, angry skin. Newly formed blisters beaded the tops of their nimble digits. "Hot…"

"Oh." *That's why…*

I bowed, trying to get a closer look. "Come here, let me see."

They pulled away, watching with distrust.

"I promise I won't hurt you." They didn't seem convinced.

Thinking a moment, I rose and wandered through the room pulling open boxes and checking tables. "Just you wait," I called out. "I'm getting something to help—ah," I tugged out a tin first aid kit and lugged it back to the spot I left the wounded creature.

Hot, however, was absent. "Hot?" I looked around the copper poles. "Hot, I've got something to help."

Examining the sundry of junk, I wondered what I had gotten myself into; I was already on a time-sensitive task. If I lost my chance to find the *Market Myrrd*, then I might as well say goodbye to my sister forever.

My nerves seized at the thought, and I nearly missed the hollow scratching sounding from inside the elevator. Quietly, I rubbed grime from the window, peering inside.

From what I could decipher there was a large mass of miscellaneous pieces of material, all folded together to form a nest of sorts. Crumpled paper, straw sleeves, napkins, old shredded towel scraps, and coffee filters were a few I could count in the moving mass. Hot was burrowing.

Taking a few steps back, I tried figuring out how to get to them.

When the building was first erected in the early 1900s, Eugene said the elevator was once used to bring shipments in from the street. As time passed, and the building changed hands, the cab was put to the basement. The shaft gutted and pulled.

If I worked it hard enough, I could get the metal gate open. However, the door was another story. The wood had rotted and warped, either it was sealed to the frame, or it would pop out with less than a tug. I wasn't sure if I was prepared to make a mess, much less expose Hot's hideout.

I wiggled the cage.

"Ho-o-ot," called a grumbling complaint inside.

"You need to come out." Gripping the metal awkwardly by the fingertips, I tugged back on the gate. Rusted pivots groaned as I leaned in, putting weight into the motion. Abruptly it gave way, spilling open halfway with a rusted squeal.

"Hot hot HOT hot ho-o-ot!" the creature chattered angrily.

My body smacked against the wall, nails thrumming with momentary pain in the exertion. "You don't want me coming in, then you best be coming out!" I bit out.

Scurrying and scratching, Hot popped out beside me with fur bristled.

"Hot."

"Yep," I rubbed my hands to my leggings, finding Hot more cute than intimidating. "How else was I going to get your attention?" Settling to the ground, I balanced my phone to a knee. The angle of light gave me the ability to sift through the tin box's contents with near clarity.

There wasn't much left, but I pulled together a few packets of sterile wipes and an old tube of Neosporin with a split down the side.

"This will hurt for only a few seconds," I warned, tugging open a towelette.

Shaking its head, Hot remained stubborn until I unleashed the expression I reserved for Abigail's particularly nasty fits. Hot surrendered quickly, hands rising to show me the damage inflicted.

Close quarters with the being allowed me to view them with fuller detail. I realized then that the burns extended to the left side of their body. Spatters of boils and heated flesh swelled beneath their fur. I had seen something similar when a co-worker stumbled with the electric teakettle, spilling boiled water across her legs.

Why would Hot be that close to boiling water?

"You really got yourself into something nasty, didn't you?" I spoke gently.

Hot's presence was only raising more questions in my mind. *Had they been living in the building long? Were there more of them? Why now, could I see this creature?*

There was an angry squeal as I dabbed the fragile skin. Apologetically, I took slower measures, finishing with a little pea-sized dab of Neosporin to each area.

"Hot..."

"You'll have to figure out another word to describe the feeling of Neosporin," I chuckled, resting the opened tin to

103

the top of a pallet of wood trimmings. Leaving the lid ajar, I instructed the tiny being on how to manage the next day.

I showed the tube. "Keep your hands clean and uncovered so they can breathe. You'll heal sooner."

"Emma?"

Heather's voice called down the stairs, startling us both.

Hot gave a frightened twitch.

"Yeah?"

"What are you doing down in the basement?"

"I'm coming up," I called back, rising quickly. "Sssh," I whispered, pressing a finger to my lips.

They shook their head, leaning against my leg with soft little chirps of fright.

"Hot hot-hot-hot, hot," They squeaked over and over in a jumble of pleas.

"I'll make sure you're safe."

"Emma?"

Distracted, I hadn't noticed Heather descend the steps. She stood at the base, staring at me with an odd sheen in her eyes.

"Jeez, Heather?" My body twisted awkwardly toward her, trying to feign indifference as an odd sensation of small claws trekked up the back of my leg. Hot climbed across my side, curling securely into my coat pocket.

"Who are you talking to, the *ghosts*?"

"Right. You know me, ghosts and ghouls galore." Snapping off the light from my phone, relieved for the darkness, I quickly gathered my keys. "Hey, it's creepy down here. Let's go up."

"If you say so…" she peered beyond me skeptically until I ushered her upstairs.

"Oh look, customers," it relieved me to see a couple there, standing and peering around expectantly.

Heather pursed her lips, agitated but compliant. She passed me without a word.

Her acute attention had me paranoid.

Rubbing my pocket gently—if only for the confirmation of my sanity—I quickly closed up the basement and tried to sneak out the door.

"Emma? Did you find it?" Heather called out, handing the to-go cups to the sheepish customers.

"Yes," I gripped the door, feeling myself dragging in the effort to look back at the dark-haired girl.

Perched precariously on the edge of her stool, Heather's somber eyes observed me.

Something wasn't right... I shivered.

"Oh..." She sounded disappointed. "You know, there are rats downstairs. I must ask Eugene to set up traps. I saw one yesterday."

"You sure?"

"Oh, I'm sure," she smirked, an offbeat look for the rather stoic girl. "I got it good with the espresso water last night." *No wonder Hot is terrified,* "Everything okay?"

I must have let a look slip. "Yeah, of course, why wouldn't I be?"

"Well, they found your mother murdered."

"She wasn't murdered..."

"My mistake," she replied, "Must be wrong about going to the hospital too, hmm."

"What?" I felt myself going rigid. Trying to digest what was being said. She didn't explain herself either. We stood quietly for a long moment before I stepped out the door. "Right, see you, Heather."

"Bye, Emma."

I couldn't leave fast enough.

Escaping, I hooked around the corner and down the alley, pressing against a brick wall when I felt there was enough distance to breathe. Taking in a gulp of air, I tried to settle my nerves in the rain.

I forgot my freaking coffee!

"Hot..." My companion poked their head from the comfort of my coat, looking about nervously.

"Yeah," I mumbled. "I'm just as confused," I wasn't sure which direction to take now. Too many questions were leading me astray from what was important.

Sliding down into a crouching position, back against the wall, I rubbed my face. "I just... I need to focus. Myrrd," I reminded myself. "Where is Myrrd?"

Coffee would have been flipping fantastic right about now.

"Hot," chirped a reply. I felt the momentary tug of tacky claws as the small being unfolded from its hideout, climbing up my arm. There, to my shoulder, is where Hot settled. Long tail curled about my neck. "Hot." Their round padded fingers pressed against my cheek, trying to catch my attention.

"Hmm? What is it?"

Nose wiggling emphatically, Hot made a flailed gesture down the alley.

"I guess you'd like to be taken back?" There was a frightened squeak, marble eyes dilated as their tail tightened. "Okay, okay," I frowned. "Show me where you want to go. Okay?"

Hot's directions were more like a game of Marco Polo. Looping about the block, I was tugged here and there by squeaks and tail gestures until I finally stood across the street, facing Country Acre again.

I had to remind myself continuously that I was the only one that could see Hot. Entering the sliding doors, my eyes darted around nervously, picking at my already tender digits.

"Why have you taken me here?" I murmured to my companion.

"Hot."

"Hot, I don't have time for this. I have to find Myrrd." The small magical rodent gave my hair a tug, gesturing, until I glanced at the machinery suspended above the isles.

Everything seemed to crash into place. Basle's voice whispered to the forefront of my mind.

'High upon the throne, the monsters perched on stable stone.'

The clues were screaming at me, forcing me to make sense of the scenario.

'Sharp teeth gleam with envy, its eaten bones of many.'

I made a passionate display of hurrying back over to the green tractor, gawking upward to size up the hoe.

'While it sleeps it guards the keep, down the steps is what you seek...'

"Sharp teeth, envy, bones of many..." What was the phrase, green with envy? I gave Hot a gentle pat, attempting to think like a Faery. "Perched on stable stone..." Cement wasn't exactly stone but the massive machine attested to the strength of the building's foundation. "Sleeps, guards the keep... down the steps, is what I seek."

Shuffling back, I studied how the John Deere was positioned. There wasn't an entrance directly below the hefty contraption, but it had been pointing at a secondary tractor which safeguarded entries leading into the bowels of the building. They blocked the door with an 'Employee's Only' sign.

Did we solve the riddle? Was Country Acre's basement the hub for monster activity? My palms were itching with the need to find out.

"Is that the entrance to Myrrd?" I whispered to Hot, already lifting my hand to take a peek inside. "Hot?"

"Is there something I can help you with?" An even tone called behind me.

Tensing, I turned around to face a broad-shouldered man, wearing a deep gray polo shirt and slacks. His expression was polite but calculating behind thick eyebrows.

Why was I surprised, considering my dodgy behavior?

"Oh, yeah!" I laughed. For the first time in days, I felt light-hearted at the discovery. "There's just so much to take in."

He nodded, giving a slight smirk.

"Yes, we're proud of the store. It has great energy. Many people from all over the world tell us they've never experienced anywhere quite like this."

Yeah, I guess crazy Faery voodoo had that effect on people.

"I'm not surprised." I feigned a look of wonder on my face.

"Was there something I could direct you toward?"

"Oh, I was wondering where the honey was."

"Isle eight, on the end cap. Anything else?"

"No, no, I think I can find the rest. Thanks."

"If you change your mind, don't hesitate. I'll be just around the corner," a veiled promise from an ever watchful manager.

Did he think I was casing the place? Well, he wasn't wrong…

"Thanks." My pleasantries faltered when I caught his gaze flickering to my neck.

Gesturing casually with a slight nod, the gentleman shifted on his polished leather shoes. "Have a good day…"

Did he just see Hot? I waited for him to leave before walking steadily toward the door. My investigation had sputtered to a close.

Almost out the door, the squeaking in my ear steered me down an aisle where I squatted in front of the honey shelf, attempting to appear like I was making a selection.

"You okay?"

"Hot."

"Thank you," I peered to my shoulder with sincerity.

"Hot," They squeaked in reply, giving an unblinkingly dewy gaze, and just like that, the little prickling paws scuttled onto the top of my head.

Looking up, I caught the last harrowing bits of their leap, outstretching their attached appendages to glide from perch to perch until they finished to the rafters above.

"Wow…" I stood, taking in Hot's achievements, watching as a few more fuzzy faces poking over the beams. That answered one question. A little wave came from my tiny companion, making my heart melt.

Waving back, I drug myself from the store. I had gained important information in my long riddle of clues, but *Myrrd* would undoubtedly bring its own set of trials.

Shoving my hands into my pockets, I stood beneath the overhang, willing myself to move toward my thawing car. There was something foreign to the town, an abnormality I hadn't notice until the kidnapping of my sister.

Walking along the streets, individuals wore a whitewash across their forms; almost like glass gleaming in the sunlight, too much to look at straight on. The more I saw, the more details I could pick up. Some had speckled orbs, a few had haloed outlines. There was one in particular with a general fuzziness that kept them out of my focus. Then there were just the dull, ordinary characters. *Normal.* Either my eyes were failing or half the town was supernatural.

I could hear James now, saying I was reading too much into things. His practical thinking would have leveled out my over-anxious ideas, calm me to the idea that not everything had to be in my control. I really missed him.

Time to go.

The smell of crisp rain permeated the interior of the car as it shook and raddled itself back to the house. The waiting game was tiring. I was alone. James had disappeared in the time I had been absent. He had a landscaping job, yet it was odd he would be out in this weather. There was the likelihood he had found himself a new interest of the female persuasion, but he had mentioned no one other than my cousin.

Really, I wasn't about to complain. The consuming quiet gave me time to shut down my obsessive thinking, long enough to achieve a few essential human functions.

I spent the afternoon keeping the fire going, prepping for the worst.

At some point, I found myself famished and made a sloppy stovetop hash, with any salvageable veggies left in the fridge. I sank into a coma-like state, eating with a fevered pace until the pan was empty.

A shower was next. Leaving my mess, I trailed upstairs to stand lazily under the hot cascade of water until it ran cold.

In a daze, I climbed into loose fitted clothes and circled my room aimlessly until I picked up laundry scattered about. I tossed them together into the washer, the bag of berries falling from my coat pocket.

After pouring in the detergent, I drug them up from the floor, staring mindlessly to my hands until salt and iron trickled through. If I had known such simple things could keep Abby safe, I would've riddled the house with nonsensical items sooner.

My notes! I nearly ruined them in the wash.

I brought my findings to the kitchen to dry out on the counter before turning my energy elsewhere.

Directing my eyes out the sink windows, I methodically portioned salt into sandwich baggies, lightly observing the snail tracks straggling lazily upward against the glass.

Odd.

I finally paused, leaning over the dish pit to peek outside. A slug dropped into view, spooking me.

Very odd...

Leaving my work, I made my way out and around the house to see what was happening. Disgust twisted my face while taking in the sight of my family's home.

Slugs and snails, hundreds of them, infested the expanse of the siding, tirelessly trailing upward in aimless directions. I watched a few dropping off to disappear into the newly made ruin of fallen carcasses lying curled and dried to the grass below. *Dead.*

This wasn't normal.

The house was under attack—*Faery-stricken.*

Rubbing my head on instinct, my skin crawled with imaginary insects. Every tuft of hair caused me to smack at myself in paranoia.

Panicked, I tossed handfuls of salt at the roaming mollusks, willing them to leave.

That's how James found me. "What are you doing?"

"Don't you see it?" I knew I sounded manic. "Don't you see all the snails and slugs? They weren't there this morning. This isn't normal James!"

"Tossing lumps of salt at them will not make them run scared," he said calmly. "Come on, get back inside. I'll take care of this, Em. Come on." He courage gently, taking me by the shoulders he steered me up the steps.

I stood to the living room window overseeing him snatching up a straw broom to brush roughly against the siding, scrapping their bodies off like unwanted barnacles on the underside of a boat.

By the time he had finished, they were curled up writhing slowly in their agony on the ground.

Cheering as he came in, I offered a smile.

He didn't look pleased though, disturbed really.

"Something is going on... You will sit and tell me what it is." He gestured to the couch.

My moment of triumph disintegrated into caution. "Like what?"

"Like, where did you go last night and this morning?" He draped himself against the banister.

"I didn't realize I had to report to you now."

"What the hell is wrong?" he tossed his keys toward the couch, folding his arms over his chest.

"Really, you don't want me to get started." I mirrored his stance, shifting my weight to one side.

"Is this about Abigail?" his eyes were imploring, searching.

"It's everything," I concluded, knowing the moment I opened my mouth the words would fall out like vomit. Acidic and stinking of the surreal only a broken mind could rationalize.

"Emma," he sounded patronizing.

"What? What do you want me to say?"

"It's been a long week. You're stressed, raw. Maybe it's a good thing they think Abigail is with your grandparents for a while. Just for a while, Em."

I had to laugh.

"Oh, I wish it was as simple as that." I ran my fingers through my hair, seizing the roots in a moment of pure frustration. "But you don't even know the half of it." *There.* I said enough to either close the conversation down or tell him everything, maybe then I wouldn't feel like I was drowning from swimming in circles.

"Em..." he began carefully. I examined his face, trying to figure out what was on his mind. "Your grandparents may have money, but that means nothing. You're Abigail's guardian. It said so in the will. They can take you to court, but that won't mean they will win."

I regretted eating now. Digging my fingertips into my sides, I flinched as the knot in my stomach flared painfully. *Anxiety.*

"You're missing the point. You won't get it. I'll do what I need to. Just—" I shifted, digging into my hip bones further, eyebrows furling. "do what you want but don't get in my way. I have shit to do."

I wanted to back out of the conversation as quickly as I had entered it.

James followed.

"So, what? You're just going to shut me out?"

"Yes." I snapped back.

"I think you are making a mistake."

"Well then, it's lucky I don't care," I spat back. He noticeably flinched, withering under my temper. "You don't get what I'm going through."

"Right, because I don't give a fuck, right? I don't care as much because I'm not a part of your family. That's bullshit, and you know it." He glared. "I'd kill for Abby. You don't think I would?"

My heart was beating loudly in my ears.

I stared at the redhead, long and unblinking. The town thought I was as mad as my mother. That James was just a figment of my imagination, and that Abigail safely tucked away with my grandparents.

And where was James during all of this?

"If that's true, then why aren't you listening?" I paled.

"What exactly am I supposed to take from this conversation? What's between the lines I'm not picking up, Emma? I'm not a mind reader. Spit it out."

114

"Why did you suddenly disappear yesterday when the cops were here?"

He was right. *Why was I dancing around the subject of Fae?* What I wanted to ask was what he had really killed at my grandparents. *Why wasn't he talking about the run-in with Basle?*

"Because I don't want to lose you!" His fist came down hard onto the buffet table, with such a heated fury I could hear the wood crack and splinter under crunching bone.

I stared in horrified fascination as he completely annihilated the surface. The lamp and an assortment of knickknacks scattered in the destruction. When he pulled his hand back from the wreckage, there were large fractures of wood lodged up under his skin.

"J-James… James, you're hurt. Are you okay?"

He drew his hand quickly away; an opaque liquid drizzled and dripped across the flooring.

That wasn't blood. It couldn't have been.

"I'm fine." He turned away from me.

"You just broke the table! You aren't fine. I heard popping. You dislocated or broke something." I leaned in, trying to see the damage. He shifted away again. "James!"

"I'm fine, Emma."

Sighing in frustration, I threw up my arms in defeat. "Fine, fine!" I checked the clock and shook my head. I could feel the tension of my brows. "I'm gone. If you don't want my help, then you don't get it. Congrats, you've won the argument by default."

I crossed back into the kitchen, snatching up my notes and what was left of my arsenal for tonight's events.

"Where are you going?" His irises seemed to enlarge, turning to stare at me with unease.

This was for the best, I told myself.

"I'm done," I repeated, tucking the items into one of my mom's coats hanging on the pantry door. "I'm not talking to another person who wants to bullshit about whether my sister is safe. The longer she's gone, the more this place makes me want to throw up."

"Then, I'll go with you." James yanked out the slivers of wood in his skin. He shrugged off his over shirt, wrapping it up before I could get a closer inspection.

Blood should have been everywhere. He was freaking me out. Unable to make a clear decision, he grabbed his keys and hooked my elbow, tugging me out the door. "Why do you always have to act stupid and do everything by yourself? You can't be an island all the time. You need to ask for help."

I wasn't going to answer him. If he wanted to come, then let him feel firsthand what I was riding out.

That is what all this boiled down to.

We parked to the far west end of the parking lot of Country Acre, facing the alleyway. Hunkered down, I sat devouring a fast-food burger, like some greedy imp half-starved to death.

"What is this even going to accomplish?"

I gave him a grunt in response, not willing to give up savoring the food just yet.

"Emma."

"I told you," I spoke past a cheek full of fries. "If you were coming, you can't ask questions."

116

"Right..." he readjusted his hand inside the large plastic cup of ice. James had protested against the hospital, so, we had agreed that if I didn't nag him, he wouldn't bother me with the details. The sloshing was telling me it was half-thawed already.

Shaking my head, I wondered if I would see a monster going inside the store tonight, now I had uncovered this newfound ability to look at Them for what they were. Although, if someone asked me, I couldn't pinpoint when they came crashing into my existence. *The Pale Man? The letter? Basle?* Maybe it really didn't even matter when or how. The trouble was, *why?*

Pausing from my gorging, I rubbed at my tired eyes before checking myself in the car mirror. "I look like a demented panda," I massaged at the dark circles, frowning at my sickly image.

James snorted into his drink, gaining a surprised chuckle from me. "No comment."

"Yeah, yeah," I cheered up after my binge, wondering if I would regret it.

Slipping out of the truck, I stared up at the sky. Neon pink and tangerine colors peaked through the gloom of the clouds. The rain had held off, but the evening was as cold as the ones before. Shops had closed no later than 6:00 PM, less they were a bar or restaurant catering to dinner. The only individuals seen mulling about were the displaced.

Camping out, waiting for something to happen, wasn't any thrill to be had. Tonight was pure masochism, and I cursed myself for not bringing a hat or scarf.

117

I leaned against the vehicle and fixated on the lower alleyway door of the natural food store, honestly wondering what I was doing. The cold crisp air had seeped into my clothes, and I found that my fingers had grown numb. I had to tell myself that this was little to sacrifice when dealing with Faeries, but after a long anxious spell of watching went by—when I was obsessing at the thought of a good hot cup of coffee—a person slowly turned down the alleyway.

After a minor delayed reaction, I quickly scrambled back, ducking down behind the truck to observe.

Slowly strolling, whistling, they dressed in tattered jeans and a greased up hoodie. They looked nothing more than an unruly youth until they paused suspiciously to the back of the building where a small white shed stood precariously against the rear of the store.

He looked around. I could have sworn his eyes gave a sheen, like an animal in the dark, reflecting light.

My heart was fluttering in excitement. I swallowed and flexed my neck muscles, trying to calm my nerves.

Finally, after a long moment of loitering and fumbling with his pockets, the teen gave a light rhythmic tap against the wood.

Staring at James through the window, I motioned for him to duck down. He rolled his eyes but sank, just in time for the door to open and close behind the kid.

"What just happened," I craned my neck up at the darkened sky, finding the full moon half clouded. Despite its shyness, I could see a distinct orange tint haloing the sphere.

"Harvest Moon," James muttered beside me, causing my skin to prickle.

"Sssh," I warned. "Didn't you see that?"

"See what?"

Giving an exasperated sigh, I pulled myself down the grassy slope that divided the car lot from the alley. James melded in like a second shadow, accompanying me with silent speculation.

Sidling up to the whitewashed door, I tried discreetly to make anything out from beyond. It was hard to tell, but I saw light coming from the haphazard gap between the entrance and cement floor. The knob was locked when tried.

I squirmed in nervousness. Only then did I realize the magnitude of what I was doing.

Could we get killed? Would the Faeries kill us if they found out I had known about their secret marketplace?

Almost jumping out of my skin, I felt James rest a hand to my shoulder in warning. Dragging me toward the compactor, he tugged me into the fitted space between the building and the exposed machinery. There, we sank into a huddle, the earth smelling damp and pungent with wet pulp. Cigarette butts and a cheap malt liquor bottle sat three-fourths empty, tucked away against the underbelly of our hideout.

My cheek was cold against the speckled brown wall we settled close to, I could hear feet shuffling down the hill now.

"Don't move," James's words were hot and hushed in my ear, making me shiver.

A creature with a lumbering torso came into view, where they paused to the door, shifting itself this way and that, before glancing in our direction.

I held my breath.

Down a long sloping neck, I could see its head resting level to its immense bulbous shoulders. The beast snorted and grunted slowly toward our hideout, alley lights revealing a meaty face with small inset eyes that peeked out over its whiskered snout.

Like a pig looking for truffles, they tasted the air for our scent.

James hugged me closer, reminding me with a squeeze not to speak while the pig-thing scrutinized us wordlessly. After a few long precarious moments, the Fae finally turned back to slap a fist against the shed's entrance.

When the door opened, a squealing grunt fell from its lips. *"Thistle,"* was hard to make out, but I was sure I heard it.

We watched it disappear beyond, and I felt James soften his restraint.

"Was this the plan all along?" He finally looked at me. "This looks like a drug ring."

His words were enough to shake fear into my caffeine-riddled body. *What was I doing getting us in the middle of all this? Was I crazy?*

"I think you should go wait in the car. Keep the engine running," I eventually managed.

"Oh no, you aren't going anywhere without me."

"James," I tried giving the most convincing look I could muster. Not that it helped, that, deep down, I desperately didn't want to do this alone, even if my actions meant putting us both in danger.

Damn, I was selfish.

"Emma." He countered, missing the entirety of my personal plight.

"Just. Stay close, real close," I snatched up his good hand, knocking on the door before I lost all my nerves entirely.

I thought of Basle and the probability that there could be something much heftier than him guarding this door. Imagining what that was, and that it could jump out and eat us whole, I shifted halfway toward the road.

But what I had not prepared myself to see was the door opening to reveal a broad-shouldered man, with the head of a sheep.

Leaning back, I stared unblinkingly up at the massive horns curling about his head. Murky horizontal pupils peered, widening the door so that the individual could take a fuller look at the both of us.

Was he a Satyr? He exhaled, cold air streamed from his nose like the steam of a kettle top. A pattern was plain see, we smelt.

What was he waiting for?

James nudged me.

OH, password!

"Thistle," I managed, squeezing my eyes shut.

I could only imagine how James must feel realizing what I had only grasped myself a few days prior. Fairy tales were real, or at least, the creatures of legend weren't myths at all.

While I waited to feel the edge of the Ram's horns, I silently apologized to my friend for shortening his lifespan.

The being only opened the door further and James didn't hesitate before pushing us past the shaggy being.

CHAPTER 7

SATURDAY EVENING

Paying little mind to the silent doorman, James was swift in his pace, leaving me to duck awkwardly after him.

Nearly smacking into a low hanging pillar to the rear, I wasn't sure what we were looking for. The shed was a collection of odd tools, building supplies, and the unexpected home of a worn 1965 Chevrolet pickup. Dark and cluttered, the ground dipped inward—edges threatening to snap and fold beneath our feet. There were no other doors inside this magpie's nest. *Was this some elaborate plan to trap us?*

Heavy breathing and shuffling feet broke the stale air. I was ready to grab for a tire iron when our eyes adjusted enough to discern the outline of light trickling through the seams of the far wall.

James quietly made his way over. Taking his time, he leaned in across a pile of boxes, scaling his hands along the crack of light; he hooked his fingers and tugged at the plywood. Staring in awe, I realized he had just unwittingly exposed a secret hallway.

We gave each other grave expressions.

I looked back at the exit; the goat man was nowhere to be seen.

"Let's go," my friend uttered.

I followed him dutifully into the passage. Glowing orbs floated across the ceiling in small clusters of pastel tones, illuminating just enough to see the narrow dirt pathway before us. My hands trailed across the walls, steadying myself against uneven treading. I observed no nails in the patchwork of wood composites tiling the sides, only charred cedar trunks offering their support from collapse. If we were following the streets right, the sidewalk would be to the upper left.

Breathlessly, we shuffled down, away from the mundane living. Dirt crumbled aside, exposing the deserted cobbled street of the entombed Underground, where blackened storefronts stood like hollowed faces.

I followed James's form closely, unsure of how long we'd been wandering. The Underground was a labyrinth of dead ends, thick air, and an ever-pervading sense of silence; a dull pressure of stillness that thrummed against my ears, making my eyes widen further to the eerie globes lulling overhead.

I thought, perhaps, we'd inevitably be consumed by the lacking.

I gripped the redhead's sleeve as the passage dropped into a low hanging octangular room comprising several doors of different hews.

"James..." I finally tempted to speak, yet the other hadn't reacted. Was he in shock? "Hey, are you okay?" I looked up when I heard a car pass overhead. The momentum was enough to rattle the walls, shaking the hinges and doorknobs, reminding me of where we were—secret world beneath Port Angeles.

"Are you sure you want to do this?" Brown eyes shifted to me in question. "You don't know what's passed here... do you really want us to take this chance?"

"It's not a matter of wanting to. It's that I have to." Our words seemed to shatter the hushed spell following us. The Underground exhaled a soft yawning breath, sending shivers down our bodies. What proceeded was the abrupt and disorderly noises of a chattering crowd, conversations intertwining in a hum of swelled excitement, all fighting to outdo each other above a ribbon of music.

Gripping the hood of my coat, I stared in rapt attention while the spheres of light shifted down along the walls to alight the boisterous entrance before us. James nodded in a resigned sort of way, gripping the knob to push slowly against the doors.

The volume expanded, mixing with the sensations of sticky sweet carnival foods. Fatty roasted meats fused with the syrupy smells of fried bread and pastries while spices mingled amidst the distinct aroma of fresh kettle corn. Nostalgia trickled in low hanging waves, wrapping delightfully around me to reminisce on fair rides in hot summer afternoons—tongues stained by dyed slushies, and hands tacky with cotton candy.

The euphoria nearly swept me away, but James pulled me discreetly to the side, letting a rotund toad-creature pass us, stinking of rotten fish and stagnant pond water. Curling my nose, I turned to glimpse *The Market of Myrrd*.

The street stood dramatically on an uneven footing, running below the entirety of downtown Port Angeles to showcase long forgotten storefronts from days of old. Short corridors and rooms led to sealed exits, doors opening to cement blocks. Windows exuded layers of led paint, caked on for privacy.

The bazaar was pieced together as a beautifully crude structure made of discarded objects. Glass jugs protruded through organically shaped divider walls, creating a stained glass effect. Candles littered the low rising ceiling, some adorning the heads of creatures mulling about. Laded shelves, sagging with copious amounts of mysterious objects, hinted to the macabre, as mason jars glistened with neon liquids and pickled creations. Herbs and animal parts dangled, strung up by knotting rope.

Beasts yelled over one another, calling out bargains at their makeshift booths. Animals lay curled in wooden crates, stacked precariously together. Their masters stood auctioning them off to the highest bidder. A large copper pot held bubbling with smoke, while a creature with four arms balanced to a stool, plucking feathers from a chicken carcass.

It was a marvel that so much could hide from the naked eye.

This Port Angeles ghost street had served well for sheltering the local Faery folk. They filled the entire underground with bright, bustling activity of all kinds.

After we adjusted somewhat to the organized chaos, I caught sight of the assortment of banners attached to the wooden braces lining the red brick walls; their images obscured by the wear and tear of age.

Grabbing James's elbow, I smacked it lightly in my enthusiasm. "James, holy hell…"

"Yeah, yeah," he tried to disentangle his limbs in agitation.

"Why aren't you freaking out right now?"

"How did you find this place, anyway? Oh, for fuck's sake, let me guess, Weatherly, right?" I gave him a dark look. "I freaking knew it," he opened his mouth to start in when I cut him off.

"Not now," Giving me a critical look, he dragged me backward just as a massive bipedal hedgehog brushed passed. Their pale green fur swept lightly across our exposed flesh, enacting a prickling sensation that only furthered when I caught sight of the unblinking eyeballs attached to several of their whisker-like spines. I felt I could breathe just after we lost sight of it in the crowd.

We kept our walking slow, entering the hallway carefully. It was hard not to stare. Every creature was both fascinating and frightening to watch. At one point or another, I had the hope of catching sight of another human, only to realize they bore a tail, or perhaps cloven feet. Repetitive patterns of animalistic features blended seamlessly with the lush vegetation that draped their bodies, mundane elements that created an alien impression.

126

The oddest sights were of those impersonating humans. I saw a fox in a hoodie. Then a boar outfitted in construction gear, complete with his hard hat and orange reflective vest. There were gangly winged beings in designer jeans and cardigans, looking anorexic within their oversized clothing. Did I see someone wearing Romeos? An older rat gentleman was pulling along his wooden walker, sporting a ball cap of the Seattle Mariners; two holes were cut crudely to the sides to make room for his folded ears.

"Come buy, come buy our blueberry pie!" hollered a plump Nordic man with a braided beard trailing to the middle of his gut. Hair slicked back to a top bun. Two furry tufts wiggled with his pointed Elven ears.

"Spells, potions and more," Cawed a molting raven. "Come to our booth and see what's in store!" When we passed, it gave us an unusual head twist, neck feathers unexpectedly splaying while its beak opened to provide us with rapt attention.

We hurried along.

"Human Repellent, get your Human Repellent right here!" The stand displayed several crystal perfume bottles containing a yellow fluid—tags titled 'Pisky Poison' and 'Glamour Guise' amongst the other options.

"Rare fruits from the sunlit skies of the Seelie Courts. Taste the fruit of your people." The blue eyes of a female peered at us closely. Her sharp angular features intimidated, even as she spoke with a soft rhythmic lull. "Would you like a nibble?" She inquired directly. Humming gossamer wings, slick and oily, peeked passed the cloak she wore.

"No, thanks," James frowned, drawing me closer.

"Are you sure? The girl looks famished. Wouldn't you like to try nostalgia? Utter bliss?" She held out a fleshy, plump piece with her four digit hand.

Sticky and inviting, like a piece of peach or nectarine, light blue liquid oozed and beaded to the corners of the fruit. Not realizing I had been reaching to take it from the blue-eyed woman, James drug me quickly back into the flow of the foot traffic.

"Don't," he growled in my ear.

Frowning, I nibbled on my thumbnail.

There were so many strange sights, glowing eerie and enticing to someone like myself, that the deeper we stepped into their world, I found my fears melting away. I had all but neglected the reason to us attending *Myrrd* until a familiar name caught my attention. Painted eloquently across a hanging sign was, '*Almarik, Lord of Prophecy.*'

Stopping James from moving on, we settled our sights to a sage green caravan dripping in lavishly highlighted trimmings. Hitched to its side, was the bright kaleidoscope patchwork of a cloth pavilion, marking the entrance where wicker chairs and oriental rugs standing just beyond the hazy backdrop.

"Are you looking for Almarik?" announced a squat creature, large ears perked forward inattention. Peering at us carefully through coke-bottle glasses, they stationed themselves before a small table of incense and resins. Green-tinged smoke lazily trailed curls up into a murky cloud above its head.

"Yes…" James stepped halfway in front of me. "Is he in?"

"Oh, the bloody man is always in." it chattered sourly. "Never sleeps, never gives discounts," they waved dismissively toward the caravan, trying to take a closer peek at me.

I shrank away. "Thanks…"

"I wouldn't give him much in return. The man takes a mile when you give him a millimeter of information," He squeaked, making blatant motions to see around James.

I moved further away, unnerved by how curious the creature was.

My friend took my hand in the same movement the creature pushed his spectacles further up its nose, tiny hands curled about the edge of the table to peer closer at us. "Who are you? I've never seen you around here before… do you descend of Seelie or Unseelie?"

"Neither" he muttered and pushed me into the tent.

Oriental rugs overlapped the flooring as low sitting whicker hassocks and chairs peeked through copious amounts of cushions and throw pillows. Oil lamps hung dangerously from the tops of the silk ceiling, giving an eerie multifaceted appeal with the various stained glass windows.

We were alone.

The quiet was enough to allow me to my thoughts, which proved dangerous in the past.

"What now…" James murmured, sharp eyes glancing to corners suspiciously.

"There is an air of magic about you, making your true form obscure to the Fae," called a voice from within. "If they are not looking for it, I believe you could pass as one of them easily. Though, you are just a mere mortal, aren't you?"

James and I stiffened. His hand gripped mine just as tightly as I grasped his.

"Come in." The voice beckoned.

Looking uneasily to one another, we stepped up the rickety stairs to enter the caravan. A gentleman waited patiently, lazing into a leather-bound high back, with a Chinese jade pipe hanging from his lips. One leg sat poised to a knee, hands steeple in thought. He adorned himself in a cobalt robe, loosely tied about his profoundly British attire. Azure crystalline irises popped with the paisley ascot snug about his neck. The man wasn't exceptionally tall, but he had a strong appearance, finely groomed mutton chops added to his vintage appeal.

When he settled his sight to us, James took a step back.

I plopped down before him without thinking. "Are you Almarik?"

He blew lavender smoke up into the air.

"Basle sent me," I continued eagerly, watching him rise silently, looping about my fidgety friend to close the door behind us.

"Careful girl, a name is a powerful weapon in these parts, especially to a Fae." He pulled a hanging silk rope, and all the curtains dropped.

"You aren't Fae?" I shivered when he gave me a side-look.

"You seem unsure."

"I... you don't glow like the rest," That was a stupid response.

James stared me down with a questioning look, quiet and stormy in his state of trepidation.

"As studious as your observations are, your hypothesis isn't correct. Almost, but not quite," he graced us with a smile before blowing more smoke. Rather than tasting foul it smelt of sandalwood. "Are you afraid, Emmaline? For a human, such responsibilities thrust upon one of your age…" he trailed off with a headshake.

My shoulders sagged. "Well, kidnapping is a crime."

"You find yourself abandoned in a hidden world of harsh brutality," He murmured. "It is a secluding road you tread. I am sure I do not have to tell you it is unwise to tell the surrounding mortals of this place?" He shifted his attention to James a moment.

James straightened and gave him a steady wrathful expression.

"Do you know what kind of pressure that is? We live in a world where a kid going missing is a felony. You don't report it, and you are front-line suspect."

"And knowing what you do now, do you think your past actions have led to the best outcome for the safety of the child?"

There was a long-drawn pause before the redhead beside me nodded firmly. "There has been nothing else to do but wait."

"Bullshit," I smacked my hand to my armrest. "Utter malarkey. You haven't heard a word I've said."

"You can go on as many treasure hunts as you want and you'll never be able to get Abigail back on your own."

"Why do you think I'm here? I'm trying to get help!" I patted myself and gave a frustrated look. I left my wallet in the car. "I don't have money with me."

131

James shook his head.

"Your paper currency is useless to me," The man leaned forward, giving me a long and thoughtful stare. After our short outburst, I wouldn't want to deal with us either. "However, I would like to see that birthmark on your shoulder."

"Whoa-ho-ho. No one is showing anyone anything. Come on," James gestured toward the door. "Emma, let's go."

"How did you know I had a birthmark?"

"It is only a simple request."

"Why do you want to see it?"

He gave a cheeky smile and tilted his head, not answering.

"The man isn't giving you an answer. Let's go, Em, the guy's a freak."

"Wait," I held up a hand to James. "If that's all he wants..." The gentleman before us nodded calmly. "Then that's what he'll get. It's the least I can do, literally."

James growled, hands gripping tightly to his sides before he walked toward the door, "Fine. Just fine. I'm waiting outside." Jerking the door open, he stepped out of sight.

"Sorry, he's just—he really IS a good guy."

"He is a noble friend." The man concluded with a sympathetic simper. "I only need a peek. I assure you, no ill intent is taking place."

Nodding, I tugged off my sweatshirt before pulling at the collar of my t-shirt. Wiggling out my right shoulder, the man took a sweeping gander over the freckled skin where the faded, brown blotch resided.

"Old Soul," He concluded.

"What?"

"The butterfly," He moved back around to face me.

"Butterfly…" I gave him an odd look.

"They represent transition, a symbolic process which involves shifting from one life to another. It is an evolution of multiple lives to create one being."

Slipping my sweatshirt back on, I blinked to the worn wooden planks beneath my feet, trying to form an adequate response to what he was saying.

I found none.

"So… what does that mean?"

"It means…" he trailed off. When I looked up our eyes had settled to the same level as he had dipped forward in wait of my attention. He continued. "It means, dear Emmaline, that you are who I am to see."

"Cryptic of you."

"Well, you came to see a prophet, did you not?" He nodded without waiting for an answer, popping his pipe back into his mouth, straitening to pace casually across what little space was available.

"How do you know so much about me?" I watched the man's robes curl and flow airily behind him. "Why does everyone seem to know me, yet I know nothing of them?" It was more of a statement really, my eyes unfocused with the numbing of my mind.

Too much.

"Tell me, have you ever heard of the story of Rumpelstiltskin?"

"Yeah, sure, what kid hasn't?"

"You would be surprised," He chuckled pleasantly, clearing his throat. "Do you remember the plight of the miller's daughter? Her father, being a boast and a liar, told the king that his daughter could spin straw into gold. Because of this, the maiden was forced into a tower filled with hay and threatened with her life to produce a miracle no mere mortal could accomplish."

I watched his hands dramatically gesture while the purple smoke danced gracefully around his fingers. What was Almarik getting at? What did this have to do with me? "As the story goes, a small man visited the miller's daughter."

He peered at me in question until I nodded in understanding.

"This man agreed to spin the straw into gold for the girl, but at a cost. The first room was at the price of the girl's necklace, the second of the ring she wore. When the maiden had yet one more room to be spun into gold, she no longer owned anything to offer the man, and, out of desperation, had agreed to give him her firstborn."

My head tilted with his words, trying to find the hidden meaning behind the story time. If Almarik knew of my confusion, he gave no sign, continuing his speech with an air of gentle sophistication rare to this modern age.

"When the spools were complete, and the straw was gone, the king had been so pleased with the maiden, that he had taken her for his bride. When the queen had birthed her first child, it was then that the little man reappeared before her, insisting on taking what they had agreed." The Lord of Prophecy pursed his lips in thought, smoke trickling from his nostrils at that point. "But because of her bold unwillingness to give up her only child, she offered the greedy man into another bargain. If she could not guess the imps name in three days' time, then the child would be his to take."

"She figured out his name though, right? Something about overhearing his name."

"Yes."

"And then he tore himself in two?" I shivered. "Is this supposed to be a real story?"

"No, Rumpelstiltskin has never been a Fae recorded in history as anything but a myth; however, the story still rings true in various forms. I chose this tale because there are lessons to learn and apply to your situation."

"The problem is I've never gotten the chance to screw up. My sister was stolen, no rhyme or reason."

"It is all about the smoke and mirrors, Emmaline."

I gave a concentrated expression to my folded hands, sighing.

"Shall we take it step by step? What is your current situation?"

"Abigail is missing."

"More specific dear."

"Faeries took *my* sister?" He gave an encouraging smile. "My sister was taken, from our home, by Faeries without a probable cause."

"Better, but perhaps they had a reason. Who was the child to be taken from in the story?"

"The miller's daughter, the mother," There was a pointed look in his gaze. Attempting to think hard on what I was saying, I rubbed at my face in frustration. "I don't know. I don't know."

"You do know," He countered. "Think harder," His jaw flexed, parting his lips to have light mauve smoke seep through the cracks of his teeth.

"I don't!" I knew I was whining; I could hear it grinding at my eardrums. Thinking was just too hard at that moment.

"Emmaline, yell me what you just said."

"Miller's daughter is the mother of the child," I slurred. "That has no relevance."

"It does."

"Who is she?" I frowned.

Thoughts trickled forward.

'On her death fate was cast, through dealings of the past.'

"None of this was an accident," I voiced the Pale Man's words. "It's just all plans leading up to some chaotic ending for us," Looking up I frowned. "This has to do with my mom, she's the miller's daughter, isn't she?"

He gave a slow nod, moving forward to reply when the caravan abruptly shook with the connected tent collapsing. There was a rush of loud struggling voices, James yelled for me to run, while the door flung open as creatures hurried inside to greet us.

There was a lot of grabbing, tugging and pulling; a whirl of colors invaded my senses while I was being carried off into the crowd of whispering Fae, staring at us with wrinkled noses.

Everyone around us was in a panic; the words *'human'* and *'mortal'* thrown around like one would call out 'murder' or 'fire.' It was a chilling thought to know we were surrounded by a race of creatures that presumably wished us ill will.

"Whaaaaaaaaaaaaaat? Human? What is this?"
"What? A human here in our market?"
"Where did it come from?"
"How did it get passed Nuaal?"
"Who?"
"The Goat man at the door, you idiot!"
"What, a human?!?"
"That's what I said, you cotton headed brute!"

James was cussing up a storm somewhere near me, struggling apparently from the looks on the offenders face.

The action was swift. One moment we were being dragged along, the next shoved into chairs in a room off shooting the large hallway. I blinked stupidly around, trying to understand the situation before me. It seemed I was always trying to catch up.

What surprised me was that they had brought Almarik with us. He stood in the corner, near a rusted boiler, shadows casting an ominous image.

"Fuck," James scrambled, yanking me closer at the elbow, glaring at a hunched-over creature that blocked the door.

Black beady eyes peeped through gangly matted fur while its long gnarled nose twitched at us in distaste. Their massive form took up the entire exit, making it impossible for us to dart away. "Back off," James seethed, rising to stand in front of me.

That didn't hinder my view of the situation, giving me a good look at the shifting creature.

"Be it poison at the hand of mortal man, wrecking, ssstealing, driven mad. Wretched humans, ssstinking drones, filling up the

137

catacombsss." It hissed softly. *"The day shall arise when you meet your demise and resume your role as foal."*

"Let us go, Troll."

This was getting out of hand. Passed the Troll were Fae gathering into a writhing crowd. Everyone was trying to get a good look at the captured humans.

"Prometheus," Almarik rumbled, "This is highly uncivilized. Where is Odhrun? Where is your Lord?" He bore his teeth, revealing four sharp incisors.

I made a choking noise triggering the prophet to relax a fraction.

"Let us out," James insisted. "You can't keep us down here forever."

"We just came here to talk to Almarik. We aren't here to cause trouble." I chimed in tentatively. I wasn't even sure they heard me. The three individuals were having a staring contest to see who would cave first.

"Lying furless stink!" Someone shouted from the crowd, a hum of agreement followed.

"You cannot reason with backward-thinking individuals," Almarik said under his breath. "It is best to speak with Odhrun. There is a reason for him being in charge here."

He settled to a seat, bending to steeple his hands against his forehead, elbows to knees.

The Troll took his time to shuffle back and out of the entryway, ducking its head to keep from hitting the brace. He made no bother to answer.

Our exit was closed. We only had the orbs above our heads for lighting as I had painted the room's windows.

"If this goes fucking sour, I'm holding you responsible, Vampyre." James took a stab at the man beside me.

I wasn't going to lie. I was now extremely uneasy around him too.

"You must understand," He closed his eyes. "This is their refuge. You cannot blame them for being terrified. A human has not stepped into the market in 15 years."

"You speak as if you aren't one. Tell me, why are you supplying this information?" I blurted out.

"That is because I am not a local. I settled here to talk to the one in my visions, the girl with the butterfly."

"You were talking about my mom."

James suddenly gripped my shoulder. "Em—"

"No, I need to talk about this. I need answers, not riddles. You told me this started with my mom, but why? Why is this all happening?"

"Fae live entirely too long." He sighed. "The games can be, well, troublesome at best," Shifting he watched me eagerly, "Emmaline, I know you can get this. Try to concentrate. We have now discovered the miller's daughter to be your mother, but who might the child be?"

"My sister," He exhaled in resignation, looking disappointed. "Well, isn't she? They took her just like the Queen's child."

"Are you seriously talking about fairy tales right now?" James paced in front of us, not knowing what to do with himself.

"Would someone seek to take your sister but then contact you afterward if he really planned to keep her? Don't you think that if that were so, he would have stolen her and then left you to wonder, rather than dropping breadcrumbs? What would a Fae have any business doing making ransom letters to a mortal girl he can easily overpower?"

"You are taking this too far!" James suddenly shoved Almarik up against the brick wall, the man's chair tipped back to its hind legs as he sat calmly pinned.

"Hey! James!?"

"He needs to shut up," He glared directly at the fortuneteller. "You are sticking your nose into other's business. She doesn't need you filling her head up with shit. You got that?"

"It's my duty. You should understand that," He gave him a pointed look, hands staying rooted to his lap.

The redhead's nostrils flared, stress evident in his posture before he dropped Almarik. He went back to pacing.

"Go on Emmaline," The gentleman turned to me.

Restless, I followed James's movements while trying to concentrate. "Okay, maybe," picking at my nails, I shifted. "Maybe he doesn't even plan on keeping her," There was a commotion going on outside of the room. I quickened my pace. "Maybe, it's like the story. He wants the firstborn." When there was no reply, I leaned away from the other. "You can't be serious."

"Did I chuckle?"

"My mom made a deal for her firstborn?" My voice sounded smaller than I had ever intended it to be. Suddenly, I couldn't look the other in the eyes. "Me... she gave me away."

"Smoke and mirrors, remember the first half of the story. There may be more to it than there seems."

"There really isn't a difference between myself and Abby. Either way, when you give up a child for the sake of a deal..."

I felt a hand rest to my shoulder.

"If she had given any of her children away, wouldn't he have taken one or all of you sooner, why now Emmaline?"

"I don't know!" I rose to my feet, and James kept a steady grip, leaning to my side.

"Why is FK baiting me with my sister? Why did my mother make the deal in the first place? I don't know. I don't have all the answers. I don't understand them well enough. That's why I came to seek help. I know nothing about supernatural beings. I don't know how any of this works. My mother just died, Almarik. She died and left me to deal with all of this. Why now? Why now after she died?" I was crying then, slumping back down to my chair, hiding my face behind a mop of messy locks.

James settled to his haunches, searching for what to say. "Em, your mom loved you guys. She's fought hard for you. When she died, she couldn't protect you any longer. She isn't the one to blame."

"I don't know how to," I muttered, taking the offered handkerchief Almarik had stashed away in his chest pocket.

"Know how to, what?"

"Not blame."

James frowned, looking disturbed but understanding. "Look, I need to tell you something—"

"Now isn't the time for pillow talk," Almarik warned just as a knock sounded to the door.

"How quaint, they're being cordial."

141

The two men rose. I followed sluggishly.

"I'm not interrupting, am I?" A faintly familiar voice rang from outside in the crowded hallway.

Prometheus hunched lower in a strange attempt at a greeting before shuffling off the side, taking creatures with him so that an ordinary human-looking man could step through.

Shifting back in confusion, I watched as Country Acre's Manager slip through the entrance. He greeted with a civil nod, "Ah, the skittish little girl from earlier."

"Hi..."

"What are you doing in my market?" his voice echoed a little too forcefully. "How did you manage to sneak in here? Prometheus, the password is being changed tonight. Nuaal is fired."

"I just—" I began, cutting short with a nudge from James. just—" I began, cutting short with a nudge from James.

"I invited them."

Odhrun gave Almarik a hawk-eyed stare. I wondered what exactly the man was. He appeared to be so human.

"Seeing as you are under an invitation yourself, what makes you think you can invite human's into this place? You aren't a resident, Lord Fable."

"You know very well who sent me."

"These are the Wildlands and Iron Ruins. Requests by the Courts are acknowledged but not heeded here. You understand? She has no control here."

"I understand." Almarik bowed his head slightly. "I apologize for my brash behavior. It was of my own making."

James was listening acutely to the conversation, giving me time to shove a hand into my pockets to work open the bag full of salt.

It was an idiotic idea. I knew that. Almarik seemed to know what he was doing, but that did not mean this pardon he was given carried to us. We were, for all I knew, deep in the bowels of Underground Port Angeles.

The eyes of the creatures beyond the painted windows hovered jeering and curious. I had put us into the hands of a culture outnumbering us a hundred to two. Who was to say Almarik wouldn't turn on us to save his own skin?

"Amuse us, why would a human see the Lord of Prophecy?"

Stilling my movements, I gawked at our captor. *Did he realize what I was doing?*

"My sister is missing," my companions didn't seem to enjoy hearing me divulge such information to the man.

He cracked a slight smile. "Oh? What a petty human problem to take up with the Queen's most favored advisor." He shifted back to Almarik, "And for the Queen's advisor to cater to such a pesky little girl."

"The Queen's letter explicitly requests the discretion of your band of brothers, Odhrun."

"That didn't answer my question." Odhrun strolled before us, his leather-bound shoes clicked lightly against the floors as he shifted from one side to the other.

When no one was willing to answer, he paused. "I'm waiting."

"Odhrun, you're far from the courts, but I doubt news has gone deaf to your ears."

"And?"

"And," Almarik intoned, "Age-old prophecies ring further true than not as of late."

They exchanged quiet looks.

Prometheus went rigid from behind the gentlemen.

"From traitor'sss womb the child doth hatch..." his trickling waspish voice rang across the throng of onlookers, sending chills along the spines of those who understood the statement within his riddled words.

Twisting, his beetled eyes stared long and hard in my direction. He was a vision derived straight from the writings of Grimm's fairytales of a nightmarish creature looming tall and haggish, dripping with a promise of slow death to its victims.

James and I stepped back on instinct.

My hand gripped a fist full of salt. Stiff with fright I couldn't will myself to move yet. I found James slipping his hand into my pocket, wrapping his fingers about my wrist.

"Let go." He murmured against the side of my head. In a swift motion, he withdrew my hand and flicked it with a sharp snap. I released the fistful, watching the salt fling and disperse, grazing the individuals that stood between us and our escape.

Prometheus reared back with a baleful wale. Everyone scattered in panic.

James lurched forward through the confused tide of Fae, pulling us between the stampede of flailing appendages.

I tried to keep up, feeling another hand wrap over my shoulder and pull me back.

Crying out, I punched and kicked at my assailant. Stumbling, James and I broke apart.

"EMMA!?" My friend's eyes were the last thing I saw of him, large and panicked, as he was forced away with the flow.

I was hit to my left and smacked against the cemented wall beside me.

In an attempt to turn and confront my attacker, I scraped my face against the rough surface, catching sight of Odhrun who towered over a frog Goblin laying curled to my feet. Their large egg yolk irises ogled up in confused horror, four arms clutching a cloth bag full of bruised produce.

We gawked at each other until its four nostrils flared, taking a strong whiff in my direction. Rows of dull, uneven teeth peeked through warty lips as their jaw slacked in disbelief.

Panicking, I shoved away from Odhrun while the small creature shrieked. I managed to hastily hook my arm over the frame of a broken window, hoisting my body through it in an attempt to get away.

Odhrun, a few paces behind, reached in to grab fistfuls of my hair, jerking me backward.

I yelped, shoulders striking the wall, narrowly missing the sharper edges of the windowpane. Clutching my scalp, I twisted painfully back to look at him.

"Humans corrupt with chemicals and waste, killing your own for the sake of convenience." His handsome face contorted in loathing. "We'd let you ruin yourselves, but you're dragging us into your mess."

"What do you want?" I pleaded.

"Your presence brings bad things, little girl. Don't you understand? You tread onto our lands and brought disaster behind you!"

"But I didn't do anything—that hurts!" I dug the tips of my fingers into his skin, feeling him grip my hair tighter in his rise of anger.

"This is a kingless city, and you're marked. You've guided attention to us."

"I didn't mean to!"

"Your actions speak louder than your intent, stupid girl. If you are what the Lord of Prophecy claims and I let you go now, we would have no leverage for what is coming." The tension on my scalp suddenly released, and I stumbled away, quickly glancing over to him. Odhrun's irises were submerged entirely in black, making him look devilish.

"Fuck off!" bellowed a familiar voice. James pushed against the thinning mass of panic.

"I was wondering where your pet went."

They stared each other down until James leaped with abandon. Grabbing for bottles littering the tops of carts, he quickly threw tonics and potions haphazardly at the feet of the market leader.

Shattered glass echoed down the hall, smoke expanding swiftly as colored fumes mixed into the vent-less air. Coughing, I watched their bodies disappear, swallowed in the massive bomb of color.

The two had lunged at each other, I could hear struggling, and glass from windows rattling as bodies hit walls.

"James!?" I cried out, not sure where to look.

We need to get out of here.

I picked myself up and dash around the crumbling hallway, struggling to zip up my hoodie and cover my nose.

Limbs flung in and out of my limited view. Ducking a few times to avoid involvement, I caught sight of red hair. "James!" He turned in surprise, getting a fist in the face by Odhrun. "Oh shit," I stooped down, trying to find where they were.

A shoulder came into view. I grabbed at it, taking a handful of shirt belonging to my friend's aggressor. Flailing, I hesitated for a split second before giving his face an inevitable smack. *Ouch.*

James barked out a surprised laugh, choking as the fumes worsened. Odhrun snarled, becoming just as disoriented as us, lurching to grab at me.

Dodging, I pulled my friend at the arm and ran.

"I will find you!" His voice trailed after us. The cries of anger cut short when the heavy metal door swung open and shut, cold crisp air hitting us full force while we clambered up the stairs.

My legs shook like Jell-O.

"Damn, you are one crazy broad," James gave a gasping laugh, releasing an apprehensive gulp of air he had been holding.

I wanted to stop and catch my breath, lean against the locked gate to steady my nerves, but James would have nothing of it. He pulled us over and off down the road, recognizing the side street as Laurel, with the mural 'Sluicing of the Hogback' before us.

We were at least five blocks away from our starting point.

"Are you okay?" I realized, while the other may have been acting normal, he had just had a fistfight with a Fae with a hurt hand.

"The guy throws a good punch, but he wasn't that impressive."

"You just fought with a Faery. You're lucky you didn't get turned into a toad!"

"He's not full-blooded," James muttered, rubbing his thumb along his jaw. "He's basically a really strong human, that's it."

"How do you know?" I looked around while we walked, paranoia was sinking in again. Rubbing my head, I frowned. "I hope Almarik is okay."

"Em, not everything is in your power to control. You need to let some stuff go." He took up my hand. "You're going to tell me everything now, and your hair has pink in it."

"What!?"

CHAPTER 8

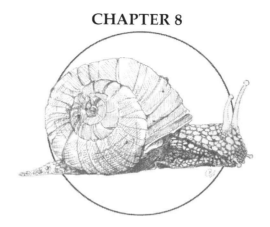

SUNDAY MORNING—PART 1

M*yrrd* was an unhinged floodgate, forcing us to acknowledge the tangible proof of Faeries existence.

We tucked ourselves within the foliage of Lincoln Park, shivering and snacking on cold fries. James was quiet and attentive, listening as I tumbled out a tangled twist of fantastical retellings. My teeth chattered with the swell of excited emotions. When I ran out of things to tell, we sat there, silence weighing thick with our muddled thoughts.

James let out a loud sigh.

"Well…" He started, "Looks like we have no other options."

"Options?"

"Then to find her ourselves," he supplemented.

"We?" I looked up, watching him. "You'll help me?"

"I won't let you go on your own, Em. You'd completely destroy yourself."

"Thanks a lot," I hugged myself, frowning.

"I'm not saying you aren't capable."

"You think I'm a screw-up."

"No, I don't think that. Come on." My friend shifted in his seat, craning his upper body to look at me fully. "This isn't like accidentally leaving her at the grocery store, Em. Magical beings kidnapped your little sister, replacing her with a freak of nature while erasing me from everyone's memories, all that, to manipulate you into trading places with her. Have I left anything out?" He ruffled his curls, trying to release pent-up tension. "This is crazy shit that is WAY over anyone's head. I won't lie, I'm freaked out we'll lose. We can't help Abby if we lose."

His words sank into my bones, instilling a new perception of my quickly changing reality. I had once thought I had paved a defined path for myself. I was the tragedy of a small-town girl, aspiring to be more than her cookie cutter depiction. The adventure of college was the key to living a life beyond the Darling stigma where no one knew the stories of my ancestor's tragic ends into madness. I just never expected the direction would turn into a twisted game.

Out of all my uncertainty, one thing was clear. My mom had made a deal with FK, and in turn, lost her firstborn. Me. I still had questions that needed answering and hoped Basle was agreeable tonight.

We pulled up into the driveway slowly, seeing a police car parked alongside the street.

"I thought you said they didn't believe you?" James frowned.

"They didn't." I registered the silhouette of an individual settled to the porch steps, stooped in a hunched position with their head bowed. The snails and slugs that plagued the house overtook the officer's form.

Was he dead?

James slowly made his way toward the unmoving person. "Hello?" He quietly inquired. "Officer Crowe?"

I shut the door of the truck, making a sizeable strained screech. The policeman would have moved from that.

"James, we should call the police." I frowned.

"This IS the police." He looked back at me, mirroring my expression. He leaned in to check his pulse. "Officer Crowe — holy shit!?" His forearm was abruptly grabbed.

"Mm-ah..." an undertone gurgle slipped past the police officer's lips. "Em-ma..."

James hastily pulled from the man, watching him lurch precariously forward, almost spilling him onto the ground.

I crept closer, crunching on snail shells.

"Officer Crowe? Are you alright?" The idea of the unsuspecting policeman being hurt by Fae gave a whole new twist. *If the law enforcement was no match, who's to say, I was?* "Officer Crowe."

"Em-ma... you can't... escape... fate. He... won't let you."

We both leaned away when his head rolled backward, showing Crowe's eyes lacking pupils, glazed over with a milky hew. Guttural breathing escaped his partially opened jaw. Other than the insects slipping across his uniform, the man appeared unharmed. *What was this, some exorcism knock-off? Were they trying to scare us?*

151

"Who are you?" I demanded, reaching out to shake him, despite the repulsion I felt. "What do you want?!"

"Butter... fly..." Saliva built up and drizzle down his chin. "Heed... my... words... fight... with caution..." A hand rose slowly before me. "Butterfly..."

"Almarik?" Wriggling out from the man's collar, I felt—too late—the crawling of a centipede fluttering its legs up against my hand.

The sensation sent my head spinning. Physically paralyzed, my eyes dropped closed. Images pulled from the darkness that shrouded my sight, shifting quickly in a jarred and hazy string of events.

Obscured colors shaped the landscape, tugging me along the strip of a dark highway we traveled westward, roaming across stretches of everlasting green. My journey seemed endless—shades of pine melded with a marmalade backdrop, pooling like watercolor against white parchment, wet, fuzzy and warped.

Abruptly, drawn into a slow roll, the picturesque image affixed itself to a large arrowhead sign, reading 'Olympic National Park: Hoh Rainforest.'

My breath caught, pitching headfirst into a tunnel of trees, where we slithered through the twisted and cracked road of the park. More greens overwhelmed my vision until signs marking The Hall of Moss, and Spruce Nature Trail burst into view. They swooped me up and over the canopy, making my stomach drop away from me.

In the small opening above, I could glimpse the flourishing buzz of brightly colored creatures. Faces so startling and breathtaking, my heart skipped a few paces. They did not notice me spying.

I ogled freely, drinking in the hues like a drug-induced vision.

Then my sight abruptly caught in flame, smearing the attractive foliage with edges of rust. Two orbs, diluted in blue, blinked into existence. A human shape took form, tall and fixed like a tree's trunk. Striking red hair framed the sightless expression of the individual.

'**Where are you? Come here**.' *they mouthed.*

The other beings sniffed around attentively, trying to discover the hidden watcher.

Panic riddled, suction pulled me backward, removing me from the trance.

I vomited onto Officer Crowe.

"Em?!" James smacked my back. "Fuck, what happened? Where did you go? I was shaking you, calling you. You wouldn't respond."

Wiping my lips, I peered wearily up at him.

"I know where to go," I was kneeling then. My whole body thrummed with aching fear until pinpricks of numbness evaded my legs, urging me to shake feeling into them.

Resting a hand on the knee of the unconscious middle-aged man before me, I rose unsteadily.

James took my hand then, ignoring the comatose officer to tug me across the yard toward the Troll's house. He pounded unrelenting on the door, keeping me close.

"James" I murmured, glancing back at the street with paranoia.

Basle's lights snapped off ceremoniously before I could hear his low voice on the other side. *"Who'sss there…?"*

"Who the fuck do you think?" My friend retorted.

"Go ahead, draw attention to yourself, whelp."

"Let us in!" James yelled.

153

Locks were unlatched before the door opened wide. I stared unblinking as they tugged me into the Troll's house and pushed onto a chair, like extra luggage.

"I take it the Market did not go in your favor?"

"We could have been killed, or bartered into some freakish slave trade. What the hell were you thinking!?"

The Troll inflated as high as he could with the low rising ceiling, sizing my friend up.

"We all have rollsss to play, mine doesss not entail hero."

"And what does it entail, huh!? Creepy Peeping Tom?"

"That's enough, James," I sank into the cushions, feeling pressure in my head. I distracted myself with the floral print of the chair as the other two fell silent. A few lights snapped back on while Basle shifted about the dwelling.

"Tea? Coffee?" The Troll called from the kitchen. My brain had a hard time deciding over such a simple question. When it finally registered coffee, I was more than eager to accept.

"Coffee, please," I twitched in alarm when a fire suddenly burst to life in the hearth. James was jumpy; having toppled backward over the sofa he was in the act of sitting on. I faintly heard a hissing laugh in the kitchen.

"Wytch wood, cream or sssugar?" he replied, as if that somehow explained everything.

"Both, for James, black for me," I blinked, watching the hint of green flicker at the base of the flames, feeling it draw me near as heat permeated the living room.

While we sat waiting for our host, I took the time to peer around my neighbor's home. It wasn't as large as my family's living room, but it had been the largest in Basle's. With floors carpeted in soft cream and walls eggshell white, what it lacked in color made up through the porcelain trinkets, furniture, and drapes that stood stark with floral prints. Clearly, Basle had no hand in the decoration of an elderly female. I didn't recall ever meeting a Mrs. Weatherly, doubting she existed.

The cleanliness of the house was unexpected; the initial smells were deceptive.

"What are you thinking?" James rested to the arm of the couch, eyes flicking back and forth in the attempt at reading my expression.

"I'm wondering about the previous Mr. Weatherly…"

"*Andrew Weatherly.*"

"And was he…" I trailed off, shying away from the word Fae. Should I even bother asking? The question raised the suspicion of how Basle came to reside in this household.

"*Fae? No, no, he wasss very much human AND mortal.*"

"Ah," I looked around vaguely, wondering if there was even a difference between the two. I really should have delved deeper into what Basle was saying, but the evening was evidently catching up with me. "Is the whole house like this?"

"*Like what?*" Basle finally emerged from the bowels of his kitchen as his all-encompassing self.

I couldn't help but stare as I momentarily lapsed in my thought process.

Gaping, he lumbered across the creaking floorboards and shifted to avoid the ceiling fan. His hunched over form was frightening and awe-inspiring. Tawny matted locks of hair encased everything but his cheeks and palms. Long stalky limbs painstakingly balanced a small silver tray of chinaware.

Basle with his ferocious exterior, holding porcelain as a host, made an awfully confusing picture for my nerves.

He rode his knuckles like an ape would, broad shoulders rippling as the muscles beneath his coat shifted. He didn't look comfortable by any means, but the action of setting the tray to the coffee table didn't look like a foreign action to him. When he finally looked up his dark lips spread back to attempt a welcoming smile. *Did I look scared?* He looked away. I wasn't sure if he realized that sharp teeth were little-to-no comfort for a human so newly introduced to his kind. He looked like he was trying though.

James leaned in, making his own silent judgments. Distrust was clear.

Basle set about, shakily pouring the dark liquid into three cups. His hands held an extra digit, the smallest finger barely able to hook about the handle of the cup he was attending to.

"I've got this." I finally laid a hand to the cup rim.

He retracted his fingers instantly, letting me make the coffee. There was the awareness he could just have easily reached out and snatched me up like a rag doll.

Everyone tried not to feel self-conscious around one another. I finished his work, sitting back to sip at the contents. "I was talking about the room," I responded to his question, "The interior decorating."

James smartly kept to himself, taking up a cup to peer into its contents.

"Ah, yesss well, you can thank Andrewsss wife for that bit." Basle muttered. *"Did you find what you were ssseeking Emmaline?"*

"As much as allowed, answers only create more questions." I smiled at him, feeling myself melt back into the cushions. Coffee was just what I needed. *Blessed coffee.*

He was contemplative again; bushy eyebrows curled to meet his brow.

"I'll do my best in assisting." He was so somber. His eyes felt more human to me than the rest of him, so I focused on those.

"And if you can't will you point me to another direction?"

I looked to James who was watching us closely.

"There is a half-dead police officer outside, and we are sitting here having coffee."

I let out a long sigh.

"Welcome to the ssstrange."

James rose, giving the Troll a look.

"I guess since I'm the designated rule breaker, I'll go deal with Officer Crowe." He put his untouched cup back to the tray. "You give it to her straight, Troll. I'm telling you, no bullshit. Okay? You hear me?"

Basle seemed to struggle with his internal dialogue. James wouldn't leave until the Troll responded, earning a locked door when he slipped out to deal with the police officer.

We fell into an uncomfortable silence where my mind could roll over the retellings of the Grimm's Fairy Tale. Dawn Darling played the role of the maiden with F.K. the dastardly child snatcher. I now knew the source for the crimes committed these past few days. *What plagued me was why?*

Pulling the notes from my pocket, I considered my thoughts.

"Tell me, what isss on your mind?"

What did I need to know?

157

"I want to know, why FK needs a first-born child. What can I do to get Abby back?" Guilt was seeping into my gut, tightening its hold on my heart. *I wasn't a heroine in a fairy tale. I was no liberator.* My thoughts weren't righteous by any means; I just wanted to save Abigail and keep myself free in the process.

"Whoever sssaid you had any freedom, to begin with, Emmaline?" The lines around Basle's lips tugged down, in a look of concern. His statement was cold but honest.

I grimaced, digging the tips of my fingers into the fabric of the chair.

The thought of being at the mercy of someone cruel and unknown frightened me, angered me.

"There were times before she left when mom fell into episodes; I thought she was just talking nonsense."

To the corner of my eye, Basle seemed to straighten and twist his head to watch me. I was a bit alarmed, but he hadn't interrupted. "She explained, in a broken sort of way, that she had made a bargain with someone. She didn't know the weight of the deal until it was too late."

"Ssso, you were unknowingly warned." He reached over, easily snatching up two logs with one hand to toss them into the embers of the fire.

I shrunk back, watching sparks jumping out, imagining they looked somewhat like fireflies, tiny and dazzling. Washington was too cold to get them. *"Continue."*

"Just before she left, she told me she kept someone away." My hands seemed interesting at that point, only to realize I had been doodling lazily across the notepad. The very initials that haunted me since they stole my sister, sat scrawled

158

haphazardly through the lines—bleeding together to form a strange web. "… I'm positive it's FK." Snatching up the paper, I crumbled it until my knuckles turned white. "A person that everyone seems to know of, yet do not acknowledge." *I wasn't stupid.* "My mom took something of his and hid it so he couldn't get to me." Chucking the paper to the fire, I sat back and smiled as it was engulfed in flames.

"Do you know what that may be?"

"No." I pursed my lips. The small victory I felt had gone. "Honestly, I have no clue. What could be important enough to create such a charade and then hide from me? I'll need to go to him."

"I see Lord Fable was more help than your friend led to believe."

"Well, I wouldn't have known where to look without his insight."

Basle shifted, looking as if he wanted to say something in response, but the quick rapping on the door kept our conversation short.

James frothed a ribbon of curses from the other side of the locked door, jiggling the knob with impatience.

"Your imp isss going to wake up the neighborhood, then where would we be?"

Giving an apologetic look, I put my cup down, quickly crossing the room to unlock the front entry.

"You locked the door on me? Are you fucking insane?" My friend forced his head through the crack of the exposed entrance, staring at Basle. "There's an Officer practically dead outside, sprawled on the lawn and you lock me out?"

"Inssstinct," Basle shot back, glowering.

159

"How is he?" I interjected, getting the redhead's attention by a push to the shoulder.

"He won't wake up." James looked sweaty and nervous. "He won't wake up, and his radio is going off. I don't know what I should do with him. He keeps saying your name, Emma." He gripped my shoulder. "We are completely screwed."

"*Where isss the man?*"

"Why do you care? You're probably in on the whole thing." James shot back.

"James!"

"He's inside. I wouldn't be surprised if your neighbor, Mrs. In-Everyone's-Shit, saw me dragging his body up the steps from across the street. I'm going to prison, for life."

"*Ssshow me,*" Basle arched over my head, resting his claws to the top of the door frame, forcing it open. "*Go on.*"

Pressing on James, I guided him back a few paces before steering him off the porch. I had to agree. The idea of being convicted of killing an officer was enough to make my mind snap. Was this all a part of the plan?

The police car settled tauntingly alongside the street before my house. A reminder that humanity would continue on despite the tricks the Fae could play.

"*It does not bode well to dwell on thingsss out of your control.*" Basle murmured behind us. I looked back to his hulking body, moving swiftly across the opened lawn.

"Everyone seems to say that lately." Shells and bugs crunched below the soles of my feet, smearing grime across the porch as I made my way to the partly open door.

There, the policeman was discovered sprawled across the entrance floor.

"James, he isn't a doormat," I stepped around the unconscious man, peering at him closely for any vital signs of breathing. Basle squeezed inside, disregarding my trepidation entirely as he scooped the man up to deposit him abruptly to the couch.

Our ceiling was high, giving the Troll a sufficient amount of space to sit straight on his haunches. He seemed pleased with the change as he peered closely at the man.

"This house is being watched," Basle commented. *"Hard to tell by whom, though..."*

He pulled a beetle from his fur, piercing it between two claws before flicking out toward the open door. *"Tell me, how wasss he when you first approached him?"*

"He was on the porch, just sitting there. No movement," I muttered.

"He called out Emma's name. When she tried touching him, she dropped unconscious."

"You're quite the sought-after individual... It seems it has already started."

"What has?" I frowned.

"You'll be hunted, for one reason or another." The Troll nudged the unconscious man before pressing the soft pad of his thumb against the officer's eyelid, forcing it open to show the lack of pupil. *"He is possessed. A witch must exorcize him."*

"Oh right, a witch. That's just what we need to bring the dead policeman back to life." James drawled, looking less than pleased.

161

I blinked. "Crowe warned me before I went 'under,'" I expressed physical quotations with my fingers.

James gave me a look, nudging me slightly.

"*Warned you?*" Basle peered down across his knotted nose, watching me intently.

"Almarik," I frowned, watching Officer Crowe with the growing guilt of drawing him into all of this.

"*A Lord Vampyre's possession, no matter how neutral in restraint they appear, involves a proper outlet to disconnect from their sired.*" He took up the others limp appendages, studying them carefully.

"Sired, what does that mean?" I followed Basle's movements as he hook a claw to the policeman's collar and peeled it back to show four fresh puncture marks against the other's neck. "Basle, what did Almarik do to Officer Crowe?"

"*He has marked him.*" The Troll finally said. "*He could have used the wrist, but he marked him.*"

"Is he a Vamp now?" James moved back from the couch, drawing me away in the process.

"*No, Almarik left him with enough blood to continue living. I informed him of the Officer's role within these chains of events; however, that does not mean the human isn't bound to the Prophet.*" He leaned back. "*He has bitten the carotid artery that pumps blood into the brain. When a Vampyre bites this, they secrete a sort of chemical, if you will, that keeps them mentally connected. It is why you see him the way you do now. His body is trying to fight the anomaly, and has possibly had a stroke.*"

"Then there is no hope for him?"

"*In most cases, he would be. It is lucky for him that I happen to know a witch who specializes in Faery curses.*" Basle tilted his

162

head when he noticed the confusion on my face. *"Almarik isss not Undead. He is a species of Unseelie, part of a courtship which claims the dark side by birthright. Some say they are one of the closest kinships to humans, the constant need for their blood, which is quite toxic to almost all Fae varieties."*

Now he was just throwing around nonsense. *This was not a Twilight novel.*

"He's trying to say he isn't a satanic bloodthirsty creature." James muttered.

"Okay," I slowly said, tucking these bits of information away for a later date.

"For now, you must get him to Raewyn Hughes as quickly as possible. Are you writing this down imp?" he directed to James, giving him a look.

My friend offered his own exchange in looks, but that didn't stop him from placing the contact into his phone.

I picked up Officer Crowe's feet while James took his upper body. As discreetly as possible, we folded him up into the back seat of the beetle. The hinges popped and groaned in dissatisfaction while we piled inside.

A thin line of navy blue drew itself over the horizon, reminding us of another day with Abigail being in the hands of F.K.

Basle watched us from behind the sheer curtains of his living room window, expression deep in thought. No words of advice, no encouragement. The moment the headlights flipped on, he disappeared.

That made me uneasy.

"It's okay. I doubt we're going to a witch that can turn people into toads, so…"

163

"Yeah, but she can exorcize people who are Faery-stricken."

We both peeked at Crowe behind us and grimaced.

"You could have been like him, Em, you need to be careful."

James didn't spare any caution in our journey out to Joyce, a small town hugging P.A. westward, comprised of a single grocery store dating back to their founding in 1912. Houses sat away from the highway, nesting in the forests and farmlands that families have owned for generations.

Finding the witch would prove difficult if we weren't alert. Most roads had little-to-no indication of address markers, and GPS APPS would only pick up half of the dirt roads.

I watched out the window, dragging my attention to every other tree that drooped over the path we took, purposefully disorienting myself. I could have sworn there were reflective eyes peeking through the underbrush — *watching* us.

Were they the eyes of the Fae?

Officer Crowe hadn't voluntarily moved an inch since being bent up into the back of the car. I tried hard to keep from being unnerved by every jolt of a pothole that made his limbs toss or his head twitch. He wasn't dead. I had to remind myself Crowe was just in a magic-induced coma I was responsible for. *Why was he at my house to begin with?*

Looking straight ahead, I pinched the skin between my thumb and index to keep my mind on the present.

Turning right onto Wasankari Road we traveled straight within a cocoon of silence. Neither one of us bothered to talk. The situation was enough to keep us preoccupied in our own heads.

164

The extended bout of nothing under prepared us for the sudden green address marker of #885 peeking through the ferns. James gripped the steering wheel and veered a sharp right.

"James!?" I seized the handle of the door, eyes wide as we nearly hit a large hydrangea bush growing at the center of the residence driveway.

The car suddenly stalled and died.

CHAPTER 9

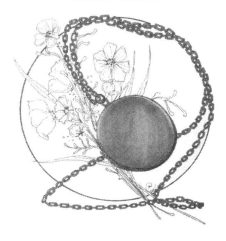

SUNDAY MORNING—PART 2

Jerking the car door open, looking to the back, I hissed at my friend, "James, we're screwed if you killed the car."

"If your car had a good battery, this wouldn't happen," James muttered, popping the trunk to look at the cab.

"Maybe we can roll the car toward the cabin?" I pointed up the road, seeing the flickering of soft lights coming off the residence home.

Peering passed me James furled his eyebrows in concentration.

"I think you need to go and talk to the witch first. I'll stay with Crowe and tinker with this heap of junk."

"My car has a personality, that doesn't mean she's junk."

"Sometimes you need to let things die," James shot back, giving me a look over the hood. "Go."

I decided his sarcasm wasn't worth the last bits of my energy. Turning, I took my time walking up the dirt driveway, the smells of campfire catching my attention a moment before I approached the dwelling.

Glittering in the early morning light, the porch entry was wreathed in variously sized wind chimes, weather-worn dream catchers and evil eye paraphernalia. A beaded medicine bag sat to the door knocker.

Instead, I rang the doorbell; muffled ringing intermingled with the sudden chorus of hollow chiming that washed across the expanse of the property, sending an eerie shiver along my spine.

Strange.

I barely registered the entirety of my surroundings when the light switched on overhead, the door swinging open to reveal a vividly dressed woman wrapped in a baby sling. She gave me a dazzling smile, bronze painted lips quirking playfully to the corners of her dimpled cheeks. Eyes of sunflower green regarded me with bold curiosity.

"Emmaline Darling." Her hands went to her hips, viewing me thoughtfully. "I hear you gave quite the stir to the local Fae market." She was clearly entertained by the mortal girl able to work her way into their super-secret hidey-hole.

"Uh, yeah, it was a riot," I replied not-so enthusiastically.

She startled me then, reaching out to graze my cheek with a feather-light caress of a palm. "Please, take the afflicted one around the back of the house. Bring that handsome boy with."

167

Nodding stupidly, I watched her slip into the bowels of her home, patting the back of her wiggling babe consolingly. "Time for a new nappy, hmm? Then some sleep."

I heard the sounds of the car revving up, a moment later James drove slowly along the trail, parking alongside the cabin to peer at me thoughtfully through the glass. We worked the comatose man slowly from the backseat, an act of teamwork proving almost too much for our nerves.

There were a few comical drops, smacks, and tugs before Crowe's body was finally brought about the witch's cabin into the backyard.

In the early daybreak, a low burning fire crackled to the center of a small clearing. Overgrown grass grew thick about a crowd of waterlogged benches, situated along the pyre in a half circle. They faced a rough path leading toward a wickiup, a squat domed structure built up of rocks, plaster, and wood. Decomposing leaves and fallen pinecones littered the area, setting an autumn mood.

James all but dropped Crowe the moment we stopped

"We need to get him into the purification lodge. Let him sweat out the influence over him." The woman ducked under the porch overhang to greet us, no longer carrying the baby backpack.

There was a distant cry of a disgruntled child from inside the lodge.

"You're Raewyn?" James gave the shapely female a blatant look over, "the witch exorcist?"

"Isn't that obvious?" She chuckled airily. "We could stand here and exchange relations, but the longer we wait, the more brittle his mind will get." She gestured to the small lodging past the fire, "Please, join me."

Raewyn's stride was seamless within the turquoise skirts she wore, tattooed feet peeking out as she bent to gather Officer Crowe up over her shoulder.

We watched in mild amazement as she made slow, steady steps in the lodge's direction—trailing along a line of loose tobacco.

"I didn't expect that." James said nonchalantly, poking lightly at my shoulder.

"You think we can trust her?"

"Well, we just let her drag away the cop so, we'll have to." He seemed more resolute with the situation than I was.

Raewyn was depositing Crowe to a bench near the wickiup entry. Crouching before the coals of the collapsed fire pit, she quietly offered a cutting of hair to the flame. A wind picked up around us, sending a licking spark to greet the presented gift. Only when the tree's stopped swaying did the witch did the witch take out a bundle of dried herbs and bury them halfway into the embers.

The billow of sweet musk met our senses. In those few short moments, I was satisfied. Raewyn spun around me, waving wisps of smoke over my form with a huge variegated feathered fan. When she finished with James, she doused herself and settled her tools to the side.

Smudging wasn't foreign to me. The idea was that burning certain herbs created a sacred space, a blank uncontaminated area for energy work. Mom enacted smoke cleansing during sporadic bouts of her lifelong paranoia. She had often used this as a way to deal with her resentment toward her mother.

When I was younger, I had thought it was amusing. Not so much anymore.

James made himself useful, rolling up the pelt door while the witch carried the police officer inside. He crawled in after, leaving me to stand alone in the backyard.

The eyes hadn't followed us this deep into the property. Maybe Raewyn Hughes was more promising than I had given her credit for. If Fae did not tread on her lands, then perhaps she really could cure Officer Crowe.

Mustering up the courage, I kneeled to peek inside; a waft of muggy heat hit my face, disorienting me.

"Come in, have a drink." Raewyn encouraged while she avidly circled the room to light the five richly colored lanterns hanging from the ceiling. "It will get hotter when we begin. You'll want to keep hydrated."

They left officer Crowe to the far side of the room, on top four mats encircling a small pit of large blackened rocks. James was moving at his own pace, looping a strange assortment of herbs up around the bound sticks that were shaping the underside of the structure. Their labor illuminated the odd shapes painted to the interior of the hut.

"What symbols are these from?" The redhead commented, looking closely to a drawing above his head. "These aren't all Klallam…"

"You know what they say. A bit of every religion is a sure way to keep the demons away."

"Do they say that?" I tucked myself nearest to the door, looking to James.

"She's joking, Em."

"But that doesn't mean it isn't true." Raewyn chuckled, handing me a canteen from a small pile of bags tucked close to the unmoving Officer Crowe.

I drank slowly, trying to find any life coming from him.

"He's breathing," James finally finished, sitting to his haunches. "I checked."

There was no correct way of answering him. Nodding I nestled the canteen between my legs, melding into the moment of the low humming exhaustion radiating through my body. I could have quickly fallen asleep within the mellow warmth of the heated rocks.

"This will be difficult to watch, you do not have to stay James." The witch discussed. "Though, Emmaline is a trigger point. You'll need to help me draw out the bad seed within him."

I made an audible noise of discomfort at the idea, quickly grabbing at James when I saw him shifting in his spot.

"Chill, I'm staying," he affirmed, shrugging his shoulder in my desperate hold.

Raewyn only nodded, keeping her hands in motion she pulled out various odd objects. An egg, a black drawstring sack, and mason jars of different sizes and hues, before settling them aside. When she took out a dagger, I doubted her intentions again. Leaning on my friend, I stared closely at the female before us.

"We aren't sacrificing anything, are we?"

"If I wanted to kill someone with this, I wouldn't do a very good job." She leaned into the light, sliding it along her fingers to show no beads of blood sprouting. "Dull on each side, see? It's not designed to cut flesh, but to direct energy. If

171

I were to somehow draw blood, it is customary in most practices to destroy it."

"That's weird," *A knife that isn't meant to cut?*

She chuckled and held it out, possibly for the benefit of trying to reassure me. Grasping it gently, I balanced it onto my palm.

"Are they all beautiful?"

Under the lamp I could see it was about elbow-to-wrist length, a Celtic Faery etched into its brass blade. The handle was plain black with a sapphire end. Running my hand along the edge tentatively, I could feel they were rounded.

"No no, I just like my tools to physically represent the area of my expertise. When you make your items more personal to you, they become a part of who you are."

The faery confused me.

"Aren't you a Faery exorcist?"

"Not quite. I deal with mortals afflicted by the sway of a Fae's lure, and curses they've bestowed to man. I exorcize their influence so that that the individual can live as normally as possible. Yet, there are just some things I cannot remove, emotional scarring, paranoia, anxiety."

"So, you don't hate Fae?"

"That would be like lumping every person together to say I don't like people." She smiled.

"I haven't met one I've liked so far," I admitted.

"People?"

"Fae."

"You don't like Basle?"

"Well, I'm not sure," I felt a prickle of a flush, but it could have just been the heat getting to me. "I guess I just never thought of Trolls as Faeries before."

"Well, the term really is Fae, babe," Raewyn smirked at James who was looking uncomfortable with the entire conversation. "Fae is an umbrella term expressing many types of magical creatures of the Unseen world. Trolls, Brownies, Changelings, Nymphs, Sprites, Sidhe, and the like are just sub-types within Fae. A Fae could also be a proper term for representing a single individual you are unaware of their heritage, but Fae as a species doesn't exist."

"Well, that's not complicated," I noted cynically.

"You'll get used to it." She settled the dagger gently to its leather pouch before pulling out a slim printed cloth box, a leather cord wrapped tightly about its center. "After all, once you can see you cannot unsee. That is the gift and curse of being a Witness." Raewyn began to slowly move again, shifting her form to settle between the policeman and the wall.

She unlaced and tugged his shoes from his form, tucking them away with his socks, while unzipping his uniform coat, and unbuttoning his shirt. Collecting his belt and gun holster, she placed them outside the entrance and dropped the flap door closed.

The room grew uncomfortably humid, the air stuffy with a low ebbing of heat. Multifaceted colors illuminated our view, mystifying the place further.

What was to come of this exorcism? Surely it wouldn't be as graphic or messy as the horror films. He wouldn't be projectile vomiting pea soup or spinning his head in circles, right?

173

There had to be some sort of a fine line between fantasy and fiction in all of this, but I hadn't found it yet.

The witch settled the box in front of herself, looking contemplative. A deep quiet pause lived inside the small space we shared. No one seemed to draw breath for fear of being the one to break it.

"Last chance," Raewyn said unabashedly, gathering up a clay jug into her arms to watch us closely.

Neither one of us budged.

Taking that as a sign, in a clockwise motion, she let a splash of water roll off onto the heated rocks to the center of the lodge. An offering to each cardinal direction, the rocks hissed and spat with steam rolling up into the air in high waves.

I recoiled in surprise, the knot in my stomach curling up in flaring anger as my breathing became labored. Telling myself this would be over soon, I clenched my hands into fists.

"Sacred Ones, Grandfather," Raewyn hummed with a slow rocking to her upper body. "I humbly call upon you to erect the four watchtowers in guidance through our journey." She settled the clay jug down. "Sacred Ones, Great Mother," the witch took up a small amber jar that sat cushioned to her side.

Unscrewing the lid, she scooped up a healthy amount of the contents with her thumb. "Give us strength and spirit to lead ourselves through the darkness we have encountered." Leaning over the Officer, she drew a turmeric-stained cross to the other's forehead, followed closely by a clockwise circle connected to each point. "Teach us to heal ourselves and help heal those who cannot do so themselves." Her fingers traced

174

a three-pronged symbol, similar to a triton or pitchfork, to his upturned palms then to the exposed soles of his feet.

To his chest, she drew a more elaborate design. One with a squat looking cross, with two short lines drawn halfway up each branch, before finishing with a half circle. She hummed and gave unpronounced chanting with every stroke, eyes growing distant.

Raewyn left him in a face-up, sprawled position, plucking the black satchel from her throng of goodies to empty its contents over his ribs. Small metal shavings, bleach white eggshell pieces, and curled up tendrils of seaweed littered his exposed skin. A low guttural moan escaped Crowe's gaping lips, making me shrink back again.

Zombies came to mind...

"I hunt for the seed of darkness driven deep within this man." Raewyn's voice bounced off the walls. The small box on her lap was pulled open, revealing a single row of long thin acupuncture-like needles.

Selecting the first, she leaned over Crowe to place it on the top of his head. The next, to his exposed neck where his Adam's apple lay. "I cast this prayer to break the chains to his sired soul, with rule and purity." She continued with four more needles, each to his palms and the tops of his feet.

Raewyn rose to all four and suddenly straddled Crowe, driving needle after needle into his chest along the pattern staining his skin. "As earth meets air, the sway unravels. As water meets fire, the hold severs."

He convulsed below her. "Mm-ah," he gurgled, "Em-ma."

Tipping sideways toward James, my body doubled over in a sharp ebbing throb that pulsed in a festering nest of anxiety and ache.

"I return all poisoned arrows that have been launched against this man!" She hit his chest with her palm, a rattled breath escaping through his mouth.

"Mm-ah," large knots began to visibly travel up his esophagus. Sticky mucus drizzled out of the corners of his lips until he started choking.

Desperately, the witch pushed against his diaphragm until she all but pried open his mouth and dug her fingers down his throat. With her free hand, she took up the egg, holding it to his breathless lips.

"Whether constrained by chains or returned to darkness, may this man never be disturbed by the wicked again! By the holy names above, he is free. So it will be!"

His head twisted in her grip, skin shading into a dusky blue as his neck swelled several times its standard size.

She hit his chest again, keeping the egg securely rooted despite his flailing.

Twisting desperately, Officer Crowe's stomach finally rejected half-digested forms of snails and slugs onto the mat below. Black veins crawled up the sides of the bone white egg, marking it with darkness.

"Open the jar," she directed firmly, pointing out a quart mason jar filled with a liquid the consistency of murky apple juice. "Hurry..."

Once James managed to pop the lid off, she crossed her athame through the space between the tainted object and

176

Crowes trembling lips, releasing the egg into the awaiting vessel.

Instantaneously, the egg fizzed and festered while turning its environment into a thick bronze green sludge, completely submerging itself into obscurity.

The odor of vinegar with Crowe's bile was unbearable. Looking as if it would crack, Raewyn quickly tucked the jar to the black drawstring satchel and promptly dashed from the purification lodge.

Following, I stumbled to a bush outside to dry heave. The humid air riddled with the stench of vomit finally making a mark.

"Em," James spoke in hushed tones, resting a hesitant hand to my back. "Are you okay?"

"I'll be okay with some air," The cramping subsided the moment I could breathe. "How's Officer Crowe?"

"He's breathing, and looks like hell, but I think he'll be okay." He looked off to the clearing where Raewyn could be seen kneeling waist deep in grass. "She's getting rid of it…"

Nodding I straightened slowly, feeling the edges of my vision darken with the threat of a dizzy spell. I had to tell myself that it would all be over soon. Abigail was only forty-five minutes away. If we jumped into the car, we could be there in no time. We would have her back, and we could pretend like none of this ever happened.

That's what I needed to believe.

"He will have some trauma when he wakes," Raewyn called tiredly, making her way toward us.

Her skirts clung to her legs, damp and littered with autumn debris from the dying vegetation around us. Despite

177

how chilly it was, she didn't seem to mind it. "It is your decision whether you want to explain what has happened to him or keep him in the dark."

"So, we can't just dump him back into his car?" My friend teased lightly, giving a sour look at the idea of babysitting the confused officer.

"He isn't my priority." I blurted out.

"He isn't my responsibility pass this point," Raewyn replied. "The break will cause a sore spot with the Lord of Prophecy and, while I make a mean protective barrier, I would prefer not having confrontations with a Vampyre Lord on my turf. You must remove him."

"You can't keep him just while we get my sister?" I frowned, watching her.

"That's a lot to expect, don't you think, babe?" She watched me with a kind but weary stare. "The fee was paid, but I cannot have my daughter around this. Whispers are spreading through the trees," she expressed with a drag of her arm. "They know you are here even if they cannot see you. Tread with caution," She warned. "Be aware of your surroundings, not all is as it seems in their world."

James wrapped a sturdy arm about my shoulders and nodded.

"Thanks, Raewyn. You saved Crowe's ass today."

I felt my face flushing, realizing how much of a whiny brat I sounded like. Shrinking under my best friend's hold, I shifted my gaze.

"It was an honor to help," she smiled, a bit of that original charm resurfaced as she watched us refold the man into the beetle. We had the sense to place him upfront at this point where he could sleep off the worst experience of his life.

"Before you leave… I have a token Basle wanted me to obtain for you, babe." She gestured toward the house with a beckoning of her hand. "It will be quick, I promise," she called to James.

Giving him a side glance I shrugged and followed her, wondering what she could offer me at this point.

"You've already helped so much…"

My eyes ran along the low rising ceilings of the dark wooded interior, bundles of herbs hung by paperclips, intermingling with hemp-tied ropes of various animal bones and amulets.

In the background, a small whirring sound of a humidifier was present.

"And one day, I can do more." She replied gently, guiding me through a short hallway where it hooked left, passed a few closely standing doors. One was ajar, exposing a dimly lit jade green bathroom with red accents. "Clara is asleep, finally."

She took me into an opened space of high ceilings, split between a large kitchen and living room. A stairwell was tucked to the corner, near the fireplace, where they led up to a loft created of whole cedar logs.

Large emphasized windows allowed the light of the morning sun to stream into the room, showcasing the floor-to-ceiling cupboards that were built into the pantry wall. If kitchenette implements weren't hanging from the ceiling, plants cascaded down in happy tendrils. Lushly vibrant paintings or tapestry's cut up the dark wall spaces with warm spring colors.

The witch wove around eclectic yellow printed chairs facing the hearth, sidling up to a massive curio cabinet with glass doors, mirrored shelves housing an assortment of animal skulls.

Pulling open one of the lower drawers to the left of her, she obstructed the view of her actions. When she finally turned, in her hands she clutched an object wrapped in plain cotton cloth. "Take this."

Raewyn brought it over, placing it into my waiting grasp.

Feeling the weight, I slowly undressed the item to expose a palm-sized wooden box. A rusted weave work of designs encapsulated the frame. There was a hint of metallic on my tongue, with something else I couldn't place.

Peeking up at Raewyn I gave a nervous look, holding the object unsure of what to expect. "What am I supposed to do with it?"

"Babe, you open it." She ran her nails across my shoulder blades in a gesture of care, passing by me to start her electric kettle.

The blood rushing to my face sparked a brain cell or two. Quickly, I fumbled with the latch, a few pieces of dried herbs falling to the floor.

When the lid of the box was drawn back, I held my breath while gazing at the entrails blanketed in herbal remains.

"It won't bite you, babe." Raewyn chuckled from her spot at the kitchen counter.

"You can't be too careful," I muttered, curiosity driving me to dip my fingertips into the small sealed crypt, coating them with dust as everything around them crumbled into powder. The real treasure lay settled upon a faded silk bed of fabric.

Hooking it to my middle digit, I drug upwards, revealing a black tarnished chain attached to a perfectly round locket. When I studied the seam, a seal of stone glistened more vibrantly than the rest of its whole. I licked my lips and moved to open it. Raewyn made a noise.

"You'll make a mess with all the trappings. I should warn you that locket, and all of its contents, is old magic. It will keep you safe should the Fae attempt to pixy-lead you."

I bit my bottom lip, nibbling unconsciously while wavering slightly in emotion.

"How did you find something like this?" The sensation that omitted was something I had never felt before, chilling, feather-light, but ever present.

"Let's just say I have a lot of extended feelers internationally. Take it, I found it for you."

"Thank you Raewyn," I had nothing to offer, all I could do was be sincere.

"Thank Basle, he's paying for it." She poured a deep, robust liquid into a mug, extending it to me. "Drink this. I'll see you again when the time comes. Good luck, Emmaline."

There was a strong smell of lemongrass and ginger emanating from the mug. Carefully bringing it outside, I stood to wait while my partner in crime slipped from the driver's side and pulled down the seat.

Climbing in, I held the cup close.

"You went in for tea?" He sat in front of me, twisting to give a light look.

"She gave me something," I coddled the vessel, keeping the tea close, like a treasured relic in need of safeguarding. I thought a long quiet moment, trying to describe the locket without James getting utterly suspicious of the Trolls actions.

"We are too deep in the game to be coy, Em." He slowly drew out of the driveway, stalling halfway through to shiver when we felt ourselves passing across a strange energy surge.

Shifting, I looked back to witness a whitewash of light penetrating through the storm clouds above; when it cleared, the field was void of Raewyn's cabin. Odd didn't come close to describing the supernatural things unfolding before me. I knew I had to stop being so shocked. *How many days had it been now since mom's funeral? Four?*

"Emma," James called lightly, looking at me through the rearview mirror.

"Basle hired her to find an object to keep the bearer from being pixy-led." I wasn't sure how to take the unexpected generosity of the Troll. *Was this a favor? Did I need to repay him somehow?*

"No shit? Get it out, I want to see it," wiggling his fingers the other gestured with his free hand.

"Okay, okay." Digging into my pocket, I took out the pendant and stuck it between the two chairs. When he glanced down, James swerved, trying to shrink away in shock.

"What *is* that?" He stared back between the road and the dangling locket, trying to keep his arm from touching it like it was made of something offensive to his senses.

"Seriously?" leaning, I gave him a look.

182

"I'm not stupid. I know *what* it looks like," my friend quickly became frustrated, restless even. "What's inside it?"

"I'm not sure. There's stuff inside it to keep me safe." I pressed my side to the passenger's seat, halfway bent over where Crowe sat limply, trying hard not to pay attention to his noticeable body odor.

James drove quietly, digesting the information, slowly drawing out a heavy frown.

"Okay, fine. I trust your judgment."

"That's unlike you," I lightly bumped his shoulder with my forehead before sinking to the back. He snorted, turning the heat on.

"So what's the plan, Stan?"

Rolling my shoulders, I popped my neck to release a bit of tension. Taking out my phone I figured the best option would be to look at P. Whimsy's website. Perhaps he had some advice to inspire me.

"You aren't going to find the answer in your phone. We won't really know anything until we face the Fae," the other grabbed my tea, taking a sip. "Ginger? This is seriously the spiciest shit on the planet."

I made an amused noise, going over the '3 *Rules of Faery Protection*.' The second rule ran through my mind in a sluggish rinse cycle.

"'Carry Iron, its poison to Fae and should be used as a precaution,'" I recited out loud to the other while holding up the tarnished locket. I rubbed the top of it slowly.

"You aren't even listening to me, are you?"

"But that's what this is made of, isn't it? Iron..." There was a glimmer of excitement growing inside me at the thought of

183

tearing into the Hoh Rainforest, iron clad with Fae scurrying for cover.

"Yeah, it is." James agreed. "I get it, iron. It's all saving iron. Praise iron." He raised his hands to the air, giving mocking bows to the wheel.

"Keep your hands on the wheel crazy man!" I smacked his arm again. "What the hell has gotten into you?" I roughly drug the locket over my head, tucking it up under my shirt where it sat mildly warm to my skin.

"Emmaline, get over it. We got to stick to what's going on right now. We need to get in there and get out."

He deviated right, rolling off of the highway and into the dirt parking lot where we settled in front of *Grammy's Café*, a small seasonal restaurant established in 1956.

Patched together, throughout the years with reclaimed lumber, the small summer hotspot was rustic with a countryside kitchen appeal. Barnyard knickknacks lined the shelves and windowsills, creating a clustered but appropriate likability against the rough wooden walls. Modest plastic-wrapped tables grouped together to the main room, decorated with Coca-Cola napkin holders, a vase of wildflowers, and matching animal pepper and salt shakers.

We shoved our bodies into the corner by the window where we could keep an eye on Officer Crowe.

"If anyone notices," James watched the beetle closely before looking around us.

"Only the waitress and the cook are here, James. They close in a few weeks. Stop looking so suspicious."

"I can't help it. I'm so tired my skin crawls, and I'm pretty sure Officer Crowe's stench has permanently saturated our clothes."

"Jamie, I think we just stink," I looked up when a short female with tribal tattoos sidled up to the table.

She gave a disinterested look at me over her pointed nose, lime green eyeshadow and rose gold hair looked unusual in the current setting.

"Can I get you some coffee to start with?" She gestured to the glass coffeepot in her hand, smiling at James. We both nodded, flipping up our mugs to let her pour. "Do you know what you want or should I give you time to look at the menu?"

"Menu please," I spoke. Unamused by the subtle treatments the girl was giving my friend. Usually, it was hilarious. *Today I just want some damn coffee.* Staring the girl down, she finally turned and went to the back before I aimed my attention to the ginger.

"Going back to your comment in the car, you're the one that has always told me to think things through, hence the research, *capiche?*"

"Okay, mafia lord." He poured copious amounts of sugar into his cup and gave a sour look. Turning onto the bowl of self-serve cream cups, he took his time peeling back each lid and dropping it into the small diluted pool before him.

"I didn't write this manual James, but I am following it. The salt at the market proved there is weight to superstitions." I sipped the coffee, tapping down the menu list.

"One superstition," he corrected. "You tried one, and it worked. That was stupid lucky. Whatever you are reading, it isn't a manual. It's a clump of rubbish probably written up by a pagan who trips out on belladonna every night and claims their hallucinations are real. Cults are bad, Emma. Don't get caught up in the babble."

"You're acting like you didn't just witness a Faery Market and an exorcism on a cop," I inclined. "Who is currently in the car sleeping off the insects he just barfed up, by-the-way." James stayed in his lazed position; stirring his coffee with his pinky. "Hey, you are either in this with me, or you can stay here and babysit Officer Crowe. I'm tired of fighting tooth and nail with you."

That got his attention.

James sat up straighter in his seat. "Hey, where you go, I go." He insisted.

The girl was walking back to us; her plaid over shirt was readjusted to stress her cleavage. I wanted to gag again. "Don't get it twisted. Even if you make me wear a leprechaun outfit to get me to blend in, I'll still follow you."

Shaking my head, I looked to the girl. "Can I get the breakfast sandwich with Swiss?"

"And you?" She glanced to my companion.

"Same." He drank his milk coffee with little interest to her relevancy. "What's the website you're looking at?" After sending him the site's address, he stared at his phone screen with a skeptical expression, "PNW Ghouls and Goblins." He cocked his head, saying in a showman's voice, "A simple guide to the fantastical secrets within the Pacific Northwest. What a *boob*."

"He's clever," I retorted, earning a snicker. "How would you know, anyway?" I was getting irritated. "You know no more than I do, so don't act like that." He was utterly undermining my entire work, and it stung.

I started ignoring him, which he didn't seem to mind. We both needed a time out.

Taking my time, I searched the unending internet world for breadcrumbs. I had every intention of flipping through countless documents to pinpoint the information; however, with a stroke of luck, I was quick in my studies.

A website called, 'Ancient Metals,' left little to question about the fundamentals of Iron. Curling up in my spot, I scrolled the page, finding little nuggets of helpful material.

'Origin unknown, the society of great ancient Egypt is the first to record their contact with the element iron. Even before the age of smelting*, iron meteorites were crafted into jewelry and revered as the "Stone of the Heavens," associating the metal to power and prestige.

Smelting* — the process of heating and melting metal from its ore.'

'(. . .) by nature, iron is quite a coarse and brittle metallic. Its purest form corrodes quickly from moisture and high temperatures. By diluting and mixing other metals to iron, creating an alloy*, its forthcomings become void in the succession of furthering revolutionary quests. From constructing buildings to kitchen cutlery, appliances and vehicles, 90% of all refined metal in present society is iron.'

Alloy* — Mixing metallic elements to create a stronger product.'

'(. . .) Iron, broad and most abundant of all metals, is a fundamental key in sustaining life on Earth. In plants, iron

187

is a primary component in creating chlorophyll* while also a crucial factor in animals where it helps carry oxygen to the blood.

Chlorophyll — *The green pigment within plants that is in charge of capturing light to deliver energy.'*

My concentration broke when the waitress settled our food in front of us.

"It's good." He commented after taking a bite, riffling through the layers of the sandwich like he was combing the records of a filing cabinet. "Could use bacon though," he slipped out of his seat, sidling up to the counter and leaned in to talk to the staff.

Shaking my head, I nibbled on my breakfast, maneuvering my phone with one hand while attempting to have functional thoughts.

My answered questions only created more to solve, but I didn't have time to be swirling around in the hypothesis pool of how a species could exist naturally on a planet they were primarily allergic to. I needed to focus on what I could do now.

If iron was fragile in its pure state, would an alloy of iron be just as good?

Scrolling the search engine for alloys of iron, I settled my phone to the tabletop when realizing the simplicity of the answer.

Steel. Steel was iron's alloy in all of its various forms. I looked to the fork on the table, taking it slowly into my hands and looking at it carefully.

"I take it you've cracked?" James plopped back down, nibbling on some bacon while watching me with suspicion on his face.

"Steel is an iron alloy," I said proudly, wagging the fork in front of his ridiculously handsome face. "This is stainless steel. Which means there is over—" I paused, checking the contents on my phone, "Over *at least* fifty percent iron in this sucker. If it were just steel, I would look at ninety to ninety-five percent iron."

His face contorted, looking annoyed.

"What are you planning to do, stab them with the fork? Cook them up and eat them for dinner?"

"Why are you so irritated?" *Where was all of this aggression coming from?* I tried giving him the utensil to tuck away in the inner pocket of his coat, but he shrugged from it.

"Because if that shit kills Fae, imagine the repercussions of your actions."

I shoved the fork into my jacket, lips pursing into an angry line. *Stealing was something old Emmaline would have never even considered, but it was to eat or be eaten.*

"Like I get my jollies off of threatening someone's life," I was bitter. Mad that he was making me feel guilty for wanting to protect us in such an abnormal situation. If James wasn't even willing to cooperate, then he left me no choice. Smacking a twenty-dollar bill onto the table, I snatched at the keys and walked off.

"Where are you going, Em?"

I disregarded his question, listening to the tinkle of the doorbell as I left the restaurant. Making it into the driver's seat, I quickly shut the door with a concluding snap.

189

"Emmaline," I could hear his voice coming closer.

I leaned over Officer Crowe to lock the door on the passenger side. "Oh, like hell you are doing this," the redhead pulled forcefully on the door, staring excitedly at me.

Refusing to look him in the eye, I locked my side before he thought about getting his long legs around the vehicle to force me from my seat.

He began to pound on the window in irritation, despite the attention it would draw. "EMMA, you aren't going alone!" I started the car and made a low lurch back like I was about to leave him in the parking lot. "EMMALINE DARLING!!!"

He grabbed the front bumper and held on, jaw clenching in the exertion. His eyes blackened against the backdrop of the cloudy sky. When the car unexpectedly stalled, I slammed on the breaks in shock. *Did we park over a pothole?*

In the moment of my confusion, James quickly worked his fingers against the right rear window, where he knew was mechanically unsound, and forced it down slowly. By the time I realized what he was doing, he was already opening the door beside the comatose officer.

"Are you insane?" I looked to Grammy's Café, seeing if anyone was spying on us. "I could have hurt you." Clenching the wheel, I pulled my body back to face him. He took little interest in the police officer as he forced the chair forward and climbed into the backseat.

"Yeah, but you didn't." He ran a hand through his hair, gripping it for a moment before folding both to his chest. "We're going to do this." He concluded, primarily to himself. "But there will be no heroics, no confrontations, and no revenge. Realize that if something happens to you, who will Abby come home to, huh? She'd be losing her whole world in one week. Do you really think it's a good idea for her to grow up without you? I've seen what this type of shit does to kids, Emma. You don't want her growing up with screwed up ideas about the world. I'd be so much different if I had someone like you when I was growing up."

"Shut up, James. That's not happening." I replied heatedly.

"You're lying to yourself and me if you think we can go in guns blazing and come out unscathed." He breathed in, resting his head against the seat and closed his eyes.

I observed him to the corner of my eye, the wear and tear rolled over him slowly and, for a moment, I saw an older man sitting beside me. Lines of stress painted his forehead, creasing the corners of his eyes. "There is so much out there. So much that we don't understand," He murmured.

"I didn't choose this," pulling out of our parking spot, I peered through the mirror and caught sight of our server watching us. I could have sworn there was a glimmer of something reflective—a phone screen.

That didn't bode well.

The humming of anxiety played in the air like a bad radio station, physically abrasive and emotionally daunting. James was quiet, staring to the evergreen pines flitting by.

There was little to no cars on the road this far out. The only ones that happened to pass had boats attached to them from fishermen trying their hand at chum salmon fishing this time of year.

What day was it, Saturday? I glanced at my phone. *No, it was Sunday morning.* There was no surprise that the roadway was vacant, the whole peninsula shut down on Sundays.

Shivering, I stared at the black strip before me.

The drive out there was listless. I could focus my attention on the sensation of the twists and turns of the path leading us through the small valley hugging the Olympic Mountains.

We ran alongside Crescent Lake's deep foreboding depths. James examined me for any signs of breakage as it was my first time out this far since mom's death. My best defense was disregarding the lake altogether, compartmentalizing my feelings for another day, this wasn't the moment to digest that information.

Once we passed the small town of Forks, it would be easy to find the Hoh Rainforest. The only stop we had was just before the single light in the middle of Forks. People stared at us, knowing we were strangers in their tiny world.

"It would be good to get gas." James peeked through the seats.

"Yeah, I guess."

"You guess?" He raised a brow. "You're nearly empty."

"Yeah, but the last time we stopped the waitress saw Officer Crowe. If there are any warrants…"

"I get it." He sighed. "I just don't think it's a good idea to be in a getaway car that can't *'get away.'* We still have a good 18 miles into the park."

"Alright," I conceded, veering into the gas station *Tesoro.* "I'm going to get Crowe a blanket from the trunk, can you… can you deal with the gas?" I wasn't up for the locals ogling.

James got out of the vehicle with a nod, making his way inside.

Taking my own time, I opened the front trunk to retrieve a wool throw. I should have tended to the policeman sooner. I knew that, yet it seemed Raewyn Hughes had done a number on his ability to intimidate. Without his personality, he was as useless as luggage. I wanted to tuck the man in so that no one saw his uniform. There was relief in knowing I could stash him away.

He was the physical reminder of the family and town who would call me crazy. He represented the slandering of my mom's death, the ignorance of my sister's disappearance, even the stack of bills piling up on the matt at my door. He was everything wrong in my life. He had the power to break me. I hated him at that moment.

Strapping the officer in roughly, I tucked the blanket snuggly up to his chin. I glared at him.

"You don't even know. You think you know, but you know nothing."

My phone blinked at me, letting me know it was less than 15% battery life. I pulled out the portable USB charger from the glove box, popping it into place before connecting my phone. Slanting sideways, onto my seat, I stared across the way. *I must be a pretty shitty person.*

"Hey, pop the gas tank," James called, tapping on the door.

Twitching, I leaned over to tug the handle from up under the glovebox. The door released.

Our final trek seemed very unnatural, the musing of déjà vu. Turning left we took the long twisted 18-mile journey into

193

the Olympic National Forest. Robust young pines thinned away, leaving ample room for colossal old growth to bend across the cracking roadway. Life all around us was dripping with soft, succulent moss, glistening with the early morning showers. Ferns climbed the expanse of tree trunks, taking roost in the elbows of branches and knotted holes. Maple leaves blanketed the undergrowth. Rusty reds, decaying yellows, and burnt oranges swept across the mulchy earth, leaving their hosts barren.

Watching the leaves trickle down from the canopy above, the distant whirr of the Hoh River sounded from afar. The scene brought us into a welcoming numbness.

Death, in the Hoh Rainforest, was truly breathtaking.

Driving was slow, for the sake of the domesticated animals around us. Elk and the common black-tailed deer had the irrational tendency to dart out into traffic. I wasn't about to come this far only to be rushed back into town from a car wreck with an animal, which could be severe enough to total a car.

We weren't in a hurry to be anywhere yet anyway, James and I decided it would be best to storm the forest in the dark, out of reach of the rangers. Ten miles in we paused at the *Rainshowers Café and Mercantile*. The marker before the park entrance with the sign, 'Last Chance: Film, Food, Drinks', to prove it.

Rustic in the exterior, the dark wooded cabin had been maintained remarkably well for a café out in the middle of Forks, Washington. Hubcaps decorated the side of the cabin facing the forest entrance, the only remembrance of how the restaurant had been when I was a kid.

Green metal roofing was its prominent upgrade, jutting out over the deck where matching picnic tables resided. Whoever kept the place running, was well adjusted to Washington gardening, the landscaping catered well to the homey atmosphere conveyed.

There was no point in going further. Having a whole day to wait before it was safe to sneak in we parked the car a good ways from the windows of the restaurant. James bought us some coffee and watched me closely, walking along a painted log in front of the car.

"What are you looking for?" He asked finally, watching me rifle through the small first aid box mom forced me into procuring.

"If I tell you, you'll just get angry." I tossed him the multi-tool, watching him catch it with an initial flinch before he pocketed it. "Sorry." *That's right.* He messed up his hand pretty badly yesterday.

"It's fine Em." He didn't look like it though, flexing his fingers like he was having a muscle spasm.

"Are you sure?"

"Yeah, yeah," He drank his heavily sugared drip, continuing his escapade of walking on precarious ledges.

Sighing, I turned back to the trunk. I really didn't have anything in here with iron. The multi-tool would come in handy, despite its make. The only other metal I could find was an old box of paperclips.

"What are you going to do? Make a paperclip chain and choke them to death?" James was snickering up until he realized I was putting serious consideration into it. "You're a freak. Seriously, I think this is topping anything you've ever done in the past year."

"Thank you," I responded dryly, sitting cross-legged to a plastic chair I stole from the café porch.

The paperclips were a well-needed distraction. Small in size and easy to bend, I took my time playing with a few until I had a rhythm of pulling and twisting. By drawing each looped end straight out, I linked each piece together with a kink of the hooked ends. The finished result created barbed wire with semi-fluent capabilities.

Rising slowly, with a two foot chain, I walked around until I found a lovely green egg-shaped pinecone to work with. Spearing the end, I tested the elasticity and gave a few swings. The results were satisfying.

I wrapped it over my left wrist and carefully tugged my sleeve down.

Prickly as it was, the bracelet came with security.

"Weirdo," James had settled to the roof of the car.

"I don't see you coming up with anything that is going to help us."

"Hey," he shrugged lightly. "I came up with the brilliant plan to insert myself into your less-than-stellar strategy. Without me, you'd definitely be Fae chow."

"Tell me again why we're friends?"

"You couldn't stand to be without me." He grinned, earning a laugh.

After all the twisting, testing and thinking, I finally didn't know what to do with myself. Crowe was checked on— *yes, still breathing*— and unconscious as ever. James seemed to have a mind of his own, slipping in and out of the clearing, appearing to be overlooking the animal trails.

Settling myself into the back of the car, I pulled myself flat against the seat with one leg crossed over the other. My energy was so depleted that my eyes were itching from the exertion. The more I rubbed, the more anxiety filled me, leaving me to squirm slightly in my spot.

Should I sleep? Could I? What would happen if I fell asleep and Officer Crowe woke up? I shifted and looked to the underside of the chair.

Good, his gun wasn't easily accessible.

Cheek pressed against the worn leather chair, my eyes began crossing from spacing out.

Then there were those haunting eyes again, suspended just out of reach; watching, taunting and waiting, they were of a foreboding nature. The boogeyman, being no more friend than a foe in the darkness, with mirrored pools that painted a picture of my humanity. Softly, my name was called, a mournful sound that drove deep into the madness of my own loss, cleverly wrapping me into a cocoon of suffrage where I settled into obscurity.

The tale that webbed around me started in the innocence of comfortable nothingness, a place that I hadn't recognized as a dreamscape until I watched it physically churn into a lively backdrop of vibrant colors. I felt no real physical embodiment of my own until it was brought to my attention. With a brush of nimble fingers, I was made into this world unlike my own.

'**Emmaline... come to us,**' the timbering voice murmured with a sultry temperament.

197

My legs did so obediently. I followed the blind eyes, like a beacon to my salvation. Cold, wet grass brushed against my legs, tickling my ankles and sending shudders up my body.

Danger…

Forbidden…

Run…

There was an alarm sounding in my mind, screaming for me to pull away.

'**Emmaline**,' ire stained his voice. *Had he heard my thoughts? My doubts?* '**Emmaline, I know you better than most.**' He knew nothing of me! There was a chuckle in reply.

Darkness bled into molten hues of autumn, twisting upward as heavily laden trees smothered out the sky with their brilliant presentation of colors. Knotted roots tore through the sloping ground, tangling the saplings together, connecting the hall with a wooden wall. The only way forward was through the carpet of deep cyan grasslands, the trembling of a harp mixed delicately with the loud rush of a river.

I was able to stubbornly hold off on my journey for a few moments until I felt my knees buckle, hitting the ground from the strain. My hands sprawled before me, curling into the perfectly shaped blades of grass, digging into the flesh of the earth before I managed to rise onto unstable footing. My feet lurched forward.

'**Emmaline…**' The voice was eager to demand my attention. A single leaf tumbled off its branch, catching my attention as it was caught halfway by an invisible snare. Dancing helplessly by the stem, it dangled above me.

Was such an ensnarement my fate?

'Emmaline!'

Blinking, I turned, taking in the decaying throne at the end of the great hall. Worn stone stitched together by the moss and ivy clinging to its form. It sat empty.

The minutes ticked by, counted with the clicks of my nails hitting together until a shadow found its way over my shoulder. My throat hitched, knowing it was him. His breath teased the wisps of my hair before a hand rose to comb them aside. I didn't understand him. There could have been so many other things more fascinating than to waste time plaguing my dreams, yet he settled to mocking me.

'**You are very cold, Emmaline,**' he droned, '**The world you live in has made you brittle and unforgiving. Aren't you tired?**' *Yes, I was tired.* '**Then come and join us.**' I felt his spidery fingers slip along my lower back, gently urging me toward the crumbling seat. But I didn't want to.

Danger…

Run…

RUN…

The alarm deafened my ears, thrumming to the rhythm of my heart.

His hand snuck into the back of my shirt and faintly rested against my shoulder. My shoulder suddenly flared with heat, all but blistering to his touch. *NO.*

Staggering forward I caught myself on the arm of the throne, looking swiftly over the shoulder to my abductor. Utter rage cracked his perfectly chiseled face, giving me only a second's glance before it shattered into hundreds upon thousands of blue-winged butterflies.

199

Every leaf unraveled from their limbs, dispersing into a gust of wind where they swallowed up the delicate creatures in a storm of flames.

'**In the end, you will,**' He promised.

I ran from the horrific scene and covered my head.

My body lurched out of its night terror state, heart beating so quickly that it hurt my chest. My surroundings were foreign, and for a moment I panicked in the dim lighting.

Staring long and hard at the back of the leather seat, I finally recognized my car.

Quietly, I shed a few relieving tears.

CHAPTER 10

SUNDAY DUSK—PART 1

We had flipped the lights low to creep past the park ranger's cabin. Old maple trees wilted low overhead, dripping with mosses plump and juicy to their branches. Even this late into fall, the area was so congested with greenery that the canopy created a dark tunnel around us.

James was wide-eyed, staring hard ahead while he white-knuckled the steering wheel.

"I better not see a bear," he grumbled to himself. "Or a lion or even a tiger…"

I hadn't noticed the fog until thick strings slipped through the wall of trees, like cobwebs, dense and foreboding. Forced to turn the floodlights on, we drove with the sounds of the Hoh River rushing loudly to the right of us.

James was staring at me again.

I opened my mouth to retort sarcastically when something heavy tumbled atop of the car hood. The momentum was so fast it dented the roof, causing James to fishtail across the roadway. We screamed.

My friend corrected himself and slammed on the breaks. A massive body went rolling off and disappeared into the churning mist.

"Did a bear just jump the car?"

Chilling cries bounced around us, calling out like a pack of laughing hyenas as a figure lumbered past the glare of the Volkswagen lights.

Cracking of tree limbs shot through the dark. Rustling leaves sounded to the vibration of a massive creature on foot.

Leaning in, I gripped the other's shoulder.

"James, move the car." I breathed.

He shivered. The car lurched forward at a snail's pace, time slipping by just as slowly. We were quiet, tense.

"They are playing with us," James finally breathed in frustration. "I'd prefer the bears." Slowly speeding up, the engine revved loudly.

Giggling erupted around us.

"Screw it." He stepped hard on the pedal.

We booked it down the road, swerving dangerously passed boulders and stumps, careening around the river's edge. I watched from the back seat as shadows of massive furred bodies bounded joyously alongside us.

I fell forward, hitting the back of Crowe's seat when James pumped the brakes.

The fog thinned, revealing the sunken eyes of a creature stooping to the center of the road. Coarse grassy hair rippled over their shoulders as they shuffled closer to the car. Shadows etched deep creases across the face, creating the resemblance to a native mask. There was a long chilling moment before their bearded jaw seemed to unhinge, shifting to the side to reveal rows of sharp stained teeth. A tongue lulled down as it laughed maniacally.

Gripping the other's shoulder, I stared horrified. Their ears perked inattention to our movement.

"What... what *is* THAT!?"

The creature uttered gibberish between mouthfuls of cackling. Their head twitched back and forth, deep-pocketed eyes watching. Leaning on the knuckles of their front appendages, they lumbered forward on all four.

"What's it trying to say?" James murmured, listening to the gurgling squeaks.

The babbling shifted up an octave, adjusting and crackling to suit the voice of a small child.

"I don't know," I frowned.

"*Peek...*" it said. "*Peek!*"

The voices chimed all around us.

'*Peek*'

'*Pe-e-ek*'

'***PEEK***'

'*Peek*'

'*Peek!*'

'*Peek, Peek Peek!*'

Catching movement to the corner of my eye I turned just as one creature slammed to the frame of the car. Flashing a Cheshire grin, it clawed its way onto the roof.

The vehicle groaned, swaying with the monster's movements.

"James," I smacked him insistently on the arm, looking all around with wide eyes. We were afraid to move.

"Peek..."

He shuttered when a face peered down through the window.

"Peek-ah-BOO!" Pressing their slender black claws against the glass of the driver's door, we flinched when the sounds of cracking glass began.

Our bodies hit back into our seats when James swiftly punched against the gas pedal, launching the car precariously down the hall of trees.

Some monsters reverted into their hyena call at the sheer delight of the chase while the rest continued their mimicry to the one on the roof.

'Peek-a-boo!'

How could a mere child's game become so deadly?

"It's trying to get in through the roof!" James roared.

Shifting to lay flat, I raised my legs, stomping swiftly up against the ceiling where nails were puncturing through. Even if the animal's cries turned sour, it was still weaseling the hood open.

The roof was being opened like a can of sardines!

One glimmering eye stared down at us, giggling. I kicked angrily — my poor car.

"I have an idea, keep the wheel steady."

"What?" He peered at me in the rearview mirror, face paler than usual.

I leaned and honked the horn angrily at the animals until he pushed me away. "Are you crazy? What if there's more of them!?"

"Just trust me!"

I pressed my face to the side of Crowe's seat, tilting in to dig for the lever. With a quick pop, the seat fell back, jostling the man further. His head turned on its own accord, alarming me as I gripped his shoulder. Awkwardly, I climbed up and over him, rolling the window manually down.

James threw out a slew of cuss words when he realized what I was about to do.

"You are NOT in an action movie, EMMA!!! Those things can kill you!!!"

I ignored him. Hooking a leg about one of Crowe's and gripping the safety handle, I twist up and out of the car. Balancing precariously, I stared directly into the creature's eyes.

They bobbled, chattering excitedly. I watched in rapt fascination as their head rotated upside down, staring up with a toothy grin.

What the hell was this thing!?

My hand was shaking as I roughly yanked the fork from my pocket, stabbing at its stupid face.

The beast screamed like a wounded child, falling off the side of the car to writhe in its place. My hair tossed into my eyes as I turned to watch with a repulsed satisfaction.

"Emma!" James called out. I quickly slipped back in, awkwardly hunching over the unconscious gentleman.

"Never do that again," He was wide-eyed. "You hear me?! No heroics!"

"I just saved our asses, thank me for being prepared!" The victory was short lived when we pulled into the unlocked parking lot.

We knew the rest would be on foot. James could drive in circles all evening, but eventually, we would need to get out. That, or run out of gas.

"Ssssh, sssh…" his eyes darted, listening intently. "Are they leaving?" He slowed the car. I couldn't hear over my labored breathing. "I'm going to step outside." Parking the car, he moved to get out.

"Hey, the orders go both ways." I grabbed his sleeve. "James, you aren't the knight in shining armor material."

Snorting, he gave me a peculiar look before ruffling my bangs.

"Thanks. Just, stay in here Emmaline. I'll be right back, okay? Keep. The. Car. *Going*." He didn't leave much of an option; I stared after my best friend as he slipped out and away from me.

Unsure of what to do next, I used my free hand to roll up Crowe's window. The glass stuck halfway, giving me an insecure feeling.

"James," I tentatively called out the window. "Can you see anything?"

There was no reply.

I twisted, peeking out the rear window. All I could see was within the range of my car lights. Desperation clawed up my throat.

Nothing was out there.

The Peek-a-boo were quiet.

The forest was silent.

"Hey, James!" I found my voice, calling out the broken window. "James, James Beasley!" He was scaring me. "JAMES!"

"Shut it." The redhead appeared by the car, crouching down to peek through at me.

"Holy shit," I swallowed my heart. "I thought you were captured or eaten."

"Scoot over, for real. They are everywhere, blocking the route we came in." Squeezing between the seats, I crouched with my hood up over my head. "I don't get it." He muttered, resting his hand to the back of Crowe's seat, looking behind us. "They aren't chasing us. I've got a bad feeling, Emma."

"What now, the trails aren't large enough to take the car."

"Even if they were, we could get into some serious trouble if we drove through a protected forest." He stared grimly toward the deserted parking lot.

"Going to jail or getting eaten by the giant monkey Fae, huh," I replied mockingly. "I can't believe you're worried about the park ranger."

"I'm not just worried about him."

We both glanced to the officer when he muttered incoherently. Quieting down, we eased the Volkswagen up and over parking blocks. Driving along the walkways, James expertly maneuvered past the Visitor's Center and on up onto the trailhead.

We didn't make it far before he realized the path ran through marshlands. The route nestled directly between several towering skeletal maples. Branches oozing of spike

207

moss and ferns, twisted outward in an ominous display. *This was not a place for the faint of heart,* they said, *turn back.*

James accidentally knocked over a few directory signs while he inched backward. The comical display did little to steer my mind from the impending figures in the darkness.

"Who're you?" Crowe cleared his throat, coughing heavily with dried phlegm. "Where is this?"

We both froze.

The man gripped the door handle and drew himself upward. The wool blanket dropped to his lap.

"Why d'you feel like I've just been hit?" Clearly, the man was suffering from brain damage.

James glanced tensely back at me.

"Officer Crowe, you've... suffered a stroke." I finally spoke.

"Miss Darlin'?"

Oh great, he can't structure sentences, but he remembers my name?

"Yeah, that's right."

"I was... waiting outside." He blinked slowly toward James, registering but not quite understanding. His hand rose, rubbing the fading bruise on his neck, "Bitten."

"Bitten, Officer Crowe?"

"Attacked," He said more clearly. "Attacked and bitten." He peered around, settling his sights to his soiled shirt. The smell of dried vomit still lingered from when we both upchucked.

There was a long moment until he calmly settled his hands to his knees. "If you take me to the hospital, we can negotiate a pleas bargain for you. You don't have to do this, Emmaline..."

I stared at him, disturbed that he thought we meant to harm him.

"We didn't attack you, Crowe." James stared the other down. "Emma saved your life. You'd be dead if it weren't for us."

"Where are we?" His grey eyes—dull with exhaustion—took careful calculation of the details in the car. When he registered the ceiling, he glanced back to me. "Apparently I've missed the action."

"We were being chased. Look," I muttered. "You are welcome to go. We'll even give you your gun. But we found Abigail's kidnapper. I'm going to get her back."

"Emmaline," he replied slowly. "Why're you saying 'we'?"

"James," I gestured to my friend.

"There are only two of us here."

James' expression melded from surprise to uneasy. I wanted to rip my hair out.

"Tell me something, why were you at my house? If you were so convinced that Abigail was safe, that James Beasley was just a figment of my imagination, why did you come back?"

He sat rigidly, "I didn't think things added up."

"Yeah? Like?"

"The red truck in your driveway, it was gone when we went to leave. I thought it was strange." He mumbled.

"Yeah?" I avoided eye contact with James, trying hard not initially to seem that insane to the officer. "What did you come up with?"

What was the hold FK had on him?

"I was given the name of a James Beasley." He stated calmly.

"So, you know I've been telling the truth."

"I know that you have a history of psychosis in your family, Emmaline. Your mother had been just as vivid in her tales when Ethan went missing. I do not doubt you know a James Beasley, but you can't contradict the facts. Your sister is with your grandparents. This charade you are pulling is only hurting you. Please, take me back to Port Angeles. We can talk through this. I can get you the help you need."

James was gripping the steering wheel.

"I don't expect you to understand," My cheeks were burning, ears stinging. "But you need to know they are watching us. They attacked us. If you try to leave this area, they will find you and probably kill you. Your best bet is to come with me."

"Where are we?" He repeated.

"The Hoh Rainforest," James grunted getting out slowly, shoving his hands into his coat pockets. I could understand why the conversation was making him uncomfortable.

Crowe blinked owlishly at the opening door.

"The Hoh Rainforest," I mimicked.

"Let's say I believe you. Will you let me use your phone to call for backup?"

"And let more people die? No."

James was pacing restlessly outside. "No offense Crowe, but your people suck. They'd get themselves killed." He finally peeked in, directing his attention toward me, "I was rooting for him in the beginning, but then he went and got himself a hickey."

"James." I gave him a look.

"What exactly are you scared of?" The officer shifted in his spot.

"Don't you remember anything from your attacker?" I pushed impatiently.

"No," he said flatly. "I was attacked, at the steps from behind."

"He doesn't remember any mental attacks? His mind separating from his body while someone probed his innermost thoughts, forcing him to succumb to their control?" James leaned further into the car, regarding the policeman. "He can't tell you he doesn't remember something, I see it on his face. For Christ's sake, he has fang marks on his neck."

Crowe's hand darted up to his neck.

"Did he just hear me?" James' deep eyes darted toward me in question.

"I found you on my porch after someone attacked you, Crowe," I pressed. "You weren't well, unconscious. When I moved closer, you were calling out my name. You grabbed me," I scratched at my hand anxiously. "Someone spoke through you. You gave me a vision, guiding me here."

"Any hallucination during my attack was because of fear and adrenaline. Vampires aren't real."

"Ah-*HA*." James grabbed the steering wheel excitedly, halfway bent back into the car again.

"I never mentioned vampires, Officer Crowe. You aren't telling me something."

211

"It's what you are hinting at," he insisted. "Mind control, vision quests, and fangs?" The man was getting restless, eyes darting around.

My companion went back to patrolling, breath coming out in puffs of hot steam.

"Do you want to know what we had to do to save you? We took you to a witch to exorcize your soul."

"You are insane. Give me my gun." He threw the blanket away from his body, staring at his feet. "Where are my shoes, my socks? What is on my feet?" He pulled up his foot, staring at the sole. "This is all crazy," He registered the smeared markings to the palms of his hands. "Where are my shoes and gun? Give me my belt." Reaching down, I tugged out his things and wordlessly handed them over.

He quickly pulled the Smith & Wesson revolver from its holster, checking the condition. He dropped the magazine to inspect the ammunition. When he felt satisfied, he popped everything back into place.

"He'd be smart not to bring us in by gunpoint," James muttered.

I ignored the other, seeing Crowe quickly lean down to pull on his gear.

He was apparently having difficulty. Beads of sweat were sprouting on his forehead. His breath came out labored.

"Do you need help?"

"I'm old, but I'm not THAT old." His reply was gruff, hoisting himself out of the car and fastening his utility belt.

"You had a stroke."

Maybe it would be more comfortable if he left. His denial was slowing us down, taking us off course. What if he walked away now

212

and went missing? He wouldn't be much of a problem then. My stomach churned with the ideas sprouting in my head. Unfolding from the back, I shut off the car and tossed the keys to James.

"Do what you need to do, but we need to continue." The cold was already seeping through my clothes, taking the spirit from me.

Crowe looked like he was digesting what I was saying, possibly figuring out whether he would take me back at gunpoint. "There's a phone booth near the visitor's center." Fishing into the ashtray, I accumulated 50 cents and pushed it into his hands. Not that the phone worked. They gutted the box and left the booth a few years back. "Or, there's the cafe down the road, maybe two miles tops." *That was a lie.* It was nearly thirteen miles away.

"Give me the keys." He rested a hand to the holstered gun, causing James' nerves to snap. The other threw the keys at the man, satisfied when Crowe stumbled back in surprise.

"What?" He looked at me then to the direction of my friend.

"That's our only exit!" I gaped.

"We'll find another way," he nodded toward the officer. "Let him see for himself."

Clenching my jaw, I begrudgingly took my phone out and pulled the flashlight from the dropped keychain. Shoving the keys back into his hands, we exchanged a glance.

"If you actually do get out, don't you forget what you've seen tonight," I warned.

Crowe never responded. Climbing into the car, the officer snapped the door closed and revved the engine. He avoided looking at me as he switched the headlights on then backed up slowly, disappearing across the parking lot.

James and I looked to each other.

"We'll be alright." Taking my hand, he led me off toward the trails.

The trees had eyes. All around us we felt the gaze of the monsters piercing our flesh, creating prickling goose pumps along our forearms.

Did FK know we had already arrived?

Was he waiting for me?

We sifted through the spruce infested walkway, coming up to a split in the trail where we bore left. I jumped when the cracking split of gunfire jetted through the air, disturbing the silence.

"If he gets killed…" I whispered, glancing back to where we came.

"Well, then they can't claim we kidnapped him," James replied flatly, tugging me onward.

Three more shots fired. I could hear the distant screeching of the beetle's horn.

"Oh god, shouldn't we go help him?"

"He chose this, Emma. Remember, we are here for Abigail."

Nodding gravely, I had to cover my ears while James took the lead with the light.

The further we traveled the more massive trunks of trees became. Long gone were spruce, replaced by the heartier standing conifer evergreens and ancient big leaf maples. Moss climbed every which way, dripping off every surface. Timeless moss clothed the naked few who competed for light, mingling with the licorice ferns to give the faux appearance of plump, luscious branches of the leafless individuals. This place would have been devastatingly beautiful in the safety of ignorance.

Even as the musk of cedar filled our lungs, not knowing what was beyond, bore heavily on our minds. I could understand why the Fae made camp here. This was a perfect nesting ground to frolic freely without untold dangers of mankind's steel. The evidence lay to the pathway itself, where the forest reclaimed what humans had forged through it.

More shots fragmented through the air.

Birds took flight above.

We paused at the bridge, facing an incline in the pathway. Below us, only a few feet deep, was a stream choked in wispy strands of water weed. James drew the light across its slow trickling surface, producing an emerald glow from the depths.

"I think they're distracted by Crowe, but that doesn't mean we shouldn't be careful, though. Keep that fork on hand."

Heeding his cautionary advice, I kept the fork clenched to my fist. I peeked up into the canopy. The innocence of rustling leaves turned sour in my mind when reflective eyes blinked back at me.

We were definitely being watched.

"You should take these," I pulled out the bag of rowan berries, all but crushed to powder in my pocket. Salt were merely granules piled to the deserted corners of my pocket after the *Myrrd* incident. The berries were my only offering. "We both need something if we get separated."

"I have the multi-tool, remember?" He grunted when I shoved the berries unzipped into his pocket.

"I have a locket, fork, and paperclips. Take the berries, please," I urged.

"I—fine, fine," he murmured, taking up my hand again. "Just, don't plan on getting lost, okay?"

Smiling at him, we took the broad stone steps as fast and quietly as we could, while our audience scurried noisily after us.

Pinecones and upturned roots scattered our trail, leaving us to stumble through the darkness. Tripping once, I caught myself on a nursing log before James pulled me upright. He was having an easier time finding his way through the gloom than I was, but the Olympic National Park was his playground when home life had been rough. Anything, he said, to get out of Port Angeles for a while.

I could tell he was annoyed that I was slowing him down. We didn't have time to waste. I knew that. But James had longer legs. So I fell into a rhythm of gripping his coat anytime he was pulling out of reach. We worked that way for several minutes, time ticking by with nothing but the sound of our shallow breathing and the shuffle from the canopy above.

We scaled our way up the side of the mount, successfully unscathed until the pathway evened. Ducking under the knotted roots of an enormously overturned tree, we quietly discussed options. Before us, the path split into the 'Hall of Moss' and the 'Spruce Nature Trail,' the two names I recalled Lord Fable showing me.

Beyond that, there were no specifics. Both were easy day hikes. 'Spruce' was a longer trek around and went along the Hoh River while the 'Moss' was short, looping deeper into the forest. *Would the Fae prefer to camp near water or go further into the wood?*

One was in plain sight, the other better unseen. Something inclined me to think they would want to be as far away from the eyes of man as they could. James agreed that 'The Hall of Moss' would be our best potential choice.

If we were wrong, then there was all night to get the directions right, but I had the feeling someone wouldn't allow us to flail too long before making himself known. *Was I ready for that?*

"This sucks," James ground out, talking to himself while kicking something against a tree.

"I'm sorry I got you stuck in the middle of this," I admitted, my voice cracking from the fear of being overheard. "This... entire scenario is so messed up. Why can't Fae be cute little cherub-faced things that give out candy?"

"Don't be sorry. I'm just hungry. I'm about to build a fire and go hunting for a squirrel." At least he could find humor in our situation. I made a face, nudging him slightly to watch him stumble, snickering.

"I should have grabbed something, who knows how long we'll be out here."

"Don't sound so ominous, we'll get out of here." James stopped to the right of me, catching my arm as I bumped into him. "Hey wait, do you hear that?"

"The sound of your stomach," I suggested, waiting for him to crack another joke.

"No," he shook his head while stepping off of the path a few feet.

Shocked, I watched him scale along a large fallen trunk like a perfectly poised feline. "Music…" he murmured to himself. "Why music now…?"

"James, I hear nothing." Apprehension crept up my spine. *What was he hearing that I couldn't?*

"You don't think there are campers out here, do you?" He looked over his shoulder, eyes reflecting an unknown light source.

A chill ran through me.

"No, James," I stepped over to the base of the corpse tree, leaning up to tug at his pant leg. "Hey, get down from there. If we get off the path, we'll get lost. Then we really will be in trouble."

"Don't you hear it though?" He seemed aggravated, hyper-aware and twitchy like someone on drugs. "It's over there, just beyond that clump of pine I bet…"

"There's pine everywhere," I complained

"Give me a minute. I just want to check it out." He pulled from my grip, sneaking along the trunk and disappearing beyond my view.

"James!" Scrambling feebly along the slick bark, I tried to follow. "James Beasley," I felt the wood below me flex as my friend jumped from his makeshift bridge, dropping to the forest beyond.

I shivered helplessly, my mind scrambling in a bed of chaos trying to come up with a plan of action. Something just happened between the trail and the tree I couldn't explain.

Clambering for my phone, I switched on my flashlight APP before wedging the end of the phone snuggly between my chest and bra strap. I wanted to look up but knew better than to push my luck. My watchers were calm now, but that didn't mean it would last.

I clambered blindly after my friend, the light beam swung precariously across vegetation as I stumbled over fallen logs. It wasn't long until my legs were licked with scrapes and bruises, my boots crunching across the ground in quick strides.

While running through a small circle of old growth cedar, every sensation exploded at once. The music finally found my ears with the whispers shifting all about in baleful sighs. Small glowing eyes blinked curiously through the bushes while the Peekaboo howled and laughed.

I was being stalked and taunted.

The nightmarish running was burning my thighs and seizing my lungs. My mind struggled to keep hopeful while my body was shutting down from the shock.

'Jamie, Jamie, Jamie' was my personal mantra when a prickly object smacked to the side of my face. I came to a confused stop as another bounced off the top of my head, then another. I ducked quickly when an onslaught began.

"What the hell?" One hit me in the back of the head, prompting me to run.

The ground shook with the Peekaboo dropping from the trees.

My heart clawed its way up my throat with heavy irregular thumps. So loudly that I was terrified the forest could hear. I held my breath painfully, darting under tree

219

branches and flung myself further into the direction of where the music was loudest. It mingled with laughing and merriment, a different buzzing of noise I hadn't heard until that moment.

Dodging more items, I rolled over a large nurse log to stumble under the safety of red cedar. Shrinking down, I pulled my phone out and directed the beam straight on, trying to make out what the voices were saying. *Was there a party going on?* I was so sure of the noise as if I could drop directly into a Mardi Gras celebration by stepping past the tree line ahead.

"James?" I whispered as if he could hear me over the ruckus the festivities were making.

There was a tug to my hair.

Crying out, I smacked at the creature, watching it plummet to the ground like a dead fly before it scuttled back up the bark of the tree I leaned against. Shrinking away I stared up in disgust.

"*Iron! Iron!*" erupted above in tiny chatter.

"*Iron?*"

"*Nasty, stinky rot!*"

"*She's gots iron in her mop.*"

There was more pulling.

"*Poke it, pinch it, make it squeals!*"

"*Let her know how iron feels!*"

They confused me. What the hell were they talking about? I felt my hair and then realized the band that held it up had a metal clamp holding it together.

Trying to tug back on my limbs, I felt small fingers scratch, pinch and prod any available flesh I had bare. Scrambling to pull back my sleeve, I gave it a good shake around my head.

Screams of fright sounded, their little bodies scattering out of harm's way. I felt myself smirking. Satisfied I could at least give them back a taste of their own medicine.

"Filthy foul frump!"

"Frump?" glowering in the darkness I tried to see the things that insulted me.

"Grumpy grump."

"Ugly retch!" one clicked.

"Human meat sack!" another wailed.

"Mortal waste of space!!!"

"Iron filth, iron filth. Put her in the roasting pot and make a meal!"

I shivered horribly and grabbed my fork, swinging it about recklessly.

"Who are you!?"

There were hisses and a few words I didn't know the language of.

"She's got a pokey iron."

"Prong that tares, prong that bites, prong that boils the blood and turns the flesh black. Tell the King!!!"

"TELL THE KING!"

"Tell the King!"

"Maybe she came in with the other thing?"

Were they talking about James? I sprung up, gripping the fork close and ran toward the parting. I didn't realize the music and voices had stalled until I broke out into a small clearing laden with moss and fern. A glow I hadn't seen

221

before erupted before my eyes, causing me to shrink back and cover my face momentarily with blindness.

When I could blink away the spots, I peeked through my fingers to stare in astonishment. Faeries, big and small, thin and full, ugly and breathtaking were standing silently with rapt attention. Foul sharp teeth smiled beneath thin stained lips while numerous glossy eyes sparkled with glee.

They were staring at me.

Every...

Single...

One...

CHAPTER 11

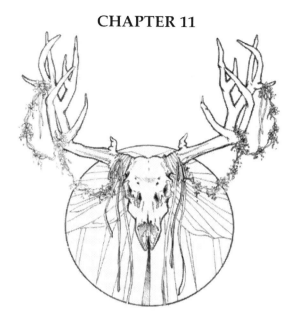

SUNDAY DUSK—PART 2

I cringed, letting out a shaky breath while they openly scrutinized.

No one uttered a word until the little voices caught up to me. Circling overhead, they chattered excitedly.

"She's got iron!"

"Iron in her hair!"

"In her clothes and on her skin!"

"It tears the throat!"

"It boils the flesh."

"She's a nasty creature!"

"Rabid thing!"

I glanced behind me, catching sight of small muddy colored bodies with bird eyes, sharp teeth, and gasoline glazed wings. They clutched pinecones within their tiny fists. When one rebounded off my forehead, I realized exactly what had been thrown earlier.

I shouldn't forget who the real threat was...

Giving the little creatures a dirty look, I shifted my attention toward the gathering of Fae before me, caught in bewilderment when they began to step back from me.

Did I scare them? I had alarmed the Fae within the Market of Myrrd... were these wild Fae the same?

Holding the fork to my side—having a bit of a confidence boost—I approached them. "Where is my friend? He ran this way, so I know you must have him." That came out bolder than expected. *Go me!*

"Grueling, aren't you?" A feminine voice rose out amongst the small assembling crowd. "So, this is the girl we have been expecting?" Her chilling laugh echoed throughout the clearing, while the others parted to make way for a wispy being that watched from the rear. "What a joke." She sauntered toward me with a golden goblet clutched lazily between her spindly fingers. Four black eyes regarded me with a desperate loathing only an old enemy might have.

My lungs shriveled with a breathy sigh at the scene of the sentient tree woman. Hollow malice settled to her eyes as if she was the outcome of a collective pain produced from the millions of trees that fell at the hands of man's evolution. Baring nothing but accented pieces of moss to decorate her shapely hips and shoulders, her frost-tinged redwood skin held a stark contrast against her wild snow-white hair of

224

thick, loose dreadlocks and wilted leafy branches. "You are a mortal child who is surrounded by Fae," she demonstrated to the crowd. "Do you really think you should demand anything from us? Perhaps you should look for our pardon instead. Then maybe we shall consider leaving you dumb and senseless, but alive, alongside the road. Would you like that child?" There were shared grins and mutters of agreement among a few of the fairfolk before me.

I gripped my fork hard, trying to keep from audibly shivering at the image she painted in my mind.

"What do you think?" I didn't give her a chance to reply, having the feeling she had a tendency to give good comebacks. "Of course I wouldn't!" There was cheering from above before pinecones rained against my shoulders. "QUIT IT!!!" I snapped up at them. "I have plenty of wire to string you all up by your ankles and toss you into the river for fish bait."

They scurried like ants, seemingly frightened.

I felt a budding sense of accomplishment until I witnessed the real reason for their departure. They were making way for the larger Peekaboo who popped up out of the tree line behind me, taking guard over the exit.

Well, there went my escape…

"Are you the Fae who follow the leadership of FK?" I glanced around, hoping to get some information from the expressions crossing their faces. When they laughed, I stood perplexed.

"*F… K?*"

"*FK!*"

Some roared in amusement.

225

"O-o-o-o-oh she means HIM, doesn't she?"

"What an idiotic mortal!"

"Although, clever enough to find our camp..."

At least some of them gave me credit.

"Shall there be more attending?"

"There IS that one before her..."

So James was here... The news relieved me, but only for a moment.

Counting heads, I had just attracted a few more dozen Fae, but the perimeter of lights revealed an area great enough to hold several hundred more.

How large of a group had I walked into? Where were the rest? If James had found his way inside then where were they keeping him?

"Am I wrong?" I answered the unruly insults thrown my direction. I settled to the woman, looking between her eyes, unclear which set to stare at. "You all scoff, but you aren't answering my question."

"You are a bold little twit. I'll give you that... but not sharp." She looked livid, like she had to suppress herself physically from slapping me across the face.

Instinctively, I moved back from her reach, knowing this creature had it out for me, I just didn't understand why.

"Louella... hush," drawled a brogue voice I was all too familiar with. "You'll scare her away." The faery troop split again, making way for a white-clad male with amber eyes.

Everyone seemed to shiver in his arrival, the area dropping a few degrees.

"You..." My lips scrunched into an indignant pucker. "So THIS is where you've been hiding?" The Pale Man bowed before me with a glimmer of smugness etched to his sharp porcelain features. "Where is James? Where is my sister!?"

This was a Fae I wasn't afraid to confront. Walking straight up to him I gave his arm a ruffling, willing to wrinkle his perfectly pressed jacket. I hoped he had to burn it to get rid of the smell that all of these Fae seemed to think I omitted.

"You won't be getting anything with a tantrum, Miss Darling. I suggest you compose yourself and proceed with caution. Oh, and Miss Darling, it is about time you showed up." His top had swayed from side to side as he tilted his head to survey me. "You really are rattled, aren't you? Did the little Pigsies do that?" I adjusted my jaw and continued glowering. "Oh very well, very well, always so stubborn." He stroked his goatee. "I do not understand where your charm lies, but perhaps it's the challenge."

Louella gave a simpering laugh.

"The more stubborn they are, the harder they fall when they finally break," the tree sentient spit out in my direction.

"Take advice from your quiet companions, Louella, and bite your tongue. Make yourself useful. Ready the child."

The Pale Man stared the tree woman down with a brittle expression. Earth had no challenge to winters bane. She stepped backward indignantly until cold air filtered through his nostrils. Louella turned and left wordlessly.

I was growing entirely too impatient in dealing with the squabbling of my enemy's henchmen. Feeling like the village rejects I wondered when they would become bored with their sideshow so I could continue on with my rescue mission. I needed to find James so we could get Abigail and get the hell out of here before they tried burning the *stink* off us.

227

"Are you going to stand there and throw insults or will you take me to my family?" If I could help it, as futile as it was, I wanted to avoid FK. There was something entirely too familiar with His presence, but I was too scared to know why after that nightmarish dream.

"You are too rash, Miss Darling."

"I think I am reasonable. In fact, seeing as you stole Abby from her home, I'm being calm under the circumstances." Gripping my fork, I held it in front of me, "I think we are both smart enough to know I am about to be very reckless if I am not taken seriously."

The Fae watched my movements closely, trying to decipher if I was bold enough to take a swing at the ice Fae. From what I could tell, most of them revered him highly, leading me to wonder what sort of social structure their people held. So far, it didn't seem like they had very high morals; although, they were taking orders from an upper chain of command. *So who did I need to be wary of?*

"Well, come along Miss Darling."

Once the throng of onlookers realized the excitement was done, for the time being, Fae dissipated back into their holes and hideouts.

"Abandoner of kin of iron and sin."

"She reeks of death that pours from her skin." Murmurs trailed around me.

"Danger."

"Stranger."

"Mortal sting."

The Pale Man was already several steps ahead of me by the time I shook free of the foreboding whispers echoing through the night. Afraid of what would happen if he left me behind, I wound around various makeshift structures with haste, trying to keep from losing pace with the man.

Moss blanketed the spired tents like patchwork quilts cascading in wildflowers that should have long since gone into hibernation. Bird's nests and beehives decorated some of their walls, like yard ornaments, while others had manmade treasures fixed to roofs.

I slipped and stumbled past their lamp-lit entrances, catching the view of a few curious individuals who seemed to seek us out in greeting. Only when they fixed their sight on us did they quickly shut the flap of their entrances, snuffing out their lamps to hide away in the dark. Some creatures had the same expression as Louella, a crippling shrewd sense of superiority that only old blood or status held. It was a stare my grandmother perfected. *Were humans seen that lowly in the Fae realm? Was there some form of universal hatred for my entire race that made them judgmental toward me?* Other than the iron I bore around my neck and hand, I saw no advantage to counter their magic tricks. *Why hide in the shadows? Why cower to a pasty frazzled human like me?*

Listening intently, the festivities suddenly dampened to a shivering gust of wind that swept through the field. The lamps rattled on their hinges, banners blew battered and astray. The lights licked dangerously low during the deafness at the height in the squall, until it cut short and a burst of activity ignited the clearing once more.

What was that? The whispers above had stopped their murmuring for the time being.

I trembled in my drenched shoes, trying to decipher my surroundings. If we were to get out of this place unharmed, I needed to take careful notes on where we entered the clearing.

Even so, everything appeared similar just enough to create a chaotic uniformity. When I turned to look behind me, the trail was overbearingly contorted in my mind, as if the campground itself had its own sense of consciousness, purposefully trying to cloud my judgment from escaping its confinement.

I wasn't sure what I should have been watching out for at that point. The path was becoming slicker the deeper we went, but fewer tents to weave through. Structures rose higher and sturdier, while the lights brightened, and the noises were more acute. People were laughing and singing along to the passionate strings of the never-ending song surrounding us.

I was having a hard time concentrating when we finally broke into the heart of the camp. A blazing fire licked the air, swaying near the source of the haunting melody—an enchanted band of instruments.

Flocks of beings danced like wild animals around the bonfire. Whooping and hollering madly with glamour-struck faces, those who bothered to clothe themselves were adorned in foreign garb molded from autumn flora and a crochet mesh. Others were like the Pale man, who favored an aristocratic flair. Homage to Victorian vintage, their smocked outfits were constructed in the finest silks and polished leathers.

Until this point, there was no sign of modern attire; yet, the further I examined the dancing creatures, I realized I could pick out sneakers and jean jackets. These Fae lacked the grace I had seen from their more civilized kin, and it wasn't hard to realize exactly what was happening.

My stomach twisted appallingly.

These were Fae-stricken humans dancing in an everlasting game. Soiled with their own filth and mud, they looked as if they had stumbled several times, gotten up, and continued to play on. A few held limp appendages to their side, broken or pulled from the socket. Fae let them continue their dance, despite how injured or sleep deprived they were. Their faces were twisted abnormally with maddened expressions of glee, masking the blind internal pain they felt.

I watched one drop.

Looking horrified, I was grabbed firmly about the elbow and steered away before the scene could stir up anything else inside me.

"It never bodes well for a human to doddle during a cursed orchestras crescendo," he murmured in my ear.

Shivering, I twisted in the other's grasp staring back to the raving humans. The one on the ground was drug away. *Was this where James ran to?* I wanted to go closer to the warmth of the flame, examine their faces. "Miss Darling," He squeezes my elbow tighter, "I assure you, the boy is not there."

"How can I trust your word?"

"Have I lied to you yet, girl?" He gave a bored look. "The boy is not over there." He drew me a few steps more, "I am many things but an untruth I shall not wield. Remember that of the Fae, Miss Darling, for it may save you one day."

231

I tried not to seize up with more tension, knowing the other would find it more appealing to knock me out than to deal with a disruptive nuisance. Stumbling, I slid against a muddied patch of earth. With the combination of his strained help, and gravity, I was pitched forward.

My wrist gave an audible pop.

Dropping my fork with a sharp intake of breath, I curled about my hand. Pain throbbed through my tendons in waves, blinding my vision in a dizzying moment of time.

"Did you hurt yourself?" He hovered, trying to look at the appendage I was cradling. "Let me see." The gold of his eyes shifted to burnt citrine while he jerked sternly at my elbow, "Miss Darling."

"Give me a moment," I bit out. "Let me breathe a second."

"Humans and their inadequacy to adapt," he gave a foggy breath out. The cool breeze passed through my hair, coating it in frost. "I can fix it. That is the least I can do to rectify the situation."

"Don't worry." I grinned bitterly, "I won't tell your 'Master' you broke me."

The Pale Man observed me. "You are quite the spitfire when you choose to be, aren't you?"

Shaking my head in retort, I stared hard at the ground, trying to subliminally will him to leave. It was then I realized what I had fallen from, frozen footprints that trailed behind my captor. They led in the direction we had come from.

Knowing I had found our way out, my nerves trembled with a surge of anticipation, that is, until I was abruptly scooped up into the Pale Man's arms. I left behind the feeling of hope in the startled moment.

Yelping, I kicked my legs, biting away the pain as I pushed on his chest with my arms. "LET ME DOWN!!!"

"Calm yourself," He bore his pointed teeth, rigidly walking while I seized up in his hold.

I refused to look at him. Adrenaline was surging through my neck and jaw, causing a dull pulsing pain. There was something very personal about being this close to another being, and I didn't feel comfortable with it, especially with the henchman of my enemy.

Why hadn't he turned his nose away like the rest of his kind? Why did this winter-clad creature hold more say than others? Was he F.K.'s super special henchman? Was he in charge of depositing me into F.K.'s presence without causing a scene? I was tumbling into a knot of questions when I should have been paying attention.

Mentally scolding myself, I focused on the pixy-like creatures that flitted about. Their hairless angular frames worked quickly to braid knots into the manes of those who slept out in the open air.

In the trees sat winged animals, with the form akin to a howler monkey but more feline in expression. Plumbing ashen mane framed their wide-eyed gazes, short snout curling as its lips pulled up to bare teeth.

When we passed, three gathered to swivel their heads unnaturally around to watch us walk from behind.

I saw individuals with skin the color of coal. Impressively large tusks jutted between their chops or directly out of the sides of their jaws, devilish eyes avoided mine all together.

There was one broad-shouldered character of quiet observation. Thorny spikes prickled their shoulders and protruding through their brow. Scale plated tail drug heavily back and forth, easily tripping a few jittery bystanders.

Centaur men trotted about small throngs of earthen folk who were clad in moss, barely covering essential bits.

Flawless obsidian skin intermingled with opaque cream. Ethereal beings of sharp contrast, all with silken hair and fine garb settled to a circle of massive pillows. They sipped mead quietly chatting amongst each other, a discreet hum of wings intermingled their melodious voices.

A few peeked over to observe us, hazel irises speaking of tantalizing promises of the utmost deepest desires. I could almost smell their sweet peach breath, the soft downy of their skin.

Shivering mentally, I cut them out. A darker male rose to watch us in audible wonder.

Were they tempting me on purpose?

I didn't have time to ponder. Whisked away by my ice guard, I was swallowed up in the mulling drove of chattering Fae.

Squat toad-like creatures, with warty wrinkled bodies, darted in and out of the various collections of open-faced pavilions.

Drinks and appetizers were passed around to sedate the boisterous parties. The vibrant emerald cloth of each sect, hand stitched with large embossed crests, distinctly showed the aristocracy in the camp that evening.

There were the beautiful and the beastly alike. Some were hard to decipher in comparison. They were all so strange, lovely and forbidden; it was hard not to feel breathless.

The Fae were a terrifyingly beautiful race to behold.

Ignoring all of it, the Pale Man turned right, leading us down a new pathway of torch lights, where they bled into the thicket of trees. Our road became thinner but comfortable enough.

Young trees bowed above our heads in perfectly braided arbors, directing us toward a tent made of white cloth and thick wooden poles. Gauzy umber stained drapes cascaded along the entrance and looped about the spires that jutted into the canopy above.

I gave a weary look to the elk skull fashioned at the center rod; longhorns bleached white with a decorated flower chain and bits of ribbon.

"Here we are, Miss Darling." The other settled me to the ground, catching my chin before I could go through the door. "Clean yourself up. Do you understand me?"

I swallowed thickly, watching him with weary mistrust.

"Where is my sister?"

"Little Miss will be in attendance the sooner you freshen up. Are we in an understanding, Miss Darling?" I didn't want to agree to that. I wanted her now. "Miss Darling," his voice became thicker, deeper as he stressed the L in my name.

"Got it..."

"Good." Quietly examining me, he pulled back the cloth. "The clock is ticking, and my Master isn't the most patient of folk," He pushed me through the entrance of the structure. "The quicker you are the better temperament he'll be."

I barely noticed the plush interior as the curtain dropped closed in front of me, cutting off my view of the woods. The near silence began a crawling itch up my spine, exciting a twitch in my hands.

235

I was alone. Truly alone, and it scared me far more than any reckless drive through the woods full of Fae could ever induce. Gulping down a few calming breaths, I swiveled on my heels to take in the chamber.

Divided by silken cream draperies, drawn back with red rope, I stood awkwardly in a common room of white wooded furnishing. Loud patterned cushions of rustic tones offset the fresh snow appearance, while sheepskin rugs ran the length of the tent.

A feast of fruits, nuts, and cheeses lay to a crystalline tray established on top of a low rising table, at the center of a small lounge. I reached out instinctively, stomach gurgling in indignation before P. Whimsy's warning echoed from the depths of my mind.

'Never EVER drink or dine on the foods of the Faery Folk.'

I slowly sidestepped the table, like it was a spitting cobra, peeking into the bedroom. My gaze drug across the large poster bed sitting to the heart of the space, blushing blends of reds and browns contrasted the alabaster furniture. Inviting smells of incense trailed from the direction of the washbasin and a copper tub, steaming water waited invitingly for me.

Was bathing in Fae water against a rule? Everything was mushing up in my mind.

I wasn't in any delusion about my appearance. My hair was tousled, frizzy, and possibly filled with pine needles. My skin itched in need to slough off my journey's wears. It would take a heavy rinse cycle to get my outfit into a subnormal state of liveliness, which meant I wouldn't be anywhere near as prepared as they were expecting. I was a hot mess and expectations were low.

236

"You need to play along," I muttered out loud. My shoes were doing a lovely job at rubbing deep porous prints below me, a physical representation of my sheer indecisiveness over the situation. A hot soak sounded very enticing, except it was hard to believe I could relax when I was far from relaxed. Then there was the bed. I wasn't planning on staying the night. I wasn't planning on staying at all. But... if I had to rub off a bit of 'stink' to see Abigail and James, then so be it.

Growling to myself I kicked off my shoes. Hollow rings echoed as they bounced against the side of the tub, settling dejectedly away from me.

My eyes kept to the door, paranoia kicking in while I stripped down quickly.

Disentangling from the locket, I placed it gently to a neat pile along with the chain of paperclips before jumping into the steaming pool. Initially, my body tensed, shocked by the heat encasing my miserably exhausted form.

Moments ticked by, when the fear subsided, one by one, each muscle slacked into a pile of immovable sludge to the bottom of the bath. I blew bubbles on the surface of the water, my mind daring to trail over the perfectly fashioned face I had encountered in my dreams.

His deep timbering voice was overwhelming, like the rush of a river carving its way through the earth in a slow but persistent path. I felt myself being pulled under, drug into the cavern of his bottomless eyes where I drifted... drowning quietly.

I suddenly squeezed my eyes shut tightly, embarrassed that I was even entertaining the intrusion he had on my psyche. Gripping the sides of the bath, I submerged my body.

Taking a long deafening moment to myself, I let my breath slowly escape in trickling bubbles.

When my lungs sent signals to my brain to breathe, I flipped around and settled upright onto my knees with a sharp intake of breath.

Splashing water noisily, I scrubbed roughly at my freckled form with the complimentary sponge that sat on a side table along with some bottled oils and salts. Scowling at the hospitality, I threw the sponge at the tent wall.

What was this, a hotel?

Leaning out of the tub, I ran my gaze along the assortment of bath goods. There were no labels to see, no instructions to read, just a collection of highly suspicious bottles and ointments at my disposal. "Nope... Nope. Aaand nope," Grabbing a cotton sheet, I rose and wrapped it protectively around my form. "I said I'd clean myself up, not smell like them."

Tugging the locket back on, feeling lopsided without it, I shuffled aimlessly around.

My wrist was stiff, but the heat had done it some good. Swelling had taken its course, but at least I didn't have to deal with a broken bone. There was something to be said about that.

After a few more loops around the bed, I stood in front of the washbasin. A comb was sitting innocently to the left of a large abalone shell bowl. The mirror hung in as a smoggy reflective backdrop, showing a warped figure of what must have been my face.

Blotchy complexion, wet hair, and cold, they would have me clean but begrudgingly so. As soon as I stepped out of this little oasis, I'd be frostbitten.

What did they think I was supposed to wear? I looked for my clothes then, half a mind to clean them with a bit of soap and water when I realized they were nowhere to be seen.

"Oh shit." That was alarming. I scurried around in short quick strides. The sheet kicked out behind me in fervor while I checked over and under the bed, around the tub, and then back under the bed again. There were only so many places I could check!

Apprehension was making the home in the pit of my stomach.

Was this a game to them? Was this a test to see if I really would snap? Louella made it very clear I wasn't welcome. Perhaps this was her way of trying to degrade my dignity? Maybe the plan all along was to force me out of the tent… naked. What a cruel world I had stumbled into. I shook, pulling the sheet up around my face and waddled over to the ever going fire.

I was falling emotionally, tumbling into that chasm F.K. had so cleverly wore through my spirit with his menacing presence. When I believed the worst had yet to come, I looked up to find a woven basket settled onto a hassock beside that tempting display of treats.

Slipping over tentatively, I crouched down to stare at the multi-wooded siding, stripped and faceted to create a modest display. Thin cotton was wrapped about the package, tied with red ribbon and a single bottle blue anemone flower.

That did not bode well in my mind. Taking up the flower, I twirled into my thumb and index, Deja vu tapping on the side of my head with a flustered sense of paranoia. I took in a well needed inhale of air as I dropped the bud. Removing the trimming, I peeked within the package.

Relief embraced the intensity that permeated my form, momentarily distracting me while I carefully pulled a dusty green dress out from its packaging.

The gown was thick linen in texture, a hearty material to cut out the cold of the Pacific Northwest in fall. The frock span was long, possibly too long, but the Celtic sleeves would run the length of my arms, snug and inviting. A gilded band was the only elaborate detail that scooped the collar.

Ankle-high leather boots were tucked under a heavy quilted shawl of creams, burnt orange, and sage. Gold thread stitched intricate designs across the entirety of its scheme, adorning the emblem that I had noticed earlier on the tents of the aristocrats.

Gathering everything I crossed back into the bedroom and dropped the divider. I managed to pull the dress on and lace the sides myself, but the boots proved harder than expected. Leather and a swollen wrist did not mix well. Sitting flustered and disoriented I flopped back onto the bed, staring up at the ceiling. *Why was I trying so hard?* I was a far cry from the ethereal beauties that traipsed around the campground, and they weren't going to make me feel like someone had stuck a pig in a dress to pass it off as something other than it already was.

"Are you decent?"

"That's a question I should be asking you," I glared at the closed curtains.

"I'm coming in."

"If you dare to," the top hat of my icy warden peeked through, parting the gauzy draperies to give me an unamused expression.

"Why are you not dressed?"

"If you plan on taking a paranoid person's clothes, do them a favor and replace them in the last place they left them! I thought you were planning on making me walk out there with only a sheet!"

"Indeed, you are lucky that wasn't the plan, that the Master found it prudent to be mindful of your modest temperament."

"Did you just call me a prude?"

"I called you *shy*," He drawled, "A word that holds little meaning in my world." He stood a bit more erect, folding his arms behind his back as he surveyed his surroundings. "You still stink of iron, but the stench of sweat is gone. Why are your boots not bound, your hair not done? Did you not like the flower?"

"Was that you?" I stared.

"I took note of it. The Master found it to be a sensible interjection."

"You're cruel," I muttered, staring at the floor quietly. "I can't get them on," I finally told him, "My wrist."

"Frail." He countered, walking over to directly kneel before me. "Rise, Miss Darling." His gloved fingers worked quickly along the laces, stretching the leafy tongue of the shoes so that I could sit up and guide my feet into them. He brusquely popped each heel inside before fastening them up.

I slipped from the bed, shuffling back from him when he gathered the shawl to hold it out for me.

"I can dress myself," snatching it, I threw it around my shoulders.

"That can be debated. Your hair," he commented with the indication of a slender finger. "Take out that band and turn around."

Blinking I pulled the tie out slowly, watching him wearily again.

"Your appearance reflects on my aptitude to prepare you for the audience of my Master."

"Oh *god*, that's what this is all about?" I rotated around, rolling my eyes. "I'm sorry, but you can't turn me into a Faery princess."

"I assure you, no one expects that."

Watching from the corner of my eye, he pulled off his gloves to uncork a thin amber vial that sat next to the large silver comb on top of the washbasin.

"What is that?" I tried turning when he grabbed a bit of my hair to force me to look straight ahead.

"It's nothing but scented olive oil to help with tangles."

So I stood, awkwardly, letting the ice warden work the tangles from my hair. He was quiet and looked displeased, pulling the begrudgingly stubborn vegetation from my locks.

When he was done, my hair had dried somewhat in the heat, allowing the natural curls to bounce up a sleek uniformity. He finished his work off by twisting and pulling back a section to either side of my head, tying them off with the red ribbon I rejected, this was a style my hair hadn't seen in years. I felt strange and awkward that he had been the one to do it. There was the itch to yank it out immediately, like a petulant child, and stomp on his foot. I still might do that. For

242

now, I waited and watched him pull his gloves back on, indicating to the door.

"This way," he affirmed, taking up my wrist and guiding me off into the night.

My involuntary supervision led us toward the lovely wafting scents of roasted meats that intermingled with sautéed herbs and root vegetables.

"You promised me, my family." I frowned, "Not dinner."

Servants dodged in and out of the multiple elongated shelters in the backdrop of the campground, structures of plain but strong high walls to fit kitchen implements of massive proportions. Smoke trailed high above the tree line, suggesting another fire was crackling in the servant's quarters for culinary purposes.

"Miss Darling, kindly stop spinning those wheels of yours and sit down." He pulled me into the largest pavilion yet, where a colossal black granite table resided as the prime decor.

A maroon runner offset the ebony surface. Garlands of threaded leaves, moss, and fall edibles wove about large crystalline vases that sat provocatively between pumpkins and squash. Cattails, sunflowers, and blooming red cabbage were some of the few dazzling details in each vessel. The prime centerpiece held branches laden with apples that drooped low over the arrangement so that individuals could grab as they pleased.

Small mysterious orbs flickered, trapped inside the bouquets. Leaning in, I recognized the similarity to those from the *Market Myrrd*. When I looked up, I found more trailing lazily about hanging glass bulbs, flickering with the candlelight. Wax dripped from them in delicate tendrils. When a chance wind trickled through, they danced in a mesmerizing sway.

I wasn't the first guest to be guided into one of the chairs. A figure sat with its head drooped into an empty porcelain plate. From what I could see he wore a disheveled smock of sorts like he had been forced into wearing it.

"Hello?" I sounded more alarmed then I meant.

When the stranger didn't move, I turned to question the Pale Man and found that he had vanished.

Alone again.

Sighing, I looked around, seeing modestly garbed Fae slipping in and out of the expansive room, getting it ready for the anticipated dinner party. I groaned loudly, listening to it echo above.

This would be a waiting game.

So I waited.

CHAPTER 12

SUNDAY DUSK PART 3

Fae and humans alike began to meander slowly into the hall. I sat near the center, watching as they filtered through with their loud raucous laughing and chattering. Those who sat beside me leaned away in distaste, making it obvious that they were intent to ignore my presence.

I didn't mind. It was better treatment than what the unconscious man was being given. He was being poked and prodded. Creatures hovered around him to decorate his hair with twigs and leaves, and when they weren't getting the response they desired, someone finished with dousing his head with a pitcher of wine.

They roared in pure amusement.

I watched him bolt upright, bloated and bruised—face nearly unrecognizable—but it was Crowe. His eyes darted around the table of onlookers with a mad sort of alertness, terrified. The response only served to delight his audience further.

When they were becoming too destructive with the officer, quiet assistance swarmed him from either side of the entry, cleaning him up before they caused too much of a scene.

I found that most of the help were pallid looking humans, with glazed over eyes and trembling hands. Even the pampered few, who sat behind, or to their master's lap, were in the same sickly state.

Noticing familiarities, I regarded my own outfit and found my heart dropping. *I was dressed like the rest of them.*

Were they my fate should I lose? Quivering, clumsy mortals at the beckoning call of the Fae and beast alike?

Gulping, I steered myself to rise and make the long alarming trek around the table. Fae audibly gasped, as if they had only just realized I was in attendance. They leaned away, pulling out fans to bat boisterously toward my direction, speaking loudly behind an upturned palm, and even hissing insults in my direction.

Ignore them, ignore them, ignore them…

Finding myself to Crowe's side, I gripped his shoulder, leaning in, even as he flinched. "Crowe," I murmured. "Crowe, it's me, Emma Darling."

Grey eyes, clouded by panic, flitted back and forth, trying to extract recognition from my face.

"There were dozens of them." He grabbed my hand roughly, holding firmly. "I fired all my rounds, but they kept coming."

"I know," I felt myself shriveling in on myself in guilt, seeing this confident man crippled by the ugliness surrounding us. *No one deserved this.* "I'm so sorry you've been dragged into this."

Candles flickered about us as another trickle of wind passed through.

Gaze unfocused, Crowe stared beyond me while stiffening. "**You are late, Emmaline...**"

How could I miss the sudden smell of earthy mulch that came in with the breeze? There was something else too, something spiced, ancient. Was that what old magic smelt like?

The crowd of Fae simmered to a hum of expectation. All of their stares and whispers permeating my skin, making me feel more transparent than ever. Finally, very slowly, I twisted my head to gaze in the direction of the resounding voice. He stood, towering alongside the high-back chair at the head of the table, sightlessly staring to me with all the poised strength a powerful aristocratic creature could behold.

Fiery curls framed his strong-jawed expression, intermingling with the striking branch antlers that knotted and twisted upward on his temple. Greyish green skin contrasted against the faded blue of his robes, webbed delicately with designs of a glistening thread. The collar was lined with the silver-tinged fur from a great opposing beast. When he moved to sit, a few leaves tumbled from his earthy crown, settling aimlessly to his braided mane that roped about his waist.

247

His thin fingers wrapped about a goblet to the table, pulling it against his thin lips to take a sip.

"**Did the Pigsies catch your tongue?**" He looked disappointed. "**Where is that clever wit we've heard so much of?**"

I had forgotten I could speak until they were laughing around me.

"*What a senseless mortal girl.*"

"*Doesn't she know she's been had?*"

"*Poor ugly little thing.*"

"*Our King, pleeease make her take off the iron stink! She's putting us off our meal!*"

"*Humans, so ridiculously hapless it sets my whiskers to curl.*"

Rubbing my hands together I let the dull of my nails bite into my flesh, reminding myself to keep from running. A large part of me wanted to give into their insults and cower like the pathetic fool they thought I was.

FK's hand rose to silence the whining brood.

"**Let darling Emmaline speak,**" he almost purred in simmering triumph, looking like a cat that was playing with his meal.

"I was promised to see Abigail and my friend James," I rested a steadying grip to Crowe's shoulder, feeling him quivering.

"**Ah, were you?**" The lord raised his palm, twirling a ringed finger where the Pale Man suddenly appeared in a swirl of cold air and ice flakes.

The spectators noticeably shuddered, hunkering down in their furs and frills.

"You called for me, Sire?"

"Corrigan, did you promise our guest she may see her sister and... companion?"

"Yes, Sire, I believe I did." The Pale Man rested his arms, poised to his back, surveying only his lord with a light bow inattention.

"**Then we must comply. The only question being, once you see them, what do you propose you'll do with that knowledge?**" He asked me.

"We all leave together," I locked my jaw tightly shut as uproar rippled down the table in a wave.

"**Ah...**" His perfect face seemed to consider what I said until he rested ever-so-slightly toward my direction. "**And what, pray tell, will you be bargaining for, in the return of such prized possessions?**"

"They aren't property!" I blurted out, regretting the action by the flicker of pleasure crossing the noble's features. "You had no right to take her."

"**Oh, but we did.**" He placed his drink down to rest his elbows on the armrests of his imposing seat. Fingers steepled, he watched me through dark lashes. "**You see, your mother wished her first born child away. A bargain we were all too happy to comply with.**"

I was rubbing my throat uneasily then.

"You tricked her."

"**Oh, really?**" he looked about the room with his spectral sight. "**Is that what you truly believe, Emmaline?**"

"Yes," I whispered. "You trick and steal. You have no consideration for the lives you're destroying." Biting my tongue, I physically had to keep myself from erupting. All the

249

loneliness of abandonment seized my ribcage, squeezing my heart.

He took everyone from me, my mom, my sister, my friend, my life, everything.

Even as he lazed back in his chair, looking unfazed by my surge of emotion, leaves dropped down one by one from his budding crown.

"Contracts were made long before you were thought of." He had a steely calmness that produced an involuntary shudder from me, **"A contract broken by a traitor who thought to outwit us with a game of hide-and-seek."**

"That isn't fair. Don't you people understand that?" I looked around at the alluringly strange creatures surrounding me. "We weren't born. It isn't fair to play with peoples will. I had no way to stick up for myself."

"Will you stick up for yourself now, Emmaline?" The lights played shadows across his face, sharpening his edges, making him look more dangerous than ever—eyes glowing white, with barely any blue visible. He smiled at me.

No comfort could be felt anywhere around me.

"Y-yes."

"Then we will strike a new deal, between the two of us."

"What could I possibly have that would interest the likes of you?"

Our audience was cleverly quiet, only the faint tone of fluttering wings could be heard from time to time. Corrigan, formerly the Pale Man, kept motionlessly rooted to his master's side, as if FK had powered him down for the time being.

While I was already presumably told what the creature before me bargained for, I doubted it. *Who could want me this much as to create such a loud ruckus? What was the point? What did I have to offer?*

"**It isn't a question of what you have, Emmaline. You've done a perfectly good job at bringing yourself to the table. It's what you will find that is of interest.**" Then the whispering started, a peculiar purr of words passed across each mouth, creating a quivering singsong rhythm.

"*From traitor's womb the child doth hatch…*" The very phrase Prometheus the Troll had voiced in the marketplace.

"What can I possibly bring you?" I muttered, trying to think back on the exchanges I have had and seen throughout the five days my sister had been taken. Odhrun said my presence brought terrible things, that I was marked.

Was he talking of my mother's dealings with FK?

"There are holes in your puzzle," I finally said with sureness in my voice. "If you owned me, why not take me when I was a child? All of these hoops to jump through, all of these challenges. You need to trick me because you can't actually have me." The lights died low. I could almost make out a low guttural growl before his lips curled.

"**Clever, curious girl,**" He rose, stepping from his chair while drawing up his goblet. "**Our sight,**" he indicated passively toward his face while slowly sauntering in my direction.

I felt my feet shuffling back, pulling from officer Crowe.

"**She took our sight and left us blind to wander like a fool amongst our people. She did this so that we could not** see you. Take you." He chuckled then. **"The moment of her passing, a new deal could be struck."**

Swallowing hard, I found myself backed into a cedar trunk that helped hold the tent upright. Staring wide, I felt my mind breaking under the cement of his words. I didn't have time to digest my feelings, however; the hordes of Fae were all turning to stare at me.

"And while we cannot force you to stay, your sister, by rights, is a suitable replacement."

"You can't have her!"

"Oh? We can't?"

Neither one of us looked so sure of that. I didn't exactly have a campground of magic-wielding beings at my side.

"I came here to free my family. That is the deal I want to bargain for."

"Then we have a deal to discuss," one of his hands rose as he laughed with sudden rich enthusiasm. He drank from his glass, gesturing to his people.

The candles burst into life as the table of individuals began to cackle and tease. More servants poured through with massive vats of delicious smelling roasted goods. Large platters of root vegetables, tossed with herbs, were placed to the merry table. Quartz bowls, brimming with sweet and savory sauces, heaping piles of quiche tarts, cheeseballs rolled in nuts, stuffed mushrooms, and other vastly delightful foods found their places. Dried fruits and nuts were settled to every other placeholder for quick grabbing.

There were freshly baked honeyed buns, croissants, heavy thick slices of artisan nut bread, pots of jam and butter to top them all. Six humans carried in a fully roasted pig, while others pushed trollies dedicated to placing a stuffed Cornish game hen to each plate at the table. Jugs, of what I could only assume where wine, were passed from hand to hand with everyone wishing to be drunk and jolly.

I almost became lost in the vibrant atmosphere. No longer being scowled or snarled at, I blended for a split moment, into the background while merriment took place.

"Come here, child." FK had established himself back to the head of his court, waving me closer with a flick of his finger.

Perched to the chair beside Crowe, a hybrid creature akin to barn owl, took it upon itself to try and feed him with a clawed foot. Crooning in distress, it chattered in a broken language as the lentil soup drizzled down his chin. No matter how insistent the creature was with its spoon, he kept his mouth shut tightly.

We locked eyes as I neared him, trying to give a reassuring smile. Self-blame saturated my already tense form as I consciously passed him. Completely evading the situation he had fallen into.

"E-Emma? Emma!" I could hear him calling out, before gagging slightly as the being finally could shove food into his mouth.

FK motioned to the empty seat to the left of himself. I knew he had been observing me. He may have been blind in a sense, but that didn't mean the man couldn't take in the scene before him.

Sitting quietly to the seat, nervous mortals quickly began to flock around me, pouring drinks and placing food to my plate. It was forced hospitality that held a dangerous essence of control. When a young girl bent to begin cutting up my offered meal, I had had enough of their hovering.

"FK—" I stopped, hearing chattering snickers.

Three watery ashen females sat side by side across from me, dressed in moss gowns of similar design. Flower petals decorated the edges of their cheeks and temples, making an intricate mask across their faces. Branches and ribbon bits interwove their bird nest hairstyles; one even contained robin's eggs.

"FK? Is she still on about that business?" The middle twittered.

"He is the KING, stupid girl," jabbed the shortest of the three.

"I cannot believe she did not piece that together," the last of them laughed, giving me an insensitive stare.

"Humans are so mind-numbing. They're only good for two things."

"Servants..."

"And sex."

The women cooed in their fun, watching me coolly.

Clenching my jaw, too late, my face was burning in embarrassment.

"Don't look so forlorn, Emmaline. Sadness does not suit you."

"Is that a request, or an order, King?" I bit out. Giving him side looks while he reached to pluck up a vine of red grapes.

"Are we going to play like that now?" He held out his glass, shocking me a bit. **"Drink and we will strike our deal."**

254

"No," I replied flatly. "I may be naive to your tricks but that one I will not partake in."

To those around, who overheard our conversation, lowered their chattering to whispers of sharp indignation.

"**Quiet.**" The King held up his hand. "**She speaks the truth, our clever girl.**" He seemed almost pleased. "**But that is what that amulet around your neck protects you from.**"

"I—"

"**Drink, Emmaline. You are protected from our sway. We would not come this far only now to betray your trust.**"

Betray my trust? If that was what he was aiming for he missed his mark by a long shot. I wearily stretched to take up the chalice, making a confused noise when he held on a moment longer.

"**We wish to have you come to us of your own free accord, despite the ties that bind us.**" His fingers brushed the tips of mine before sitting back, releasing the drink. He smirked, "**It is good, we promise.**"

Anything to keep me from sinking into the degrading moment, with a slight pause, I timidly took a sip. Sweet warmth trickled down my throat, spreading into every nerve ending, letting the intensity in my body subside. There was an underlying mood of compulsive giddiness bubbling up, but I could easily maneuver it into submission. The mental strength brought an interesting awareness. Making me question just how strong the pull of Fae food could really be if I had no protection. "**Were we correct?**"

I nodded absentmindedly, staring into the ochre liquid.

There was a core itch to comply with his every word, to please him no matter what manner. *That scared me.* Mostly because there was a small part of me that actually liked the attention I was receiving.

"F— King. I want to strike the deal so that my friends, family and I can go home…" Crowe was halfway down the hall from me, succumbing to the bizarre and provocative influence of his onlookers. He settled unnerved in his chair, gulping from the various cups offered and accepting each fork full of food. The officer was purged of one supernatural influence only to submit himself to another.

He was literally stuffing himself to death.

"Often than not, mortals are powerless to the influence of Fae."

That could be me in Crowe's shoes. *I had to think, remember.*

"Don't let them do that to him, please." Looking back at the ancient being, hysteria tried overthrowing the fuzzy heat tingling across my spine. "Please, it isn't fair."

"Nothing rarely is, but…" he gestured with a sweep of his arm, dismissing the creatures back to their seats.

Crowe was left abruptly to slide off his chair, toppling to the side with a loud clatter. I heard dry heaving and Fae squealing while the officer began to purge on the ground. **"You should let him be their distraction,"** the Fae King hummed, settling back again. **"Fae are cruel when the mood strikes them. Let us hope they do not turn toward the ones you really want to fight for, hmm?"**

Gulping more of the drink down, I squeezed the cup and stared unfocused to its depths. As I began to swirl the contents absentmindedly, bitterness crashed against the lonely cliff side called my life. I stood at its edge, staring

256

down into the writhing yellow waves that would surely destroy me.

I snapped into the moment when I felt a hand to my jaw. Staring up into pale blue irises, like facetted opals, the Fae King brushed his thumb against the single tear that rolled down my cheek, then brought it up to his lips to taste it.

I wasn't getting out of this mess. There was only one thing he wanted back, so there was only one option I could make, my freedom or my families.

"How do I know my family isn't already dead?"

There was a chuckle, his breath tickling my ear.

"The first smart thing you've asked all night," Louella's dead voice filtered through the hall.

Grinding my teeth, I reeled in my dignity to watch for the woman.

"**Look across the table,**" the nobleman gestured before us, pointing out the little blonde head bobbing in and out of the mingling crowd.

I jumped up from my spot, forgetful of the offensive tree spirit, making a hasty dash around the King. I pushed myself through the gathering Fae, hoping this wasn't just a cruel trick of the eye.

Yet there she was, fussy hair stuck with pine needles. Her large eyes glanced up at all the onlookers with quiet contemplation.

"ABBY!!!"

She perked up at my voice, looking around quickly with a slightly awed expression until we finally made eye contact.

"Emmy!" she squealed. "I found you!" Her small pudgy finger pointed with glee. I pushed through the crowd, falling onto my skirts in front of her. "Emmy, don't cry. I didn't really go away." Abby mumbled while leaning her whole body against me. "I was just hiding."

Draping myself forward, I drew her into my arms to hold her there.

She was here. I can feel her, this isn't a trick.

"Were you?" I forgot to respond. "No, you didn't really go away, smart girl." Laughing weakly, watching her face go through the motions of feeling alarmed from my upset. *Had she not understood what happened to her? Did she not know by now that Fae had taken her from me?*

"It's your turn to hide, Emmy." She smiled at me.

"We're going home soon…" I pulled her up slowly, steadying my foothold.

"But you said," She whined, wiggling in her frustration. "When I find you, you find me. That's the rules."

A sense of foreboding hung in the air.

"Abby, when did I say we would play hide-and-seek?" I was confused and more alarmingly aware than ever before.

"Just now," She looked at me as if I had gained a twin.

"Oh," I smiled evenly, trying to digest what she was saying without frightening her too much. "I did?"

"Yeah, Jamie's still hiding. Can we find him?"

"You've seen James?" My eyebrows rose before glancing around, hoping to catch a glimpse of rusty hair.

Abigail tugged on my dress lightly, giving a pout. "Emmy, can't we play?"

"We can play later," I was growing paranoid again, looking distractedly over her to make sure she wasn't harmed. She was a bit dirty, but I could tell someone had recently washed her pajamas. There was no need to be this alarmed. Abby didn't look frightened. Someone had been taking care of her in my stead, an individual who was playing a clever charade of guardian.

"There you are. I've found you." Louella's voice called over in an unusually gentle nature.

Turning to retort the tree Fae's words, I halted, staring at a mirror image of myself. Abigail looked back and forth between us, making a whining groan in discomfort.

"E-Emmy?"

We were both tangled up in confusion.

"How about we go play, Abby?" Louella's voice—*my lips*—hummed softly.

My sister's curls bounced back and forth as she stubbornly shook 'no,' hiding her face in my shoulder.

I stared angrily into my own face. "Louella, what the hell do you think you're playing at?" I stepped back, glaring.

Her face shifted slightly, the second set of black eyes blinked into existence, making my image look unearthly.

"How lucky you are to have the favor of the King," she murmured, fingers dancing at her sides as if she were itching to wrap them around my throat. "I would have drowned you in the lake along with your mother." She hissed.

"Louella," Corrigan glided casually to my side, giving her a frosty stare. "The King wishes to see you."

Her four eyes blinked steadily to him before brushing passed me irritably.

"Do not encourage her." He adjusted his felt top hat, watching the woman slip over to the King's chair. "Do not go near her," he warned just as a hollow slap echoed through the air.

A few Fae decided to part ways with the dining hall, giving me enough of a view to watch Louella kneel before the Fae King in her true form. She was talking in quiet, submissive tones, bowing her head. He seemed to be having nothing of it, speaking with little words before ignoring her completely.

I watched her slowly rise after a long moment of being ignored. Her snow white mane tossed as she turned sharply to look our way.

"Stop staring," my guardian warned, raising his chin in dismissal when Louella returned to us. Her cheek was flush with the promising mark of a bruise.

Baring her teeth at me, she looked to Corrigan.

"I'll be taking the brat."

"No, you won't," I twisted away from her, holding Abigail closer.

"She will," he agreed.

"She will NOT."

Louella reached out, and I smacked her hands away. *No one was taking my sister away, especially not her!*

Rage flickered across her features before she brazenly seized my wrist in response, twisting with a pop. I yelled and kicked, trying my hardest to make contact with her disgustingly slender legs until Corrigan broke us both apart with a firm push.

"Louella," fog escaped between his teeth as he seethed. "Take the girl and *go*." He scooped up Abigail and dropped her to the arms of the tree.

"Just remember," Louella shifted to me again, dressed in the outfit I currently wore. "She may be absent in your life, but you won't go amiss in hers. I'll always be here to watch her."

In one fell swoop, Abigail was taken from me, again.

"EMMY!" Abigail wailed. Her cry caused the little orbs above to crawl into the cracks of the building and hide.

"NO! YOU CAN'T DO THIS."

Corrigan spun back, feet shifting apart to hold me firmly into place. I felt his fingers slide across my shoulders to my upper arms, trying to keep me rooted by a half hug. Cold lips pressed to the side of my temple as he squeezed lightly. "Calm yourself, do not let the King see you distressed."

Blind with tears, I struggled to pull away, watching through a blurry gaze as Abigail disappeared into the crowd. When she was no longer in sight, I slacked against him in defeat.

"You have a visitor, Emmaline, steer yourself. There are more surprises in store…"

"No, I can't," I muttered even as I allowed him to guide me back to the front of the table.

Not noticing where I was placed, I went to fall bedraggled to my seat and found my cushions shifting below me. Looking down two strong but slender hands pulled me further up the resting spot. My gaze ran up the arms to see my enemy staring back at me.

I was sitting on the Fae King's lap.

"**The deal…**" He replied softly, lacing his fingers together in front of me, daring me with his expression to struggle free.

"**Our sight for your sister,**" as if the deal hadn't already been evident.

While my cheeks were raw with crying, a mark of weakness to some, utter repulsion surged through me. I wanted nothing to do with this man. Cruel, calm, collected but utterly sweet and sticky, with a lace of arsenic in the blend, he was everything that was wrong in my life.

I hate him.

I hate the Fae King.

"And when I find your sight," there was no *ifs*. "You will assure me my family is given back with no physical, mental, or emotional scarring?"

"**That is up to you,**" was there disappointment in his voice. "**The longer you take and the more you stumble, the closer she becomes a part of this world, forever.**"

"James, he is a part of this, and Crowe, you give them back to me," I warned him.

"**Or, what?**" He was closer than needed, hovering over me with the shadows playing across his devastatingly handsome features.

Being this near, with his sweet, crisp breath exhaling across me, I could see hairline cracks running down across his temple. Any further away and I wouldn't have noticed the imperfections of his otherwise godly stature.

What was wrong with him? The more I followed the trail of veined fissures. I realized they spread throughout his brow and under his ghostly eyes.

FaeKing was breaking.

He must have realized I had seen. A hand rose up to cup the nape of my neck.

262

I suddenly tensed, eyeing him wearily.

"**Virgin Darling,**" he hummed, tilting his face to observe me closer. "**Yes… bring him in, Corrigan. Let us take a look at Emmaline's beloved family and see his worth.**"

The Pale Man watched the scene for a split moment with a slight hesitation, before he slipped away. When he returned his hand guided the arm of a hostile male, his rusty red hair covering his face as he turned away from us.

"James, was it?" FaeKing was smiling now, gesturing for him to sit into the chair on the right side of the King's seat.

Something was off. His build was right, the hair was spot on, but the clothes were all… wrong… his skin, too ashen.

I growled, knowing this must be a trick like Louella took part in.

"You can't fool me like my sister. If my friend was hurt—"

"**James,**" The Fae ignored me, too keen on driving the individual to speak for him. "**She's confused, why not tell her?**" The Fae in question shook its head distractedly. "**Are you afraid her compassion for you will be broken?**"

"This isn't funny!" I cried out, even when my body was beginning to shiver, having an uncontrollable chatter to my teeth. My eyes were growing wide again, unblinking. "W-where is J-James? Where is J-James!?"

"Em…" his voice trailed from the hunched-over creature. "It's me…"

"You aren't him," I stabbed at him. "James's my friend, my best friend. He'd never do this. NEVER."

Slowly sitting up straighter, dressed in the pale blue of the king, with brown fur and silver accents, the creature folded his arms over his chest protectively. He had eyes, black and

263

glittering like polished obsidian, with flesh, so pale green, it looked almost stone. Veins could be seen pulsing beneath his fragile skin. His appearance made him seem like some sort of inspired heartthrob off of a supernatural drama.

"**James,**" FaeKing hissed the presentation into my ear. Another quiver racked my form. He was the devil to my shoulder, speaking seedy lies into my ear.

"No, he can't be..."

The rusty-haired Fae offered me a slight twitch of a smile before looking to the King with begrudging betrayal on his face. All the tics and undertones of a James-like face were there.

Nostrils flaring, I took an intake of breath when the magnitude of the situation hit home. "No... nononono," wanting to hide, I could do nothing but cover my face with my hands.

Maybe if I shut them out, I would realize this was all just a dream.

"**Do you still wish to fight for his freedom?**" purred my captor. The steel that laced the veiled sweetness was far more chilling than any breath the Pale Man could muster.

"What's the point...?"

"**And your sister?**" The timbering roll of his lowered voice would make any girl tremble with giddiness. *Not me.* Now knowing he was the devil himself. "**We know life is burdensome. Your footings unsettled in the wake of your recent loss, you only have but to ask.**"

"Ask?" It was my turn to question. *Where was he going with this?*

My ears pricked inattention when I heard my own voice speaking softly back to me. *"No more worry about the future and what it entails. Leave her. Leave Abby with the Fae, no one would blame you for letting her go..."*

"Don't listen to that bullshit." James rose. "Let. Go. Corrigan!" He struggled to brush the ice Fae's frosted fingers from his shoulder, watching me in anger then. "I'll never forgive you, Emma. Don't you let Abby go! Don't let her go to HIM."

"Make the deal for your own freedom," FaeKing smiled down at me, despite the words of my traitorous friend.

I slapped him then. Not sure who was surprised, the Fae or myself, I pushed from his form in aggravation. The King seemed to have expected nothing less; his appearance lit with an elated satisfaction over my assault.

Stepping back with exasperation, he angered me more in every twitch of his chiseled appearance.

"You... listen here you son-of-a—" I stopped to adjust my jaw, rearranging my words. "I don't care how much my life goes to shit. It doesn't matter who tries to take her from me. I will ALWAYS find her, and I will NEVER give her up willingly to YOU."

"Very well," He cocked his head to the side, chuckling proudly. As if there was some underlined battle we had been fighting and he had somehow finished victoriously. **"If that is what you desire, Emmaline, then so it shall be."** He raised his hand, a parchment appearing with a familiar swirled cursive lettering of brownish red ink. **"Here are our documented bargains of trade. If you should complete held tasks, then we shall render your family free of any treaties**

265

previously made by your mother, Dawn Daphne Darling. If the failure of your task pursues, the fealty is ours as follows."

He handed over the document. I stared at it for any inconsistencies or tricks. Irritatingly it was a perfected document. Not a word out of place. Not a fault of smudge in sight.

"Emmali—" James's voice was cut off by a sheet of frost sealing his lips together.

We watched an unsteady mortal female slip down past the rows of seats, an engraved box clutched in her hand. She was beautiful. Even if her skin was reduced to a pallid russet and her eyes as vacant as all the other before her, I imagined her being native to somewhere warm like Hawaii or the Canary Islands. She had crimped dark locks, pulled back and decorated like a doll.

I was having a hard time looking at her as she set the box before the King, shrinking back tamely to sit on the balls of her feet.

Did she have a family still looking for her? Were they long since dead or were the memories erased of her existence? Then again, I couldn't imagine Fae caring enough about the relatives of the pixy-led victims they've collected.

Inside the wooden craft, FaeKing plucked instruments made of a foggy quartz crystal and laid them studiously before his self after servants took away his plate and utensils.

I piously studied the dish, dagger, quill, and the jar, wondering exactly his intentions.

"Hold out your hand Emmaline."

"Why?" Staring at the delicate objects suspiciously, the situation was more heightened with James fussing on the sidelines. The King gave me a look. Relenting I held out my hand in the intent to grasp something. Instead, he gently seized my index finger, puckering the skin, to quickly slice into the pad.

Yelping in surprise, I drew back, more irritated at the fact that I hadn't realized his objective sooner. Further creatures and monsters left the large pavilion while others turned their noses in disgust. Few stared in rapt fascination.

I closed my eyes tightly as the other kept my hand rooted firmly into his, milking the crimson liquid into the offered bowl. When the pressure released, a cooling sensation wrapped about the fresh wound. I recoiled, finding a sticky sap coating my fingertip.

"**It is to close the wound.**" He said sensibly, plucking a leaf from his antlers. "**If you wish to keep the wound clean, press this to the poultice.**"

Snatching at it, I pressed it along the curve of my digit, watching it adhere smoothly to my skin. I didn't want to know where the 'poultice' came from. There was an angry mark on the Fae King's wrist that was quickly healing.

Even if the King had an issue with my blood in the bowl or the steel around my neck, he made no expression of discomfort. He merely plucked up the glass quill, offering it to me obligingly.

"What am I supposed to be doing here?" I knew very well what was going on, not that I wanted to really believe it.

"**This is a blood bonding treaty.**"

Taking it slowly, I dipped the writing utensil carefully into the dish, raising it, the red liquid twisted down along the spiraled point, waiting, plump and beading, at the sharp tip.

I signed slowly and carefully, knowing my efforts would never be as elegant as the rest of the document. *Was I trying to impress him?* I wasn't sure, but I needed to get out of here before anything else was dealt into his hands.

"We are going to leave now."

"**We?**" It was his turn to parrot my words. The ancient immortal passed the parchment off to his icy butler, turning to face me with a curious look.

I gave him a blanched expression. The riddles were growing tiring.

"Abigail, Crowe," I had to rethink who was in my band of brothers. *James was no longer one of us, he never was...* "I came with the intention of bringing my sister home. That is what I intend to do. We made a deal, FK, my sister for your sight."

"**Whoever said you were allowed to take her home? No, no. We still need leverage, Emmaline. Who isn't to say you'll trick us as your mother had?**"

"I have a family looking after a dangerous creature! Crowe is half dead because of you. Do you realize what will happen if this continues? I'll be blamed for all of this and be thrown into prison for kidnap and murder. Then where will your sight lye?"

"Hmmm," he didn't seem impressed. "**We will spare you some difficulties and take care of a few loose ends.**"

"How will you—"

"**Do not ask if you are not prepared to hear the answer.**"

268

"How do I know you will keep up your end of the bargain?"

"**One for one… Yes that does seem fair. You may keep the gentleman that was brought in by the surviving Peekaboo,**" he added casually. "**Your companion may return with you if he wishes. His pilgrimage has not yet ended with you.**"

My gaze turned to James, now standing on his own. His lips were still sealed, but his eyes were giving me all the begging I could take. He moved to speak to me, growing frustrated by the spell sealing his lips shut. Turning to Corrigan, he grabbed him by the perfectly groomed smock and shook him.

"**Let him speak,**" the King drawled, rising.

If Corrigan thought that was unwise, he wasn't showing it. Unbinding the young man's lips the frost Fae watched the King dutifully.

Rising from the table, FaeKing passed the younger man. Nearly a foot taller indifference, he paused to turn his regal head and glance sparingly to him.

"**I expect you to return home soon.**" He spoke briefly, offering James a sardonic grin before he called to the escort of the wooden box.

She stepped up to the King's seat agreeably, taking careful measure in placing the tools back in their holding.

"Emma. Don't watch her," James spoke— too late— the girl dipped her face into the bowl, licking it eagerly clean of its contents.

My blood had shown brightly in the fire glow as it drizzled down her chin. She was able to set the bowl down, just as she crumpled cleanly to the floor, her heart stopping. Knowing it had to have been the iron in my blood, I walked away quickly.

Inadvertently, I had killed the girl.

CHAPTER 13

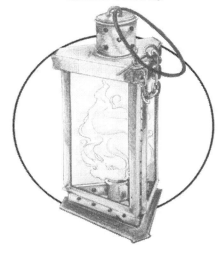

MONDAY MORNING—PART 1

Kneeling beside the officer, I shook him until he drew in a sharp gasp, glancing up with foggy recognition. I took the time to guide the man to his feet, trying to keep him from embarrassing himself, quietly steering him toward the exit.

There, Corrigan stood to wait.

"A butler, an imp, and a cop, yet none of you can do anything," I stated blandly, regarding the ice Fae with discontentment.

He took in my words with no physical reaction. "The imp wishes to know the traveling arrangements," He gestured across the way, where James stayed awkwardly, his hands in his pockets.

"He can go screw himself," I lugged the officer out into the night.

Another day was almost done, and *Failure* stung my forehead. Our journey felt futile. I did not gain my sisters freedom back, only another task to add to my list, another knife in my back to keep me suspicious.

I trailed after Corrigan, to the tent I had dressed in, where I insisted he returned my clothes. *I wouldn't be leaving in Fae servant garb.*

"Your things were tattered and soiled, Miss Darling. There is a high chance that they were thrown into the fire."

"Then take that magical Popsicle stick lodged up your arrogant ass, wave it around, and give me some of my own clothes." I gave my best, '*this wasn't a discussion,*' tone. Most of the fear I had for the man had all but dissolved.

I sat Crowe to a chair, turning my back to the ice Fae completely. Positioning him near the washbasin, I stripped him of his soiled shirt, and began wiping down his face. I imagined him as an oversized toddler, a messy one at that, rubbing firmly across the incrusted bile drying near his earlobe. I reminded myself I had dealt with worse.

Abigail had the worst colic when she was an infant. No matter what concoction mom made for her to drink or rub on her gums, the girl had the constant upset stomach. Colic turned to horrid teething problems, then on into terrible twos. The girl was a handful.

"Thank you."

"What?" I blinked, inspecting the officer closely.

He watched me with leaden grey eyes. "Thank you... for saving my life."

272

Sighing, I tossed the rag into the bowl, kneeling beside him and staring wearily. "Yeah… of course," I rested my elbow to my knee, rubbing at my eyes. "But you need to pull yourself together, we can't fall apart. Not yet. I'm going to get my sister back from them, but until then, I need to know any information you have, okay? We need to keep our story straight." I peeked at him again. "Do you understand? This is bigger than all of us."

He nodded, looking older than before.

I needed to caution myself. Crowe had gone through his own turmoil. He had been drug through the mud, stamped on, and then left ragged. He would require time to digest what had happened… but I couldn't afford to stand back and let him too long.

"Good…" I took the offered clothes Corrigan had appeared with. Our old outfits were washed and pressed, but there was no steel given back. While Crowe had permanently lost his gun, we were each given the additional warmth of a wool poncho. I kept the leather boots on, begrudgingly accepting that my shoes were beyond salvation.

"And these," The ice warden added, holding out two triangular brass lanterns. One held a brightly burning candle while the other kept a lazy honey-colored orb, with a trailing green tail. "The Wisp will show you to your carriage, should you give it direction."

"Does the beetle even work still?" I glanced over to the officer who was shifting nervously.

"I ran it into a tree, but I think it's okay…"

I steadied myself for the trek back into the park, knowing we would walk further if the car couldn't start.

Corrigan led us toward the entrance of the campground, by then, most Fae had gathered up by the large bonfire, making it all but vacant in the outskirt areas.

James was standing in his human form, waiting nervously with his hands to his back pockets. His clothes had gone through the same dry-cleaning process, only his hoodie had a few tares that needed mending. When he saw us, his initial reaction was to flash his infamously dazzling smile.

I must have forgotten to conceal my expression. His mood had sobered quickly into a melancholy nod of agreement. In any normal circumstance, my friend's presence would have been a relief, but now I was too bothered by that gaping wound festering between my shoulders.

"Miss Darling," Corrigan stood before the three of us, looking disinterested but obliged to stay and instruct. "You must keep in mind that the Wisp will only bond to one individual. You must whisper your name into its ear, and it will lead you to your desired location; however, never let the Wisp go," He warned. "If you do, the freed Wisp will lead you astray. Keep the Wisp close, keep the latch closed, and it will be your greatest compass."

"Thanks," I muttered at the ominous instructions. *Did we even need the Wisp?*

Giving James a look, he shrugged his shoulders.

"They switch the camp around. I wouldn't know how to get back."

"Nice…" I replied sarcastically, watching the three men. "Shall we?" I took the Wisp naturally, accepting this was my cross to bear. Staring at the small entity, I sucked in a steadying breath before tilting close to whisper my name, *"Emmaline NovaLee Darling."*

The orb seemed to expand in response, bouncing about in its cage like a hyperactive child on sugar before resolving into an even pace of an up and down pattern.

It hushed, *"This way…"* with a sigh hanging to the edge of its sentence.

Without looking back, I walked out of the boundaries of the Faery Troop. The world swallowed up the sounds and lights behind me, placing me in a dark and cold stretch of old-growth trees. It was as if the camp never existed. Only the sound was of an owl hooting distantly in the background and the light of the Wisp casting a low ebbing light before me.

"This way…" the Wisp hummed.

Then a warped popping arose, Crowe appeared beside me, expanding the light source to a good 10-feet in front of us. James soon followed, pulling out two phones and handing mine over.

"Thought you might want this back," he settled it into my free hand.

"I forgot about it." Staring at the screen, I wondered if the GPS would have saved me the dangers of the Wisp.

"We are out of range," James replied, knowing what I must have been rolling around in my mind. "That, and magic has a funny way of messing with technology."

"Good to know, would have been helpful a few days ago."

He didn't reply.

"This way," the little voice repeated patiently.

Marching onward was our only option. The sooner we started, the better chance of getting back to the car before a ranger noticed the suspicious white vehicle.

Abigail was hovering in my forethoughts, a self-shaming ritual of obsessively replaying the scene in my mind. Re-afflicting the damages I had already received. The process was draining and miserable, but it kept me walking, thinking through the drudgery of the hours walk from the Faery dwelling to a marked trail where we followed it back to the parking lot.

By then the sky was a navy blue, laden with angry strings of clouds that hid the waning moon from our view.

Crowe was struggling, feet dragging, making him stumble frequently. James was indulgent enough, taking him firmly about the waist to guide him across the pavement behind my guiding lights.

The Wisp itself was refreshingly quiet, speaking only when we were going off its directed path. When the car drew near, its tail melded into its body, tinging the yellow with sickly green hews.

Humming, it glowed like a signaling beacon. Taking us along the road, and on out of the carpark, we walked a good 50 yards down before the Wisp instigated quiet remarks of location.

"There, there, there…"

"Where?" I lifted the lantern, trying to view our location.

"The crying cedar," It whirred.

"Oh, that's sad," James frowned.

"I'm sorry," Crowe repeated. "Those things... they kept jumping, I couldn't see." He was getting worked up, his frame shrinking in the stress of remembering.

"It's alright Crowe."

"Call me John," he muttered, "where are the bodies?" He pulled from the redhead, stumbling down the slight incline. "I hit at least five. They dropped around here..."

He shuffled around until he found his bearings, taking us to a dirt mound where a colossal cedar stood. There, the Volkswagen sat perched halfway up the roots of the tree, where its bumper could be seen lodged into its flesh. If it weren't for the cedar, the beetle would have rolled right off into the river.

No Fae bodies were in sight, just the tracks of where the car had veered off course, and a few disturbed patches of dirt. James took it upon himself to slip into the car, trying the keys that were still in the ignition.

"You are lucky you aren't dead," I told Crowe, watching the man fidget as James tried turning the engine. It sputtered, dying a few times before the lights flickered into existence. The engine roared to life with a tap of the pedal.

"I wish I was." He said miserably, moving away to go help dislodge the car from the tree.

There was a long, uncertain pause in our journey.

I settled uselessly to the side, watching the two men figure out how to extract the car from the tree. The imp had the officer climb into the car, place it into gear and rev the engine. When that wasn't enough, he then tried situating himself in-between the tree and machine. Pressing his back to the trunk, he pushed hard against the hood of the car.

Burning rubber screeched. Dirt flew as the earth was upturned below them. The sickening tear of metal sounded, and then the car rolled quickly backward and away from its front bumper. Crowe slammed on the breaks before it hit another tree.

I watched James fall down, yelping as the sudden release dropped him onto the machine's lost appendage. Slipping down, I ran over to him. "James, did you break anything? Don't move."

He groaned, shifting, trying to stand. "Metal on my back, fuck, that smarts." He straightened, lifting his shirt to show a red mark streaking down his right side. His skin wasn't broken or bleeding. He would have a rug burn, but he would be okay.

I gave it a smart smack, rubbing my hand against it. "Looks like you'll survive."

Squealing, he glowered before I rivaled him with my own. "Right… thanks."

Yeah, that was mean.

That was a mean thing to do, but it was satisfying.

We pushed the bedraggled car back onto the road. Blowing out the candle and settling the lanterns inside, we piled into the car driving slowly to see how much the vehicle could take. Like the champ that it was, the white Volkswagen beetle made its way all the way back onto the highway.

I gripped the wheel, giving it kind words of encouragement. We took the trip at a solid forty-miles-an-hour, in a zone of sixty. The caution took us longer to get home, but we were in one piece. Two and a half hours later I pulled out my orbs lantern and tossed the door closed. We were home.

In a series of forgetful moments, I somehow found myself inside my room with a lovely bottle of coconut rum. By the time I had fallen asleep; one arm was securely wrapped about my mother's locked journal, with my face pressed against my new alcoholic lover.

The alarm clock squawked deafly in the background as I lay in bed, trying to form thoughts. Sun streamed through the plated sections of my multicolored window, dust particles shimmering lazily through the air. From the dresser came a soft tapping of glass.

"Who's there?" I managed, picking up the twitter of incoherent talking. I listened acutely, but the noise had since settled. Chalking it up to mice in the walls, I rolled over intending to fall asleep again.

More pattering sounded.

Pulling my body up finally, I found my footing to glance around.

On top of the bureau, amongst various hairpins and clips, laid the brass lantern from the night before—toppled to a glass side. I was amazed the entity hadn't gotten out.

Small and lazy, the Wisp tapped against the glass in greeting. "*Morning…*"

"Good morning… do you have a name?"

"*Forgotten…*"

"Oh… that's too bad." I rubbed at my swollen lower lids, trying to brush away the eye goo. "What exactly are you?"

"*Lost*" it murmured, trailing after its green tail.

"Oh, is that because you're far away from the camp?" I felt a tinge of responsibility.

"No home."

"So you aren't missing your little Wisp family? You don't have little Wisplets needing to be fed?"

"Alone."

This was probably the singularly most depressing conversation I've had with another individual.

"Right, uhm… Well, I'm going to go take a shower… are you fine where you are?"

"Anywhere, nowhere…"

"Okay…" I replied slowly, quickly gathering clothes. Shuffling toward the bathroom, feeling disturbed, I hung my locket to a hook on the back of the door and hopped into the shower.

I remained motionless beneath the showerhead, wondering what I was trying to accomplish. The water wasn't washing away any of the previous emotional upheavals. Watching my fingers wrinkle was only prolonging the apprehension of taking on the next feat of the day—facing my so-called best friend, but anxiety was enough to keep me rooted until the water ran cold.

Out of everything had happened the one thing consistent in my life was James. *What was I going to do now?*

Sighing, I stepped out into the fresh air. Wrapping myself into a soft oversized towel, I dragged back to the room, feeling displaced. So I sat, checking my almost-dead phone. There were several messages since the last time I checked. They must have happened while I was in the rainforest, dealing with pesky Fae. Unsettled, I listened to the voicemails wondering who was trying to contact me.

Gram's voice suddenly jarred my attention, sharp and berating. *'Emmaline, why aren't you calling me back? Do you know how worried your grandfather and I are—?'* I didn't hesitate to delete the message before the rant could go on, realizing the next several were a slew of awkward family messages, all stacked up on top of each other.

AUNT DYNA: Em, any time you want to talk, you're more than welcome.

AUNT DYNA: Emmaline, contact Gram. She's really worried.

MARTHA: Emmaline, why aren't you home? We wanted to come to see Abigail.

DILLAN: Emma. Gram is going nuts. Call her.

AUNT DOT: Emmaline, why aren't you picking up the phone?

MAY: Emma, call the grandparents already. Grandma's about ready to break down your door!

DILLAN: Em, the grandparents are planning on fighting for custody.

DILLAN: I thought you should know...

They all screamed for my attention, making me restless. It had been several days since I notified the police of Abigail's disappearance, when Gram showed up at my door with the Thing, discrediting my claims, the gossip must have spread to the rest of the family.

Honestly, I thought they would have been calling sooner.

'That boy called—' I paused in my slew of canceling voicemails, *'That Beasley boy, he said you are doing fine, and that*

281

you are thankful for the time spent to sort things out while Abigail is with us.'

What was she talking about?

'… While you may be as self-seeking as you please, Abigail has no place in it. She is a child, needing a proper upbringing…' I felt myself slowly checking out while her voice droned on. '… I wanted to discuss this in person, but since I can't seem to reach you, I'll say it now. We aren't planning on just keeping her for a few days…' I was trembling, trying to pull my thoughts together. 'You'll need to steer yourself, realize that we've raised several children and have decided we are her best option. In the meantime, she'll need a few items while we figure out paperwork…'

James called her?

Who gave him the right?

'… We've contacted the attorney in charge of your mother's assets. You must tell them you'll comply with handing over guardianship. If you could write these things down: Change of clothes, a list of dietary restrictions. I'll be pulling her out of daycare. She doesn't need to be babysat by strangers.' Unable to stomach her voice any further, I erased the message from my phone. I knew the act wouldn't solve my problems, but it was satisfying.

Fumbling for the charger, I paused. The phone was blinking incessantly up at me still.

"Monday Madness," mumbling, I peeked into my text messages. Pulling up Eugene's contact, I realized he had sent me a post at 10:23 AM two days ago, and again at 7:15 AM this morning. His voice seemed tentative, asking if Abigail and I were doing okay, before bridging into the next text to inquire if I had seen Heather. She hadn't shown up here for her evening shift yesterday.

I knew where this was leading.

Eugene continued to explain Sunshine was in the middle of training the new girl, and he himself had his monthly foraging class that Monday. He backtracked, saying he could cancel, but two people were coming out from Seattle. If I could, he wanted me to call him. Rachel was on back dial, but she was already working at Oak Boutique today.

Flopping backward, I stared over to the lazy Wisp who continued to circle its tail.

What was a person supposed to do after a week like I've had?

Curl up and rot?

I dialed Eugene. Perhaps a dose of normality was what I needed. "Hey Eugene," I put as much chipper into my voice as possible.

"Emma! How are you?"

"I'm fine, I'm really sorry I didn't get back to you sooner. I'll come in as soon as I pull myself together. When is the class?"

"The class starts at ten, but I need to head out around nine-thirty. Thank you, Emma, we appreciate it."

"I'll see you soon, okay?"

"Yeah, thank you, tell Sunshine I'll be right in."

I could hear his soft short chuckle through the phone. "I'll tell the boss," he responded kindly.

This was a good thing, distraction, and avoidance. Hanging up I threw on some black leggings and an oversized t-shirt. With my footwear, I wanted nothing better than to raid my mom's closet for something, anything, but there was a high possibility I would walk in on James, and that would not happen.

I stared resentfully to the Faeling boots. "Just so you understand I'm not wearing these because I like them," I shot to the uninterested Wisp. Pulling on the begrudgingly comfortable footwear, I witnessed the accented leaves magically shift to match my outfit with uncanny precision. Inspired, I put a bit of makeup on and drew my hair into a sloppy bun.

'Fake it 'til you make it,' was the mantra of the day.

Sneaking down the steps for my habitual pot of morning coffee, I stumbled on the sight of Crowe passed out on the living room couch. *Didn't the man have a family to get home to? Didn't he have friends or co-workers wondering what had happened to him?*

I wasn't sure why I was so surprised. The man had a raging storm of questions, concerns, and reports to stamp out. Perhaps he wasn't ready to face his own dilemmas yet, but if he were still here by the time I got home, I'd have to confront him.

Frowning, I snugged on a coat and headed out toward my shamefully battered beetle. The car was scruffy, but it otherwise had made it to work.

When I arrived at the door, they greeted me with smiles and warm welcomes. There was a physical sigh of relief being able to meld into a familiar routine. Even with the odd shimmering of particular customers, the abnormality was feeling natural at Easy Street. I could handle this new layer of life because I felt control here.

I could look those magical individuals in the eyes, smile, take their orders, and make them their organic coffees without letting on that I knew. When I took my break, I was even confident enough to grab lunch from the pizza place across the street, going as far as strolling down to enjoy the ocean air at Hollywood Beach. While I didn't linger, there was enough to reassure myself that I could cope with this knowing and still function.

Upon returning, I left my pizza crust to the bottom steps of the basement, hoping my little friend was okay. I needed to follow my gut more. Something was wrong with Heather, and it worried me it somehow tied her strange behavior to my circumstance. All I could do was hope I had been wrong.

"Nice lunch?" Laura looked up from her biscotti to give a charming smile. She was cute. Dishwater blonde hair cut to a long bob. She wore black-rimmed glasses, styled fashionably with her vintage long-sleeved sweater and floral dress. It shocked me she could bust tables so quickly in the heeled penny loafers she wore.

"Yeah."

"Hmm," she snacked happily, peering closely at me over the rim of her glasses. "So, not to intrude but a handsome ginger came by. He said he wanted to talk to you. He was really serious." She gave a lopsided smile. "He wanted you to call him as soon as you had a moment."

James never came to my work. This was quite the desperate act to get my attention.

"Thanks."

"Is he your boyfriend?" she smiled. "Must have had a fight? He was really worried about you."

"Don't worry," I waved my hand slightly, knowing the girl was just trying to get to know me. *She couldn't possibly be trying to pick him up, right?* "Just squabbling..."

"James is Darling's friend," Sunshine interjected, smiling from her roost near the kitchen door on the counter. Laura smiled more in response, nodding from Eugene's stool.

Yes, that was something rational to say, an ordinary answer for someone to understand and let be without too much of a concern.

I tucked my coat away and trailed around, readjusting tables or wiping down the door. The workflow was based primarily on the lunch rush of downtown PA. By the time 1:00 PM rolled around, the occurrence of customers was at an ebb, giving me time to check my phone.

Staring at the texts and missed calls from James, I made a closed throat noise. The other was finished subjecting himself to loneliness, his own version of purgatory, which meant he would then be confrontational. I didn't want to leave the *Easy Street* now; I wasn't finished revering in my blind sense of security. Gently urging Sunshine to leave early, that Laura and I could close the coffee house by ourselves, I took the extra hours to prepare myself for my personal life.

When I went home, the house was lit downstairs—the chimney trailing smoke. James's pickup truck stood in the driveway. While my game face was on, my emotions were still uncertain. I needed to work on finding FaeKing's sight, and James's fussing wasn't the key to that happening.

Sulking, I walked up to the door, unlocking it slowly to make a gentle entrance.

That didn't happen.

"I've been trying to get ahold of you all day. I went to your work to look for you. Did the chick there tell you I was trying to see you? I asked her to have you call me back when you got the chance. Why didn't you call me back? Didn't you get any of my messages? Why the fuck didn't you answer? I thought something horrible happened. I thought you might have—"

"Have?" I interjected, tired suddenly. "Have, what? Have I done something drastic because my life is a complete shit storm? Or maybe I went a little crazy because one by one I find myself surrounded by liars and traitors with extraordinary capabilities beyond anything I could have ever previously imagined," I sucked in a deep breath, feeling it turn to stones in the pit of my stomach.

"You hate me, don't you?" He stood with his hands in his pockets, devastation evident on his face.

I gave him a sour look. "After all the shit that's fallen out of your mouth the past few days, and you say something so selfish? News flash, I have bigger things to worry about then to fry your ass with an iron skillet."

"I didn't lie," He said feebly.

"Did you have to? Withholding information is JUST as bad. Steering me from the truth is worse."

"I... you're right." He curled his hands into fists but nodded slowly. "You're right. I was deceptive."

"I don't want to hear it," I stressed, pulling off my coat and tossing it onto the coat tree.

"You need to hear it."

"You want me to even consider the thought of forgiving you? Then save it for when I'm done taking down your King

287

and ridding my family of this stupid mess. This, for once, is on my terms. Got it?"

James sighed and slumped to the couch arm, resigned. I knew I had won, but he still looked up pleadingly. "There's other stuff we need to talk about."

"Grandma called if that's what you're talking about."

"She did…"

"Yeah, apparently you took it upon yourself to tell her I'm relieved she took Abby. Why the hell did you say that to her?"

"I didn't…" he frowned, opening his mouth to say something more when a familiar voice cleared their throat.

Crowe leaned against the kitchen entrance, a mug in his hands. His hair was disheveled, clothes wrinkled from sleeping in them.

"Hey, John," I got out slowly, finding it strange being on a first name basis with the policeman. "Sleep okay?"

"If you could call it that," he murmured.

"We need to come up with a story before anyone else leaves this house." The redhead stated frankly.

"Let's get a notepad… and coffee." I had a feeling this would be a rough night.

"How much did you have at work?" James followed behind me slowly. The policeman had reverted back inside the bowels of the kitchen, settling to the corner chair of the table.

"Not enough, apparently…"

James frowned, moving to perch himself on his usual post, an arm propped to the back of his seat with his chin resting attentively.

Taking a notepad from the fridge door, I tossed it rather abruptly across the tabletop. The cop sat staring with eyebrows furling in deep consideration. He grimaced like he had just eaten something gross. Was he going to bail?

"You agreed." I prompted.

"Just give me a moment." He leaned against the table with his elbows, rubbing his face with callused hands. Stubble was turning to a beard, a far cry from his carefully groomed appearance just a few days back. "What exactly are you expecting me to do?" He gazed up at me, signifying with his hands. "This is my job. I don't distort the truth. It'll break everything I stand for.

"You mean that high pedestal they have put you on?" James leaned in, watching him with a tap of his finger to the notepad. "Your title, that persuasion you've maintained all these years? You are telling me you've had no idea, not even a hint, of what has been going on in this town?"

"What do you want me to say? That I knew all along demons riddled the town and I did nothing about it?" Crowe shook his head. "I've been on the force, half my life. I've witnessed unspeakable acts of human cruelty... but never... this," he trailed off. "No. Life isn't a fairy tale. None of this makes sense."

"Then you're blind," the other muttered. "Did you forget what happened to you in the forest?"

Crowe suddenly stood. "Never," he barked. "I was chased, run down, tossed through the trees like a rag. I was drugged, influenced, violated, left in my filth while they just laughed and laughed... for what?" He grabbed at the back of a chair, leaning in with a wild look in his eyes. "What was the point in it all?"

"Then you need to do yourself a favor and get smart. Cover your tracks. You never saw Emma. She isn't a part of the equation," James regarded the older man. "Make this go away… or they might make you go away."

"And you?" John gestured bluntly to the redhead. "Where do you stand in all this? If I'm monster chow, what does that make you? You're one of them, why are you even here?"

"Why I'm here isn't important. Taking sides might get me screwed over." James shrugged his shoulders, "but I'm not the one who's spare parts."

Crowe looked clammy, shaky even. He dropped back into his seat, picking up his cup absentmindedly.

"Oh, it's important." I shot at him.

"Em," He stressed. "Do we have to talk about it now?"

"I dunno, do we?" I looked to John Crowe, cocking my head to the side. The man looked toward James wearily.

"There's more," James tried shifting the conversation, grabbing and releasing the notepad on impulse.

"More?" My brain was still trying to wrap around the idea that Fae had a stronghold in Port Angeles politics.

Didn't Odhrun say this was a Kingdom-less area?

"Your grandparents want us to bring the imp clothes." He paused when I disappeared into the pantry, pulling out potatoes to deposit them into the empty side of the sink. They were sprouting. I took out a paring knife, slowly shaving off the greens. I needed a distraction. "Emma," he called for my attention. "Changelings can be dangerous if left unchecked."

"… and?" I didn't feel particularly obliged to help my grandparents.

"Emma. The King didn't just give them a block of wood, or some other inanimate object. He could have, but he didn't. He gave them an Unseelie child posing as a human. Do you get that?" I heard the frown in his voice. "It's chaotic and manipulative."

"Unseelie?" I peered over my shoulder. "People keep using that word. What exactly does it mean?" When there was no reply, I shifted taking in the uncomfortable display of two grown men staring absentmindedly away from each other. "Well?" I demanded.

"That's a sticky subject," James took up fiddling with the pad of paper again. "Hard to explain without getting more questions. Unseelie are arguably the darker alignment of the Fae… but there is a grey scale. Majority enjoys bathing in baby's blood."

"What?"

"Okay, the last part was a little dramatic. Then again, I wouldn't put it passed a few. Look, the changeling is dangerous and prone to throw tantrums. Duende aren't the easiest to work with, but the upside is that they do eventually forget."

"I'm not going to let it get comfortable."

"Right…" he muttered. "So if you really want to do that… we'll need a plan. Abby wasn't just snatched up by just any Fae. The action was calculated and filled with loopholes." James gestured toward the living room. "I may have destroyed the poppet that the Duende had been feeding on, but that apparently hasn't severed the bond…"

291

"So what do we do?"

"The real question is obvious," Crowe spoke up behind steepled hands. "You're looking at a situation where your family has been duped into believing life is normal. Do you really want to bring them into this world?" His eyes were growing sullen. "If I could just get back to my old life, forget... somehow. Not that before was especially happy." He shook his head as if he were trying to shake out memories he didn't particularly want.

"Yeah... I get it." I mundanely placed the potato wedges onto a sheet, popping them into the oven before it had time to preheat. Turning back around, I leaned against the handle of the door, gripping it from behind. "But would you really?" I muttered. "You're a cop, don't you have unsolved mysteries?" I gestured toward the window. "There's probably your answer. *Fae.*"

"Just be grateful." The younger male shrugged toward Crowe. "Grateful that he let you go with your mind intact." There was a twinge of bitterness in James's own voice. I wondered vaguely what his deal was.

"Be grateful?" Crowe twisted in his seat, rising, looking like James had grown three heads. "You know, we're in line with those crack jobs on the History Channel, raving about aliens that abducted them from cornfields. I used to watch it for laughs..." he sank into his seat, staring at a spot in the room.

That would have been amusing if he weren't so devastated.

"He could have easily denied you passage home, but he didn't Crowe." James sighed. "I'm not defending him. I'm

292

just saying that this is what they do. This is what HE does. Distractions don't make his game as fun."

"So the Changeling was a leg up?"

"Yeah, why not? He made the gesture because he's an arrogant jerk. He thinks he can give you all the help you need and STILL you won't be able to win."

"I thought the idea was for me to bring him his sight back?"

"Don't you think he can already make you do that? You should have made a deal for your own sake. Get your own life back." He sighed.

I clenched my fist a moment. "It's his loss for underestimating me..." Rolling my shoulders, I tried to relieve some tension before opening the fridge. I peered inside to find something edible enough to pair with potatoes.

Pulling out an egg I shook it curiously to my ear, still good. I moved to make scrambled eggs, but James sidled up and beat me to the pan.

"Sit down... please. Let me finish."

"I'm not as useless as everyone thinks I am."

"You know I don't think you're useless."

"Stop lying, James. It isn't working anymore." Drawing away from him quickly, I pulled a chair haphazardly back and sat down myself.

Well, apparently I was still agitated.

He settled a mug of coffee in front of me, holding up his hands in peace. "If you won't listen maybe your P. Whimsy will have ideas about how to send a Changeling screaming back through the veil." James moved around the table. Taking up the eggs, he took his time cracking each one.

That wasn't a bad idea. Dragging up my legs I rested in a comfortable position, slouching over to take a peek at my screen.

'WHAT IS A CHANGELING?

The belief of Changelings is older than that of written language and laced throughout every culture. Many theories shroud their significance, yet one is certain. If your loved one is fancied, a Changeling will replace them.

For those with children, it's speculated that they leave behind an unsatisfied imp so that a mortal mother may nurse them to health. Other accounts state they may leave behind a sickly old Fae intending to wither and pass.

Wood Stock, shaped to your beloved's likeness, may be a substitute. They eventually fade away into nothingness where the grieving family then buries it.

In this age of iron, Fae are dwindling further into extinction. Desperation to replenish their brood is a primary driver for the higher levels of Changeling activity in today's society. If you are worried your loved one has been swapped, here are ways to...

IDENTIFY A CHANGELING:
-Mood swings
-Abnormal sleeping patterns
-Constant hunger
-Eyes: *Bulging, Dark, Sullen*
-Skin: *Thin, papery, and wrinkled*
-A frame that doesn't fit its skin
-Abnormally long fingers and toes
-Wanderlust
*NOTE: Changelings are known to try and return to their origins of birth, leaving you childless.'

FAERY PROTECTION:

NOTE: See my blog entry about 'Faery Protection.'

If your gut tells you that you are dealing with a Changeling. Here are tried and true ways of dealing with Fae abduction.

TO EXPEL A CHANGELING:

WARNING: These are all HIGHLY DANGEROUS acts of banishing a Changeling. These are NOT for the faint of heart.

1. Iron to the skin
2. Prick the child's finger with an iron needle
3. Feeding the child fresh iron-rich blood at midnight
4. Bathing them in a solution of foxglove or Mandrake
5. Starving the Faery away
6. Smoking the Faery out
7. Tossing the child toward the fireplace

If there is no doubt in your mind you are dealing with a Changeling, these methods should not worry you. Fae are not our friends.

Best Wishes,
P. Whimsy'

I felt my lips turn down. This was not good.

"You don't look happy." The older gentleman commented, settling a pen to the table. He had been working on something on the notepad. "That bad?"

"That bad," I exhaled. "I can't do any of this. It's cruel," I passed my phone off to the officer.

His eyes darted back and forth, quickly reading each line. "I don't see how any of this differs from what I received back in the woods."

"There has to be a line drawn somewhere. I will not fight like them." Rubbing my eyelids I took back my phone, staring for a long moment until an idea came. "Raewyn, I want her number." Twisting my body, I stared expectantly to James.

"Raewyn?" John Crowe questioned.

"The Witch," we both replied.

Wiggling my fingers expectantly, palm up, the redhead tossed his phone. Catching it, I scrolled through his contacts realizing the list was vastly unmarked. The only numbers with any familiarity were moms, the grandparents, and my own.

I took a moment to stare at the picture of mom's face.

James had her logged as 'MOM.'

"Can't you find it? It's under—"

"Hottie? Or is she Hottie 2?"

"She's actually under RH." James licked his lips.

"The Devil is a nice touch for Gram."

Crow interjected, "I need to go home."

"I'm sure James can take you there," I sent her number to my phone. "I'll make up the couch when you get back."

"I don't plan on coming back, Emmaline." His voice held a reminiscence of his self-assurance, making me waver. Having him part ways would lift a complication in the process of retrieving FK's sight, but I wasn't sure the other was emotionally stable enough to be on his own.

"Do you have someone you should get home to right now? Anyone you could be with?"

"Yes," He shifted his gaze toward James. "And I'll need to take the car back to the station."

"You're lying." James pulled the eggs off the burner. "Not once have you mentioned a wife or kids. You've been gone for days."

The other looked agitated by the statement. "I'm an officer of the law, I know my rights. You cannot keep me in this house against my will."

"Woah, jeez," James threw up his hands. "Sorry if the truth hurts."

I audibly groaned. "We will not force you to stay. This is all on your terms. I'm just... I'm offering a place to stay where people understand what's going on with you." I peered at the gentleman, "I don't like this any more than you do. I didn't ask for any of this to happen, it just happened. But I get it. If running far away from this situation will help you, then I applaud your efforts. I'm pretty jealous, really."

Both men crossed gazes for a moment before the officer rose. He paused, hesitant before giving my shoulder a tentative pat. "Just, keep this away from innocent bystanders, Emmaline. The world may be cruel, but it isn't ready for monsters."

"I have no control over what the Fae do," I grimaced. *That escalated quickly.*

I wasn't a troublemaker. I wasn't.

The trouble came knocking on my door.

I didn't seek it out.

"Either way, keep it out of town."

"Don't worry. Peekaboo won't be swinging from the buildings." I promised, earning a flinch.

We told him. We warned him and yet he drove off into the night by himself. My car was in worse shape because of his actions. That affected me.

"… Good." He walked out of the kitchen then.

James sighed to the right of me, watching. "I'll go follow him home. Make sure he's fine, give you some space. Please, don't go anywhere while I'm gone?" he waited a moment for a response but silence evaded the space between us. His quiet steps were only noticed by the squeaking floorboards as he slipped away.

I released the breath I'd been holding.

CHAPTER 14

MONDAY MORNING—PART 2

Soft unrecognizable words carried from the hallway before the door opened and closed behind them. Rubbing at my face, I listened for the two cars starting before my shoulders relaxed. I tried to stay focused and shot Raewyn a concise text.

ME: Raewyn, this is Emma. Do you have any advice for removing Changelings and/or keeping it... tame?

I wasn't expecting a prompt response

"Alone," I said aloud, glancing to the scribbles on Crowe's notepad. The only thing he left behind was a rough doodle of large black swirled eyes, with sharp crude teeth to match. They reminded me of my mother's drawings.

'Secrets inked with blood and tears, marking pages filled with fears.' I reminisced on Corrigan's riddle.

Looking to the ceiling, chills trailed along my arms, as I rose to make my way to the stairway.

'Bound uptight, then tucked away... hidden safely from the Fae.'

I slowly made my way up to my room, checking carefully on the Wisp. They had settled themselves into the candleholder of the lantern. With its tail pointed up and swaying, they resembled a lovely ambient flame from afar. *I was almost fooled.* They made a tinkling sigh, peeking one eye in my direction.

"Sleeping?" I asked tentatively. Not sure how to converse with the depressed little being. I leaned in, casually picking up my mom's journal.

"Waiting..."

"Would you like to come downstairs?" I offered.

"Fine, here..."

I shook my head, walking over to settle its home to the windowsill overlooking the street. "There... the least you can do is look outside. You won't attract other Fae, will you?"

"Maybe... maybe not" it hunkered back down in the candle inset, peeking out at me with its dotted eyes.

"Okay..." So, it was almost cute. Fae can sometimes be cute. *Who knew?* "Are you hungry?"

"No," It sighed.

"Alright..." Shifting to leave, I rubbed the edge of the book with my thumb.

"Ironless."

"What?"

"Ironless..." it repeated.

Giving the creature a look, I suddenly patted my chest. "Ironless," I responded, realizing the locket was missing. "Where did I put it?"

The Wisp sighed and hid its face, offering no direction other than resuming its flame imitation.

I was in a sudden panic. For one flustered moment I thought, somehow, it had disappeared.

"Wash," I heard a gentle voice.

That's right, I took a shower.

Dashing into my bathroom, I craned my body around the door to look at the hooks. Reaching out, I quickly snatched at the locket and yanked it hastily over my head.

I kept it close, attempting to slow my heartbeat. *That was close.* It was a good lesson. Hearing the oven beeping, I went back and flipped the wedges over, sprinkling them with spices before popping them back in for another set time.

I found myself back to the table, sipping on my lukewarm cup of Jo and contemplating. My hand glided across the edge of the book cover, digging into the lock with my fingertips, I tried prying it open one-handed.

"This is impossible," I muttered, leaning away from the journal in disappointment. I sat gazing unfocused with numbing thought when my mug met the counter again. Grabbing the edges of the front and back covers, I gave a heaving pull.

Nope.

I could still picture the sketches my mom drew of those gruesome beasts. They gazed up from the pages, watching and waiting for that right moment to jump out and gobble me whole. There were so many nuggets of advice she had left me, and I had taken them for granted. We made dream catchers for night terrors, each crystal bead representing a good feeling or thought. Mom washed the floors with a concoction she called 4 Thieves and drew little doodles on our clothing tags for 'safe journeys.'

Meeting the creatures of her nightmares, I have since understood the depth of her sorrow. Festering deep in her soul, those fears that shrouded her had slowly killed her. Perhaps, it was just my imaginings, a wish for a dead mother's advice from beyond the veil, but I needed her secret.

I needed the key to this journal.

"Mom, I need to find it," I didn't even remember her having a key. *Where would she put it?* She had the booklet opened until nearly the moment she passed.

Tapping the surface in thought, I cringed at the idea of her really being buried with it. "No, no." I gave myself a pep talk. I knew I was reading too much into things that weren't there. "Emma, *calm* down." I tried shaking off the image of being the grave robber to my own mother's plot.

Rising, I made the quick business of completing the half-cooked eggs, demanding my mind to form a game plan. I was trying to feel somewhat productive.

I could cut the book open… That wouldn't do much for appearance for the beautiful-looking leaflet, but at least I could read its contents.

My palms were itching. Dragging the finished scramble off the burner, I flipped a light switch on flooding the kitchen with more light. I leaned over it, inspecting its threaded seams where the two leather sides joined. "Mom locked it up for a reason. Cutting it up wouldn't make sense," I logically told myself.

That's what the Fae wanted me to do. *Clearly,* it was sealed shut to keep someone out. *I just didn't think it was from me.*

Tracing an index finger around the green stenciled border, I shifted to feel along the spine. Nothing seemed out of place. I flipped it over and touched the backing, continuing to toss the book around and around until I finally found something off. Considering the book was in almost impeccable order, the missing thread in the bottom corner was something to be interested in.

Trying not to get too excited, I bolted up and grabbed a butter knife. Bringing it back, I wiggled it along the sides with small, studious motions. Almost too quickly, did the utensil slide up in-between the leather layers of the back. With a mental jerk to my psyche, I almost thought I had damaged the book.

"Huh…" I looked around with hairs rising on my neck, expecting someone to be spying on me. *I saw no one.*

When I could calm down long enough, I checked the insides slowly, feeling around for anything foreign that my mother could have stashed away. An ever-so-slight clink of metal hitting metal occurred. "Thank you, thank you, thank you, THANKYOU." My heart fluttered erratically against my chest, coaxing the object from its hiding place.

In a matter of moments, I sat holding a small iron key in the palm of my hand.

Barely containing my excitement, I placed it to the lock and turned.

The buckle popped open.

I rose from my spot, needing to pace in my moment of anticipation. Taking careful strides, I served myself some eggs with ketchup, refilled my coffee, and then settled back to my seat. There was no need to get myself worked up, especially if there was nothing to gain but the maddened words of what my crumbling mother.

Slowly, painfully, I peeled the cover back. I felt the handmade paper beneath the pads of my fingers, stroking the gold edges while dragging my eyes along the familiar penmanship that snuck across the front page.

This was my mother's handwriting.

To Emmaline, when times are difficult———

With bated breath, I turned the page…

October 3rd, 2001

Emmaline,

I wrote this in hopes you'd never need it, that I would still be there to fix all the mistakes. If you're reading this, then something has happened and I haven't finished what I was intended to do.

I'm writing this down. You have a right to know. I promised you to the Fae.

And yes, that's insane to say. Even when I write it out on paper, I know I sound bonkers. But you need to know that I regret it. You need to believe I regret it all. I love you, with every fiber of my being, to the moon and beyond. I was a kid when this all started. Selfish and lonely, I was brazen, unconcerned for the consequences.

October 4th, 2001

The beginning was when I was 7.

304

Only little things happened first. I would glimpse gauzy wings, and hear voices that trailed through the winds, laughing in the woods. Those piercing eyes that watched through the branches in the trees...

Then there was the Oaktree. That was my first Fae encounter. A dryad that had long forgotten language after it took root within the property. The moment it let itself be known was the instant they all squirmed out of the woodwork, like termites. They inhabited the woods, the yard, even the basement of the house. I heard them moving in the walls, snickering outside of the window.

My parents took me to a psychiatrist, positive I was mentally ill because of my night terrors. The doctor put me on depression medication and, for a moment, they melted into the background.

When I was 16, I was with a group of friends at Salt Creek, during low tide on a full moon. Drunk on cheap beer, and full of spite for my parents, when Keith Richards dared me to jump off the edge of The Tongue, I agreed—so as long as he did too.

Everyone thought we were mad. We stripped down to our underwear, crawling across the rocks, and stood at the very most point of The Tongue. Listening to the waves, there was a voice, but I stupidly dismissed it. And when we jumped, the undertow pulled us with such a sudden speed we lost our bearings. There were eyes under the whitecaps, sleek bodies pushing me to the rocks. I still can remember the sharp fingers, pinching and prodding, forcing me onto land.

They saved me, but Keith was... just gone.

My parents sent to Western State Hospital after my breakdown. No pills or treatments could rid me of the things I saw. The trauma was too real. My sight was permanently unlocked to the creatures beyond the veil.

305

I hid away for a year. By then, I had befriended a man like me. He saw what I have seen, witnessed the unspeakable things lurking out from under the layers of mundane existence. He saw the Fae for what they really were. He said he was in that place because of them too, and that his daughter was a Witness and was taken. He swore he would get her back one day. I wonder now if he had.

Who knows why he took a liking to me, but when I left he gave me a trinket bracelet... told me it was hers and that I should wear it to bring me luck.

Turning the page, I stared at the ripped seam where a sheet had once stood. I had to take in a gulp of air, long enough to try swallowing the butterflies rising from my gut. *Where had it gone?*

October 24th, 2001
The summer of 1997, you were three-and-a-half.

I had gone down to my parent's house, an infrequent occasion, for an even scarcer family reunion. Your dad was working, so we were by ourselves.

Bad idea. Nervous near the woods, with family and my wished away toddler, I consumed much more alcohol than intended. I lost you in the crowd of members passing you around for coos and awes. Bad judgment. Terrible.

Once faced with a decision I always seem to make the wrong choice. I never should have come back to Port Angeles.

Searching and looking, no one could find you. I was in misery, thinking I had finally lost you. When the police returned from the forest search, dazed and confused (faery-struck) I was angry. He was mocking me. Showing me, he was just as confident in my lack

306

of capabilities as I was. I had lived in paranoia for too long, the fear that ate away at me, stealing my youth.

Needing you back, wanting to get even, I sought someone to help me.

Madame Wilhelmina Beatrice of Jamestown; although, I doubt that was really her name. She lived in an unmarked thicket in a large brick Victorian lodge. I stumbled across her card on a friend of a friend. Our area attracting abnormal individuals of the immortal and mortal persuasion, I thought nothing of it at first.

She was under a profession as a 'clairvoyant folk-healer.' At that point, I didn't care if she killed kittens as a part of her practice. After two days with you missing, I was desperate. I wanted you back. I remember her as a beautifully ripened woman with the appeal of silken beads and silver bangles. While she was kind to me, there was a hidden aura of steel to her, something she attempted to hide when meeting me.

Bringing me inside, I handed her a crumpled wad of cash and was steered into a dark musky room. She knew I had dealt with Fae. I told her it wasn't intentional that they tricked me.

She replied that it never was, not until the deal curdled and grew sour. The great balance demanded equality and Fae know this. Usually, when you deal with the Fae, they wind up taking more than you initially bargained.

I was angry, rattling on what He had done. Then Madame Beatrice was curious, asking about who I meant. She knew who I was speaking of, sly, devilish woman. I found myself on my knees before her, hands digging and grasping at her. I buried my face close and cried for her help.

Relenting, she gave me tea and asked if she knew why he wanted you. She didn't think I had the guts to know but resigned to tell me

307

that most Fae steal humans for servants or toys. There was a rarity to find a Fae willing to go beyond tricking to strike deals with a Witness, much less a mere human. In this case, there had been a rumor circulating for the past eons by the Name Seer.

'From traitors womb the child doth hatch.' She recited. He was seeking a mortal child. For what, was still in speculation. She warned me before she continued that I was about to break a deal with the most influential individual known to the Fae existence, the balance would be thrown into chaos until a sacrifice was given.

I just wanted you.

She lit a multitude of white candles that dotted the small room. Flame crackled to life, their glow bounced off the large unrefined crystals that sat in various corners, causing a beautiful array of glittering stars throughout the space.

She asked for something of mine, and I gave her the trinket bracelet.

Madame Beatrice set to work on calling the elements, directing a dagger to five corners of the room. She burned incense over charcoal, the smoke circling the room with disbelieving precision. Lights flickered around us while she called on ancient beings.

'Boundless Áine, I humbly seek your pardon of this passage through your plane of homage. Goddess of law, the stolen child, is what we seek. To break the bond with mother's blood as compensation for the great imbalance created by this rite. Dawn Darling, from the Port of Angels, do you accept the repercussions that will pass as Goddess Fortuna sees fit?'

I agreed. I would. I must.

She dropped the bracelet into the bowl of incense and drew closer.

'Sacrifice for balance, Dawn.' She reminded, taking my hand into hers. I barely felt the blade puncture my palm or the liquid trickling down to drop onto the charcoal with sizzling accuracy. 'Allow it to be known, blood for bondage break. Let the image of Emmaline Darling be burned from the sight of the Originator, King of Fae. Take this vessel containing such power, hold it, and guard it against its source. Let his senses be weak as she grows strong. So it shall be.'

There was a sudden pain surging up from my wound, across my arm, and into my head. Painful, blinding seconds passed, making my mind numb until it had suddenly dissipated with the snuffing of every candle flame at once.

The plea was accepted.

I think I was kneeling because she picked me up to shove the bracelet to my hands. Blood mixed with hot metal, flesh boiled in contact. She suddenly threw me out with haste.

I had asked how I would know if it worked. 'Oh, it has already,' she was hollowed in appearance, shriveled from the task. Yet a gleam of something conquered was set in her pastel green eyes.

I left, upset and feverish. It was a long anxious ride back to Port Angeles.

When I finally rounded the corner to drive down the street, I saw flashing lights with the chilling sounds of sirens. Pulling into the driveway, an officer Crowe came out to greet me. He was one of the men that had been on duty searching the woods for you.

'She's safe and home.' The best words I could have ever hoped to hear.

You were fine, dirty, but fine. We never could get anything out of you but I already knew where you'd been… You got away. I was able to bring you home.

309

Madame Wilhelmina's last and final words echoed in my mind. 'Bury it, hide it. Do what you will but put that bracelet in a place it shall never see the light of day. For your child's sake, never let the Fae get ahold of it, for it will be the undoing of the curse cast.'

Life never returned to normal. Every deal made was a piece of my fractured soul crumbling away. I realized then that normal was just an illusion of something I could never really have.

When I finished the entry, my hands were shaking. I closed the journal, pushing it away from me to think.

"Shit..."

Time ticked slowly. Rising I grabbed the garbage can and drug it over to the fridge, taking the time to toss all the perishables that had been stacking up from the previous week. Casseroles, baked goods, cold cuts, deli cheeses and more, I threw it all out. Tossing glass onto glass, satisfied with the sound of breakage.

They riddled Mom's entire life with chaos. My mind spiraled over moments in her last days, triggering the moment I stood over her cold body as the doctor wrote her time of death. *I could see her face in my mind's eye, weak and full of pain...* I thought she had become a stranger in her last days, a person I was scared to know.

In truth, she had just been broken and was too afraid to leave that little girl she worked so hard to keep safe. *Me.*

Scrambling, I grabbed her journal and stumbled my way toward my neighbor's house. My body was hyper-attentive to the cool prickles of dew soaking through my socks. The crisp nip of the evening breeze rolled through the crevices of my clothing.

Pounding restlessly, I heard nothing shift inside.

Calling out, cursing loud and long at the creature, still, there was nothing. I walked off the porch and followed the small cobblestone path that led to the rear of his property, getting a good look to his back door I gave it beating as well.

Nothing...

Silence.

Wasn't he supposed to help me, guide me? Perhaps even protect me? Where was Basle when I needed him the most?

"Go screw yourself Basle!" I kicked the door, moaning in discomfort.

Sitting directly on the porch, I pulled off my sock to inspect the damage, a swollen toe, and a lost sense of self.

What am I supposed to do now?

The sky was fading to deeper greywater tones with a hint of warm glows just across the thinly lined horizon. With the constant prevailing clouds, the night would truly become darkness.

My eyes wandered along what little lit area I could see, Basle seriously needed to clean up his yard...

The longer I sat staring at all the figurines, the less bitterness came frothing up my throat. I glanced begrudgingly behind me, not wanting to give up my grievance. It was all I could say was mine.

Shaking in the cold I curled up on myself. Pulling back the pages of the book, it drew me to my mom's words.

November 24th, 2001
Your birthday was yesterday. You turned 7.

311

They came back. They talked you into going into my dresser to take the canister, the one I kept the bracelet in.

Luckily, I corroded the seal with salt. They got a nasty surprise, their screams were loud enough to hear inside the kitchen. They were small, I didn't know what He was thinking they could accomplish, but they were spineless little things, scattering to the thicket the moment I started yelling.

I locked us in the bathroom. I spanked you for stealing and then cried when you did. Your cake was ruined, burnt by the time we walked out together. You were happy with frosting and ice cream... I'm a bad mother.

December 1st, 2001

Ethan was acting strange last night and left. Said he had things to think about.

I just don't understand what's happening Emmaline. I must be paranoid. Not everything has to do with Fae. Not everything that goes wrong in the mundane world is because of the Fae.

December 9th, 2001

There is nothing to celebrate today.

Your father's truck was left abandoned ten days ago at Lake Crescent.

January 12th, 2002

I needed an explanation.

We traveled back to seek Madame Beatrice for advice. We found the house abandoned and in ruin, collapsed from years of misuse.

I should have known. Maddening. What a cruel trick to play. Had I really kept the Fae away or was this a trick to keep me occupied?

You weren't safe. I made sure everything was in place so that the curse would keep. I took the vessel away so that no flesh could touch it again.'

She never wrote the location.

There was still that one question hovering above all the rest.

Why was I traded in the first place?

I lifted my gaze when James walked from the back of the house, passing over the fence to kneel in front of me.

Shivering, we observed each other quietly.

"James... I need help."

He reached out and took my arm, guiding me back to the house where we sank into the couch.

"Did you bust your toe open?" He frowned, leaning down to look at my exposed foot.

"It's nothing." Apparently, he didn't believe me.

Jumping over the back of the couch, he crossed the room to retrieve the large canister of medicines mom stocked in the pantry. Sauntering back over with it, he settled crisscross in front of me.

"Right" He wiggled close until his knees touched the side of the couch. Taking up my foot, he looked at it closely. "You're always getting yourself into trouble." He muttered, gingerly massaging and pressing points until I almost kicked him in the face when he touched the joint of my middle toe.

"Ouch!? Hey!?"

"It's not broken. You wiggled it. So it's probably sprained." Popping open the canister, he plucked out a brown bottle and unscrewed the lid.

"Yeah, thanks," I was sarcastic, watching him pull out a squat looking granite mortar and pestle to cradle on his lap.

When he popped open amber bottles, I leaned back in distaste as the strong smell of alcohol mingled with the curing herbal assortments. One was a lavender tincture mom had made the summer before. "Witch Hazel, Lavender, and Arnica Montana," he recited, giving me a cool stare.

"Your mom was always great at being prepared."

"Did she know…?" *I wasn't sure why I was so shy to ask.*

"Yeah… I mean, I think so. She had her suspicions." He muttered, taking out a small vial from his pocket and uncorking it. When he tapped the bottle gently, a shimmering powder escaped out into the mortar.

"What is that?"

"Piskies dust, more or less."

"Why…?"

"The Pisky dust will give the rest of it enough 'oomph' to speed up the healing." With a small wooden spoon, he sprinkled the dried herbs into the mortar with a few squirts of each tincture. Tossing the dried plants with the pestle, the liquid ingredients slowly broke it all down into a paste.

I tried not to make a face as he scooped up the muddy poultice, plopping it onto a square cut of cheesecloth before pressing it gingerly against my foot. He wrapped it up with gauze and cautioned me against walking for a while.

Tingling warmth spread through my foot. "Better, right?"

"Yeah."

314

We gave each other another awkward look before I shifted.

"So," He got up slowly, looking like he was trying to find the words to say something. I cut in before he could continue.

"There should be potato wedges ready, and eggs."

"Right," Running a hand through his hair, he gathered up the first aid and made his way to the kitchen.

Watching him a moment I finally leaned back, relaxing into the cushion. Pulling my legs up, I rested the journal against my knees, and began flipping aimlessly through the pages until the book seemed to land on a particularly ink-laden scene—one with repeatedly drawn eyes of haunted faces.

I stared at them watching me. *Was this what mom saw when she looked at the Fae, jagged teeth and evil faces? Could she see past their masks of bright colors and beauty?*

Running a finger across the paper, I noticed there was the indentation of ghostwriting. Taking it up, I peeked at the back. Words bled through from the foundation of the sketch, showing hairline traces of something more than it let on.

Dipping my nose close, I studied the blotched writing, reading carefully to myself.

'Into the watery depths where soap corpses sleep, my greatest secret she shall keep. By my blood, none shall take, unless you are my kin sake.'

"What do you see?" Jumping I closed the book with a snap, ogling up at James. "Oh, come on Em…" He frowned, "I'm not like them. Nothing's changed since yesterday morning."

315

I doubted that but held my tongue, slowly peeling the pages back again.

"It's a riddle... but I'm not sure how to take it." I admitted.

Lazing to the arm of the opposite side of the couch, eating from a bowl, he sat attentively. "Well?"

I shook my head, struggling to clear the way for new thoughts. Reciting the riddle in my head, I tried to pull about the string of words, breaking them down phrase for phrase. "Into the watery depths..." I groaned loudly. "I won't ever get it back if it's at the bottom of the Strait."

"Come on. Just tell me," He grumbled through a mouthful of potato. "How did you finally get it opened?"

"Secret key," I hummed.

"And... the book is for?" Our roles seemed to have switched.

"I'm not sure... to help me, I think." I relented, eager to share the riddle with someone. So I did, slowly and with a hint of distrust.

He stared in rapt contemplation over the words, slowly shifting the uneaten food from cheek to cheek forgetting to swallow. James was a freak but I was glad he hadn't seemed to change much since discovering his secret.

"I don't think there are any 'soapy corpses' in the Strait of Juan de Fuca." He answered my question.

"Could happen, you don't know." We gave each other a look. "Okay, who would 'she' be?"

"No idea," he said lazily, popping yet another wedge into his mouth while scooping ketchup up with a fingertip.

"Ew, James." I scolded, watching him lick it despite me. "You *are* a freak," I concluded out loud, tapping the book emphatically. "Pay attention. This is serious business."

"I know…" he sat up straighter.

Trying to decipher the riddle I pressed the pads of my fingers to my forehead. "What bodies of water are near us?"

"Uh, Strait of Juan de Fuca, Elwha River… Sol Duc River, Hoh River, Lake Sutherland, Lake Crescent, Salt Creek, Lake Erie, Lake Angeles?" He tilted his head back trying to think.

Crescent Lake sent chills down my spine, recollections filling in the puzzle piece by piece. The lake was the epicenter of everything chaotic in the history of the Darling family.

Rising swiftly, I hobbled over to put on some shoes.

"What just happened there?" James quickly popped off the couch, following me. "What is it? What's the answer?"

"I need you to go make a pack for Abigail." I stared at him, "We're going to go see my grandparents."

CHAPTER 15

MONDAY EVENING

I'll explain in the car."

"Okay but wipe your face, or Doreen will have a heyday." Gripping the handrail, he careened around the post and skipped up the steps.

I carefully teetered into the downstairs bathroom, doing a balancing act with the poultice while peering into the mirror.

Oh shit, he was right. Taking up a towel, I washed my face recklessly. There was no time for looks. I wriggled on a coat, watching the impish redhead make his way down the stairs. A princess backpack hung off his left shoulder.

"Ever fashionable," he hummed, giving a twist to show off the bag.

I snorted as he struck a pose. "Yep, that's made for you, princess." I shot at him, distracted as my phone vibrated in my pocket. I glanced to the screen, anticipation rising in my chest. Raewyn responded.

"Who is it?" James tugged on his leather jacket, fixing the collar.

RAEWYN: Find the host's doll. Destroy it.

"Raewyn, she said to find the host's doll and destroy it, but you've already done that."

"Tell her." He gestured expectantly.

ME: James has. The Changeling is still... present.

RAEWYN: Strong ties...

RAEWYN: Follow carefully.

RAEWYN: Get a satchel/bag. Anything. Find the remaining ash of the doll. Place them in the bag, along with one acorn, three cloves, a sprig of pine, nine rowan berries, one steel nail, salt, a needle (to prick yourself)... and something of the Changeling. *1of4*

RAEWYN: Fill the bag, close it tight. Prick your thumb and smear the bag. Say: 'By blood, iron, and earth, I see this Changeling for what it's worth. Truth rings control; I bind this changeling. I bind it from harming others and itself.' *2of4*

RAEWYN: Settle it into the grounds of the place it lives (Remember where you placed it, you'll be finding it again) *3of4*

RAEWYN: Good luck *4of4*

There was a plan forming in my mind.

Gaining momentum, I went around collecting each item. Cloves and salt were in the kitchen cupboard. Pine was in the

319

backyard. I retrieved Rowan berries from James, and I had an acorn nestled amongst the various items along the kitchen windowsill. Mom tended to hoard strange little items from nature; I was beginning to understand the method behind her madness.

The ashes of the poppet proved to be the most difficult to deal with, they were vast and scattered in the still-burning stove. I took the job of scooping out the coals with a shovel, depositing them into a bucket where James took them out into the yard to choke out. When he returned, I was already sifting through the ashes, growing impatient with the project.

"They need to cool down." He hovered, frowning. "They'll burn right through the cloth."

"Thank you Captain Obvious," I mumbled, leaning back. "I don't have time to let them cool."

"Just—hold on a sec." He disappeared into the kitchen to rummage about through the drawers and cupboards until an

"Ah-*HA*," met my ears. Sidling back in, he held up a flour sifter and a large bowl.

"Is it even working?"

He poured all the larger leftover bits into a pillowcase, peering inside curiously after the dust cleared. "Well, I'm definitely picking up wax. So I guess so."

"I'm worried about what's been left out."

"This is the best we can do on short notice. If it doesn't work, we'll figure something else out. I think you've proven your skills of improvising." James rose when we finished our project, tying the top of the sack with a rubber band.

"Since you have the workable car…"

320

He nodded, holding open the door where I ducked up under his arm and down the steps. Climbing into his truck, I established myself into the seat and pressed my forehead against the window. I watched the twisting road ahead while we skimmed around slick corners, keeping an eye out for the ever damnable deer.

Traveling the tunnel of trees into my grandparent's property proved to further my anxiety. The other made the wise choice of parking where escape was easily accessible. We didn't exactly have a plan walking up to the door; we just had a princess backpack and a pillow sack full of ashes.

"Well, isn't this unexpected," Darleen made the dramatic display of sweeping open the door, allowing us both in. "I'd thought you fell off the face of this earth."

James nodded to the backpack. "As prescribed," He stated lightly.

"If I would have known you'd be calling at this hour, I would have put something in the oven." She gestured to follow.

I inwardly cringed, quickly cleaning my shoes on the doormat then nudged for James to do the same. "Is Grampa here?" I crept into the sizeable encompassing house, so much larger now that there were only two living there.

"Yes, he's in his shop."

We crossed into the impeccably clean living room. Everything was a cream tone or cool grey, accenting the hard cold wood floors, matching the stagnant energy lingering in the space. Like a museum, Gram fashioned small lights over her collections of abstract paintings and secured pottery behind glass cases. Mom told me that this

321

place had once looked more organic, more vibrant, and bustling when all the children were still in the house. I couldn't imagine it.

Gram wove us through the living room, down the hall, and on into the kitchen. "Coffee, tea?" she eyed me. "You didn't take your coat off."

"We don't really plan on staying that long Gram."

"I see," She rested a hand to the counter, looking directly at me. "We? You aren't trying to take Abigail away, are you? She's perfectly content in her room."

That's right. They couldn't see James.

I wiggled my fingers toward the table, showing I wanted the princess backpack settled down. "I'm dropping the clothes off."

"Fair enough." She gave a double take to the sudden appearance of the bag. "Right, well. She's upstairs in Dot and Dyna's old room."

My mother had a vast expanse of siblings. Not including the two infants lost at birth, Aunt Dot (Dorothy) and Aunt Dyna were just two of five of my grandmother's children, making Mom the seventh child in Albert and Darleen Darling's progeny. With four girls and a single boy, Darleen had always been incessantly unsatisfied with her daughter's choices, even long after they've grown. Twisting and bending to seek her approval, family dynamics were strained, if not frayed.

I speculated whether Gram's attention on Abigail was an effort to salvage the crumbling fragments of their disappointment in my mom.

"Thanks. I'll go say hi to Grampa first," I stepped away from the older woman, giving a side look to James and trying to retreat toward the back of the house.

He followed me like a shadow, raising a brow to the woman in passing.

"She seems normal" I muttered to him.

"Hmm…" he agreed.

Stepping down into the shop I waved to the older gentleman who was stooped over a piece of half carved wood. With his keen taste in spirits, it surprised me he hadn't chopped off a finger by now.

"Emma." Albert smiled, giving a watery gaze toward me. "What brings you into the woods?"

"I'm dropping off clothes for Abigail." I shoved my hands in my pockets, giving a nervous smile. "I, uhm, have a strange question for you though, Grampa."

"Well, a strange question deserves a refill." Putting his gloves down, he dusted off the wool button up he wore, and then gestured back into the house. "What is this extraordinary question you have for me?" he looped around us to get into the bar in the living room, shuffling about to make himself a shot of whiskey on the rocks. He gestured with the crystal glass in question.

I shook my head. "Well, I wanted to know about your Great Aunt Hilly," I spoke frankly.

Albert's expression was as expected. His eyebrows rose in surprise. "Sudden and strange," swallowing all of his drink he went to make another. "What do you want to know about the Lady of the Lake?"

James turned eyes flickering in acknowledgment.

"Can you tell me anything about her?"

"I don't remember much. I was very young when she went missing. What I know is mostly based on what the newspaper stated. I believe—yes, I think I have a few things if you'd like to look."

"Yeah, thanks. That would be great." I was eager, wanting to get my hands on something substantial. Something to prove my sleuthing was correct.

The older man nodded and slipped off down the hallway, disappearing into his office.

"Clever," James whispered my way.

"Well, we'll see, we haven't seen what he has yet."

"Is this a school project of sorts?" Grampa called out.

"Yes?" I wasn't sure how to respond.

"Being invisible could be an advantage." James was whispering beside me as the click of a shutting door carried from down the hall. "I'm going to go scout."

I didn't have time to respond before my grandfather made his way back into the living room, an overly stuffed photo album tucked in his arm.

The aged and tore booklet looked abnormal against the pristinely clean scene of the house. Albert didn't seem to mind. Pulling the cover back gingerly, he showed off the top-to-bottom pages filled with newspaper clippings and photos. All centered on the Darling family.

"Wow, Grampa. You've been collecting all of this?"

"My mother started this book. A record of sorts of the scandalous endeavors the Darlings have gotten themselves into." He chuckled mildly, flipping through the card stock pages slowly. "Your grandmother doesn't like me talking

324

about the family in that light, but it isn't hard to see where the nuts fell on the family tree."

"Well, that's refreshing," I peeked at him.

"What? That I don't sweep problems under the carpet?" He snorted. "It's the whiskey talking Emma," I could hear a barking laugh from somewhere in the house. "Ah, but you are here to see about Hilly Mortimer." He overturned a few more leaves, rotating the book toward me. "Aunt Hilly Darling-Mortimer," he hummed. "Handsome woman wasn't she?" he rose to make another whiskey. "Shame she got herself killed."

I stared down at the black-and-white photo of a strong-jawed woman with a demanding expression. "Why do you say that?"

"Her husband was known for his wild ways and excitable personality. Well, go ahead, read the clipping. It will tell you."

I leaned in to read, my eyes gliding across the title.

THE LADY OF THE LAKE:
60TH ANNIVERSARY OF AN UNDYING LEGEND

The story of 'The Lady of the Lake' is one of the more popular legends amongst the Olympic Peninsula inhabitants—a macabre tale of murder, mystery, and soap corpses.

Our tale begins in 1940 at Lake Crescent of the Olympic National Park. Two fishermen were out in the early morning and discovered the body of a woman floating along the lake's surface. Hogtied and bound in a frayed blanket, it was an odd and gruesome sight.

The public's imagination flared by the horrific discovery, the murder victim becoming known as the 'Lady of the Lake' nationwide, a fitting title for a soul who emerged so suddenly from the depths of a lake with the reputation for never releasing the dead.

While her face was unrecognizable, her body had yet to decompose. They later identified this as saponification, the chemical alteration forming when the glacial waters entombed her, transforming the fats of her body into a soap-like substance.

Our victim, formerly known as Hilly Darling, was a resident of Port Angeles, Washington. Working as a waitress at 'Lake Crescent Tavern' (now known as 'Lake Crescent Lodge') she met her husband-to-be, Percy J. Mortimer, in 1933. The family reported that the couple were instantly drawn to each other, if a bit volatile, marrying not four months after.

Three years into their marriage, Hilly (Darling) Mortimer went missing shortly before Christmas in 1937, Percy claiming she had run off with another man. When Hilly did not contact her family through the holidays, they had grown worried. While Percy's claim still stood, he had moved back to California with another woman, disregarding the worry of his wife's disappearance.

July 6th, 1940, Hilly reappeared, shocking the Peninsula Coast, and those who knew her.

Percy was then apprehended a year later, shipped back to Port Angeles' Clallam County Superior Court for the trial of the murder of Hilly Mortimer. They reported that Percy insisted that the body did not belong to his late wife and that she was still alive, off gallivanting around with the man who stole her away.

However, dental plates proved as credible evidence, linking the corpse to the missing woman. If that wasn't enough to convince, Percy had rented rope from the storekeeper at the lakes nearby lodge, 'Lake Crescent Tavern,' identifying it having the same fiber matching used in tying the victim. Hilly's mother also insisted that the clothes worn on the body belonged to her daughter.

Taking the jurors four hours to reach a verdict, on March 5th, 1942, the jury found Percy guilty of second-degree murder. They sentenced him to imprisonment at Washington State Penitentiary, in Walla Walla.

As the year's pass, some tell of her spirit still dwelling within the walls of Lake Crescent Lodge, sitting and smoking a cigarette while speaking to an unsuspecting tourist. Others say they've seen her from a distance, walking the shoreline of the lake where her body was recklessly dumped. In the end, it all is left for interpretation. But who doesn't love a good ghost story, especially when they are true…'

When I finally looked up, I saw James staring at me from across the room. I nodded to him.

"Is it okay if I get a copy of this Grampa?"

"Sure, why so interested in Aunt Hilly?" He sipped his drink, watching over the rim with his watery gaze.

"School," I replied quietly. If he thought I was still in school, I would not correct him.

"Hmm, history project?"

"Something like that, thanks Grampa."

Doreen found her way slowly down the stairs, less composed than usual. Gram looked frazzled. Not that that gave me any delight. "Emmaline, Abigail wants to see you."

"Gram," I intoned, "I think I'll pass."

"Emmaline." She gave me a nostril flare. "You cannot leave without seeing your sister. I insist that you say hello. After that, you may do whatever it is that you do."

James gently nudged my elbow with his hand, having crossed the room to stand near me.

"Fine... where is she?" I didn't want to see it again. I didn't want to look at the object my grandparents adorned with clothing. Who they believed was my sister.

"She's been restless, poor girl."

"In what way?" I glanced to James who frowned, shrugging worriedly.

She guided us upstairs toward the room designated to tuck the children into during the holiday festivities. Gram firmly believed that children should not be heard.

Once a daintily laced room, adorned with rose print wallpaper, pink lace curtains, and carefully organized shelves, was now posed as a biohazard zone. The walls were caked with day old food and crude crayon drawings. Vintage bears, rabbits, and dolls were beheaded, then strung up with shoe lace strings, while their bodies were gutted and tossed to the side. Books had been compiled onto the desk in the corner. Signs of scorch marks, from a hastily stamped out fire, licked across the wood frame.

Gram rapped her knuckles against the open door, making her presence known. "Abigail," she cooed lightly. "Your sister's here."

"Oh, my god..."

How could this thing get this far without my grandparents reacting in terror?

"She's been enjoying hide-and-seek lately," Gram explained. "I've meant to ask, really. Her sleep rotation is completely off. She likes to come out at night when we are sleeping. Your grandfather caught her on the kitchen counter with a knife in her hands. I am relieved he had gotten up when he did." She leaned down, "Sweetheart, did you hear me? Emmaline is here."

There were little snickers from underneath the bunk bed, dark and greedy little chuckles that never would have come from my sister's lips. "Abigail, your sister is here to say hello to you," Doreen sounded strained.

"No, that's okay," I backed up to leave, but my grandmother blocked me. How was she tolerating this mess? Was she blind?

"Go on, say hello, she will appreciate seeing you, I expect."

Shuffling slowly and looking at the bottom bed, the darkness buzzed erratically like that of a hummingbird's wing.

"You can stay where you are. No need to come out." I managed finally. "I wanted to say that you are in a new environment, but that doesn't give you the right to mess it up."

"*Ee-emmali-i-i-ine,*" the voice called softly from below. "Why don't you come down and play with me, *Emmali-i-ine.*"

"I think I'd spoil the fun if I were to join."

"Oh *no* sissy," she replied sardonically. "We would have *so-o-o* much fun!"

"No, I am in a terrible mood right now. I doubt I would be any fun tonight."

"I insist. Come play with me." There was a warning in its tone.

I crouched but didn't move closer. I saw an old softball trophy in the corner I could use in my defense, should anything decide to jump out at me. "I have my friend waiting for me. He'll know I'm missing."

329

There was a jealous hiss. "You'd rather play with him, then me?"

"Oh, you brought a friend?" Gram rested her hand lightly to her chest as she peered down at me. "Why didn't you invite him in?"

I watched James hovering behind the older woman, holding up scissors he likely found in the kitchen.

Right, we still had to get something from this crazy little imp.

"It's fine Gram. I was just here to drop off Abby's clothes..."

"That won't due," Gram frowned. "She's been asking for you every day since she's been here."

"SHUT UP!" The Changeling suddenly screeched from her roost. "Ye manky old hag!"

"See, you're making her upset." Doreen was looking pale.

"I said, SHUT UP!" She pitched her small voice indignantly.

"Sweetheart, we don't talk to others like that."

"GET OUT! JUST GET OUT, GET OUT!!!"

Gram nodded. A blank gaze shrouded her face, leaving with the slow drag of her slippers against the hardwood. James and I were speechless. What had the King done by sending this thing to my family's home?

"Now that I have your attention..." the fake Abby said calmly. "I'm bored... come play with me, or I'll cut up the old ones..."

"You can't."

"I could."

"You won't."

"Who's stopping me?" She giggled madly, reveling in the game.

"FaeKing could stop you," the redhead muttered finally.

I gave the darkness a look, moving to peer closer and see if I could make out where it was. James grabbed my elbow and yanked me away, just as small pudgy digits with dirty claws swiped at me. We stumbled away as high squeals of laughter erupted from under the bunk bed.

"You evil little creature, who are you?"

"Do ye think I'm tha' stupid as to tell ye my name?"

It never hurt to try.

The words never left my throat, watching the creature finally peek out from under the bed. Seeing her again wasn't any easier. Her wrinkled waxed skin had settled more to her bones, but her owlish eyes remained black and ever staring. I thought I might throw up, and she just laughed, crawling slowly toward us like a spider on all four.

Backing up toward the door— too late— she seized at my ankle, nails digging into flesh.

"I dun' think so Bonnie." She grinned, an expression quickly replaced by fright. Arms reached around me to grab a fist full of her hair. "Bealin' caffler, iron!?"

"This is what you get, you little demon." James gritted his teeth as she scratched manically at his skin, drawing opaque liquid from his skin.

Her scream was piercing; the distinct smell of burning flesh and hair intermingled in the air as he cut clean up to the scalp with the scissors. "That's MINE. Ye can't have it! Robber! Stealer! Filcher!"

331

"Says the Faery that stole my sister's identity!" I growled at her, getting pulled back and out the door with a firm click of the door. We listened as miscellaneous objects were thrown; loud cursed screaming rang muffled in her tantrum.

Then she just stopped, becoming eerily quiet.

"Emma, we should go." I pressed my ear to the door, listening to the quiet skittering and rustling from beyond. The end of a knife tip sank through the wood, just inches from my eyes. I screamed unexpectedly, delayed in reaction while stumbling back with James.

We hit the wall directly across.

Small fingers sprouted out from the gap below the door, scratching shavings of mahogany finish. I stomped hastily with my heel, seeing the digits curl out of sight with a howl of pain.

"Shit! Out, out, out!" James took my hand and guided me off down the stairs hastily.

Where were my grandparents?

"Gram? Grampa?!"

"Emmaline, what are you yelling about?" I whirled around to see them both standing side by side perfectly still in the middle of the living room.

"Gram, are you alright?"

"Why wouldn't I be?" she gave a slow blinking expression.

They really weren't there mentally. Grampa had a copy of the newspaper clipping loosely clutched in his hand, eyes regarding us closely. This was set up for a horror film.

"I uhm… I have to go." I blurted.

"Emma," my grandfather called. "You're forgetting something," He held out the photocopy.

"Right, thanks..." I walked carefully toward his direction, hesitating before taking the offering from him. "Thank you, Grampa."

"You'll be seeing us again, soon?"

"Sure, Grampa," I offered a tentative smile. I stepped back, watching them closely. "Everything will be okay, okay? Just lock her in... just do it. Keep her in there. I will fix this. I'm going to keep you safe."

"Oh, and Emma," Albert called out again. "Don't let Hilly know she's dead."

My eyes widened, snapping the door closed behind us. "I just left my possessed grandparents with a deranged Changeling."

"She'll have her sulk and get over it." James gripped my wrist as we backed up slowly. "Transitioning is a hard process. Luckily, your grandparents are Faery-stricken. They won't think anything's out of the ordinary. Even if she swung from the dining room chandelier, they wouldn't treat her any different."

"That's NOT what I'm worried about. Grampa caught her in the kitchen with a knife. You heard her. She said she'd cut them up if I didn't play with her." James groaned, shaking his head. "What?"

"I got what we needed." He held up the fistful of hair he had been clinging to since he snatched it. "Let's... get this over with."

James had quickly darted about in the dark, finding a small hand trowel shoved into a potted plant. We made quick work out of the base of an Oak tree, digging up the wet mulch, enough to cover the sack.

I brought out all the ingredients from the bowels of my pockets. Tossing them haphazardly with the ashes, I coughed when I got a mouthful of dust.

James dropped the Changelings hair into the mix and shook it.

"Dust," I coughed louder, leaning away to bat at the air.

"Sorry, now what?" His eyes shimmered, making me shiver.

"I'm supposed to prick my thumb." I stared at him.

"What?" he hissed. "That's blood magic. We aren't touching that."

"It's all I have to go on. You don't get a say in this."

"That's bull." He growled, gripping the edges of the pillowcase with irritation. "I don't want you bonding yourself with a Changeling. You've already got a Wisp attached to your name. Do you realize that if it ever got loose, it could—?"

"Yeah?" I interjected, distracted in looking for the needle I had brought. "What was that? We're taking time now to list the issues in my life? As you can see, I really don't have many options—shit." I gritted my teeth.

"Forget something?"

"The needle..." James laughed until I pushed him. "This is all for nothing if I can't do it properly!" I hissed in the dark, starting toward the house.

He grabbed the cuff of my sleeve. "Hold your horses," leaning down he took up a small twig from the ground. Rolling it between his palms, he blew gently against it. I blinked once, and he was holding out a sharp-pointed needle where the stem had been seconds before.

"Holy shit," I stared with wide imploring eyes. There was just enough lighting from the floodlights to see the hairline gleam off the object. "I didn't know you could do that!?"

"*Ssssh*," James warned. "Just, be careful." He strained.

"Out of all my foes, this needle is the only I submit to." I could practically hear James rolling his eyes. Steadying myself, I had to jab my thumb a few times before I produced a pool of blood. Squatting down, I smeared the small offering against the bag. "That wasn't pleasant at all. I hope that was enough."

"Any is binding. Be careful."

I waved him away and pulled out my phone, flinching from the flash of the bright light of the screen. Taking a moment, I pulled up the words I needed to say. "By blood, iron, and earth, I see this Changeling for its worth. Truth rings control, I bind this changeling—" There was a loud crash of glass behind us, a guttural scream bellowed from the top floor of the house. Looking back, we witnessed the silhouette of the creature crawling from the wreckage of her bedroom window, scuttling across the rooftop on all four.

"Hurry up Emma! Drop it!"

"I b-bind it from harming others..."

James stooped to dig deeper with his hands, guiding the sack into the hole while I tied the top off. Something heavy fell to the bushes before hollow pattering of footfall sounded toward us. We made a shoddy job of covering the bag before dashing to the truck.

"YE WEEDY EARTH-VEXIN' MINOW!" The Changeling shouted.

James yelped, stumbling to the ground.

"James!?" I grabbed at a rock from a nearby garden bed, chucking it to the creature piggybacking my friend. Nicking it on the shoulder, she squealed and dropped, squirming her limbs like an overturned cockroach before scuttling up to grab at his heels.

"Yeasty half-faced lout! Ye won't be taken me, Emma!"

"Yeasty?" James attempted to disentangle himself, growling. "Get the truck started!!!" Yelling, she bit at his heels. "Get the fuck of me you nasty little girl!"

Why wasn't she taking after me, I made the bond? Scrambling into the car, I grabbed at the keys on the dashboard.

"EMMA!?"

"You have too many goddamn keys!" I tried them, stumbling and shaking through the course of four keys before I got the truck going, drowning out the Fae girls laughter with the roar of the engine.

Snapping the door closed, I stuck my head out the window. "Come on!" The brake lights exposed their quarrel. She had a firm grasp on James' forehead while her legs were crossed around his neck. The Changeling looked like she was trying to choke him out while he pried her off.

Dangling her upside down by a leg, she shrieked and flailed until he chucked her into a nearby bush, making a mad dash toward the car. "Go, Go, Go!" He slammed the door closed.

I put the truck into gear and backed up in a flurry of gravel and muddy water, jolting physically as I rolled into potholes.

Shifting gears, I glanced through the rearview mirror. The barefooted child stood stoically in the parking lot. Her shining eyes gleamed dangerously after us.

"What are you waiting for?" James turned to see what I was staring at.

"What's your real name?" I called out the window. This was the test if she answered me I knew the binding was working.

The creature twitched, leering angrily in her spot. She clawed frantically to her throat, face reddening while she physically willed her tongue to keep quiet.

"*Ehy-la...*" She croaked, stamping her soles irritably along the gravel.

"Ehyla, you're to be a good girl while I'm gone." I gripped the side of the door. "You understand?"

"*Y-y-yessssss,*" she hissed, pulling at her hair.

Hitting the gas, I sped away from the deranged child.

"She gave me the double middle finger..." James muttered. "The only thing we can do now is to replace her with the real thing. We can't do much until we uphold our end of the bargain." James sat back.

I nodded in agreement, slipping down the seat more. I rubbed at my face, placing the pressure of my palm against one of my eyelids. When all of this was over, I wanted to sleep for a year.

"James..."

"Yeah?"

"Are you like her?" *Did I want to know? James was still James, wasn't he? Had I known the same one this entire time, or was he replaced?* I peeked over to him when he didn't answer. "James?"

"Mom never said it out loud, but I remember the way she looked at me. I was this... robber, a monster who stole away her kid." He rubbed the back of his neck as he concentrated intently on the road. "I don't know how she knew... but she did."

"So you must have thought you were human, for a while."

"For a while," He gave a little smirk, but it didn't meet his eyes. "I tried to be a good kid for her... but well..."

What could I say?

I had questions buzzing around my head. *How was he chosen? Did he offer to be a Changeling? Why was the human James taken? When?* None of it was fair. Somehow I had a feeling Changelings didn't intentionally offer themselves up as this twisted form of cannon fodder. I was piecing together the puzzle of his jaded existence. Perhaps this was the first time I really was really getting to know him.

After we drove in silence for a while, I leaned down to awkwardly kick off my shoe. My toe was miraculously doing far better than I expected. I suppose that's magic for you. "I don't know how I'd function without you," I muttered.

"You could go on without me, Em. It would just be hard, like burying someone."

I watched the twisting of the uneven roadway, thankful I was the one driving. The highway along Crescent Lake was notorious for its lack of railing, so thirty-miles-per-hour was assigned for most of the seventeen mile stretch.

The lake, itself, still held the horror stories of those who were too reckless with their driving and had skidded off into the icy depths below. Even in the summer, her waters held an arctic chill that kept its arsenic blue and gloomy grey-green waters from warming to anything above 40 degrees. There was little to wonder on how Crescent Lake preserved its dead. Even the countless cars, an ambulance, a school bus, a ferry, and even a train still dwelt fully formed beneath its surface.

We parked at a lookout, kept the motor running and shifted to get comfortable.

"The Lady of the Lake," James started, watching me in the dim light. He waited for the story.

"It's a fool's errand," I responded dramatically.

"Careful, you're acting like them." Rolling my eyes, I unrumpled the paper Grampa had given me and passed it over for him to read. "Well damn," he said after a moment.

I unlocked my phone, trying to draw up a simple fact sheet. "Lake Crescent was carved out by a glacier. It says 'officially they have recorded the lake to be six hundred and twenty-four feet deep in areas' and that's only because the 'equipment used was limited to the technology of the time.' Unofficially, it's 'over a thousand feet, but bottomless still is often used to describe its depths. That's below sea level.'" I looked out toward the eerie body of water before us. "I can't find the King's sight in that depth of water. It's a death sentence."

"Well, the paper says there are reports of her spirit haunting the shore. You are kin. She'll come to you."

"I guess I have nothing to lose at this point. I'll probably be Faery stew. Grind my bones to make their bread or whatever the hell Fae do to humans."

"I think that's an Ogre. What would you be doing with an Ogre?"

"Nothing, I don't have Ogre companions just a Troll, a Changeling, and a cop." I flipped on the light, "Crowe, that sneaky bastard."

"What?"

"When I was a kid, he was a cop involved with my disappearance."

"What?" the other straitened this time.

"Darlings have a knack at getting themselves into trouble," I muttered.

"But why didn't he say anything…"

"Hell if I know, the man genuinely acted like he'd never seen a Fae before."

"Maybe he didn't know." James watched me. "You don't remember anything?"

"No, of course not," my eyebrows furled, "nothing."

"It's probably for the best… although it explains why you're such a loner."

"Hey!" I smacked his arm.

"Ouch! That one hurt. I'm not trying to be mean. Even if you don't remember, it obviously affected you."

"Hey, if we aren't divulging into your childhood then we aren't in mine."

"Fine, Hilly Mortimer it is…"

A wooden marker and green government sign indicated Lake Crescent Lodge. We looped around the large white prestigious lodge, where it rested just before the lake shore, hugged by old-growth woodlands.

Flipping our lights off, we situated ourselves to one of its several off-branch parking lots near the Marymere Fall's trailhead. Quietly discussing our options, the best decision was to find our way to the lakefront and see what we could make out. If we couldn't grab her attention that way, then we would wait and rent a canoe when the lodge opened.

That's where we found ourselves, shivering loudly in the dark, listening to the soft lapping of water caused by some unknown breach in the distant depths.

Skies dark as ever, the adjacent beach was not to be found in the murky expanse before us. Shuffling up to the wet marker that showed where land met water, I shoved my hands into my pockets.

"Well?" James whispered.

"Don't push the process." I cleared my throat, "Lady of the Lake?"

"Oh, come on, you know the rules." James snorted. "Full name gets the attention of the Unmentionables."

I couldn't quite see my friend's face, but that didn't stop me from giving him a look of confusion.

"The what?"

"Right," he moved beside me, "supernatural or magical peoples. Sorry."

"You call them Unmentionables? Sounds like undergarments."

"Or dirty little secrets?" James laughed. "Well, they sort of are, aren't they? When you're a person who straddles both worlds, it's good to have a lingo that can be used interchangeably."

341

"That just made the whole thing worse." I heard him snort good-naturedly, "seriously."

"Well, I didn't make it up. You're stalling."

"Transparent," I grumbled. "Hilly Mortimer…" Hesitating, I wasn't sure what to say. "I am Emmaline Darling… Dawn Darling's daughter…"

We waited quietly, and attentively.

Nothing.

"I'd like to speak with you please, Hilly Mortimer… Or would you prefer Hilly Darling?"

Still nothing.

"Sometimes it takes a while." James shifted. "Come on. Let's grab a blanket and sit this out."

"We are doing an awful lot of waiting on these excursions."

"Not everything is instantaneous. It takes time." He headed back toward the truck to grab the blanket, bringing it back and tossing it over.

"You're right," I muttered to myself, wrapping the blanket around my shoulders after he retrieved it. Looking back toward the cold waters, I could faintly make out the reflection of light trickling across the disturbed lake surface.

"Hey, Emma?"

Moving to settle down on the ground, I leaned against a log and peered up at him. Shoving his hands into his pockets he shrugged down, staring out at the body of water in front of us. "Just… never doubt I'm on your side," he murmured. "No matter what you hear, no matter what you see. No matter what, I'm your best ally."

I nudged my shoulder against his side when he sat. "Okay…"

The blanket was warm, strangely warmer than it should have been. I tried offering the other half to James, but he refused, saying the cold didn't bother him. That he ran on a different level of climate sensitivity than me. I finally backed down and cocooned myself into the wool blanket, smelling of moss and the scent of rain in the air.

Thoughtlessly, I fell asleep.

CHAPTER 16

TUESDAY MORNING

A chattering group of hikers startled me.
Sucking in a noisy breath, I sat up and regarded my surroundings until I recognized where I had left myself. I had fallen asleep by the lakeside and slept entirely through the night without freezing.

I wasn't sure how I felt about that...

Shifting my numb legs out before me, I gazed up at the slice of radiant yellow, molting from dark blues into a brilliant peachy glaze. I sucked it into my lungs, letting the scenery soak into my pores and relax my sore muscles. When I saw dots, I turned, blinking. Something felt amiss. I realized James was gone.

His truck sat idle behind me.

Pulling myself up off the ground, I dusted lazily at my dirty clothes, mustering the energy to make my way up onto the grassy embankment. My feet found themselves along the cemented pathway which took me across the shoreline toward the impressive looking white lodge.

That's where I settled. Sitting to a wicker chair amongst the empty tables, I watched the lake lighten in hew as the sun rose. Light cast across the wide-paneled windows of the sundeck, basking my face in warmth.

I sat like that for a long while, absentmindedly picking at my thumb. When the needle prick reopened easily, I wondered if that was what James meant about magic—*that there were limits.*

"Emma?" James called softly.

Leaning, I squinted toward the door-less entry leading into the lobby. James peeked in with a peeved expression, "You disappeared."

"You disappeared." I parroted.

"Right..." He seemed to collect himself. "Right, are you hungry? I can get us menus?"

Nodding, I wrapped the ever-warm blanket tighter around me, daring to rise from my comfy spot as the waiter came into the room.

"Hey Emma," The female smiled kindly. Her dimpled cheeks and brown eyes reminded me of her name.

"Sherri Johnson from senior history class," *How could I forget?* I held out an extended hand as she gave a nasal giggle in response.

Sherri was one of the top students in our grade, the president of the newsletter and a part of the dance team. Her

345

parents made sure her name was well known throughout our academic years with a handsome donation for the track and field installment.

"The one and the only, please, take a seat wherever you'd like, guys. The picking is yours."

James and the other exchanged pleasantries as she seated us. We both requested coffee and Sherri held out her menus before skirting off to gather our drinks.

I noticed James stuffing a piece of paper into his pocket, and I kicked his ankle.

"Ouch!"

"For real," I dipped forward and raised an eyebrow. "You actually got her phone number, at a time like this?"

"What? I didn't ask for it, she just gave it to me. She's heading off to France for college after she graduates from PC." He shrugged, fiddling with his folded cloth napkin.

"Right and you didn't use those Fae charms to woo her into—" I paused when Sherri flitted back into the room to chatter lightly with us, settling down our cups on saucers. "Can he get milk and sugar? Like an ungodly amount. He doesn't actually like the taste of coffee he just wants to feel like a big boy."

James snorted, staring at me in surprise.

"Well, aren't we spunky this crisp fall morning? Sleep on a pinecone?"

"Yes, but this blanket is heavenly, it must be the stuff of magic." Giving him a slightly squinted gaze, he nudged me under the table when Sherri giggled.

"You two still up to your shenanigans, it's cute. How are you doing, Emma? I saw the newspaper, I'm sorry about your

346

mum. I remember her bringing some really bomb no-bake peanut butter cookies in middle school for the bake sales."

"Ah, yeah, thanks." I shrugged awkwardly, feeling the peppiness leach out of me. "She made an amazing vegan cookie."

Sherri nodded with a genuine expression of sympathy. "James told me you're camping. How's it going? The weather's been temperamental." She noted, shifting the order pad to her apron.

"It's been uneventful, but the night wasn't bad at all." I tilted my head to James who was playing on his phone.

"Are you taking any hikes today? Marymere is a fine fit for this sort of weather."

This small talk was making me nervous.

"Maybe," the redhead looked up. "I think we're more in the mood for a quick boat ride unless that's an issue, Shay."

The girl giggled, showcasing her dimples again. She shook her head with a toss of her perfectly poised ponytail.

"Oh James, always the cutie pie of every girl's eye," I commented dryly, getting a nudge under the table again. The female flushed red at my stare.

"Oh yes, I remember that." Her laugh climbed higher in her embarrassment. I decided I wouldn't tease her further and settled down to look at my menu. "Before I forget, the breakfast special is the salmon shallot scramble with rye toast and a seasonal fruit bowl." She smiled. "I'll give you both a minute to look over the options."

"Thanks, Shay."

My nose was still in the menu, but I could hear the smile in the imp's voice.

"Don't drool," I snorted.

"Hey, come on Em. She didn't do anything to you," He looked at his own menu. "The crab omelet sounds great."

"Preppy girls are the bane of my existence," I joked, giving him a blanched look. "You're paying, you know."

"I figured." He leaned back, checking his phone. "Okay, listen to this. Their website says renting any of the boats is: twenty-two dollars for one hour, thirty-two dollars for two hours, half day is fifty-two dollars and a full day is sixty-two dollars. Extra people are a charge of five dollars."

"I take it I didn't miss much when I fell asleep."

"No, not really," James set his phone down to make his morning drink concoction.

Staring at his ever-growing pile of sugar packets, I hummed.

"I'm not sure. What do you think?" The price had escalated from what I remembered. I speculated on what my bank account must look like. A trivial thought, but something I hadn't checked in a while.

"I've got it." The other was watching me, seeing me cycle through my frame of mind. "It's the least I can do, really."

"Thank you."

He waved me off just as Sherri was shuffling back in with a toothy smile. Her slicked-back ponytail bobbed behind her, a habit from her dance days.

"Are we ready?"

"Crab omelet," He hummed, "with lots of butter on the side."

"I'd like the special, please." I handed our menus back politely, pulling my mug back into my hands.

"Would you like a coffee carafe at the table?" She asked pleasantly.

"Oh, *that* would be fantastic!" I nodded in thanks.

"Coming right up Emma," she smiled at us both then left quickly to her tasks.

"See, doesn't that make you feel bad?"

"No..." *Okay, yes,* "She's efficient."

"I'll go rent us a boat for the day, then make a few calls. I think I might know someone who has a few tips on getting a spirit's attention." He rose. "I'll be right back, okay? Just, stay here." He shuffled off, pulling up a number and giving it a ring as he slipped out into the lobby.

I waited patiently, finishing my drink.

Sherri brought the carafe, joking briefly that I didn't have to worry and that I could slow my pace. For her benefit, I chuckled.

Even after the meal was delivered, the redhead still hadn't returned. *Just how complicated was it going to be getting ahold of Hilly?* I was dreading another overly complicated summoning, like Crowe's exorcism. Halfway through my meal, James finally found his way back.

"So? How'd it go?"

Plopping down, he gave a boggled expression.

"Well, long, long, long story short, I paid for the boat. They just need a copy of your driver's license, and I got some tricks on how to get your Great Aunt's attention." He bit into a cold piece of toast.

"Long story?"

"Yeah, my resource can be long-winded when he's familiar with the subject in question." He lathered the toast in the

349

extra butter he ordered, giving a knowing smile. "An Unmentionable," he winked.

"Right, well, as long as you trust them."

It was strange to think James had been having a completely separate life since I'd known him. A life filled with secrets he had kept tightly bound up and tucked out of reach from me. I tried not to over think about it.

"You're rattling around in your brain again," he told me between large bites of food.

"I'm trying not to," I drank a good three mug's worth of coffee before feeling even remotely reasonable. "I'll be right back. I need to stretch my legs."

He nodded, watching me rise. "How's your foot?"

Blinking, I tested it out slowly, surprised by only a stiffness, "Great... actually."

"Just keep light on it. Magic may help mend, but it's not invincible."

"Aye aye, captain," I murmured, excusing myself to trail out the doorway toward the shoreline.

"There are restrictions." He called out.

Waving him away, I made my way down around the side of the building. Passing foliage and ferns, I looped about a particularly gnarled tree trunk laden with stringy moss, and hooked a sharp left across the fixed dock jetting out across the water.

The lake turned stormy that morning. The wind blowing soft but cold with low hanging grey clouds. I watched as fog crept in to blanket the mountain peaks, the crisp outline disappearing into a hazy distortion of muted colors, subduing the greens of the surrounding forest. It was an eerie beauty that unnerved me.

If this lake could speak, what would it say?

Standing to the edge, watching the water slosh against the foundation poles of the dock, I ran my sight across the shallow waters. Despite how stormy it had been, the lack of algae made the beach visible as far as ten feet deep. The flooring didn't disappear until the natural lake bed dropped, creating a marked ledge. Mesmerized, I pushed my body to the safety rail, mentally willing the lake to produce the long-lost bracelet my mom spoke of.

Crescent gifted me with the sounds of a distant splash of water. Gazing across, I witnessed the large head of a creature breaching the watery surface, dark glassy pupils gazed back unblinkingly. I hadn't even had time to take a proper breath before it dipped back down, just as quickly as it had emerged. A sleek serpentine body followed, with the slap of its slick tail.

I turned and quickly headed back into the restaurant. James was chatting softly into his phone, both our plates wholly cleaned of any food.

"I'll talk to you later..." he muttered, frowning and nodding. "Mhmm, thanks." He hung up, giving me a close look. "You look like you saw a ghost, Hilly?"

Shaking my head forcefully I shifted in my chair. "An Unmentionable," pointing to the lake, I stared. "A massive Unmentionable..."

Craning his upper body, he looked out to the water. "What did it look like?"

"Uh, hello, massive."

"Emma."

"Loch Ness Monster," I said honestly.

"Ah, you saw Cressie then," he chuckled. "A rare occurrence, but of course she'd happen to be visiting when you're here."

"Cressie?"

"Yeah, she's old. She comes in through the Strait of Juan de Fuca, through the Lyre River and into the lake. Someone told me she comes in during the winters."

"You mean she migrates?" I sat back.

"Well, it's cold, and she's got plenty to eat since they started the catch-and-release act. Although, I was told she's been seen less and less frequent by local Unmentionables." He nodded slowly, observing the scenery. "She's a quiet protector, a good sign to the native peoples. The lake has always held an ancient secret, which is why the native peoples are smart to respect it at a distance. When technology started advancing, things have gotten dangerous for large Unmentionables like her." He made a noise and regarded me. "And that spells trouble when you don't have the lake guardian willing to protect its territory. Things... slip in and take root."

Frowning, I poured another cup for myself to digest his words.

"Okay, didn't expect that. You know a lot." *Like quoting a fact book, really.* My eyes shifted around us, wondering if the Lady of the Lake was sitting and waiting for me to turn in her direction.

"Try not to upchuck, okay?" He gave me a sheepish look. "I already paid... we can leave when you're ready."

"Why aren't you freaking out?" I wrapped the blanket over my shoulders again.

"I don't think it would be smart for both of us to be scared right now… I'm nervous." He muttered, rising along with me to head out into the lobby.

Upon entering the impressive double-door entrance, a receptions booth stood to a sharp left where James had undoubtedly squared away the rental situation. Beyond, was a lofty sofa arrangement, set around the lodge's central hearth. There was a small sitting area directly across from it, where guests could enjoy the cocktails from the bar. Offshoot hallways led to the sunroom, gift area, and a larger dining room, while a stairwell led up into an off-limits section.

We stared around at the deer heads mounted to the walls and the various native artwork tastefully adorning overhangs until the lobbyist popped into the front counter to take the rest of the needed identification.

Heading out into the fresh, sharp air, we trailed back down to the shoreline where the boats sat tied and ready for the taking. We were greeted by the bundled up lifeguard and went along with their conventional explanation of how the lake was formed by a glacier over ten thousand years prior.

After the history lesson, he untied the #7 aluminum rowboat and, with the help of James, shifted the craft toward the water.

With James's insistence, I climbed first into the rocking craft nervously. Handed the set of paddles, I was instructed to tuck them to the rear of the boat where I stood awkwardly, white-knuckling the sides.

"Miss, are you sure you'll be okay doing this?"

353

"Yes. Yes, of course!" I must have looked like it was my ride into the underworld. *For all I knew, it could have been.*

"Okay... but you must sit down, so you don't tip yourself overboard." The man looked very unsure of my skills until he watched James push me the rest of the way offshore and jump into the boat himself. "Alright, before you leave, I need to go over a few ground rules for safety. By following a few basic guidelines, you can ensure your protection each time you head out into open water."

I nodded mechanically, giving James a look. He had his back to the man and was parroting wordlessly to the young lifeguard's speech. Distraction was well-meant but poorly placed.

The man continued to go over the procedure checklist, asking us to keep any form of technology in the boat rather than on our persons. We obliged, giving each other looks when we discarded our phones to the center of the craft. Once the lifeguard finally finished with the safety and boat instructions, he wished us luck and waited for us to take off before resituating himself to the dock.

"I guess this is happening..." The entire action felt more alien than the journey out to the Hoh Rainforest.

My friend leaned in, grabbing the oars and dig them into the ground, push us away from the shallows.

"You realize he wouldn't have just let us leave like this... there's a storm coming."

"Then how did you..." I trailed off, seeing the expression of the other. "Right... So, we aren't supposed to go out?"

"The forecast calls for sleet. I guess." He shrugged. "Well, you can see the wind." He gestured, fighting against the tide

354

to push us out past the dock. "But we need to go out into the middle of the lake."

"What will we do when we are in the middle?"

"I'm not sure what exactly will happen. I just know the golden rule: If you take, you need to give of equal or greater value."

"Faeries are sticky business," I sighed. "I should have thought this through. I have nothing worthy enough to give to a lake spirit. What if she won't come and see me now?"

"You know her real name." He gave an uncomfortable look, "Which means—in some respect—you hold a candle to her. That, and well, you can always offer a bit of—" He stopped.

"What?" I watched him and then raised a brow. "You were going to say blood."

"We will find something else." He looked around.

"It's fine."

What's another offering?

He frowned, inspecting me closely. "You don't get it, Em. Blood, your name, attaching yourself to these individuals... You can't take it back. Not easily."

"Abby is worth it. You know she is."

"I know, she's worth everything," James frowned. "I just hate seeing you pull yourself apart."

"You'll be there to stitch me up."

We sat quietly for a moment, watching each other.

"Of course I will." He promised. "Do you still have that needle?"

"I think?" Padding around my form, I found it interwoven in my collar.

"Let me try something." He handed me the paddles, taking up the offered implement. "I'm a piss poor excuse of a Fae... she might see right through the glamour."

"What are you going to do?"

He placed the metal between his index and thumb, holding it up to study it carefully.

"I'm going to try to disguise it further." He brought his other fingers up, grasping the center of it, he pulled upward slowly. I ogled in fascination as the tool bent and twisted to his will, glimmering with soft undertones as he reshaped it into a thin silver band.

"A ring?"

He nodded, holding it in his palm. "We don't know the nature of Hilly Mortimer, but we do know she isn't Fae." Taking up my hand, he slipped it onto my finger. "Glamour over glamour, won't last long. Maybe a few hours..."

"Are you proposing, James?" I snickered, watching him blink profusely, comprehending what he had just done.

"No." He said flatly.

"That color of red is nice on you." I shoved my arms inside my jacket, snickering to myself while his ears flushed further. I momentarily forgot the trepidation in my gut, on what we were about to do.

It had been a long time since I had done anything close to rowing but it wasn't altogether estranged from me. I remember a few scant fishing trips I made with my dad where he allowed me a few strokes in before my arms gave out. How oddly foreign those fragmented memories seemed now. "You said knowing Hilly's full name was important, why?"

"It's a powerful thing to know of someone's name, it wields strength…" he seemed to try to switch the subject. "For Fae, it's as crippling as iron," he watched me then. "Naming someone—or something—is to give purpose. But to know that name can often exercise a sense of control that brings even the most powerful of Fae to their knees."

Processing, I gave him a puzzled stare. "But you said it yourself. The Lady of the Lake isn't Fae."

"Every entity has guidelines. All have their own dealings with names. From what I've seen so far, if you forget your name, you forget yourself. If you give your name away, it's binding."

"So, keep it close. Do you have a different name, James?"

He nodded slowly, looking uncertain. "Yeah but no one gave it to me, the curse of being a Changeling. We will never hold the power of our name, our purpose isn't to lead the life of a Fae."

"Oh, jeez," I frowned.

"Yeah well, I don't know any different. So, as far as I'm concerned, I'm James." He shifted his gaze off across the water.

"Wait," I spoke up. "Ehyla gave me her name."

"If she knew her name, I'd be shocked. Then again, the girl was brought into the mundane world suddenly. Who knows, maybe severing the connection with Abigail, brought a resurgence of memories for her."

"So basically, she was putting on a show earlier?" He shrugged at me, "Why didn't you say anything!?"

"Because there was nothing we could do." He strained. "The binding may have worked, but that didn't mean you had control over her tongue."

"Damn, Fae are assholes."

"Yep…"

We fell into a grave silence as James rowed. When we were far enough out of sight, he let go, amazing me further when the boat paddled on its own. There was idle prattle, anything to distract us from the chattering of teeth and the idea we were facing a spirit which has long since been dead. *How could you really prepare for that?*

"Into the watery depths where soap corpses sleep, my greatest secret she shall keep. By my blood, none shall take, unless you are my kin sake…" I bit my lip. Closing my eyes to breathe in the cold, wet-smelling air, I expelled it noisily in frustration.

The fog continued to roll in by the tons, choking out the surrounding scenery.

"I believe we are lost." James finally stated. "Maybe reciting the riddle out loud wasn't the best move." He peered through the gauzy strands at me.

"No shit Sherlock." I groaned. We tried finding our place in the lake, but there was nothing to identify our footing. We could have been a few yards or a few hundred yards, and we would even know.

Calm settled over the water's surface. It was then I felt a chill run up my spine when a wet slap sounded not too far from where the boat was floating. Rubbing my forehead, I calmed myself before leaning down to check the time.

"Did you hear that?" My friend looked around, rising slowly to his feet.

"James! Don't do that." I hissed.

"*Ssssh,*" He motioned for me to quiet with a finger to his lips, only to stumble when the boat was smacked into from the right-hand side.

I went to grab the edges of the craft but thought better of it when the mental image of a lake creature rose from the gloom to lick at my knuckles. I shuttered, hoping that we had either bumped a fallen tree or, perhaps, a shallow area. That would mean we were close to shore, prompting me to peek over, to see if I could see anything below, I was met with dark, turbulent waters. The fog made it all the more sinister.

"Emma, it's time," the young man whispered. "Regardless of where we are, someone knows you're here..."

Flailing, I pushed my arms back into my sleeves. I gulped in some air, thrusting my hand into the water before I could over-think my actions. Adrenaline pumped through me, mixing with the bitter wind, making me almost unable to speak from my chattering teeth.

"L-Lady of the L-lake, I Emm-m-maline N-novalee D-d-darling, kin-n of D-d-dawn Daphne Darl-l-ling... call up-p-pon you, k-kin of the D-d-darlings..."

Even I didn't buy that, but I was hoping the words didn't matter, that it was the ring that stood for something.

James looked green, hands gripping the oars fiercely as he stared non-blinking at me.

There was a moment's pause.

Yelping, my arm was drug down into the water. I snatched my hand back.

359

"What happened?" He grabbed at my soaking limb. "Where are you hurt?"

"It… licked me." I shivered, disgusted.

He checked my thumb. "Were you picking at it?" He stared at me.

The boat smacked into something again we both jumped, sprawling haphazardly when more thrashing arose. Peeking over the edge with bated breath, my eyes widened, witnessing sheen of scales slice through the water and disappear into the deep.

Standing against my friend's advisement, I got a good look at the dark masses swarming around the vessel we were settled in.

"Oh. My. God…" Jerking an oar hastily from the other, I smacked at a fin. Dropping out of sight, more rose to take its place.

James steadied my waist as long webbed hands with black claws grappled the edge of the craft. Floundering fins beat against the turbulent lake water, spraying us as I attempted to dislodge the vessel from their snare.

"We're moving." The imp called over the noise, realizing we were being pushed further into the fog.

They were dragging us forward, somewhere far from safety. At this point, I had no clue where we were on the lake. We could be miles from where we once were, and that scared me. *For all, I knew these creatures tasted my blood and just wanted us as a midmorning snack.*

I sat down, sitting on the center bar where James leaned in to keep me balanced. We waited, quiet and alert, feeling the minutes ticking slowly in our troubled journey. Thirty-six minutes later, we lurched forward when the boat came to an abrupt stop. The hands sank silently away. Putting my phone down, I peeked around to see if I could recognize anything out of the gloom.

The fog was thinner at this point. I could just make out the ghostly images of the tree line as I bobbed slowly from side to side. If we could see the trees, then maybe we were close enough to make a beeline for shore.

Gripping the paddles, James put them to the test, making the boat row itself as quickly as it possibly could. There was the familiar splashing of tails that erupted, like a mass frenzy of fish competing for scraps of bread thrown into the water, a bone-chilling experience when you knew you were now running for your life.

Adrenaline kicked in while we tried hunkering down. Our eyes were wide and watering from the chilly air that surrounded us.

Then there was the screeching.

Angry, gurgling shrieks that swarmed us from all sides, they erupted and cutting short as their body's leapt in and out of the water.

Nails scratched along the boat we traveled in, attempting to slow it down. Then hands found themselves at the oars, tugging mercilessly until they flung one off into the water, causing us to turn in erratic circles with the other spellbound paddle churning water.

Screeching continued to bark around us, almost laughing.

"Un-spell it!" Seizing the wooden oar, I smacked at arms and long spindly fingers that started rocking the raft back and forth, making us unbalanced. "Shut up!" I screamed at them.

James made a last-ditch effort, grabbing the boat's rope to tie it around my ankle. Twisting it and tying clumsy knots, trying to keep it put. He rose and grabbed the paddle, forcing me down as he used the blade of the tool to hit the leathery limbs with as much impact as possible.

Even as hands fell away with screams, more took their places. A few snatched at the offensive oar, tugging back against it. The swaying became more pronounced, our phones sliding from side to side between our stumbling feet. The splashing made for slippery footing until, abruptly, I witnessed the moment James lost his tug-a-war with the creatures.

"NO!!!" I yelled, reaching out to grab him as he toppled headfirst into the murky depths.

I felt my side hit against the edge of the metal boat. The wind knocked out of me as I did an awkward tumble after my friend.

While I sputtered and wheezed, James's hand snatched at mine, trying to keep both of us afloat by grappling the side of the craft. I could get a few stabilizing breaths when the rope around my ankle was yanked. I choked on my scream, being completely submerged.

Encased in the frigid tomb, struggling with an alarm ringing wildly in my head of being drug down to the depths to die, I forced my eyes opened to look at the assaulting monsters. Foul Merbeings, with frail grass-like hair of charcoal and moss green, met my gaze. Their upper torso was leathery sickly grey with ribs and a spine that dramatically protruded with anorexic degrees. Fast moving tails were akin to the native Beardslee trout. Their scales, a deadly variation of steel and grey-blue spattered with black flecks down their sides, blended them against the backdrop of lake terrain.

Their faces were flat with ear-to-ear mouths, filled with sharp translucent teeth, which grinned even as they clicked their tongues angrily. Large half-dollar sized black eyes, reflected the soft lighting from the surface above, watching our movements like predators. Their long, spindly, webbed fingers were clawed, attesting to the legends.

If they these creatures were real, what else laid lurking in the depths?

Grabbing the rope tied to my ankle, I climbed up as quickly as possible. My lungs were burning, making me dizzy.

James got one leg over the boat, trying desperately to get enough grip to help me. It only took a moment to lose hold. I yelped, falling back from the force of their wriggling bodies, being separated from my friend.

His yell intermingled with mine, eyes black with rage. He was calling out my name. I could see his mouth moving while being carried down and away.

The movement was quick. A Merfolk wrapped its hands about the rope—my lifeline—unhinging its jaw where it snapped it clean in half.

No...

The lake surface rose away from me. My oxygen-deprived brain screamed. *This couldn't be true!?*

I needed to save Abigail. I wasn't supposed to end like this!

Wriggling...

Struggling fruitlessly...

My movements slowed as I finally faded...

Something inside me resigned. Activities flitted before my unfocused sight, a flurry of fins and limb registering in my mind before I stilled with the trailing of lake weeds in the underwater current.

CHAPTER 17

TUESDAY MIDDAY—PART 1

Then, I was breathing.
I coughed—sucking in a burning breath—eyes wide and wild in confusion. Clawed hands left my body while I purged the excess water lodged in my stomach.

"Child… of Dawn Darling," called a soft voice from beyond.

Straining my head up, feeling like it was a swelled lopsided mass on my shoulders. I focused on the glow amongst the deep gloom of Crescent. *I was still in the lake?* Blinking profusely, I tried clearing the accumulated gunk from my vision.

I shifted around, dull shock settling inside me.

Was I dead?

"No, you are very much alive and kicking. You rang me, remember?" I was having a hard time piecing together what the voice was telling me. Everything was unattached, jumbled and floating. "Come on sweets, pull yourself together," The other encouraged. "Your mother paid me visit years ago."

"H-Hilly Mortimer?" I croaked.

There was a soft, sad sigh in response. A short deafening silence pursued, manifesting unresolved feelings in my mind about my choice of words.

"I haven't heard that name in over seventy-five years." She finally responded.

"But…" I swallowed thickly. "It is you?"

The light dimmed into a softer glow, enough to where I could make out a figure floating before me. Her dark hair and decaying clothes swayed softly in the lake bed's current. Unlike I had imagined, her face and body were intact. A bruise powdered her neck and wrists, leaving the mind to imagine the other welts received by the fatal beating. Hilly was ethereal, despite the fate she was given. The only thing out of place was the charm that hung about her left wrist.

My eyes widen when I understood.

FaeKing's sight.

Hilly nodded slowly in acknowledgment, "The very same." She raised her palm in a beckoning motion, "Into the depths, where the soap woman sleeps… her greatest secret, I shall keep. By Darling blood, none shall take, unless you are our kin sake."

Her rendition of the riddle sent chills down my soaked form.

I used my arms to propel myself forward while I gazed at her wrist. To me, the bracelet was more prized than a crown of jewels. "What will happen now?"

"You will take the bracelet, and I may finally be rid of what it costs to bear it."

I wasn't following.

"You will know soon enough Emmaline... Please, take it." The wristlet dislodged itself, dropping to the sediment-laden floor below.

"What will you do now that the bracelet is not in your care?" My brain was still drifting around in the weeds, her sadness moved me.

"Me? The bracelet was not the only burden given to me, Emma. I will forever be a hostage within this watery prison."

"I'm so sorry Hilly," I grimaced. *What could I do to help?* For everything she had suffered, I couldn't just present a bespelled twig ring.

She remained hushed as the distant echoes of a siren's call drifted through the ghostly underwater land. Hilly turned finally. "I am not the only soul that dwells within Lake Crescent's womb... I just enact order so that a semblance of control may continue."

"Order? Control over what? The other lost souls?" *Why was she being kept here?*

She cocked her head to the side, a languid motion causing an odd shudder through me.

"To keep them at bay and preserve balance." She spat her words like they were a foul tasting, "These waters hold far more secrets than I care to divulge... even less to think about.

Let's just say, without a strong grip on various individuals inhabiting this crypt, there would be an awful lot of missing bodies."

I licked my lips nervously. The water gliding across my tongue reminded me I shouldn't be alive right now. This shouldn't even be possible.

"This lake never gives up its dead, especially a Darling." Her form flickered. "Because someone decided suffering is a Darlings specialty. Which raises strong stock, don't you think?"

I was unsure of how to respond. "… There's no way of escaping your fate?"

"Ah," she lifted a finger, wagging it with a smirk. "There we have it, the loophole of Crescent's deep. A soul, trapped in these waters can rest, but only if they have someone else to replace them. Foolish as I was, I gave up that right by bargaining my body for my soul. To bring justice to what that bastard had done to me."

Hilly's hatred permeated the surrounding water, working her into such a high state of excitement that something short-circuited inside her. I watched as her pupils dropped into a lifeless state, body growing limp as she floated suspended loosely before me.

She was dead… wasn't she?

Stooping sluggishly, I took the glittering piece of jewelry into my hand and pocketed it. The weight was calming enough.

I tilted back, kicking lazily, treading in my spot while the moments escaped quietly between us. I was unsure of what to do next, until, just as suddenly, the spirit before me snapped right back into motion. She gave an owlish look before taking up the lost space between us. "But I have long regretted my action. My mortal body ensnared in this tomb would have been nothing compared to the hell I've suffered since taking this deal."

The intensity in her eyes unnerved me. Dread slowly seeped in and settled to my core, shaking me into attention.

Something is wrong with this picture.

"You see, that bracelet you hold so dearly, is personally worthless to me," She gestured to my pocket. "I tried. Oh, I tried. I followed the rules. I lured in swimmers, driven vehicles to crash, and boats to sink, all to keep Crescent's darkness below its depths. I pulled their souls to the obscurest of pits, which even Cressie avoids. Hundreds of them, but nothing, no other lives are worth the measure of my bargain. No one tips the scale."

Slowly pushing my hands against the water, I backed up, staring at her.

"So for me," she leaned in. "It's costume jewelry." Her hair danced around her ghostly frame, splaying up like the trickling vegetation thriving on the lakebed. "Imagine my surprise when Dawn came stumbling back to see me, desperate to re-hide that thing. Where better than Crescent, I said? Then, I had learned that people were after you... after the bracelet. Dawn was dying and desperate. I knew it. She knew I had pulled the pieces together." She gave an endearing smile. "We both recognized I couldn't simply give the bracelet over to someone who had powers to outclass the deal I had struck with the lake. After all, by blood, none shall take unless you are of kin."

No.

"What are you saying, Hilly?"

"I'm saying, Emmaline, they can switch us."

I floundered back while she glided closer. Small particles seemed to crumble off her face and fingers.

"No, you can't... You can't do that Hilly. My mom is your niece. I'm your niece!"

"You are nothing but a stranger." She drew another deteriorating stride nearer. "You figured out the riddle, surely you know the story. I was murdered. My life was cut short, and now I am paying for it, beyond death. I want to be free. I want to be finally rid of the pain and suffering I have endured." I gaped in panic, watching the last layers of skin flake off of her jaw, showing bone. "Why can't you just accept that the Darling curse will always find its way into your life? Be it by disease, drowning, or beating... I served my time, and now it is yours. So, *take it!*" Her hands, eaten away by fish and time, lashed out in a flurry of soap suds.

I kicked away, desperately climbing back toward the surface.

The sharks swarmed again. Their mouths gnashed dangerously as they sang the mysterious song of Lake Crescent's deep.

The Lady of the Lake rose after me, laughing elatedly as she took skeletal swipes at my legs.

There was nothing but darkness around me.

Desolation of this empty place only made my brain confused on what was up or down. I struggled to maintain a firm stroke, lungs heaving from the earlier struggles. If only FaeKing had known he was so close to retrieving his sight.

370

Burning flared across my birthmark when Hilly grabbed my ankle. She yelped in surprise, letting go as if my skin had scorched her. The confusion didn't take her long. Barking orders at her minions, their mouths and claws lashed out at me, sinking into my flesh.

Screwing my eyes closed, I screamed. Skin breaking like a knife slicing through butter.

I did little to struggle then.

The more I resisted the further damage they created.

Going limp, I let them tug me back down. Any tears I may have shed were lost within the waters.

"Good..." I could hear the satisfaction in Hilly's voice. "Good, good." She grinned, swimming closer to take a good look at me. "And they say you're the Darling to meet his match? Don't make me laugh." She chuckled and circled me, slapping away the Merfolk who were leaning close to sniff hungrily at my wounds. "Get off her, you disgusting bottom feeders." She gave a repulsed look as they licked the water where the blood had dispersed.

Turning her back to them, I got a good look at her form, what was left of her face, had cracked and flaked away. The rest of her form revealed the real travesty the lake had left her in, a mere skeleton of what she had once been. I tried not to look at her mouth, already fighting the action to vomit from the pain searing up my throbbing leg.

"Where is your precious Fae King now, hmm?" She gestured emphatically around, watching me with her single eye. The other had collapsed into the socket, disappearing with the rest of her. She laughed when I turned away from her. "Bring her... and don't nibble."

Hilly glided off ahead while they gathered me, dragging me after. I was, yet again, carted from one place to another. Closing my eyes, I tried to focus on something other than the pinpricks of pain when I was jarred this way and that, surprised at my resilience. Though somehow, being bitten and scratched by these water monsters wasn't as bad as their teeth looked.

My mind and body slowed.

I could think more plainly than I had in, what it seemed like days. The feeling was probably shock, but the weighted warmth of my locket gave a reassuring pressure.

"Whatever you have in store, it won't work."

"She speaks. Really, how do you figure that?"

"I didn't come to the lake alone. I came with friends." No need to tell her it was only one.

"Even if you had a whole army of Seelie and Unseelie alike, it would do nothing for you, this land is cursed. No Fae in their right mind would touch these waters. There's too much death here and too much iron infecting the depths."

Bullshit.

"What are these things then?"

"Ah, a scavenger is what they are. They may have been just as pretty and magical as the sirens that paint the myths of the open ocean, but the scraps of metal riddling this place forced them to adapt."

"And why do they follow your command?" I couldn't imagine these creatures as anything but gruesome. Some of them held long fleshy scars along their body from where boats may have collided against them.

Now that they weren't floundering after me in attack mode, their tails were far more interesting to look at. From a distance, the dim light gave the appearance of the steel blue, but on closer inspection, the scales themselves had a translucent quality that shifted as their environment changed. This could have been the reason why no one has ever spotted them before.

"So full of questions, aren't you?" She didn't sound particularly bothered. "Well, that will have to wait."

The temperature slowly warmed as we drew away from the deeper parts of the lake. Inwardly cheering at the possibility of getting out of the water, I brushed my fingers against each other, feeling wrinkled flesh. I reminded myself that I was still intact. While rough around the edges, I could move my legs and arms. *I didn't understand why I hadn't died of hypothermia, or, you know, drowning.* But I finally decided there were far too many factors that made little sense to dissect it all.

The dead woman slowed our journey, regarding the merfolk skeptically. "You stand guard, you hear? If you even nibble on her, you'll be a chew toy for Cressie. I will be back," She fixed her good eye to me. "Try nothing. They are underdeveloped creatures with the hunger for blood. They rather enjoy chasing their food. Please do not give them a reason to disobey my orders, hmm?"

Hilly's form flowed away from us. Using the pull of the undercurrent she glitched from one spot to another, until the distance swallowed her into the gloomy backdrop of this submerged landscape.

Where was she going?

I decided not to care, studying the surrounding creatures who began to leisurely swim around me. They spoke amongst each other with an odd variation of clicks and whistles.

I deliberated on how far I could go before they noticed I was trying to slip away. So far, they were all congregating into groups. The ones that hauled me along this mysterious journey, left to join the school, while a few chased a cluster of small salmon that had run by.

Ideas churned as I noticed they kept body level with me. I managed a few lazy kicks, rising a few feet, noting that they followed with little consideration of what I was doing. I checked my pockets, taking the bracelet out to stuff in my bra, knowing it wouldn't escape me unless they stripped me of all clothing.

A few of the lake people saw my movements and stilled to watch. When I wasn't running, a few took off, trying to snag a bite of fish the others had chased down.

Peering to James's ring, amazed it hadn't shifted back into a twig yet, I was glad I had some form of a time limit. If the glamour only lasted a few hours, then that meant it was still daylight. *If I got back to shore, could I call for James? Was he still up there, struggling in the boat? Was he okay?* Not knowing only made it more imperative to get to the surface.

Being tugged along at least gave me time to recover some of my energy, but my shoes would drag me down. So I lost them. One dropped after the other, drifting slowly out of sight.

None of the merfolk seemed to notice.

Good.

I took off my socks, tucking them in my pockets, expecting a trek to get back into civilization. I only hoped James would be fine until we found each other again. The last thing I removed was my jacket. Giving me more room to move my sore arms, I rolled a sleeve up to inspect some of the crescent-shaped bites along my arm.

A feud was breaking out amongst the scavenging few, the ones who hadn't caught anything. Their argument escalated from loud trilling clicks to an all-out attack. Pulling, tearing, biting, and fin slapping, the water began to cloud with dark ink-like blood.

Wounded merfolk were quickly overtaken, being feasted upon by their greedy kin.

My heart raced.

This was something I did not want to be drawn into. Not wasting another minute, I shoved one arm back into my jacket and hastily made a dash for the surface. My body thrummed with apprehension. When I broke the surface, I wheezed and sputtered, sucking in fresh air for the first time in a while. I gave myself a few large gulps, finding my direction to shore, then took after it will all my might.

After the first few yards, it was apparent I could no longer breathe underwater, telling me, whatever spell placed over me, was now broken. Any time my head bobbed underwater, I was quickly pulled back up to gasp for breath, coughing. The taste was foul. I didn't want to imagine what was floating in it.

Finally, I had passed a striped blue buoy with the depth level reading thirty feet in black print.

So close, I was so close to land I could almost feel it. Hooking a left, I headed toward a rock that jutted out of the line of trees. There was an orange buoyed swimming hole, marking a nearby beach, but it was too far to risk.

Taking large strokes, I had to eventually pause halfway to give myself a quick break. My lungs were burning, and my limbs dully ached with the abuse I received.

So close…

Paranoid, I surveyed my environment, intending to pick up my journey again when I spotted something bobbing in the water fifty yards behind me. Peering at it closely, my heart skipped as it fell back into the water noiselessly then rose once more with several others of its kind.

"Oh god, no…" the thrill never ended.

The creatures seemed to have finally noticed I was missing and went to seek me out before their master got a whiff of their carelessness. Leaping out of the water, like dolphins in a pod, they took after me.

I twisted back toward the rock, scrambling.

When my feet hit the slippery lakebed, I cried out in a painful glee. Rocks pierced my numb feet, massaging blood back into them while I made my way up toward the overhanging saplings that lined the narrow hillside.

My fingers latched onto the branch of a young pine, just as I felt clawing up my legs.

Screaming, I kicked back, angry red lesions drew down across my limbs as three Merfolk used their nails to hook and drag me back.

I white knuckled the branch, dropping to punch one in the jaw with my free hand. It screeched and fell back from me, releasing my right foot so I could kick another one with my heel.

The pain was little consequence now. I switched hands and flung my coat at the last attacker who thrashed under the sudden substance blocking its view.

Taking the chance given, my arms bolted firmly about the tree limb, attempting to lift myself up with adrenaline seized push. Relief sounded in my head when the vegetation kept my weight. I dangled precariously over the creature-infested water, swinging my body intending to get enough momentum to push myself up onto the higher embankment.

Shrieking barks sounded below me. They changed their tactics and took turns in flinging themselves up into the air hoping to snag one of my legs.

Flailing my body, I pushed hard then suddenly let go.

Time slowed with bated breath until I stumbled onto the earthy ridge. My ankle gave out, and I crumbled to the floor. Nails dug and scraped into the graveled soil, attempting to keep a firm hold on my new found terrain, lest I should stumble back into the water.

The Merfolk beat the surface with their fins, screaming defiantly at me.

I was safe. They couldn't get me from here. At least, that's what I wanted to tell myself. I made that mistake, caught in the disbelief of what it was to be in a safe position. Then the moment was quickly snatched from me.

A hollow thump sounded.

Loose gravel rolled down, spattering lightly into the water below.

Twisting my head back, I saw the bruised faced of a Merfolk digging her arms into the soil, dragging her lower limb across the rough ground.

Eyes widening, I kicked and shouted while the animal wormed its body up after me. Gnashing her teeth dangerously in my direction, she took a swipe and missed.

Tucking my legs away from her I grappled for anything I could use as a weapon. Rock! My fingers registered the solid object, bringing it down onto her reaching hand.

They all screamed together with the sounds of their wounded kin, but I knew what they did to their injured. They didn't favor the weak. If they scented blood, it would all be over for this one.

Snapping at me, she squealed with another blow of the rock.

Retaliation was swift.

The Merfolk knocked against the side of my head with her splayed webbed fingers, grabbing a fistful of my hair.

"NO," I tore back, clenching my teeth while hitting the blunt object along its clammy form. "GET OFF ME!!!" I shrieked bloody murder while we toppled backward.

Her body hit the rocks below, snapping her neck and cushioning my fall. I stared in horror as the light faded from her wide gaping eyes. Black oozed from the back of her head, spreading in cancerous tendrils across the water's surface— like an oil spill.

They had a new sound I hadn't foreseen, a strange whirring hoot with nostrils flaring. Sniffing the air, their chins tipped up in search of our scent. *Could they not see us? Me?*

Pulling back, I hugged the side of the hill where the water met land. The area was shallow and jagged with large boulders. They could get at me from here, but it wouldn't be as easy as swimming.

I watched them pin their fallen sister about the neck to pull her under the lake surface.

Hunger was their primary attention. They couldn't see me. Hilly mentioned they were bottom feeders. Their eyes were large pools for viewing in dark spaces. That meant they could only smell me. *What do you do when an animal can smell you?*

I grabbed fistfuls of damp earth, rubbing it along my body, favoring my weak ankle; a desperate act in the last ditch effort to save my skin proved its weight in gold. When a few reemerged to sniff the air, barking, and chirping, they looked through me.

Taking a step over to another rock, they only slapped their tails. I made a few more careful steps, holding my balance by leaning to the side of the embankment. They heard me, I noted, but they couldn't identify my location.

My journey was precariously slow. One rock after the other I crossed the side of Crescent until I made it up to the orange buoys of East Beach. I could just spot a few cars in the distance. The rock hopping ended. I had to go up to make it over to the beach side. There, I could call for help. Hope fluttered at the sight.

Turning, I crawled up the side of the slanting embankment on all four. Body favoring my right ankle, I dragged myself onto a well-worn trail and settled a moment. I lugged out my wool socks, squeezing them dry as much as I could.

Observing my foot, I realized it was the same one I had damaged on Basle's door.

I found that amusing and stared at the swelling limb, laughing.

Stress had gotten to me as I wiped at my running nose, sniffling but not quite crying.

CHAPTER 18

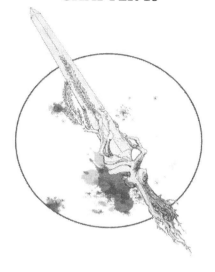

TUESDAY MIDDAY—PART 2

Now that my body was calming down, the crisp air was getting to me more and more.
Cold, filthy, in pain, and completely shell-shocked, I don't think there was anything on me that wasn't throbbing.

Peering around at my environment, I regarded the branches of the pine and cedar with a bland outlook, using them to lift myself up in a standing position. With measured breathing, I took uneven steps along the pathway, picking a sturdy stick to take pressure off my lame foot. I used that moment to try dissecting what had just happened.

I had just gone through hell for the sake of a cheap bracelet. The least my mom could have done was get something of value.

Perhaps an epic passage into the lake to retrieve a gold ring belonging to an ancient sorcerer—*too close to Lord of the Rings...* Or a family necklace bearing sapphires made of enchanted dragon's tears. Maybe a bottle carrying a letter from William Dyrling that spoke of a missing talisman that would break the family curse? *You know... something extraordinary.*

If I was being honest though, my sarcasm was deflecting how absurd I felt for getting this rattled. I never thought of myself as weak, many things, brooding, insecure, cynical, and unforgiving, but *not* weak.

There were those who had gone through so much worse. Losing their families to fires, human trafficking, watching a child wither away from a disease their bodies can't fight. Yet here I was, sniveling over scratches from some mutated fish.

"Screw you, *Ariel.*" I growled. No one ever said anything about Fae curses, deals, and magic. No one ever wrote a self-help book on how to overcome the trauma of mythological monsters that use your family as a plaything.

"EMMALINE!?!?!?"

The cry shattered my seething thoughts. Jerking my head, I peeked through the saplings, toward the lake below. Hilly's voice rolled over my body, crippling me with fear. She had finally found me gone.

Fog stretched across the freshwater, rolling softly up the hillside toward me. The image sent the memory of the newspaper clipping to the forefront of my mind. *'Some say her spirit still dwells within the walls of Lake Crescent Lodge, sitting and smoking a cigarette, while speaking to unsuspecting tourists... others say they have seen her from a distance walking the shoreline of the lake where her body was recklessly dumped...'*

Could she really walk that far onto shore? The lodge was over a hundred feet away from the shoreline yet there had been reports of her inside the building. If that were true, at this moment, I wasn't even fifteen feet away from the lake. I paled.

"EMMALINE, I KNOW YOU ARE OUT THERE. I AM OWED A DEBT YOU MUST RIGHTFULLY PAY."

What was she talking about? I had no debts to her! How was it that she could scream her head off and only Unmentionables hear her?

I looked around as if I could find the perfect bush to hide under. I would not switch with her if that's what she was implying. That wasn't my fate. I'd be damned if I got back into that water, alive.

"Oh god..." *Was that really what she wanted? Why did she leave if she wanted to see me dead and floating in the water as a corpse?*

"Emmaline!?" Her voice was closer. Her minions must have divulged the spot I had disappeared to.

Taking off along the forest trail, I bit the inside of my cheeks, gearing the pain away from my ankle. My future continuously seemed less than stellar. When the trail opened toward the swimming hole, I dug the stick deep into the ground; carefully descending the precarious footholds made of root and molded earth.

There it was, the gravel driveway leading up and away from the lake toward the main road. It could bring me back to civilization, back to James. Then again, I could make a beeline for the cars I had spotted earlier. Even if the fog had settled, I could still make out the outline of a red Trailblazer parked not forty feet from me. I knew they must have a cellphone. I could call James.

The Lady of the Lake wouldn't come out when humans were present, would she?

So I screamed, like a madwoman who got her jollies from watching people pee their pants from jump scares.

I waved my stick as I hobbled along toward the vehicles. "HELP! HELP! PLEASE, HELP!!!" I made it to the first car. My hopes soared as I knocked on the glass quickly. "Hello? Hello, please! I need help! I'm hurt!"

I pressed close, cupping my hand against the glass to see inside.

There was *no one*. In fact, there was nothing inside I could see. Not even a purse tucked between the two front seats or an ornament that hung from the rearview mirror.

I went to the other car, a green Jeep Cherokee, smacking on the windows with the palm of my hands.

It was just as empty as the first. I was hyperventilating.

Did she take them? Did she possess them and force them to walk into the water, disappearing forever?

I hurried across the parking lot toward the picnic tables beyond. *Maybe they were in the bathroom...*

"Really, if I thought you would have been this fun to watch, I would have brought a human or two and strewn them around to watch how you would react to their corpses."

384

That wasn't Hilly's voice, alarmingly familiar, but yes, nothing to be thrilled about. "Well, little twit. What do you have to say for yourself?"

Twit...

"Shut up Louella, you'll only make her scream."

"Then shall we? I'd rather take her and be done with all this nonsense... the bitch can rot in that lake with her little cretins for all I care."

"C-Corrigan?" I gasped in disbelief. The British brogue of his voice was far too unique to forget. I felt faint, leaning against the Trailblazer for balance. "Corrigan, is FaeKing with you?"

"No." Louella cut in. "This is the diversion... So, why don't you hand over the bracelet before the lake weed realizes we are here?"

I had no reason not to, but something unsettled my gut. A feeling called *bullshit.*

They stepped closer within the veil of mist shrouding overhead. I could finally make out their forms. Corrigan, his amber eyes were deadly calm.

"How do you know about the bracelet?"

Louella bristled branches on her back rustling in irritation. "The Lady of the Lake," she concluded, "has a very large unhinged mouth. You let it be known you have a certain stature in the Unseen realm and words just fall out," She gestured a twirl with her hands.

Fae cannot lie, they have told me, and so why was this feeling so... wrong?

"Corrigan?" I focused on him again. "Is this true?"

"Demanding. Why would it not be true?" Louella spoke for him.

"Because the only people who know of the bracelet are Hilly, my mom, and I," I gave a look. "How would you know that she had it in the first place? And no, I won't give FaeKing the bracelet back until Abigail is safe and sound."

"You've been hurt," Corrigan finally spoke, stepping forward. "And dirty... and I am sure, quite tired. Come with me, I'll take you from this place."

"Corrigan," Louella hissed at him, giving him an expression I couldn't quite follow. "Just hand over the bracelet." She demanded, grabbing toward me with bruising strength.

"Trying to leave with my prize, are you?"

"Oh look, the Lady of the Lake finally graced us with her presence." The tree woman gave a dirty glance toward Hilly's untimely appearance. Her own unearthly beauty had since twisted into something disturbing and evil.

That was when I realized this wasn't about me, at least not directly; this was about the Kings sight. *Were these two here on the order of FaeKing or someone else?*

At this point, I wasn't sure if I was glad or sickened that the Lady of the Lake was here. For all the hurt and pain she'd been through, she, herself, had returned it threefold. I hadn't much sympathy for her plight anymore. Especially as it could be a life and death situation. *Luckily, she was doing an excellent job at averting the attention from me.* Louella was easily one for dramatics, making the pair perfect to feed off each other.

"We had a deal, Louella. Your master needs to uphold her end of the bargain. I upheld mine." She stepped from the water but wavered in appearance. She disappeared from her spot, and then came back a few feet from the other female.

"And what exactly were you promised, *soap spirit?*" Louella hadn't budged an inch.

"I was told someone would set me free, that She had ways of manipulating the balance. That, if you regained the vessel from Crescent's depths, She could take it... wield it in my favor."

"She did, spirit. It failed."

"That was the mother. She was overly spent as it was." Hilly pointed toward me, and I stiffened. She was getting angry and desperate. "She said Emmaline was the key. She was strong enough to tip the scales!!!"

Something inside me lurched uncomfortably, picking up bits of the confusing conversation to roll them around like rough, unpolished rocks in my mind.

The mother...

"Ah, I see your confusion." Louella hummed. "You may have given over the bracelet to the girl, Lady of the Lake. But as far as 'handing' the twit over, you did no such thing." Hilly's eyebrows furled when she got the other had scammed her. "You let her escape your grasp. She fell for our trick. You lose. We win. Tata, now. shoo." She gave a dismissive flick of her hand.

A storm crackled overhead in Hilly's anger. "Do. NOT. Dismiss me like I am some lowly being you can toss and toy with, Louella. You aren't powerful enough."

"You do not seem to get it, spirit, you're already dead." The other female laughed maliciously. "The only power you hold is linked to this forsaken mud puddle you call home." All four of her eyes widening with glee, "and you, you are simply a pile of soap suds, held together by grief and a curse."

Hilly Mortimer screamed in a rage. Fog swirled about the shoreline further coating it in a dense curtain. I could no longer see the supernatural beings, but I could hear their continued banter. The ground shook as cedar trees bent to lend their strength to the tree woman while water crashed against the shore to meet the challenge.

Shivering, I turned to look at the cars hoping they were unlocked. Tugging on a door handle, I stumble back as it came clean off the side of the Trailblazer. My eyes went wide when I watched it melt into a piece of vegetation, paint flaking off and crumbling into glistening flecks of sand. The vehicles were just a rotted patch of squash.

How could I not have seen that? Dropping the vine with disgust, I wiped the oozing juice off my hand and onto my shirt.

Hobbling toward the long inclined driveway, I knew if I got onto East Beach Road and headed toward the highway, I could flag someone down.

A brilliant plan with poor execution, I forgot Corrigan.

"And where are you off too, Miss Darling?"

"Attempting not to drown... or get frisked by a tree." I bit out.

"That isn't how this will go, Miss Darling." His image appeared unexpectedly, white top hat looming as he leaned in to inspect me.

I lost my footing, gasping.

388

The frost Fae reached out with biting hands, grabbing me about the waist and upper arm to keep me from toppling backward. He leaned in and softly murmured, "You are supposed to act like a good little damsel, let the girls tear themselves apart so I may step in and take you to FaeKing."

"What is the point in that?" I hissed, shoving him away.

"There are plots arising you have yet to know of, Emmaline."

I clenched my hands tightly to my crudely made walking stick, giving him a look. "Get to the point."

"Pull your thoughts to the present. Were you not listening? Louella has persuasion to another authority." His hands ran down to my wrists, tensing as weighted ice encased them.

"Hey!?"

"Sssh, you have his sight?"

"Yes. So get me the HELL out of here."

"Emmaline," he held my forearms and shook firmly, giving a stern look. "I am trying to assist you. You must understand we are being watched and not by those who favor us living." Corrigan was trying very hard to stay calm while the commotion sounded behind us.

He forced me down into a crouch as the body of a Merfolk flew overhead. Hitting the trunk of a stationary pine, she dropped limp a few feet away. Something had broken her jaw. Blood seeped through her chest where a branch was protruding.

Shivering, my eyes stared transfixed on the carcass until Corrigan guided me off into the obscurity.

Stepping down onto the bark laden shoreline, the chaos ensued. There were large towering western red cedar and

389

white pine trees animated before me, the ground shaking as their twisted bodies drove to pull from their resting spots. They swayed, roots coiled and curled like snakes as they made their way toward the lake, intent to attack the Mercreatures.

In the short time it took Corrigan to reason with me, Louella had fought the lake spirit into the shallows.

"Get out of the water Louella." He called in warning. "Do not fight outside your element!"

"I have this!" She insisted, looking smug as the trees passed her.

In the command to protect, the saplings arched over and scooped their aggressors up, tossing them away in haphazard directions. Their trunks sliced through the water, dropping limbs down onto the shrieking entities to trap them underwater. With firm pressure, pools of black rose to the surface in their stead.

"Your abominations have nothing on the ancients of this forest, Lake Weed." Louella leered, walking farther into the water to taunt Hilly.

"You will pay for this Louella," The Lady of the Lake bellowed shrilly. "I will make sure you drowned in these waters!"

A distinct sucking echoed from out of the gloom beyond. When the treading Merfolk began to be swept outward—*too late*—I registered the colossal wave rising high above the depths of Crescent, climbing clear to the tree line.

Hilly laughed elatedly as the Fae stumbled unexpectedly forward.

"Louella!" Corrigan shifted to assist her, but she had already toppled into the groundswell, pulling her body out into the water thrashing.

Tails slapped behind the Merfolk as they dove after her in avid excitement. I stared in horror as the surge gained its peak, rolling down toward the beach.

Doubling back, Corrigan was swift to react. Looping an arm about my shoulders, he raised his hand to have crackling ice from where his skin met water. Dragging his fingers up and overhead, they molded a precariously formed a pocket of safety, narrowly beating the flood.

Brittle cracks let water trickle in while the wave crashed down and back out, dragging a few smaller animated trees with. His face looked strained, frost creeping out from his hairline, spreading across his eyebrows in his concentration.

It had happened so quickly. I hadn't had the chance to digest the sheer power it must have taken to shield both of us before the ice shattered around us.

"Holy shit," I breathed.

Louella popped up within the buoyed swimming hole, a large maple followed faithfully after her, scooping her up and out of the water.

"You vile wench," she spat out at the lake spirit. "Corrigan!? Where are you!?"

"Keeping the girl from running off," his shoulders were bedazzled in ice droplets, steadily forming dangerous looking stalagmites.

"She's half dead, Corrigan, where could she run to?"

"And you, frost man." Hilly cut in, "You think your tricks can keep me from taking what is rightfully owed to me?" she

391

glitched onto a rock protruding from the shallows, creeping closer.

The merfolk were patrolling along the deep end, diving and bobbing around the tree that held Louella.

"Yes," He replied lacing his fingers together to give them a pop. "I will give you on the count of three to either slither back into the depths where you belong or meet my challenge. My patience grows thin."

"Kill her already!" Louella growled. "Put me down," she barked dismissively to her savior.

Compliantly the old plant bowed, shivering in the wake of her power.

"One…" Corrigan ignored the irritations that came along with being saddled up with the wooden woman. He kept his sights on the lake spirit. Hilly hesitated but didn't back down. "Two…"

She played the appearance of weighing out her options while a patch of water vented a few hundred feet offshore. Bubbles foamed and ruptured with the agitated excitement as a swirling pool began to spread. It abruptly exploded inwardly with a massive bursting splash. More waves crashed across the shoreline with the weight of a sizeable rusted barge rising off the lakebed. The corroded heap of metal was hurtled toward us. She gave her answer.

Corrigan glided up off the ground, leaving skidded ice tracks behind him as he scooped me up abruptly and tossed me out of range.

Falling and rolling into a patch of dead grass, I inhaled a sharp breath.

The ground thundered below us as the barge smashed into the earth. Peeking back, it had taken out half the embankment where a picnic table had once stood. Louella had collapsed somewhere to the other side of the eroded machinery and was screaming about her leg being caught.

Liquid drew up magnetically to Corrigan's feet, keeping the frost Fae from sinking into the poisoned water. He was ignoring the screams, sights dead set to the lake spirit before him.

Hilly's dead eyes widened. Another wave swelled with a boost of her hand, attempting to force him back.

The Fae dodged, coming at her.

Get yourself together…

Breathing, I grabbed a fistful of grass using it to guide me into an upright position. Louella's words turned pleading, landing me in an uncomfortable moral standpoint. She wanted me dead the moment we met, but she sounded trapped, in pain. *Could I really leave her like that?* I could get up, walk myself up the driveway and get away from them all. I could flag someone down and call James.

"Twit… Emmaline…" She called out. "Emmaline, I need help," she begged.

"Louella… are you badly hurt?" I carefully stepped around the crumpled raft, making my way to the tree woman's side to see the damage.

She was in bad shape. Her body lay twisted, with an arm splintered in several sections, while the barge had trapped her leg from the knee down, hemorrhaging sap across the gravel. "What the fuck does it look like?" She moaned in

393

pain. "Oh god... you... you have to cut it off." She was twitching, watching me with a tortured expression.

"What!?" I was appalled.

"I-iron... the iron! The iron..." her eyes closed while swallowing thickly. "It's spreading through my veins. If you don't cut it off, I'll die."

"B-but... how?"

She gestured toward a branch lying askew a few feet away. "My branch... take it up and dip the broken end in my sap." She gestured to the puddle forming by her leg.

I grimaced.

Awkwardly taking up Louella's limb between cuffed hands, I rolled it carefully in her blood as instructed.

"Now hold out the other end. No, keep hold," She ordered. "I don't have the strength to operate it."

Gripping the stick halfway, I shivered while observing her sap drizzle down across my fingers. When she clutched the fractured end, her branch grew roots and embedded into her palm. I felt it shift under my fingers, turning to a hilt before me. The amber liquid rippled and fanned out to form a resin blade. The edge appeared sharp but could it pierce wood? "Stop gawking and cut it off!"

"I... Louella, it's your leg," I stared down into her four eyes, glaring in disbelief.

"I'm a fucking tree." She disentangled herself from the sword, dropping motionless. Her remaining energy spent. "I'll grow it back. Cut. It. Off," she wheezed.

"O-oh." *Like a starfish...*

Why me? Why, out of anyone, did it have to be me?

"CUT IT OFF!!!"

394

I gritted my teeth, bringing it down hard—an ax to kindling, five inches from the kneecap— the blade shattered when hitting the ground.

Her tormented shriek rang in my ears, unsettling my soul.

Stepping back, I watched her desperately dig her fingers into the soil. Small white hairs sprouted from her barked skin, reaching for the earth. They grew in thickness, maturing into dense roots while her lithe body melded together to form the trunk of an albino redwood. Expanding where she laid the white needles plumed across her limbs, leaving a ghostly watermark within the mist.

"Louella?" She was quiet. "Louella, are you alive?" Not even a twitch.

She left me standing on the shore, helplessly watching old growth warriors blunder in disarray. They were awoken and then left deserted in a restless state of wandering. Corrigan skated passed the largest of the maple, unaware of Louella's current state, and got knocked across the water like a hockey puck.

Luckily he didn't sink, leaving patches of ice to melt into slush.

I couldn't keep up with the madness.

He was struggling to rise back onto his feet when hands of a few Merfolk caught up to him. They were reaching up with their webbed hands, attempting to pull him down.

Hilly was glitching from one spot to another, darting around with madness in her gaze. When he was preoccupied with her underlings, she drew herself closer. Her toes skimming the waterline as her hair and tattered clothes flowed out in a suspended state.

Her skeletal fingers wrapped about his throat, squeezing. "CORRIGAN!?"

He was clearly choking. I pushed out into the water, feeling my chest surge with a painful wave of heat.

"Fool, get up the hill!" He coughed out, deep freezing a few hands. An iceberg formed below his feet, pushing him up and away from the beings so he could blast the spirit away with a gust of blistering cold air.

Where was Hilly's power coming from? How could a mortal spirit hold such sway over the elements?

I searched across the ebbing fog. "Get up the hill Emmaline!!!" Corrigan called again. "I can't protect yo—WATCH OUT!!!"

There was nothing but black for a split moment. Static prickled the corners of my vision, feeling pressure in my eardrums and chest. I hit something hard then took in water.

Sputtering, coughing, trying to find something to grab onto. There was nothing. My arms were trapped in ice.

Panicking, I was sinking.

"EMMALINE!?" Corrigan's eyes were uncommonly wide as I dipped below the waterline.

CHAPTER 19

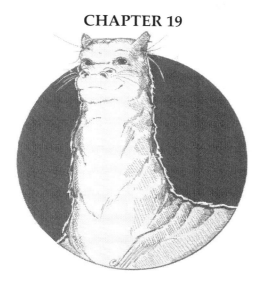

TUESDAY AFTERNOON

Silence evaded, encasing me in a hyper sense of mind. I hurt from a pain that seemed to pulse through every inch of my being. I must have been hit by a tree, there was no other explanation.

Abigail…

Movement flickered in the murky waters before me as my body settled to the lakebed, toes skimming the sediment. *When would be the moment my brain shut off?* I forced my eyes opened, despite the burn, watching a rippling shadow slither across the sunken landscape. Fish were scattered in fear. The grasses were thrown into disarray while the mass churned the water.

My chest flushed, radiating with a fever.

Was this drowning?

The gliding string of darkness steadily solidified, growing larger the closer it drew toward the shoreline. When it seemed to pass the designated swimming hole, it whirled about, picking off Merfolk who were still teeming in the undertow.

I tossed about like a weed in the upsurge created, my hair clouding my vision. Tensing, I felt something solid collide against me, driving me upwards. Hands joined the action, hooking under my arms to force me out of the muck. We broke the surface, spray erupting from—what it sounded like—flaring nostrils of the creature cradling me to its back. My chest expanded painfully as I gulped the fresh air, distracted, while hands wordlessly pulled me closer. A chin resting to my shoulder as we pushed back toward the beach.

Taken the appearance of a snow globe, a flurry of sleet consumed the area. It slithered along the hillside, forcing rooted vegetation to bow from the weight. Merfolk had frozen halfway in their places, others trapped on top of the frozen terrain, where their fins grew stuck. Old growth had become so top heavy that they fell forward into the freshwater, glazing over with frost nipping across their sodden branches. The larger, aggressive oak tree had been hastily pulling his roots from the skating rink, a few cracking off, still protruding out from the freeze keeping him hostage.

Louella was nothing but a specter in the widespread devastation Corrigan had fashioned. *But where was he?*

Nervously, I finally mustered up enough sense to peer over my shoulder. James's dark eyes stared back through the

398

damp curls sticking to his face. He gave a reassuring grin, display a row of unnaturally sharp teeth.

"I came just in time."

"James... how did—"

"Long story," he muttered, reaching around me to work at the ice on my wrists. "We need to end this before the bigger fish step in." His hands made quick action in placing pressure to either side of the block until it cracked and collapsed.

"Thank god," I rotated my hands, finding it odd I hadn't gotten frostbitten or grown numb from the cool, another magical thing to not become distracted with. I focused on the slick muted fur that ran along the body of the creature. Muscles rippled while they shifted to lead us directly up against the ice. Our bodies lurched forward on impact, a massive otter-like paw rose from the deep to hook about the side of the floating tundra, keeping us stationary.

When the creature finally bowed their head to me, I was staring into the softball-sized eyes of Cressie.

"Oh, wow..."

She blinked twice with both lids, short rounded tufts rotated toward us to listen and wait patiently. I could see creamy grey flecking her under neck, melding into the soft muddy tones of her back. Four nostrils flared at James as he slid from her to the ice carefully, snapping underfoot, causing her to slap the end of her tail nervously.

She was worried about him.

"Emma, Corrigan went too far. I need to get this under control before the neighborhood gets curious. Cressie will bring you back to the lodge," I went to protest, but he shook his head firmly. "I want you to get as far away from the lake as you can. I'll find you again, but get out of the water." He stepped backward, facing me with a grin, "We have a bunch of Umends throwing their weight around, Emma. We can't have that."

"How is that your job? Why are you supposed to fix it? W-wait! Don't leave!" I was anxious, watching him trudge away from me. Cressie pushed slowly form the sheet of ice, making a soft whirring noise.

I hunched down quickly, gripping her hair to steady myself.

"Who else will do it?" He turned halfway toward me, glancing back to give me a steady look. "Get out of here Emma. Whatever you might see, just get out." He took off toward the shore, toward a frosty lump of spikes that shifted across the tundra.

Cupping my hand to my brow, I peered steadily toward the fighting scene. The armor was thick, dangerous. Enveloped with raw crystal-like points, pikes crowned the snow creature's forehead where they slated down along its spine to gather into a pattern of moving scales. Their central core radiated beneath the protection of a translucent breastplate while two pinpricks of orange blazed angrily across a sharp frosted face.

They were making swift hasty punches toward the presence of the Lady of the Lake who was listlessly popping in and out of the ice knight's view.

Corrigan...

What had he done to himself?

I didn't get to find out. James was just reaching him when the lake monster pulled around the curve of the lake, blocking my view.

We headed back toward open waters. Quiet, peaceful and attentive, Cressie twisted her head back to give me a lopsided stare when I couldn't seem to sit still. I calmed then, resting my head to her back, running my fingers through her fur, watching the scenic view roll by.

"I'm useless..." I told her. "All of this fuss over a stupid piece of jewelry." Reaching down, I felt the lump for reassurance.

There was a soft rumbling of warning coming from my ride before she flattened her body into the water. Panicking, I had flashes of being re-submerged until the distant sound of a motorboat met my ears. Understanding, I huddled down to tuck my legs behind me, looking as small as possible without pressing my face into the water. We both kept this way until the bystander passed.

Cressie looked back at me again, blinking her eyelids, the four nostrils lining her snout flexed. For a moment we shared a quiet expression, curving my mental pain if only for a moment.

Slowly, she resumed our travel.

Shy creature...

The weather was cold, yet somehow I was withstanding the temperature. The mysteries of this unraveling world boggled what I knew as common sense. Breathing underwater was not normal. Riding a lake monster, wet, in frigid weather... That was not normal. I could never do these things before. *What was protecting me?*

Cutting through the lake with ease, Cressie took me serenely up to a deserted cove where a paved trail could be seen beyond a mass of reeds. Around the corner Crescent Lodge was just a few hundred yards away, meaning we made a long roundabout trail to the other side of Crescent Lodge, where Bovee's Cove lied. A clearing, surrounded by old growth stood with vacant picnic tables, a perfect time for Crescent Lake's monster to drop me off without wandering eyes.

"I don't know how to thank you..." I stood to the water, ankle deep, favoring my foot. I watched her vast webbed feet unsettle the silt of the shallows as she adjusted her large breast against the floor. Leaning down, her face brushed along my forehead, nostrils taking turns to blow hot misty air on me. Long whiskers brushed across my cheeks. "Will I see you again?"

Peering up, I raised a hand hesitantly where she abruptly butted her chin against my knuckles. She allowed me to rub the underside of her head long enough to have a quiet rumbling purr escape. Oh... damn, that's adorable. Her gills flared when she flexed her neck to look back. The lake guardian's ear nubs twitched forward, staring at the water intently.

"What are you looking at... fish?" Smiling, despite the circumstance, I peered past her massive body to see a pair of eyes peeking out from the water, long tendril air fanned about the face.

I stumbled back into the reeds in fear. *Not again...* Wondering when the torment would end. Feeling my hands through the muck, I could catch hold of the slope, where I tried climbing backward as quickly as feasible.

"Emmy…" the wind whispered. "Don't be afraid…"

I shrank still. My eyes felt wide and imploring.

Only two people call me that…

The entity pulled closer, wet curls and clothing drawing snug against her flesh as she took a few more careful steps toward me. Her body had taken on subdued opaque tones, but her eyes shown a brilliant blue with flecks of brown, showcasing the light of her soul.

She smiled tenderly.

"M-mom?" My eyes were stinging. "No, that isn't fair… that isn't fair at all."

It petrified me, my breathing hitched.

Out of all the dirty tricks the Lady of the Lake could do, to take on the form of my mom was spiteful. I was panicking. I could hear it in the irregular pattering of my heart, pulsing up my neck and into my ears.

I couldn't catch my breath.

"We haven't much time." She halted when she must have realized how scared I really was. A devastated look crossed her lovely face before she squatted down to peer up at me. "Emmy…"

"You died." I bit out. "You freaking died, how… how can you be here?"

She looked troubled, glancing briefly to the lake. "How can any of this be? They tricked me." She breathed, "Hilly thought I was the ticket to replace her, but she was dead wrong." She snorted at her own morose joke. "Sweetheart,

403

I'm here for a reason, and sadly, these encounters may only happen when a dire circumstance arises."

I crab-walked my way back down through the weeds, staring wearily. Cressie was resting her head down, watching us with one glassy eye open.

Which meant…?

I launched myself at her form, trying to hold her, keep her close.

"Oh, sweetheart…" I went right through, stumbling to my knees and jarring my foot. "I'm so sorry…" Her voice was in soft, sad strokes, making me shiver. *What else could she say?*

Digging my fingers painfully into the rocks, my face reddened with tears. I held my breath, scrunching my eyes before pressing the palms of my hands against them. "H-he's got, Abigail." I choked out. "I don't know what to do anymore."

"I'll tell you…" she promised. When I blinked away the spots, I found her kneeling in front of me. She reached up in instinct to brush away my tears. The action was futile.

We peered quietly to each other before I let out the breath I had been holding.

"Hilly will not stop. There is a deeper more ancient power settled in this valley… one that has twisted her into something other than human or Fae. She will tear this place apart. She will hurt others to get to you." she lightly pointed to the locket on my chest, "I can stop her… but I need your help, do you understand?"

Taking up the piece of jewelry, I gawked at it in confusion. "This is keeping me from being swayed by Fae." She nodded sympathetically, "Mom, it's kept me from being under the influence of magic, you want me to give that away?"

"Emmy, Fae can't influence you. This locket is doing nothing but be bug repellent." She held up three fingers. "Scout's honor, you're stronger than you're giving yourself credit for."

I moved to retort when Cressie stirred from her spot, nostrils flaring her ears rotated again. "She hears the Ceasg... the water people."

Hesitantly, I pulled the locket from the safe spot on my neck. Miraculously it had stayed with me all this time. Feeling the security leave me, I held it out to her. "You need to be brave, Emmaline..."

"It's hard." I stared at her. "I don't think I can do this anymore, mom."

"You can do this. I'll guide you... all you need to do is hold the necklace and I'll do the rest." Dawn drew from me slowly, backtracking into the water with the lake guardian. "I'll be watching and waiting," She encouraged. "I won't ever let you sink."

Watching my mother slip down beneath the surface, they left only but a soft ripple. The entire interaction felt like a mirage. *Was I hallucinating?* I hadn't had time to figure it out. The telltale noise of shrieking Merfolk met my ears.

Scrambling back up to the beach, I settled the locket to my unoccupied pocket, feeling dramatically under qualified for such a feat. Two Fae and a Changeling went up against the Lady of the Lake, and somehow she still walked away. What did my mom expect me to do, riddle Hilly into a pile of soap?

I tried to tell myself I wasn't alone, that I had this, but I was squirming.

My brain screamed at me to run, to curl up in a hole and make myself disappear from the insanity that picked my family off one by one. James warned me. *Yet, here I was, listening to my dead mom's advice.*

Hilly Mortimer's body twitched and appeared within the reeds several feet away. Loathing rolled off her body as heavy as the mist that surrounded us. "Emmaline Darling, how nice it must be to have so many concerned for your welfare."

My shoulders tensed. "I'm tired of running," I finally called to her.

"You're resigned? How cheeky and I've only just started."

"Well, I don't see Corrigan or James," I swallowed thickly. "So that must mean you've won."

That was bating.

"Serves him right for what he's done." She cocked her bony head to the side. "He got himself all worked up, now he's just a stationary Popsicle." She laughed at that. "As for your main squeeze, he's got a few of his own problems occupying his attention."

So, he wasn't dead... I wasn't willing to relax just yet.

"What do you mean?" daring to ask.

"Something about being halfway fused with an oak tree." She tossed her hand lightly back and forth in gesture, "Must hurt."

My jaw clenched. "If I give up, will you leave them alone?"

Glitching before me with a sudden crazed desire, her eyes narrowed to scrutinize me. "If that's all that requires you to submit..." I stiffened as she raised a bony digit in my direction. She stretched out, reaching for my neck. "By my blood..." She repeated, mesmerized. "None shall stake, less you are my kin sake."

I sucked in a stuttering breath.

An odd sensation ran along my insides. Like small tendrils of cobwebs brushing across my flesh, starting from the tips of my limbs and pooling toward her touch.

The web filtered together, forming a humming ball of warmth to my core. When she drew her finger back, soft crystalline sunbursts trickled from me.

Alarmed, I pushed from her. Splashing and flailing back into the reeds.

This was wrong.

The spirit's captivated state filtered into shock and then into a seething rage.

"I WILL HAVE WHAT IS RIGHTFULLY MINE." She drew up, soap suds dropped from her frame to spoil the shore with frothing tides. She lunged at me.

I screamed, tumbling down the embankment into the mud.

"Emmaline!" I could hear my mom calling even as the entity wrapped her skeletal hand about my neck, squeezing, pushing me down further. She gathered the points of her fingers to press them painfully against me, drawing the glistening spectral slowly from my chest.

"EMMALINE!?!?!"

Convulsing, mud squelched around my form to suction me to the ground.

It was becoming harder to move while Hilly's expression twisted above me. Her attempts to subdue me changed with the intentions of drowning me when I wouldn't submit death.

My hands inevitably slipped under strain, head falling back below the muddy liquid. Dulling my senses with an all-pervading silence...

I felt my heartbeat, the ringing of my life ticking away.

I didn't want to be trapped in this lake, consumed by fear and hate as Hilly had.

Kicking, my lungs felt tight.

I didn't want to die!

Amidst the chaos, I found warmth humming, building up to a pressure against my back. Reminiscent of a hug, the sensation took over the primitive distress of dying.

The embrace flowed across my arms, guiding the locket from its confines to force it roughly about Hilly's neck.

In that split moment, a nova explosion vented into the air, my soul colliding back into my body.

Hilly's spirit instantly released me, being flung back.

I gasped, blinking the gloom from my eyes.

Hilly Mortimer shrieked writhing in agony as her ghostly flesh sizzled where the locket touched her.

Suddenly, the pendant sprung open before her, revealing a small bound clump of charred substance within.

Sensing corruption, the locket produced a cool blue flame from its core, leeching obscure ooze that wriggled outward from her suspended frame. All the festering darkness she kept from the years of torment and twisted sense of justice, filtered inside.

When there was nothing left, I watched her form collapse into a pile of soap suds.

Falling to my rear, my eyes crossed slightly.

"*Thank you...*" Hilly's voice echoed across the lake, causing shivers to run down my spine.

She was gone.

A trace of pressure graced my temple. My tired eyes looked up to find my mom kneeling beside me. She brushed her hand across my matted hair.

"You've done so well, sweetheart..."

Snow was drifting down from the low-hanging clouds above.

"M-mom, you're going away..." she was melting slowly. "Please don't leave..."

Me.

"The lake is calling," She spoke softly, a flicker of worry crossing her face. "You get Abigail home... you get her safe." Leaning in, she whispered softly into my ear.

Snow was already sticking to the ground.

I curled over, vaguely remembering the closed locket clutched to Dawn Darlings hand before I passed out.

CHAPTER 20

TUESDAY EVENING

Dark... There was darkness all around. Sweet, peaceful darkness that was, for a minute, a vastness of eternal dreaming. I let it wrap about me, like a soft downy blanket, to cocoon me from the wears of the world beyond.

'**Em-maline...**' The darkness spoke softly, lulling me to rest.

'**Em-maline... you'll feel better soon...**' There was a gentle caress of the velvet shade.

Why would I possibly want to wake when this felt so safe?

The gloom spoke with another tone, another voice.

'**Em-ma, come on, wake up...**' *If staying here meant prolonging my healing then I would fight it.* '**Em-ma... stop fighting... you need to take this to heal!**' The second voice was frustrated. I didn't like it when it was cross... '**Em! You** can't keep yourself like this!' My world shook, and I cowered within my nest.

The softer one came back.

'Em-maline, if you wish to stay a thoughtless invalid forever... be my guest.'

There was silence for a long while, so I settled back into my black world in reflection.

'Please...' it trickled through, ever-so-softly. **'Em-maline, you've climbed so far...'**

Dark...

There was darkness all around...

...

My eyes snapped open, and I gasped in panic. Clutching my chest to take long gulps of air, I attempted to stabilize my quickening heart rate. I was in the dark. Sheets entangled in my legs as my mind tried to make sense of the fleeting traces of my dream state.

Within the recesses, I remembered two trees. One with the colors of autumn, vivid maroon and ginger leaves, stark against its mossy trunk. The other was more surreal. Plum with cobalt accents adorning a mauve body. Vibrant fleshy fruit scattered the vegetation like emerald stars.

I groped for a glass of needed water. My tongue was dry, like a cotton swab from the dentist. Clinging to the roof of my mouth with very little persuading. When I attempted to swallow, the bitter taste of medicine stuck to the back of my throat.

Finding a cup, I drank blindly, greedily sucking the cup dry from all its contents before settling back down. I rolled back over, attempting to sleep but my hand landed on a damp pile of leaves.

Sitting up in question, I drug my hazy view around. *This wasn't right.*

Did I leave my window open? I picked a sprig up in question, rubbing it slowly between my palms. *Where was I?*

Finally, I ventured to stand and shivered when my bare feet touched dew-laden grass. My ankle was splinted, gauze wrapping a few sections of my body, to show the raw evidence of what I had experienced.

Perversely, I ran fingers gingerly along the puckering skin. My mind was slowly processing I was not in my room, that I was never there to begin with. *Who was taking care of me?*

413

Taking a testing step forward, Wisps flickered on above. Their soft glow drew my attention to the moss-weighted canopy. Crowning branches bowed down into husky trunks where they lined perfectly side by side, forming walls. *Who could have a room of trees?* I took another step, flinching but not buckling. After a few leisured paces I found the exit, hidden by vines and reinforced by a red curtain. The familiar crest of a tree graced the front.

FaeKing...

"Oh..." Shivering, I peeked back to my resting spot. Someone built the bed frame up of roots from the guarding trees. They climbed up, entwining together, cradling the cushion I had been sleeping on only moments before.

Mentally blocking my overactive imagination, I pushed out through the drapery. *I had been fast asleep in the middle of the woods...*

Old growth cedar shrouded overhead, the inkling of small eyes blinked into existence at my entrance. Self-sustaining balls of flame marked my pathway, hovering along a short trail leading off into the forest. I had no other options other than the one ahead, the abnormal line of trees making up the shelter I slept in, was immense and evasive. I couldn't see any other way around it other than back into the room or down the indicated trail.

I kept to the beaten path.

My clothes had changed... again. The Fae apparently had a fetish for taking my clothes. I was cleaner than the last time I checked, but I still felt the crustiness of lake goo sticking to my scalp, stuck up under my nails and between... well, different cracks and crevices. I needed a bath.

The haunting melody of the cursed orchestra lilted through the thick foliage, gracing my ears after a few yards. I paused, frowning, remembering the dancing humans all too well. *Was this the moment I became one of them? Would I cease to exist the moment I gave FaeKing his sight?*

My eyes widened.

Quickly, I looked through the clothes they put me in. *Where was it? Where was the bracelet?* My blood pressure was rising, by the end of tonight; I would probably die of a heart attack rather than a death dance. Pulling up my long cotton sleeves the trinket innocently dropped out, dangling from my left wrist, catching light from the peculiar flickering fires illuminating my way.

"Fucking Fae," I seethed, finding new bloodlust, "Freaking Unmentionable bullshit. Screw you lake spirits, Mermaids, and all the shitty-shit that came along with this stupid bracelet."

"So, well rested I take it." Glancing down the path, my red-headed friend stood solid. His arms were folded to his chest with his head cocked to the side. An impish smile graced his green flecked face.

"Oh great, now you're better looking than before." I rolled my eyes, walking toward him. "No wonder you have no brains. Your ego smothered it out."

Opening his mouth to retort, I grabbed him into a hug, stopping him abruptly. After a moment, he slowly pulled his hands free to wrap them around my shoulders.

"Well, it's lucky you've got the wits, hmm? Wow, you stink." He laughed. "I think I prefer the iron over lake muck—ouch!" He shrank away from me, grinning while I gave his arm a good smacking. "Ouch! Hey!?"

"That's what you get for leaving and getting stuck to a tree!"

He frowned then, his emotions suddenly flipping dramatically. "Who told you that?"

"You know who."

"While the resemblance was uncanny, Hilly isn't related to Voldemort."

"Oh brother, James," I shook my head.

"That would make you related to Voldemort then, wouldn't it?"

I gave him a bored look. "James."

"Right," he shifted. "Right, I was. I have now been unstuck. I'm fine." He stated, taking hold of my upper arm. "The question is, are you? You became a chew toy the last time I saw you. How's your foot?"

"I'll live." *I think...*

He attempted to shift me back toward the tree tent, but I resisted. "No, I need to go talk to FaeKing. Where is Corrigan, is he safe? Where is Abigail?"

"Em, I will explain everything but your leg won't heal if you keep your weight on it."

"James, seriously, I don't have time for that. Where is Abby?" I pulled away from his hold, sulking. "Louella is a spy," I blurted out, "for someone else. I need to talk with Fae King. Maybe if I give him some information about what they told me, he'll let us go."

"Em, you're talking about stuff that should be said in private." His eyes rolled up to the forest canopy in sign

416

before he nudged his head toward the tree tent again. "Please, I need to tell you something, before all this goes down. I need you to know I'll always have your back, no matter what. No matter what anyone tells you—"

"That's enough," clipped a familiar brogue voice. "I thought I asked you to get her ready?" Corrigan crossed the gap of space between us, a sharper frostier version of the pale man. His vintage appeal was no more, replaced by the ice armor that was in the middle of drip drying. Spikes across his shoulders glistened sharp and smooth as they dissolved in the evening air.

The Frost Fae's jaw was tight when he looked me over. The lines between his brows spoke of a strain, a possible pain he was trying to bite back.

"I was..." James stiffened, watching the other wearily.

"That will no longer be necessary." He brushed passed my friend, his cold fingers wrapping about my upper arm. "This will have to do..."

When he released the pressure, I felt cool brush strokes crossing my skin tugging at the cotton threads of my nightwear and transfiguring it into an entirely different attire.

Encasing my body in a wavy silken material, the gown cascaded with multiple layers toward the damp moss flooring, loose fitted—in areas that counted—a gauzy plum color hung by silver and opal jewelry, and melded on into plush layers of frosted grey with little hand sewn embellished bits.

It concealed my larger bandaged areas, attempting to distract from my battered human form.

"... I don't understand," I complained, staring at the princess gown with slight distaste. *This flamboyancy made me nervous.*

Corrigan stepped back, gave me a thorough check before nodding. "Oh, do I meet your approval, Frosty the Snowman?" I was getting angry again.

"Your humor never ceases." He drawled.

"What is this for?" I asked directly. "What is happening?"

"A celebration," they both said in chorus.

"Right," I rolled my eyes, "for?"

"Em—" James started before the ice guardian gave him a look.

"I'm not going to that, whatever it is. I don't care," I gave them a look.

"Oh? I doubt the Master would stand for that."

"He doesn't own me." Even as I uttered those words, there was a sinking pit in my stomach.

That was a lie...

"Hmmm, he will care." The other added. "Come, Lady Emmaline. Let us look at that leg." He scooped me up, and I yelped in surprise. "Will you leave me alone?" I glared at him, "I'm not a doll you can flop around."

James was silent, looking miserable while he trailed behind the ice knight. They took me away from the tent and its corridor, bringing me toward one of the open-faced gazebos near the center of the labyrinth of shelters. Fae were popping out here and there to look at the spectacle we made.

I stood awkwardly when he put me down, not sitting to the stool he gestured toward.

"Sit. Let me examine your leg."

418

"Like hell," I wasn't about to let him get near me with that sharp exterior of his.

"Lady Darling," there was a metallic edge to his voice. "I suggest you sit on your own accord unless you prefer others to take your pride."

"I don't see why it does any good. Whether I'm sitting on my own or someone is making me. None of this is my choice, so why bother being mannered when it is just a fake formality."

"Ah, but at least you have some semblance of control." He knelt gracefully, gingerly brushing my gown aside to peek at my ankle, reaching to unbind the splint. Amusement seemed to glitter in his soft honeyed eyes while he inspected my swollen, discolored leg. "You could sit with annoyance or, perhaps with elegance? Although, I doubt you could ever have the grace of a Sidhe female." His white fingers brushed across the side of my foot.

"Sit, Em," James coaxed softly.

I did but not for their sake. Without the brace, a dull ache seemed to run up my bones, clear to my knee. "I don't know what happened to make it hurt so badly," I muttered, flinching when he raised my foot to roll my ankle slowly. "Ouch?"

"You've been through a huge ordeal for having the soft fleshy shell of a mortal." He focused on creating frost streaks across my skin, soothing the inflamed muscle long enough to keep the pain contained around my ankle. "When I caught up to the lake spirit, it astonished me you were still alive. You are lucky only a few of your wounds are infected." He tried raising the dress a bit more to see up my leg, but I batted him away quickly. "You have a hairline fracture. If you continue insisting on using it, you'll prolong your healing. Your fragility isn't up to such menial voyages."

"Menial voyages..." I felt my expression shift to irritation.

"That's not what he meant," my supposed friend stepped in. "Fae word things sharper, even when unintended."

"You're starting to sound just like them too." I bit out, my lips tugged into a pursed line. "You call what I've been through menial?" I pulled my foot away. While it was painful, I still had my self-respect. "Dear god, you Fae seem to think you're superior. Don't you? I swam in a damn lake. YOUR kind is too frail to touch. I went through infested waters where I was kidnapped, drowned, scratched, bit, chased, and thrown around. My soul was sucked out of my body then pulled back in. Many unnatural situations that made me wish I never met the likes of you! Oh, now," I wagged a finger. "This is where you give me some shitty deal. I chose to go after the Fae King's sight. Well, guess what? I freaking didn't have the choice! If it was you in my shoes, wouldn't you do anything you could to escape the fate I've been given!? I see what happens to my kind around your lot." I pointed toward the distant flickering of the large bonfire to the core of the camp. "Sickly, numbed and tamed to serve your kind, no one deserves a life like that."

The camp seemed to quiet with my escalated words, the two men before me attentive and curious.

"So..." Corrigan started slowly, "This is the Emmaline Darling the Master is so fond of."

"I have no idea what you're talking about."

"Righteous little Miss Darling," He chuckled to himself, grasping my ankle again with both hands.

I attempted to pull away, but his grip was vice-like. He was no longer privy to my stubbornness.

"Hey," James finally stepped in, glaring at Corrigan. "Step off. Now."

"You do not get to bark orders at me." His icy eyes bore holes into mine, dismissing the other by refusing to look at him. "The heroine of the human world, Emmaline the Virtuous, a lecturer of all great monsters and beasts by the power of a thousand brave men. Doesn't the venom of your bite get tiring? I find any human, bold enough to match words with a Fae, become overly spent with exertion."

Was this what my life would now be like arguing with creatures who didn't understand equal rights of their fellow man?

His words really shouldn't have stung as much as they did. He mocked me. Not that I hadn't done it to him, though it was easier to dish out than to have it thrown back. *I will admit that.*

I felt James rest his hand to my shoulder, trying to give reassurance.

"That's surprising news," I responded quietly. "Considering Fae numb humans to a point where they no longer can speak their minds."

Why was my mouth still running?

Why couldn't I just shut up?

I was sore and almost entirely spent, yet I continued sitting here, wasting my time arguing with a man who clearly had no respect for me. The infuriating point of all was that they considered me a weakling. A human woman wounded to where she needed to rely on her captors to heal, an obligation to continue being involved with a King who has torn my family into pieces. *Who said sexism was a dying breed?*

Clutching my wrist, I covered the bracelet with my fingers, feeling the bite of it pressing into my skin.

There was one thing to celebrate, one thing to keep in the forefronts of my mind. I had saved my sister from the same fate as myself. There was something to be hopeful for. *The rest, I had time to figure out...*

"You may be right, in that assumption, Lady Emmaline."

"At least, I can do one thing right."

"And that would be?" Corrigan asked lightly. I hadn't realized I said that out loud. He didn't seem to care either way. After replacing the splint, he tucked my dress mindfully down and rose to his feet. "I was requested to escort you to the party. Are you both ready?" He looked James up and down, looking undecided at his attire. "Yes, of course, you are..."

Corrigan didn't wait for us to reply. Sidestepping me he bent down to loop his arms about my form, lifting me up and away.

I watched the pavilions filter by, anywhere but at him.

Feeling displaced in this world, it was difficult knowing exactly how to hold myself. My mind told me it was because he was cold and sharp externally, but my heart told me it hurt. *What was I expecting, kindness?*

I finally curled my arms close to my chest, hoping I didn't seem too feeble to the creatures passing. The campground was more festive than I had last pictured it. Florals and ribbons lined the tops of tents, connecting them and drawing up toward the grand hallway.

As we entered, the oversize marble table had been broken down and removed. Trees seemed to have recently taken station along the wall, growing out through the ceiling. Chandeliers peeked through their long sprightly branches, overhanging the cleared space at the center of the room where they dripped multilayered colored candles. Cascading swirls of organic designs fell toward the floor, stopping short just before the tops of the guest's heads.

Several small round tables dotted between the vegetation, overladen with tiered stands of deliciously surreal looking sweets, fruits, and nuts. Barrels, stacked in a pyramid formation, sat behind a bar where a human servant stood pouring out vast hews of warm stained liquids.

There was music, dripping deep and robust with an aftertaste of bitterness, a feeling of autumn changing into winter.

Fae matched the part, wearing lavishly dripping gowns, even more, luxurious than the dinner I had witnessed before. They were dancing to the center of the hall, fluttering in the trees, using roots for chairs and chatting wildly with a humming expectation I was unaware of.

Across the broad stretch of space, stood a throne of worn stone fixed together with soft plush moss and climbing ivy. Two, once polished sphinxes guarded either side, hinting of ancient times long since passed.

The sight was mildly familiar, causing a shiver to run down my spine.

Corrigan slipped through the crowd of Fae, settling me to a mahogany chair brought out by human help. Looking across the group of contorted and misshapen figures, I saw expressions of contempt. I was not welcome here. *So why was I? Why bother dolling me up and placing me to a pedestal so that everyone could sneer in my direction?*

Looking for James, my heart sank when I couldn't find him.

Pressing back against the chair with pressure, my mind wandered to inevitable places...

"**Em-maline...**"

My head snapped to look at the individual settled casually to the crumbling throne. His hands were clasped before him, leaning over to give me a side smirk. "**There you are. Where did you decide to wander?**"

Leaning away, I ignored him, adjusting my jaw to look elsewhere.

What was I doing here...?

"**Em-maline...**" Fae King coaxed before lowering his voice to a softer tone. "**How are you feeling?**"

"Irritated, mainly due to your presence," I bit out, gripping the armrests of the chair I sat to.

"**Oh come now, Emmaline.**" He almost crooned.

"Don't patronize me, Fae King. You aren't my friend."

"**I could be,**" He quirked his head. Tresses of his vibrant hair swayed to frame his face, softening him momentarily with a kinder expression.

"I'll never be anything to you," I leaned away from him, stomach curdling.

424

"You realize if any other would talk to us in such a way, we could entertain the idea of punishment?"

"Then do it. Punish me. Send me off to a dungeon and starve me to death. What do I have to lose? I have what you want, my sister is free."

"Oh, really?" He abruptly clapped his hands to the audience, gaining momentary attention. "**Continue dancing, dining, and drinking. It is due to Emmaline that we are celebrating. So please her by giving your entertainment.**"

I stared at him bewildered. Sitting back, he folded one leg to another, watching the festivities over steepled hands. He ignored me adamantly, even as I blatantly sat staring.

He was subtly different from the last time I saw him. His antlers no longer held their leaves, having fallen off with the last of the departing autumn. FaeKing wore dark robes, layered and thick, hugging his form clear up to the high collar that graced his earlobes. I saw little skin, save for his hands and face.

What he couldn't hide was evident aging along his face, pronounced creases lined the corners of his eyes, and his fiery hair had tinged with rose gold streaks.

Shifting uncomfortably in my seat, I wondered what had happened to him. *Was FaeKing sick? Was this the reason why he was so adamant about retrieving his sight?* I fiddled with my mother's bracelet again, picking up the abnormally shaped trinket to get a good look at it. The form looked like a seashell of sorts, worn about the edges, making the piece look incomplete. Fastened to a silver clasp the charm was made from pale green jade. Two pearls settled to its center with an empty groove, suggesting the third had been lost.

425

As minutes ticked by, my fingers rubbed the pearls slowly. They offered various foods and drinks. I refused. I fell back into the recesses of my mind, surveying what had transpired.

"I don't understand." I finally managed out loud. "Why haven't you taken it...?" I wasn't about to stare him in the face, but I needed to know. "You've had plenty of chances to."

"**It's your medal of honor,**" Fae King replied. "**Wear it proudly... You have the King twisted tightly about your delicate little wrist.**" He stood abruptly and walked off without another word.

Did that mean he could not take it without force?

'*She looks different...*'

'*The iron is gone.*'

'*In the end, she's just a toy.*'

'*Still, it's plain she's sitting coy.*'

'*Who does she think she is? Only a queen should hold such a spot.*'

'*The creature is tactless, really...*'

I tuned out the voices and watched the King dully. Gathering my arm close, I fiddled with the band as the other flitted about the room to converse with the nobles attending.

What was this game he was playing? Why bother placing me on a pedestal, only to dismiss the arrangement he had agreed?

A prize...

That hadn't occurred before now. I was a trophy that Fae King had won. The pieces were falling into place. The pampering, the celebration, and the bestowing in the arms of his icy butler...

"Em…" There was a hushed whisper sounding behind me. I nearly jumped out of my skin, "No, don't look back. The transaction will look suspicious. People are always watching when we are together."

"Are you insane?" I smiled, despite my unenthusiastic outlook, giving a suspicious hum. "FaeKing has mimicked my voice before. Who says other Fae can't do the same with yours?"

"Because no one else but someone on your side would tell you that you still have time left…"

"Time left?" I straightened against my chair inattention, "time for what?"

"I didn't have time to tell you how Cressie found me." He muttered. "Didn't you think it was odd we paired up?"

"Well, yeah… but a lot of crazy stuff happened," I rubbed my forehead, trying to think back.

"You had no interactions before the Lady of the Lake showed up?" he hinted.

Brooding, I leaned my head back to give him a side stare. "Mom… she came to you."

"Yeah, they stranded me on the boat. In the middle of the lake, flailing… trying to figure out how to get to you. I'm not… skilled enough or old enough to figure out fancy tricks like Corrigan. That's why you heard nasty bit about the tree." He sighed in frustration. "Anyway, she called Cressie said she could help."

"That's…" Sighing softly, I closed my eyes. "That's nice."

"I didn't tell you the best part," He leaned in slowly, brushing his jaw to the side of my head, keeping his eyes on the party before us. "Strike another deal, bide yourself more time."

"More time for what?" I frowned. "He's won, he's been flaunting all evening."

"Strike a new deal."

"Why would he possibly want to do that? He already has what he wants." I wiggled along my wrist it in indication.

"Not all of it, you don't." I could practically hear the smugness exuding through his words.

I turned to him then, staring blatantly at him before looking to the trinket. "What?"

"Fae King's guard is making his rounds," James was staring across the crowd, watching Corrigan intently, becoming distracted from our talk.

"James," I hissed.

"Shit, there's so much to say. Dawn split it up—the bracelet. Hilly only had a part of the whole. Your mom hid them in different places because she worried you'd end up trapped in some stupid manipulation ploy like you are now." He backed off slowly. "Em, whatever the King tells you. I'm on *your* side."

"What?" I looked back to him, paling. "Why do you keep saying that? What did you do?" My chest flushed excitedly. Pressing a palm to my chest, I tried to steady my irregular heartbeat.

I rose, balancing on my good foot to stare out across the crowd.

"FaeKing," I demanded, the room grew hushed at the utterance.

428

The Fae had shuffled back from their King who was staring at me with a quizzical irritation.

I held up my hand as if I were waiting for the teacher to call my name, showing off the band about my left wrist. "Letting me believe I held your sight, when in reality... it is only a fragment?" I tossed out, listening to the buzzing of questioning conversations bleeding through the ocean of onlookers.

He walked quietly, spreading them back with a mere ghostly gaze.

I sank back into my seat when he moved before me, but my spite was evident.

"It seems you've been whispering to a little red-breasted bird." He grasped the back of my chair, leaning down over me. **"What exactly did he tell you?"**

"My mother left me crumbs... and I did as you asked. I found your sight. It just isn't all of it." The corners of my mouth twitched. "By right—" I took the bracelet off, shoving it into his hands. "My sister is free."

There was a long moment where nothing moved. When Fae King straitened before me he had a cruel smile gracing his features.

"Oh... is that all? Very well, she may go home. However, that does nothing for you."

"I'd like to strike a new deal, for my freedom."

He chuckled gently, but the noise didn't match his sharp face. The smile was dropped, replaced by an intense concentration. **"What could you possibly offer for such a prize?"**

"Give me time, I'll find the rest."

"How do you know we will not command for the information?"

"Do you really want to risk the rest of the pieces being found... or lost... broken?"

"**Fae negotiation suits you, Emmaline.**" He tilted his head to the side, holding out his hand. "**Very well, you have until your sister's fourth birthday. If fail to place our sight within our hand by the stroke of midnight, you are ours... regardless. Do you understand?**"

I took his hand confidently, the temperature rising against my birthmark. With a swift tug, he hugged me close.

He leaned over me then.

The music suddenly thrummed up a sharp foreboding lilt. Grasping the small of my back his hand worked the bracelet back to my wrist.

"**Let us seal the deal with a dance.**" He motioned toward the crowd, pulling me across the brightly clad throng of spectators, "**as a gesture of good faith, of course. Where is the prince? He's been shyly poking about. He has desired the chance to dance with the Lady Darling all evening. Corrigan.**" He barked.

"M-my foot," I muttered, blinking stupidly to the sudden gesture of merriment.

"He is here." The frost knight stepped forward, tugging a struggling creature behind him.

He brought the man to the centerfold, being released by the Fae servant where he stood with a pleading gaze.

"**We're sure you'll have plenty of conversation starters during this waltz. Prince James, we believe you've met the Lady Emmaline.**"

TO BE CONTINUED